QuickFame

Jason Fabbri

For Kristal, Jackson, Rhiannon and Mum

Author's note

This is a work of fiction, inspired by the real world.

We all have different lived experiences, and I can only write based on my own, however I was sure to have this story read by friends with a wide variety of beliefs and orientations.

Characters in this story come from all walks of life, and I accept them all.

Table of Contents

1.
ROMANTIC RECOVERY

An uncommonly heavy and wet snow was falling in Emmiline, the first such precipitation in years, and for a moment a hush settled over the city. To Felicia Scalding the huge white flakes shimmering in the headlights looked like tiny angels—which were promptly being crushed to death beneath the endless stream of cars.

Millions of dead angels, she half-sang to herself as the possible intro to a song, *saving me from—you? No. Death? No. Love? Come on, Felicia. Be more creative. From another Christmas alone? Maybe.*

"Front entrance, Ms. Scalding?" the driver asked.

"Take me to the back, please."

"Alright ma'am."

Felicia sighed and sat back and watched shoppers high-stepping the puddles of slush that'd suddenly appeared all over. She loved yet loathed Christmas. For Felicia, the past few holiday seasons had become nothing more than a chance for atonement. It was no longer about the guy on the cross or the pagan tree in the corner or about reuniting with family for a feast of dead pig and pecan pie; it was now a time to ask one's nearest and dearest to forgive and forget all that had been said and done the previous twelve months. The insults hurled. The fists swung. The gambling undertaken. The credit cards depleted.

The plans aborted.

The fetuses aborted and the children neglected. Yes, nothing said "let's start over" like a gold-plated iPhone or a supersonic drone with a high-definition camera or even a first-class flight to Dubai. Such gifts whitewashed the recent past better than hypnotherapy or strong drugs.

Except that Felicia Scalding was realizing she probably could not afford any of those.

She was lucky if she could manage a decent tip for her Sööper driver.

"This ok, ma'am?" the driver asked as he navigated the hordes of shoppers and edged in close to the curb at the back entrance of the mall.

"Fine, thank you." Felicia removed her smartphone and brought up the Sööper app. She'd bought the phone pretty much exclusively for this reason: to get rides in handsome cars with tinted windows driven by hopefully even more handsome men. But these devices—their functions were beyond her understanding.

Why can't they have buttons, or a click wheel like the old iPods?

"Christ on a crutch," she muttered as she dragged a finger across the screen, trying to get the app to run.

"Everything ok?"

"I just need a moment to figure out how generous a tip I should leave."

"Of course."

In truth Felicia was trying to log into her bank account to see how much was left in there, whether it was even worth it to visit the mall today, or ever again in her life, but the app was taking forever to load and the driver was drumming on the steering wheel while resetting his GPS. Felicia tapped on the phone, cursing silently but managing to spit all over the screen, until the app simply quit.

"Asshole."

"Sorry?"

Felicia brought up the Sööper app. She held her breath as the fare appeared, $49.99, then slowly exhaled as she typed in a whopping Christmas bonus tip of $5.01. *Might as well round it up for the guy.* The digital Sööper mascot smiled at her and then the app beeped and thanked her.

Simultaneously the driver's phone registered the payment and the tip. The driver was professional enough to take it all in stride, considering who his passenger was and how much money she must have had, all those royalty checks and appearance fees and all that income from merchandise sales.

"I gave you a perfect rating," Felicia said.

"As did I for you, ma'am."

Felicia took a deep breath, pushed open the door, and stepped out into the public—her first appearance in nearly a week. She steeled herself for the inevitable assault of rabid, mindless fans.

"Happy holidays!" Felicia forced herself to say with a smile as she waved goodbye to the driver.

She'd barely shut the door when the first throng headed for her, three middle-aged women clutching five or six massive shopping bags each, barreling down towards her with such momentum that she feared she might be crushed, just like that time in '95 or '96 when all those screaming teenage idiots rushed the barrier outside her hotel, toppling it onto her and fracturing her tibia. (She'd finished the tour with a cast on her leg, which only cultivated more publicity and good vibes in the media; it made Felicia smile just remembering the headlines.)

Felicia grabbed her purse, tensed up, clenched her eyes shut behind her sunglasses, and prepared to be body-slammed, all the while wondering if she would be responsible for such damage to the Sööper driver's door.

"Please, stop, I don't—"

"Watch out!" The first woman brushed past Felicia so that she could rap on the passenger-side window with her phone.

"You're the closest car! Can you take us right now?" The window came down. The woman, breathless and sweating despite the chill, said, "I'll give you an extra fifty if you get us out of here."

The trunk popped open, as did the passenger door, which bopped Felicia in the butt.

"Excuse me," the other women said, reaching past her for the door handle.

"But I—"

The woman stopped and glared at Felicia.

She had beady gray eyes and limp brown hair, and some of her lunch—pizza? Italian? raw tomatoes? —was lurking in the creases of her face. Just when it looked like the woman's greasy lips were going to separate to release some frank invective, Felicia broke away, giving her enough room to toss her bags into the car. The other women followed suit, stuffing their overpriced gifts into the trunk, and then climbing into the still-warm seat that Felicia had just vacated.

The car pulled away, leaving her standing there in a cloud of— nothing. It was an electric car.

Still, something dark hovered over her. "You idiots! I'm—"

Felicia caught herself, not quite sure what she was going to say. *Famous? Someone? Felicia Goddamn Scalding?* She tried to compose herself, stood tall in her six-inch heels—which helped boost her past the five-foot-two mark—and was about to make her way inside when she noticed a swollen brown rectangle lying at her feet like a wounded animal waiting to be taken home and fed. Or spent. When she picked it up, she realized it was a wallet. Cheap and ugly, it must have belonged to the women who'd butted her out of the way. But it felt full—of possibilities. She opened it up and inside saw a wad of the green stuff. Her heart started to race, and her hands started to tingle, her fingers already typing in the URL to her favorite gambling site.

As she thumbed through the stack, she saw that it was comprised of more than just ones and fives. It was—it was—she closed her eyes. "Shit."

Looking up, Felicia saw that the car was waiting at the corner on a no-turn red light. She clopped through the snow, her ankles growing wet and cold, and caught the car just in time, banging so hard on the window that all occupants, including the driver, bounced in their seats.

The butt-shover looked up at Felicia as if she were a mugger, panhandler, or even worse, one of those Greenpeace solicitors who stalk you with a clipboard in their arms.

"What is it?"

Felicia made a *roll down the window* gesture.

The woman lowered the window a few inches, and Felicia shoved the wallet through it like a postal worker dropping off the mail, *plop,* into the woman's lap.

She stared at it a moment, then broke into a smile as she looked up at Felicia.

Then, in an instant, her face changed yet again.

Felicia had seen it literally a million times: that moment of recognition when one realizes they're talking not to some bitter, middle-aged, mid-level sales manager but a bitter, middle-aged former pop star.

"It's—you're—"

Felicia, however, didn't want to do this right now.

The slush was wending its way down her feet and pooling in the tips of her shoes.

"Merry Goddamn Christmas!" she said, then spun and headed back to the entrance.

She made her way through the revolving doors. They drew her in, surrounding her with both manufactured and human warmth, and deposited her at the far end of the mall, just beyond the food court.

All those moist bodies encased in thick clothes, overexerting themselves, sweating through a meal of sodium and fat before returning for another round of consumerism—Felicia sneered. Then smiled. Then sneered again: for a moment she'd pictured shoppers buying the box-set reissue of 2Tone's greatest hits, then remembered that Cedric, her manager, said that no one bought those things anymore.

Everything was digital now, stored on phones or in the cloud.

She looked up, wondering if the cloud was in the mall.

Can I touch it?

Felicia debated whether to keep her sunglasses on but decided that to do so would simply bring more attention, more questioning stares, more autograph hounds, so she carefully folded them and stored them in their case (the right lens already had a big scratch on the inside, and although she was positive that Marc Bollant would send her a case of them, it was uncouth to ask—and perhaps would reveal her impoverished state).

She swept forward in her thigh-length black coat—far too thin for this time of year but much more flattering than a bulky winter thing—her heels rapping on the linoleum floor. She dodged some screaming children, stared down a few more until they wilted like every flower, she ever put on her dining room table, and headed toward Celona's department store. The store was no longer the height of upper-class commerce, but she still had a Celona's credit card and the men's department managed to retain a certain macho indulgence that people like her husband Chad were fond of.

She stepped onto the mile-long (or so it seemed) escalator and subconsciously tuned into the muzak being piped in through the PA system. At first it was nearly undetectable, the music having been watered down with flutes and keyboards, but when she realized that it was a late '80s hit by her foes on the music charts, Shayna, and the Shine, she grimaced. Then she smiled: to be reduced to background noise for something as mundane as holiday shopping sprees, something unobtrusive, comforting for its recognizability, a mere "ditty" devoid of real musicality—little was more demeaning for a band.

Felicia reeled in her smug smile as the escalator deposited her on the second floor of the mall. She strode toward the second escalator and ascended again. Up there the music was somewhat louder, and she realized that it truly was an awful song. Its fate as muzak was actually some sort of saving grace for Shayna and her Shine girls, bringing in a few pennies of royalty each month.

Celona's was at the far end of the mall, and between Felicia and the store were thousands of people yet. She caught a few overly long stares, a couple of smiles, and some people raising their phones for a quick snap. Felicia sped up. She didn't want to be "tagged," or whatever it was called, in someone's social media post. She kept moving. Celona's loomed ahead. Soon all that sat between her, and the main doors was her weakness, Scüpz, the frozen yogurt stand with a hundred types of toppings. It was tempting today, but with crowds like this, the question mark in her bank account, and the—

What in the actual fricking hell?

A trio of girls standing in line at Scüpz were doing the dance from "Mellow Out Man," 2Tone's third-biggest hit, which debuted in the top ten in 1992. The song and accompanying video had for a long time thankfully vanished from collective memory, as had the absurd dance the director had created involving a series of jerky, robotic sun-salutations with a slightly racist "native" element thrown in for good measure—until now. Recently, thanks to YouTube and the various channels of virality on the internet, the song and dance had been rediscovered, but not in the way a former pop star would hope for: some moron in Melbourne, Australia, had mashed up the video with some footage of Cheech and Chong, turning the pop song and associated dance into a viral sensation.

A "mashup." How does one even do that? How do they get a copy of the video? Are all teenagers technical wizards? In my day only the audio-visual club dorks could operate those junky VCRs.

As a result, 2Tone—mainly Felicia, since Michaela George was still in hiding two decades later—had earned some newfound notoriety. Indeed, a whole new following had been churned up by the tides of popular culture thanks to the meme. Felicia learned, however, that she wasn't making any money out of this, despite numerous inquiries into the matter. The viral nature of the video and the mashups were not, strictly speaking, legal or official or even revenue-generating, so there was really no way to stop them. As soon as the music company that had issued the main body of her work, Streemy, issued a cease-and-desist letter, a new version of the video popped up elsewhere, like an STD or a stalker. There was no way to sue, since there was technically *no one* to sue. These hackers and mashup artists were spirits, it seemed, with no real addresses or bodies.

Felicia found herself looking up again. *Do they live in the cloud?*

The thing was, "Mellow Out Man" wasn't meant to be some sort of stoner's anthem. It was a feminist riot-call, a raised palm in the face of blatant machismo. Yeah, the message was watered down with a stupid chorus and dancers in skimpy dresses and sporting hair so tall and teased with so much hair product that it threatened to catch fire under the spotlights, but Felicia and Michaela's intention had been legitimate—to basically say *fuck you* to the guys who were so desperate for attention that they'd all but beg and plead, and when that failed they resorted to affronts, threats, or outright violence. Sometimes rape.

"Oh my God, is that *her*?"

Felicia snapped out of her reverie to find the "dancers" staring at her. Their stares in turn were catching the attention of other shoppers. Felicia strode past Scüpz, both ashamed and relieved, and headed into Celona's. She beelined for the men's section, reached into her wallet for the tear-out from a GQ's gift guide, and set out looking for the "smart" golf club device that she thought Chad would like, some sort of machine that collected vital golfing data and then, no doubt, sent it to the people living in the cloud. What they did with said data she had no idea, but it sounded manly and important and she hoped it would keep Chad happy a while longer.

She located the item with the help of a smartly dressed but obscenely young sales associate who then led her to the counter and handed her off to a stunning and tall woman dressed like a flight attendant with a chic and ironic flair. Felicia hated her immediately.

"Anything else?"

"That'll be all."

"Would you like it gift wrapped?"

"Does it cost anything?"

Felicia immediately regretted asking, though the woman's face was nothing but poise, as was warranted by her profession.

"No charge. It'd be our pleasure. I'll just bring it to the gift-wrapping department on the mezzanine and—"

"Thanks, I'll pass. I'm in a rush."

"Of course."

The clerk bagged the item in a bag so tasteful that it alone would pass as gift wrapping in Felicia's somewhat pathetic standards, then rang up the device and offered the total to the ex-pop queen.

"That'll be eight hundred and fifty-five dollars."

Felicia's breath caught in her throat, but she managed to maintain her composure and hand over her Celona's credit card.

A minute later the clerk slid the card back across the counter, whispering, "I'm supposed to cut it up but I wouldn't dare to do such a thing in public. Do you have another card?"

"Oh, I, uh, of course." Felicia assumed that someone in the cloud had made a mistake. She rummaged around in her wallet until she found a card that hadn't expired or been half-chopped up under similar circumstances before she had been able to intervene. She thought she might throw up. She could feel the woman judging her from the other side of the counter and sensed that the young sales associate and his cohorts were spying on her from afar. So were the people behind the security camera located in the ceiling, which of course begged more questions as to the nature of the cloud.

"It'll just be a moment," the woman said,

"Of course," Felicia said, though she was half hoping that it would be rejected so that she wouldn't have to pay for that stupid smart golf device. What a ridiculous sport anyways. How did she end up with a man who plays golf? *Oh yeah, he's ten years younger, a former model, and has the manufactured charisma of a talk show host.*

"All set, Ms. Scalding."

"Have a lovely holiday."

Felicia took her bag and fled the store. She sped past Scüpz, the "Mellow Out Man" dancers thankfully having since departed. Back on the first floor a thought came to Felicia, and before donning her sunglasses again she spun around and headed for the music store. As she got closer and saw the signage, a feeling of dread settled into her stomach: Skyscraper Records, the venerable tastemaker of all things music and music culture, was going out of business, and not just in the mall but everywhere, according to the verbiage on their desperate clearance campaign. Felicia slowed down, her eyes wide as she assessed the carnage in the racks full of CDs and even cassette tapes (*They still make those?*). Prices had been reduced once, twice, a third time, with more slashes on the CDs than seemed dignified for a music store. Worse, almost no one was browsing the racks, despite the prices dipping into throw-away territory, mere cents on the dollar. Everything was discounted so heavily that it seemed like management was simply trying to avoid being gouged by the trash haulers.

Chin to her chest, Felicia made her way along the aisles until she reached the pop section. She refrained from making eye contact with the nerdy, portly, middle-aged ex-hipster behind the counter and the two or three bargain hunters rifling through the bins. She found the box-set section, and there it was, her collection of reissued and remastered works.

The price was a whopping $6.97.

It was supposed to have been a sure seller, even when "Mellow Out Man" went viral, but apparently, as her manager informed her, virality is fleeting: as quickly as it rose it also descended, and the kids were already onto the next viral sensation, such as the sappy video about a rescue dog and his favorite chewy toy (Felicia had watched it ten times, alternately sobbing and laughing her ass off as the dog dragged around a dinosaur four times as big as him, the foamy innards spilling out wherever the two of them went, the owner picking it up nightly and stuffing it back into the beast). On the release day of Felicia's box set, the stupid dog video had dominated the headlines, commanding twenty million views in a matter of days, and earning the animal an appearance on multiple talk shows; meanwhile, her album had sold less than two dozen copies. Here was copy number thirteen, sitting in this bin gathering slash marks like some teenage emo chick with an unhealthily low number of MySpace friends. *That's still around, right?*

"Can I help you find anything?" the old hipster asked from somewhere behind her.

Felicia dared not turn to face him. "Just browsing."

"On Friday, we're running a special. Fill a basket for ten dollars flat. Anything you can fit inside you can have, except for shirts and jewelry."

"Sounds depressing."

"It is what it is."

"Is it?"

"Indeed."

"I'll take your word for it."

"That's why they pay me the big bucks. Anyways, I'll be around if you need anything. Such as my phone number."

The clerk chuckled to himself and waddled back to his perch behind the desk. He shut off the alternative rock and switched on some pop music—K-pop, that Korean sickly cute subgenre infused with bits of cliché English and sung by tiny girls devoid of muscle tone. To Felicia it was barely music, more like aural candy: sweet for a moment, then forgotten; just a vague aftertaste that lingered before being wiped out by the next meal.

Felicia admitted that her own voice had started to wane in ferocity: it required a lot of warming up and her range wasn't what it used to be, but it remained a lovely voice, the tone still dense and rich with the vocal blemishes of a former pop diva at the forefront of her beautiful decline into maturity. But she refused to have her singing propped up with auto-tuning and masked by heavy mixing. Such a thing was akin to whitewashing a temple or filling the crevasses in a mountain with concrete.

What these producers were doing with the kids belching out this new form of pop music was criminal.

There was no security device on the box set. Felicia stuck it in her purse. She waved to the clerk on her way out. "See you Friday!"

The clerk looked up just as she slipped on her sunglasses and faded into the masses.

Close to the main entrance Felicia got out her phone and brought up the Sööper app to order a car; the app beeped and told her that she couldn't afford a Süper Sööper, so she downgraded to a Ständärd. Again, it told her no—her account was suspended due to lack of funding.

"Shit! Asshole motherfucker!"

She tried to downgrade to Büdget. The mascot laughed at her and the app closed.

She could call a cab and then ask for Chad to meet her on the street to pay for it, but then she'd be forced to expose to him the depth of her debt. And she didn't want to risk having another card declined by someone who might recognize her.

There was always mass transportation.

She got in line for the bus, though it wasn't a very long queue—until she realized that this line was merely the queue for the *real* line, which started around the corner. Hundreds of people were waiting to squeeze themselves into the stinky, overheated tube so that they could stand hip to hip and shoulder to shoulder with strangers from all over the city. Felicia forced herself to breathe and told herself she could do this. Once upon a time she had taken the bus all over Emmiline, traveling from studio to studio to hawk her demo tapes, to her shifts at the two diners where she worked, to the studio and gym where she'd bang out three hours of dance classes and a complicated fitness regimen.

She flipped up the collar on her coat, already regretting wearing such a thin thing in weather like this.

Stupid bitch. What were you thinking?

The line edged forward. A bus departed, its noisy engine leaving them in peace for a few minutes. But, for some reason, even after it was out of sight the ground continued to tremble, almost as if there were a subway line beneath them, but there wasn't one in this part of town.

"Shit, not again!"

"Move away from the building!" someone yelled.

"Why?" Felicia asked.

"I don't know!"

In the end no one moved since no one was willing to give up their spot in line.

This was not a legitimate earthquake anyways, just a tremor. The big one had yet to hit, and of late the talking heads on TV and online were not in agreement as to the cause of the shakes, since they couldn't yet pin down the locus of the seismic activity.

Still the tremors were hitting with increasing frequency, putting everyone on edge and threatening to fling ornaments from Christmas trees throughout the city.

In the wake of the minute-long tremor followed a profound silence, but that too, passed, and soon everyone was back to their surly, overspent, regret-filled selves.

Then she heard it.

At first she thought it was simply the soundtrack that plays in the background of her brain all hours of the day, but then she spotted someone up ahead doing the "Mellow Out Man" dance in synch with the tune coming out of the PA system: her song had been turned into mall muzak, just like Shayna and the Shine's.

She thought she might cry. Then vomit. Instead, she got out of her phone and brought up the messaging app.

Did I sign off on the rights to turn my best songs into shittyass mall music? Can I sue? Should I? Should I fire you?

She put away the phone. A few seconds later it buzzed and chirped, and she retrieved it.

U can fire me, her new manager, Cedric Nash, had written back, *but who is gng to rep u? Not xactly big money but lots of headaches.*

"The nerve!"

She shoved the phone back into her purse and snapped it shut. The line inched forward. Soon she'd turn the corner.

Forty minutes later, shivering, her teeth clenched against the wind, Felicia boarded a bus. According to the route map it would be at least another hour before it swung through her part of town. The irony, she thought, of the high-class part of the city being the worst-served by public transportation. She settled into a seat beside a man with earmuffs more suitable for a thirteen-year- old girl, fuzzy pink and shaped like pointy cat ears but with smiley faces. There was food in his beard, and he stunk—not like body odor but just some off-brand stink of weirdness, sharp and repulsive.

She tried leaning away from him, but that meant that every person either boarding or disembarking would slam into her.

By and by the passengers fell away and the bus was left mostly empty. Felicia had her seat to herself. She'd put on her headphones and was listening to Dreamless Sarcophagus, a band out of India that a mysterious online friend had suggested she check out. The band was really onto something, with its strange mix of didgeridoos and sitars and booming vocals, and whenever she listened to them she felt transported to a place above the Earth, not heaven exactly but a place where things mattered less—things like a smart golf device, which Felicia was now turning over in her hands.

She removed her sunglasses. She felt the need to be recognized. But, looking around the bus, no one seemed to notice her. Or didn't care. All except one person: the driver. She caught his smiling face in the mirror.

He was not an unpleasant-looking man. His skin was darker than her own Latino brown, not muscular but fit for a bus driver and well-postured, which she felt said more about a man than just about anything, including his choice of earmuffs. He was a diligent driver but continued to steal glances in the mirror every minute or two, always smiling and mouthing words like *Hello* and *Ooh yeah* and *Baby, baby*, which, while creepy, was sort of sweet in its desperate earnestness.

Felicia waved to him—just a couple of fingers, a coy hello to let him know she appreciated the attention.

The smile dropped from his face. It was replaced with a question mark and slitted eyes. Felicia slunk down slightly, then realized some signals had been crossed. She spun in her seat and saw that a couple rows back and on the opposite side of the bus, a woman seated there was tugging down her shirt to repeatedly show the driver her nipple.

The woman was older than Felicia and outweighed her by at least eighty pounds, but that didn't seem to deter either her or the target of her affections.

Felicia slunk even lower and put her sunglasses back on.

She knew that moments like this, along with the muzak horror, were supposed to be discussed on social media, that to expose oneself and laugh at one's foibles and triumphs was what it took to remain in the limelight, but she'd never gotten the hang of it.

She had a publicist for such things, though Felicia hadn't paid her in months and the social media channels had largely fallen dormant in recent days.

They'd have to be resuscitated, soon, however, when her solo career got back on track.

Because of her newfound viral fame, her name had found its way back into the mouths of people who pulled the strings in the music industry.

Among them was Dexter Rhodes, who was one of the hottest songwriters during her era and somehow managed to keep his relevancy among the latest crop of crooners.

He wanted to "rebrand" Felicia as a tough, well-travelled solo artist and to strip away the associations—both positive and negative—with 2Tone.

Not that there really were any positive associations after what'd happened at Wembley in 1998.

Dexter had a new song he wanted recorded, "Unfeeling/Feeling," but the artists he'd approached either didn't like it or he in turn didn't feel they were suited for the song: too millennial, too white, too privileged, too weird.

He wanted someone who had experienced the emotions that the song spoke of, from being left behind in a foreign country to loving someone so hard that you forgot to eat for a week. What former prom queen behind the wheel of a self-driving BMW could boast of such things, despite having a voice of gold?

Felicia said yes, recorded the song, and now it was being mixed and assessed by execs at Streemy. Still, she wasn't holding out hope. Kids don't listen to middle-aged female singers.

There are no bitches, hos, Instagram, or bling in the song, nor would there ever be. It was a good ol' pop song, full of love, longing, and pain. And drum machines. And some synthesizers. Synthesizers were back in style, apparently, though for Felicia they'd never lost their luster.

"A quill is just a feather that you use to write a love letter," she sang to herself, no longer caring if the driver or the nipple-lady heard her.

When Felicia was a star, songs had come to her by the hundreds, either through her agent or simply delivered to her desk in nice little envelopes, and she'd spend weeks sorting through them in search of something that spoke to her. Now only the orphans showed up on her digital doorstep. It wasn't supposed to be like this. For eight years in the nineties everything had gone according to plan, all those bus rides turned into a golden ticket, a hall pass through the life of luxury. 2Tone finally reached the big stage. Then the other half of the duo, Michaela George, pulled her stunt.

This is all Michaela's fault.

If Felicia ever found her, she was going to throttle her the same way Michaela had throttled her career.

Felicia reached her stop and pulled the cord to signal the driver. The breast-barer had already left and now the driver was fully focused on her, surely trying to figure out whether a famous person was riding his bus. His stares were relentless, far worse than the ogling the nipple had received.

She hopped off, using the back door.

Felicia rode the elevator to the top of the luxury apartment building, pressed her finger to the smart lock, and stepped inside, finally safe.

She heard noise in the bedroom: talking, laughing, all the typical signs of Chad being home.

"Sweetie, it's me."

Something fell over in the bedroom.

"Everything ok?" she asked, pausing.

"Yup. I'm on the phone. Just a sec."

Felicia kicked off her shoes and felt warmth pour into her body. She dropped her coat on the floor near the door, one of Chad's pet peeves, removed her earrings and tossed them into a fine China bowl, another peeve, then undid the top two buttons on her dress—not a peeve—and let herself breathe again.

She carried her handbag to the dining room table where she'd taken to working of late, having found the office too stuffy and dark. This Chad didn't mind, since he liked to have the office to himself. He spent hours behind the closed door, and what he did in there she had no idea and didn't want to ask.

Felicia slipped into her Big Comfy Slippers, which she'd been shuffling around in for nigh on five years now and plopped down in one of the dining room chairs. To her left the Emmiline skyline spread out before her; some snow drifted past. Now that she was warm and away from all those people, the Christmas glow settled into her flesh. She felt kindness towards humanity and herself.

It was immediately eradicated her mail, which for some reason she decided to open.

She started with her royalty payments, which were dwindling to Shayna and the Shine levels, muzak levels.

They were barely enough to sustain her gambling habit, a habit that she'd taken up as a hedge against the imminent decline in her musical income.

Most of the royalty payments of late were for "Cold Hearted Chance," for which she'd technically only written 25%, the chorus, while Dexter Rhodes had written the rest and earned 45%. The rest was split between her former manager and agent, as well as Dexter's.

God, how she hated that song.

She couldn't even stand to listen to the remastered version for the box set, even though the original had hit #1 on the charts for three weeks.

She'd only agreed to team up with Dexter Rhodes so that her former chart nemesis Andy Rainer wouldn't get his weird, chubby hands on the song, but then she went even further and recorded it, something she'd regretted since.

Chad emerged from the bedroom only to head to the bathroom. He shut the door; the water ran. It sounded like he was taking a shower.

Felicia looked up a moment, then shook her head and continued sorting through the pile.

A fan letter from a crazed divorcee, an invitation to lead a retreat in the Bahamas ("Release the Queen-Beast Inside You! Yoga and Voicework!"), and bills.

Her credit card had amassed tens of thousands of dollars in debt, thanks to the gambling. She'd been waiting for the new single to break out and for the advance to arrive, but thanks to stalling on Streemy's side the interest was just piling up as she continued to gamble.

She was going to have to tell Chad she was selling the boat, and then they would have to discuss what Felicia feared most—asking him to cancel his membership at that antiquarian WASPish golf club where men of color carried trays of drinks out to the green.

The water shut off.

"Chad?"

The door opened; Felicia heard wet feet slapping along the hallway and managed to catch a glimpse of Chad's glistening, muscular, naked buttocks disappearing down the hall. The bedroom door shut.

"Honey, I want to talk to you."

The door stayed shut. Felicia scooped all the mail into a pile and shoved it under some songs she was supposed to look over, then slid her laptop close. Just then a helicopter swept past, and for a moment she couldn't help but think it was paparazzi trying to catch her half-dressed or with a lover who was not her husband. But it wasn't. It was just a plain old police helicopter, perhaps scanning for signs of distress following the tremor.

Felicia typed in her password, which she changed every week to prevent Chad from snooping, and checked out her latest small-bet games that were running in the background, as well as minor wagers on trivial matters like sports events, weather systems, political turmoil, stock market shifts, and so forth. The successful ones tended to rack up big numbers, but most of them were steady losers.

She closed the window and looked at her last round of blackjack, a tournament that had taken up most of the weekend. She'd started out strong, plummeted around midnight, surged again on Sunday, and ended with a deficit of at least ten thousand dollars.

"Gotta be rigged. Fascists."

She checked the horse racing schedules, but she'd never quite gotten into the "sport." It was wrong to force those animals to do her bidding. Instead, she ran a few rounds of slots, losing five dollars every spin until her account was tanked.

Chad opened the bedroom door; Felicia slammed her laptop shut and stood up. She heard plastic scraping along the floor and her husband emerged, snappily dressed in dark winter colors, hair gelled up, face shaven, dragging two suitcases in a single hand.

"What the fuck?"

"Don't make a scene, ok?"

"A scene about what?"

Her face broke into a grin.

"We're taking a surprise vacation?"

"Not 'we.'"

"What—you're?"

Chad nodded.

Felicia crossed her arms.

"You're leaving me? Just like that? Where is this coming from?"

"From my heart. You knew it was going to happen."

"Is there someone else?"

Chad went to the refrigerator and removed a pitcher of beet juice. He poured himself a tall glass and drank half.

"There wasn't, and then there was. Your gambling doesn't help, but that's not really the gist of it. You have no ambition beyond trying to get your groove back and obtain your former glory. You think you can be a star again. You can't. I'm sorry, but the time has passed. You need to get hold of your life and figure out what's next but not with me. I can't handle this."

"But I bought you this!" Felicia grabbed her purse and removed the smart golf device.

"I spent the last of my goddamn money on your Christmas present!"

Chad glanced at it, finished the beet juice, washed the glass, then set it aside to dry.

"I don't golf anymore. I'm done with all of that. Gloria and I are going to Nepal for a three-month retreat. The first month is silent."

"Nepal? Gloria? Who—? Why—? What is going on?"

Chad went to the hallway and put on his coat and scarf.

"I think it's obvious."

"I'm selling the boat. The car. Everything."

"I'm ok with that. You paid for it all anyways. Plus, you can't even drive, so..."

"You're a piece of shit. A coward."

"You can also do whatever you want with this apartment now. Make a mess, don't shower, leave food all over the couch, have an orgy, whatever."

Felicia resisted the urge to resort to her usual tricks, namely falling to her knees and crying. That's what she did in the video for "Cry, Cry My Love," which peaked at #3 on the Billboard Top 100. She was in her twenties then, and such behavior was romantic and heartfelt. For a 43- year-old it was probably pathetic.

"When you have giardia from drinking out of the streams that pack mules shit in and Gloria sees what you're really made of—which is basically nothing, since you're a hollow, bland imitation of a man— don't come crawling back. The locks will be changed, and your stuff will be on the backs of the homeless guys living in the alley."

"I know I am empty inside. For my entire life I've been attached to material goods and locked into the idea that I am little more than my looks. That's why we're giving up everything to volunteer at an orphanage for children left behind by the Sherpas who've died while helping the privileged elite climb Mount Everest."

Felicia pointed to the watch with disgust.

"Good for you. Now hand over that watch. That was a gift. And don't take those suitcases. Those are mine."

"Felicia."

"*Chad.*"

"You're making this much worse than it has to be."

"You did this, not me."

"Don't be naive. We haven't been working as a couple for a long time." Chad pulled up his sleeve and unfastened his watch, then set it in the bowl with Felicia's earrings. The sound was too much for her, and she fell to her knees.

"Don't go. I love you, you stupid asshole. I wrote songs for you, you selfish prick."

"They weren't very good."

"Shut up!"

"They're sincere, and I know you meant it, but they were also cliché, and the choruses were so derivative of Peter Cetera and early Madonna that I couldn't bear to listen to them."

"Don't say that! I poured my soul into 'Cold Hearted Chance' and 'Broken Clouds.'"

"I'm sorry to be so blunt but this is the new me. I need to be forthright and real with people from now on. And I never loved you. I used you for your fame and money. Now both of those things are dwindling, and I've come to see the light. I apologize for being so shallow. I promise not to vlog about this."

Felicia was sobbing, her shoulders heaving and snots running down her chin.

"I'll have a courier return the luggage once I transfer my stuff to our backpacks and duffels. Again, I'm sorry. I hope you find someone who believes in you. God bless their soul."

The door opened and shut.

The helicopter circled the building.

The lyrics from "Broken Clouds" swirled through her head.

A thousand miles and poles apart
Where worlds collide and days are dark
Like swimming to the moon, only you can save me

If you'd just listen to my heart
Only always and forever
Put your key in my hand
You could have had me, you fool

Felicia sat in her underwear on the couch, spooning ice cream into her mouth. Ten tabs hosting ten different gambling websites sat open on her computer, but because her online accounts were maxed out, along with her credit cards, she was forced to use the free sites, hoping to gain enough credits to earn a few real dollars so that she could gamble for actual stakes—but every tap of the touchpad only put her further behind. She'd already created over fifty email accounts to keep getting starter points, each one of them using the same password: *ChadIsDead.*

A glob of ice cream fell onto the couch. Felicia wiped it up with a blanket.

She needed to sell the boat. A few days earlier she'd called the golf club but the refund for the year's balance wouldn't happen until next month.

"So sorry for your loss," the stuffy voice on the phone said: Felicia had summoned up some tears and a sob story about Chad's death in a twin- engine plane that'd smashed into the peak of Everest.

"At least he died doing what he loved," Felicia said and hung up.

The truth was, the sadness was becoming increasingly usurped by relief. Chad was too young, too Ken-doll-like for her tastes, and had never had an original thought in his life. His job, modeling, had consisted entirely of standing in place and being told to look pretty. At times even that was challenging for him: one time he'd been sent packing for his inability to pretend to be a boat captain. (Apparently, they're not supposed to have smarmy, lecherous looks on their face, which was pretty much Chad's default expression.)

The helicopter made another appearance mid-day. Felicia, so lonely and in fear of losing her apartment, nearly summoned it with a bed sheet. There hadn't been any more tremors, but the helicopter continued to circle the skies of Emmiline.

She set the ice cream aside and went in search of her dressing gown. Unable to find it she settled for her filthy bathrobe. She'd cancelled the maid service months ago, having promised Chad that she could handle the cleaning by herself, which they both knew was a lie. Now nearly her entire wardrobe sat on the bed and floor. Felicia kicked it as if checking to see if a dead body were underneath and slammed her toe into a dumbbell that Chad had left behind.

"Ahhhh!"

She keeled over. It was a soft landing on all those clothes.

She settled for some sweatpants and a sweater that she'd never even seen before—blue, with a gaping neck reminiscent of something from Flashdance—and returned to the couch with a bag of ice for her foot. In addition to listing the boat she needed to start auctioning off memorabilia, some of it hers and some of it gifted by or stolen from other more notable celebrities, but she couldn't bring herself to do it.

Instead, she turned on the television, landing on an interview with Andy Rainer, discussing his new saccharine Christmas single, "Love Is the Reason for the Season.

"I just hope my songs can bring people back together again," Andy was saying, "to gather around the Christmas tree, to slice the turkey or ham together, to remember why we love the ones we love."

Click.

She hoped to find something about herself on VH1. Instead, it was playing a documentary.

She changed the channel.

Then she switched it back.

The VH1 special was about Monkees, one of those bands she vaguely recalled and yet, when she thought about it, knew little about beyond the fact that the mother of one of the musicians invented White Out (something the music industry had used by the gallons before the World Wide Web had come along).

What Felicia didn't realize was that the group was the first-ever manufactured "boy band" and meant to be a comical sendup of the Beatles. Yet at their height the Monkees outsold the Beatles and the Rolling Stones combined.

The band members had been chosen from among hundreds of candidates. They were not necessarily good musicians, and more qualified players needed to be brought in for recording sessions. Their musicianship was largely irrelevant: the band was not authentic. It was their looks, their style, and their ability to engage with their target demographic—teenage girls—that propelled their mythology. The point was not to win Grammys or to write timeless ballads but to get out on tour as often as possible, to churn out merchandise as quickly as those girls could get their tiny white fingers on their fathers' dollars, and to amplify the shtick through constant radio play and a goofball television show, the latter of which was largely a conduit for their music but which remained virtually unwatchable by modern standards. They did, however, churn out a few songs of artistic merit, with infectious harmonies and mournful undertones.

Felicia watched the entire documentary, checked her gambling, then snapped her laptop shut, shut off the TV, and wrapped the ice cream-stained blanket around her.

Whatever. Idiots. Like teenagers know anything about music. Or love. If you don't know love, you don't know music.

"Shit! Write that down!"

If you don't know love, you don't know music. If you can't hit the notes, you can't... float. No, sail a boat. No, gloat? Vote?

"Argh!" Felicia threw her notepad across the room, then flailed about the apartment heaving objects left and right. Then, exhausted, she slumped over and cried herself to sleep.

She woke up hours later to a dark apartment and the sounds of a stalker closing in. She let out a quiet yelp, then stifled it with the mile of sleeve that her sweater afforded and dropped to the floor. The glow of the city afforded her some light and as her eyes slowly adjusted, she tried to remember where she and Chad had agreed to store their gun, the little peashooter they'd bought when a deranged ex-ballet dancer had started shipping her boxes of cat hair culled from his own pet. She heard it again, the footsteps in the—

"Felicia! Are you in there?"

Someone at the door. Felicia exhaled. She slowly got to her feet, her toe throbbing but apparently not broken, and shuffled through a puddle of cold water from the ice she'd left on the floor. She switched on the digital eyehole to see who was visiting and saw that it was Ernie, the concierge, along with Cheree.

"Oh God."

"I heard that! Open up. I've been calling you for a week. Is everything ok? Have you begun a crack habit like that lady from the sitcom who just died? Are you alive? Is someone holding you hostage? Knock once for yes and two for no and three for bust down the door."

Felicia rapped on the door. "Wait, was that one for 'yes, I'm ok,' or two for—what was the code, Ernie?"

Felicia rapped four times in succession and started to walk away.

"Felicia, let me in or Ernest here will summon the police."

"No, I won't," Ernie whispered from the other side of the door.

"Quiet, you. Felicia, I'm—"

Felicia unlocked the door.

Cheree covered her mouth.

"What the hell is—you look like a street whore!"

"Is that a compliment?"

Cheree brushed Felicia aside and entered.

"It's not chic right now. 'Yoga slut' is all the rage."

"Everything ok, Ms. Scalding?"

"Yes, thank you, Ernie."

The concierge tipped his hat and left. Cheree flipped on the lights. "Oh. My. God. Did you host a rager?"

"Yeah, but it was just me. Chad left."

Cheree spun around. "*Whaaaat?*"

"I guess he found himself."

"Where?"

"The Nepalese wilderness."

Cheree made an expression as if she understood.

"He fell in love with a tree of his own species, no doubt. Anyways, what in the shit is wrong with you? Why haven't you been answering your phone?"

"I needed some time to think. And I can't find it. I bet they shut it off. I'm broke, Cheree. I'm doomed! I might have to sell this place and move in with you."

"Aw, sweetie. You know the spare bedroom is always available to you. Now come on. We're going out. Girls' night on the town, just like old times."

Cheree fixed her bangs, the same curling wave of hair that she'd been sporting since leggings and shoulder pads were in style.

"Is it Christmas yet?" Felicia asked. "Where's my phone? Is it next year already?"

"Girl, you need to get your shit together."

While Felicia showered, Cheree went in search of the missing phone and in the meantime did her best to tidy up the place, mainly by piling the clothes on the bed and all the dishes and food on the dining table. The carpet was stained with ten different types of liquid and the odor of something rotten was lingering, though try as she might Cheree couldn't find the source.

More than once she had to fight off a gag reflex.

She and Felicia had been friends for twenty-five years. How their friendship had endured was a mystery. Cheree largely chalked it up to both of them belonging to the sisterhood of '90s scenesters who had fended off the hypermasculine (and often closeted) producers, singers, and backup dancers who felt it was their duty to manipulate, coerce and grope every lithe body that entered their general orbit.

36

Cheree was a dancer herself (but not a singer: she couldn't manage "Happy Birthday" without going off key), as was Felicia, at least for the first couple of years.

Unbeknownst to Cheree, however, Felicia was scrimping and saving for vocal training, piano lessons, and even taking a songwriting course at a community college.

So, when 2Tone's demo turned into a full-on offer from Streemy, Cheree was not only surprised, she was stunned. She reeled with jealousy. She cut off all ties and accepted a gig with Janet Jackson. Then that folded and Cheree was left waiting tables again at the same diner where Felicia had once worked. She had to be careful not to glance at the newspapers and magazines customers left behind, which were often populated with stories and picture of Felicia and her then- boyfriend Jesus Frazier.

Then Felicia rescued her. She popped into the diner, gave Cheree a hug, asked why she hadn't been in touch, and demanded that she sign on not only as 2Tone's lead dancer but also as choreographer. Cheree broke down crying and quit right then and there. ("*Ya gotta be kidding me!*" Ralph, the owner, bellowed, prompting Felicia to leave a $250 tip to make up for the sudden departure.) For the next eight years she toured all over the world with 2Tone. She made money, made love to men who barely spoke English, and made a promise to never turn her back on Felicia again.

"Let's go, honey!"

"Go where?"

"To celebrate the holidays."

"I'm in mourning."

"Your need to dull the pain."

"I can't afford to."

The bedroom door flew open. Cheree stood there with her hip cocked, snapping her gum. "I'll pay. Hey, what happened to your TV? It looks like someone shot it."

"I hurled a smart golf device at it. It was surprisingly sturdy. The TV wasn't."

"But why did you do that?"

"It was all, *Andy Rainer this, Andy Rainer that.*"

"His single got bumped out of number one."

Felicia yawned.

"That's almost worth celebrating."

An hour later Cheree was six drinks deep. After three drinks, however, Felicia switched to seltzer. Alcohol was never her vice, nor drugs; only dancing until her feet bled and loving until her heart was drained of life. Cheree, on the other hand, had some sort of genetic quirk that allowed her to be blazingly drunk yet still functional and charming in the company of suitors, all while barely being able to stand up.

Felicia left her to her own devices and retired to the far side of the club to scroll through her messages.

She was used to disappointment—after years in the business, she'd accustomed herself to constant letdown.

Now that Streemy had rejected her most recent single, she realized she'd never see positive headlines again. No: *Refreshingly Poppy and Unfiltered. Smart Yet Fun. Danceable Yet Classy. A Career Resuscitated: Where Has Felicia Scalding Been Hiding All These Years?*

There were no messages from Chad. Felicia's stomach turned a moment and then the relief settled in.

"Buy you a drink?" someone said.

Felicia turned on her stool.

Standing beside her was a six-foot, hipster-lumberjack sporting a thick, full beard but thankfully devoid of a topknot, dressed in a lovely gray suit with no tie but with the shirt unbuttoned to reveal a tattoo of a frigate on his chest.

"Sure. Seltzer with lime."

"What?" the hipster said.

"Seltzer."

"Sounds great." He walked off.

"What the hell?" Felicia returned to stirring her ice cubes.

"Over here," the voice said, and this time she tracked it to the mouth belonging to the man at the far end of the bar, just out of reach of the shadows. Short, balding, dumpy, wearing a cable-knit sweater, the guy was sweating with nervousness.

He ordered her another seltzer, then moved to a closer stool.

"Thanks for the water," Felicia said.

"Look, I'm not trying to hit on your or anything."

Felicia's right eyebrow arched way up, her signature expression of curiosity mixed with skepticism and mild disdain—and tinged with disappointment. "Oh?"

"I mean, not that I don't want to, but I know you're out of my league. I know who you are. Felica Scalding. I've seen the 'Mellow Out Man' clip on YouTube. Truth be told though, I'm not a fan. Of that song. Or pop music in general." He added a shrug with his narrow, sloping shoulders.

"This is going really well."

"I'm an associate producer. Here." The guy fumbled around in his pocket for a good long while, at last producing a wilted business card. *Thaddeus Goldar.*

"Actually, it's more like Associate Associate Producer."

"This is an AOL email address."

"Yeah." He shrugged. "You could say that I've been climbing up the corporate ladder a good long while. It's hard work, especially with the muscle I've added over the years." He flexed his biceps while pumping his eyebrows up and down, then chortled, waved his hand in the air, and took a long pull on his drink, which might have been Rum and Coke but could also just have been Coke.

"An associate producer for what?"

"QuickFame." He smiled and awaited her approval.

"QuickFame," he repeated.

"It sounds like something you clean your car with."

"Nah, it's a show! Haven't you seen it?"

"I've heard of it, to be honest, but have never watched it. I find it hard to stomach all those B- and C-list celebrities judging people far more talented and braver than them."

"You're missing out. It's a cultural phenomenon."

"Like Star Search? You know, I auditioned for that back in 1987. Ed McMahon liked my song, but the judges didn't. I didn't make it past the second round. Then I went on to have three number-one hits. I had a full career."

"That's why you'd make a great judge. Listen, let me get you to talk to my boss, Fay Friedman."

"Talk about what?"

"Getting you a slot on the judging panel."

Felicia turned on her stool and slid her drink away.

"Please. God no."

"Why not?"

"Because," Felicia said, half off her stool. "Because—because I am who I am."

Thaddeus smiled. "At least let me tell you how it works. The process is kinder to the talent, and we only allow viable candidates on stage so that the stakes are higher when they win and lose. The breakdowns are authentic, the tears are salty, and the moans are heartfelt, like your music."

Felicia sighed; Thaddeus moved to a closer stool.

He told her then how the show lived up to its name.

The QuickFame process was meant to fast-track talent from unknown to phenomenon in the time it would normally take to record a single. The major continents each had their own sets of judges and talent, and each continent's show lasted five days.

The first two days were for auditions, with the three separate judges working three revolving stages shuffling through the thousands of acts. The judge pressed a foot pedal to send the stage spinning around and depositing the failed acts back into the real world, while the passing acts were graded in three categories: musical ability, stage presence, and a third category called 'joie de vivre,' a combination of charm, marketability, personality, likability, and so forth. Day three featured the top thirty-three acts. From these acts ten were left standing, then three. The last day—the Grand Finale—consisted of a concert featuring the three finalists, each of them alternating songs for a full hour until it was clear who would continue. Said winner, and the judge who'd brought them this far, were then flown to the QuickFame World Championship where they would compete against the top seven contenders from around the globe. This year the final was being held on the steps of the Sydney Opera House in Australia.

"Sounds silly."

"Andy Rainer is going to be one of the judges."

Felicia sat up tall. Her mind twisted through a stream of consciousness involving various revenge scenarios. As she did so she focused on the woman in the mirror across from her.

For a moment Thaddeus faded away, as did everyone else in the club. There was no music (thudding, throbbing techno crap, all computer bloops and bleeps and record scratching). The light above her added life to her hair, bringing out the redness that had lurked there until her late twenties—and also the gray streaks and the wrinkles around her mouth and eyes, earned from tens of thousands of hours belting out the same lyrics over and over. She blinked and saw herself on television again, her name in the news, her star shining bright in the psyches of the people once again.

"No thanks."

"Please. Think about it."

"I did. It sounds awful."

"Maybe think a bit longer?"

"It's a desperate gig for desperate people whose careers are in their twilight."

"Can I at least get your phone number?"

Felicia looked at Thaddeus. Pale, sweating, terrified, he was really punching above his weight class tonight.

It was sweet and he looked like a nice guy.

"I'm in romantic recovery."

Thaddeus nodded. "Sure, of course."

Then he smiled. "That'd be a great name for an album."

Felicia nodded in agreement. "I live my art."

"Well, you've got my card in case you change your mind. But do me a favor, ok? If for some crazy reason you decide to get on board, would you please go through me? As you can tell, I'm not very adept at these things. I'm more of an intellectual than a physical guy. It would really change how my colleagues look at me."

"Of course, Ted. I'll be sure to do that."

"It's Thaddeus. Goldar. Do you need another business card?" Felicia waved him off. "How could I forget a name like that?"

"Right. Well, I mean, you already did, so perhaps—"

"I've got it, Thaddeus. Relax. Now let me enjoy my melting ice in peace before I go home to an empty apartment and cry myself to sleep."

"Of course. No problem." Thaddeus all but toppled off his stool, then got out his wallet and slapped a couple of twenties on the counter. "See ya, Felicia."

Felicia sipped her drink through a tiny straw. It tasted like toothpaste. Now she was desperately trying to avoid the woman in the mirror.

"You cowardly bitch."

Felicia surreptitiously glanced down the bar and saw that the bartender was helping some ravers at the far end, then snatched up one of the twenties, finished off Thaddeus's drink—it contained rum—and headed out to catch a cab.

The night had grown colder.

A cab rounded the corner, but as soon as Felicia's arm was in the air its Off-Duty sign came on and it raced off, into the drifting snow.

Felicia cursed Cheree: she had either gone into the bathroom to snort something or had gone home with one of the douche bags with popped collars. Felicia tried the Sööper app just to see if it had magically reset. Instead, it warned her that if she did not bring her account positive, she would be banned for life. She shoved the phone back into her purse and clutched herself and stamped her feet, wishing she'd asked Ted—no, Thaddeus—for a ride home. He would have taken that the wrong way, she imagined, and it was safer to be alone. Plus, she might have invited him in. She might have even let him touch her.

Felicia shuddered but not from the cold.

She set out walking and a few minutes later spotted a bus stop on the opposite side of the street, close to one of the few venues in the area that didn't have neon lights, velvet ropes, a 300- pound-bouncer, and queue of glossy losers waiting to bribe their way inside. Felicia, shivering, strolled past a social club called Herman's and glanced in to see a hundred people mingling, most of them white- and blue-haired old folks. They looked like they were waiting for something. Streamers dangled from the ceiling and some cheap lights tossed a kaleidoscope of primary colors around the room. When she got to the alley, however, she saw not a bunch of velvet-suited lounge singers but five kids unloading equipment from the back of a van. Lithe and handsome yet clean- cut, they were all dressed in various levels of black tastefully offset with their individual brands of panache.

A couple of them had five-day beards while the rest retained their youthful smoothness. All were possessed by an emo-heavy miasma, that telltale sign of youth already overtaken by the Dark Art of Music.

"Hm."

Felicia took a good long stare, then slipped into the bus stop and hid in the corner, out of the wind. Her feet were numb, which was a relief from the rawness caused by the stilettos she'd regretfully chosen for the night. When groups of people strolled past, she bunkered down and hid her face. Ten minutes passed. Fifteen. She was so cold she couldn't remember her own name.

Some octogenarians hooted and hollered inside the nursing home party or whatever it was. Someone shouted into the microphone. *Testes. Testes. One, two, pee.* Even though he was being carefree if not entirely too casual about the entire thing, there was a richness to the boy's voice, so assured and strong it was as if it'd sunk a hook into the top of Felicia's skull: she stood up tall, then without even thinking about it found herself ambulating toward the feedback.

She walked in just as the front man summoned his bandmates in close. "Let's do this, boys." He extended his right hand and one by one each member placed theirs on top.

"One, two, three o'clock – 4 o'clock—"

And in unison: "ROCK!"

Felicia rolled her eyes.

They took up their stations and immediately the drummer set off the beat. The lead singer sprang into the air, his heels kicking up toward the ceiling. Felicia steeled herself, ready to see the old folks keel over as the Sex Pistols or some watered-down Slayer poured out of the speakers.

But that apparently wasn't on the agenda this afternoon. "*Now I'm a believer*," he sang. "*Yeah, yeah, yeah.*"

She laughed: it was one of the Monkees's biggest hits. According to the documentary she'd watched, Neil Diamond had written the song, but it was the Monkees who'd remained forever associated with it. Only someone who'd grown up with such music could appreciate it, and half of the people in attendance were born after World War II, most of them too hard of hearing too appreciate the tone of the lead singer's voice. Felicia, though, picked up on it at once.

The guy was far too good to be doing Monkees covers at a shindig as pathetic as this. Not only that, the sound mixing was superior to that of the majority of the concerts she'd attended, something she as a producer of her own work appreciated.

Felicia went to the bar and ordered a drink: a lemon-lime-and-bitters, then looked the bartender square in the eye and told him she had five cents in her pocket.

"But here's the deal," she said.

"When I get back on my feet, I'll throw my first show here."

"That's a deal," he said, reaching across the bar. They shook. Then he said, "But the drinks are free tonight."

"I love you, Grandma!" the androgynously cute singer shouted once the song was over. "Thank you everyone else for coming out to celebrate. We are Shivvr and the Quakes."

Felicia spun around. The name would be the first thing to go.

2.
HOT PSYCHO BITCH

Despite its glossy veneer, the Emmiline Heights Hotel and Conference Center was no longer the epicenter of the city's music culture. Worse, the only mirror in Layton Coy's room was in the bathroom, forcing him to stand in the tub in order to assess his outfit. Even then he couldn't see past his thighs. He twisted and turned, knocking over the tiny bottles of shampoo and conditioner and body wash, none of which he would ever deign to apply to his hair and body.

The QuickFame production company had really outdone themselves with the accommodations. The room was supposed to be a double, but it ended up having only one narrow double-bed, and Layton was not going to share his precious dreamspace with Jai (a notorious kicker and blanket hog), so they'd asked the staff to stick a cot into the corner. The two bandmates had been trading off each night. Then the air conditioner had broken, leaving them swimming through their sweat for two days until someone finally came in and jammed a screwdriver into the machine a few times. It was working now but when it ran the ceiling light blinked ominously.

"Not exactly my color," Layton said, examining himself in the mirror. He imagined he could dye the outfit when all this was over.

There'd be lots of time then, since this whole QuickFame thing was clearly a joke.

Of course, he secretly hoped it wasn't. He and the other members of Shivvr and the Quakes— no, now they were called #Five—had mixed opinions as to whether they had a chance of getting past the first round.

Layton adjusted the collar and teased out his hair. He liked it better when it hung loose and free, falling nearly to his neck, with just enough bounce and a few of his natural curls revealing themselves.

It didn't faze him, the demands of being a front man. The girls screamed. The microphone tingled in his hands. The crowd surged forward like a wave that would literally crush him and probably consume him. *Tidal. The Wavez. Dead Ocean.* He sighed; he could think of a dozen names better than #Five. Even though Felicia Scalding had absolutely no clue what a hashtag was ("Is that some sort of Scottish dish made with lamb intestines?"), she ran the name up the flagpole, and when it came back down, she said they should go with it. It was catchy, easy to remember, inoffensive, and both inclusive and excluding at the same time. Layton supposed she was right, at least for this "experiment" she had concocted. Really all that mattered was the music, the stage, and the conquest that followed, whomever that may be.

"Ugh. You look hot but no, this hem is all wrong."

Layton stepped out of the tub, his black boots thudding against the linoleum, whipped the dress over his head, and tossed it aside. He grabbed a wad of tissue paper—couldn't use the towels or there'd be evidence—and started to wipe away the lipstick and blush. The eyeliner could stay.

Keys rattled in the door. "Oh fuck."

Layton stuffed the dress into his weekender bag, flushed away the makeup-covered toilet paper (and his last bowlful of vomit), then ran a comb through his hair and pulled it into a topknot. He hated it but it was in style, and he'd rather be criticized for something he wasn't than investigated for something he wanted to be. He kicked off his boots and put his outfit back on—black jeans with the knees ripped at the caps, tastefully tattered white t-shirt, trademark black jacket with a stub collar—and stepped out to find Jai lying on the bed, even though it was Layton's turn.

"Rows and rows of girls out there," Jai said as Layton slid past.

"And boys, right? All sorts of bands? Even old people, I heard. People pushing thirty-five, forty."

"Yeah, of course, but I mean that there will be massive amounts of sad, pretty girls looking for a shoulder to cry on. Think about it. Only a few are going on to the next round out of literally thousands. Those chicks will be absolutely crushed."

Layton sat in the stiff chair beside the tiny round table in the corner of the room and propped his feet up on the end of the bed.

"They should have whittled down the selection more before this starting. It's just too big a contest. They can't be fair to each band. That's like, what, maybe one minute each? Even the most talented guitarist in the world can break a string before the band has even belted out the first note."

"Are you saying that I'm going to mess up?"

"Come on, you know I have faith in your fingers. And in 'The Scythe,' the world's ugliest but most dependable guitar. I just hope this isn't all a waste of time. And Felicia—I just don't trust her plan. What if there are rules about meeting a judge outside of the competition? What if there is a video of us meeting with her in Britt's garage that we don't know about? She came to, what, five rehearsals?"

"Really, Layton, don't worry about it. We are going to blow away the other bands. Felicia or QuickFame or whoever is going to 'discover' us and we're all going to continue on to a recording contract, a tour, all that shit. No more filing, no more burger flipping, not more black-market apartment moving services. And no more goddamn high school."

"Not that you ever went."

"I know. My mother keeps sending me messages about failing gym and biology. I'm like, lady, look, I know *all* about human anatomy." He winked; Layton rolled his eyes and checked the time.

They still had a half-hour before their cluster was due at the audition hall downstairs.

Unlike two-thirds of the other aspirants, #Five had been able to secure a room at the Emmiline Heights Hotel Complex and Events Center where the event was being held. Though it was far from fancy it meant less stress and, more importantly, it meant that Felicia's plan was working, that she was pulling strings to make this happen.

The way Felicia had presented it the day she showed up at their rehearsal was that she had a contact, someone she'd met moments before stumbling across the gig at Layton's grandmother's eightieth birthday bash—an inside man, so to speak, who would get the band to where it needed to be. All the other Quakes balked immediately, saying that they wanted to earn their stripes the old-fashioned way, through basement shows and prom gigs, via word-of-mouth and social media strategies, all the while keeping their integrity and not risking their long-term trajectory.

"I get it, I really do," Felicia had said. "I did it the same way. And you know what? It took a decade. I slept in a closet for two years. I fractured my foot during dance practice and had to wait tables on crutches. I once fell asleep on the train and circled the city for eight hours. When I finally broke through in the music industry, it was like enlightenment or an orgasm that lasted for a week, but—"

"Woah, woah, TMI," their bassist Donovan had said.

"Please, Ms. Scalding," Grannie had said.

"Don't interrupt the lady," Britt had said. She then made two points.

First, QuickFame was rigged already, but no one yet to spill the handpicked Arabica coffee beans. Bribes had already been secured on behalf of certain high-potential acts; handshakes and winks were flying around like drunken butterflies; other judges like Andy Rainer were making good on promises made to old friends decades ago, assuring them that their tone-deaf daughters would make it to the semi-finals.

Second, #Five's talent was not something that could be faked or manufactured. Their cohesion and presence was organic, and all she could do was foster such talent—to nudge it toward the end of the diving board until it was ready to step off. Whether they flopped or dove was up to them. She and her inside man, whom she referred to as Ted, were simply "adjusting" a few key factors that needed to be arranged beforehand, such as the timing of their audition. Ted, she claimed, was going to make sure they were in her audition cluster, not in Andy Rainer's or Heidi Starr's.

"Whatever," they'd said, shrugging, already silently agreeing to play along.

"Whatever," Jai said back in the hotel room. He swung his feet off the bed and went to the bathroom to fix up his hair. His roots were dark, but the rest was white, matching the inset of his eyeglass's frames.

His "thing" was his thin, black mod-style tie over a white button-down shirt and paired with black slacks that stylishly fell a couple inches short of his wing-tips.

The ensemble suited him perfectly, especially when balanced out with his dark skin, Jai being of Indian descent. Layton admired him from afar but not romantically. Layton too had once wanted to be a guitarist, and his parents spent thousands of dollars on lessons and equipment before realizing that his fingers were only meant to caress thick things like microphone cords and not little metal strings. Following that revelation Layton moped around the house for a good six months before his mother heard him singing to the cat one night in the back yard, and that was that, his true path was revealed.

"What the hell is this?" Jai said, his wing-tip toying with something that Layton had left on the bathroom floor. He emerged with a set of women's underwear, pink and lacy.

Layton sprang up and grabbed it, then stuffed it into his weekender. "Sorry."

"What in the fucking fuck? You met someone already?"

Layton's face turned dark red. More telling, his posture had changed, something that Jai had picked up on years ago, something that would surely result in Jai losing at poker on the first hand should he ever dare to sit down for a game. He knew Layton had secrets that he would rather die than divulge.

"I didn't. It's just—something gross."

"Dude, tell me."

Layton gave him a little shrug. "Just someone I met a long time ago. I hold onto them as a memento. It's sentimental, I know."

He looked down.

He actually wasn't lying. Rather, at least half of it wasn't a lie.

"Anyways," Jai said, "I watched all of Felicia's videos, from her backup singing and dancing days to her biggest hits to her guest spots on shows and panels. She was the shit, dude. She was really legit. I get that her voice has pretty much tanked, and she wants to be a producer, but is this really the way to do it? Aren't there better channels?"

"Those channels are dead," Layton said. "This is the new way. People are tuned into this gimmick, mainly because people like seeing underdogs win and winners fail, you know? People like seeing little Jon Benet lookalikes get booed off the stage and they like to see fat, greasy lunch ladies belting out opera to standing ovations. I guess the question is, which one are we going to be?"

Jai sighed and flipped off the lights. "I know which one we are, but we don't have a good story, do we? Not collectively, anyways. We get along, we're not druggies, we're not hoodlums. We're middle-class boys who kept our noses clean and know how to dress ourselves. Maybe that's not a good enough tale."

Layton's mouth opened to say something, but he didn't finish.

Now wasn't the time. No, he thought, collectively we don't have a good story.

But individually—*if anyone ever gets hold of our diaries or interviews our families, we're fucked.*

"Yeah, she's got the tools. I think she can pull it off."

What Layton hadn't told Jai or any of the others was how much Felicia had staked on the outcome of this project. After they had all agreed to the project, she'd called him and asked to meet up, and a couple nights later a silver electric Range Rover slid to a stop in front of his house. Layton's parents and sister were home, and it was awkward and weird having this celebrity clopping her way up the walkway in her ludicrously tall heels. He demanded that his family keep the special visitor to themselves; and if they did, he promised to take them with him on the ride, destination unknown.

The portly dull guy named Ted had come with Felicia, or maybe it was Tad—she kept screwing up his name and the guy kept correcting her—and Layton had offered them seats in the living room, which his mother had been frantically cleaning for over an hour after learning that someone of such import was coming to *their* house. Ted had sat down but Felicia said no, she wanted to see Layton's room.

She wanted to know what he was all about. And they needed somewhere private to talk.

Layton could see it in her face as soon as she'd stepped inside: she knew his kind. She unearthed his secrets like some sort of metaphysical detective, though in truth she didn't have to dig very deep, since all the clues she needed were on display. Her eyes took in the posters of similarly androgynous underground stars (no obvious nods like Bowie or Prince but lesser-knowns like Suede and even the recently transitioned Laura Jane Grace).

She flipped through his vinyl collection, laughing because she only recognized a few names, scanned the books on his shelf, then, last of all, poked her head into his closet.

Layton had leapt across the room and shut the closet door, praying that she hadn't glimpsed his "real" wardrobe. As if it mattered at this point. They both knew. (Ted remained clueless, nervous, and sweating and unable to take his eyes off Felicia's rump.)

"Please, sit," Layton said, offering her a chair at his desk. Ted perched on the edge of the bed, afraid to catch whatever teenage germs were lurking under the sheets. Layton plopped down on his bean bag.

"I like you, Layton. You're different. Sorry for being blunt, but that's the way it's going to be between you and I. We're going to be totally straight-forward with one another, ok?"

Layton nodded, then looked at the other guy.

"It's ok. Ted can hear whatever I have to say. He knows that if he does anything uncouth, I'll cut his balls off and serve them in a cocktail."

Ted made a *my lips are zipped* gesture, then laughed, and Layton was pretty sure that the laughing caused the big man to eructate onto his nice clean sheets (he changed them every five days, much to his mother's chagrin).

"Look, Layton, I'm going to be honest. If you want to be famous—and judging by the looks of your room and your style, that's your intention—you have to accept the good with the bad. The good parts of the music industry are really good. The bad are supremely bad. Your life will change in ways that you cannot comprehend. Do you understand?"

"Not really."

She sighed, then took off her heels. She was so short her feet couldn't reach the floor. Her face changed, and it was the same type of shift that Jai would witness in Layton's in the hotel room, her facade breaking down as the truth pushed through her pores. She told him then about her journey, the toil, the heartache, the disaster at Wembley. She just wanted to love and be loved: love the music, love the musicians, love the men, be loved by absolutely everyone. Unfortunately, that wasn't the way it was. In fact, her closest friend didn't love her at all, apparently.

"Michaela George and I were 2Tone, two halves of the same whole," she told Layton (and Ted, though he already knew this part, having followed the tabloids religiously when it was all unfolding).

"Michaela was like half my heart. I sometimes couldn't tell her voice from mine."

All that grueling rehearsal and songwriting and travel, years, and years of it, finally got them to the top, culminating in a sold-out show in Wembley Stadium that was set to be broadcast live on pay-per-view television.

The Prime Minister had opened the night and the opening act had just taken the stage.

Then, thirty minutes before show time, George disappeared without a trace and without so much as a "ta ta, you bitch."

"She just drove off without warning?" Layton asked.

"She had her makeup on, her headset in place, she'd limbered up her body; all she had to do was stretch her vocal chords. She said, 'I'll be back in a jiffy.'"

Felicia threw her hands in the air.

"I looked up 'jiffy' in the dictionary, and it's a sailor's term, a word for lightning. That's apt because she set sail and never came back."

"So, what did you do?"

"I told them the show was off. I had no choice."

"You could have done it solo."

"The band was not called 1Tone. It wouldn't have sounded like anything. Our music was engineered for two voices, two harmonies."

"One of the backup singers must have known the words."

"You're not getting it, Layton," Ted interjected.

"It was perfect just the way it was. It was meant to be, even if no one could see it at the moment."

"He's right," Felicia said, "though at the time I didn't know it. I'll never forget looking out onto that sea of expectant, anguished faces and having to tell them the show would not go on.

The shock was almost too much to bear—their hope turning to disappointment, then to anger. But with time my skin thickened, and I started to understand that fame is very harsh mistress, not one of those vanilla ones who spank your buttocks with a feather duster. No, fame is one of those sick wenches who chain you up in some dank dungeon and smash your balls with an iron mace and demands that you smile the entire time."

Layton sighed, getting bored, the thrill of the visiting celebrity having worn off.

"Yeah, it's a sad story, and it will crush my testicles, but what's the point? That fame is rough. I know that. I read. I watch TV."

"You still don't understand," Felicia said. "Even if this entire project fails miserably, it will succeed wildly too. It's a win-win situation no matter what the outcome is. Get it? You *will* be famous no matter what."

Layton thought about that. He looked around, studying his room the way they had.

It was funny, he suddenly thought: his bandmates had never come over here. Instead, they'd pretty much always practiced in Britt's massive garage. Layton was suddenly thankful that he'd kept them at arm's length.

Felicia and Ted, however, were insinuating themselves into his lives in ways he wasn't sure he was ready for.

They were already in his head, like a little electric worm reconfiguring his neural synapses.

"What I don't get," he said to Felicia, "is your role. I mean, what's in this for you?"

Felicia leaned over, nearly falling off the chair, and in her smoky, sweet voice said, "Controversy creates cash, but it must be planned carefully, so first we're going to stir things up. I need leverage to get my music career back on track. You can help me do that. At the same time, I'll help you kickstart yours. I mean really kickstart this engine, which is not some junky dirt bike you found behind your grandfather's shed out in the country but a Japanese crotch rocket."

Felicia pictured herself on the back of a speeding motorcycle, the wind in her hair, the freedom... and then Ted snapped her out of it.

"You'll make money," he said to Layton, "and Felicia will earn back her credibility. Your careers will be launched. She'll be the Maker of Kings. She can be one of those new-style music moguls who produce albums but also make music every few years. Her plan is brilliant. I'm glad I brought her on board. And as for me, I get a better job and some respect."

"You scare, me, Ted," Layton said.

"It's Thaddeus, actually. Thaddeus Goldar."

"You sure it's not 'Golddigger'?"

Thad's face went white a moment, and then he chuckled.

He chuckled long and hard.

Then Felicia joined in.

Their laughs were so different, his chortle emanating from the back of his throat and contrasting wildly with Felicia's tender, hiccupy squeal, the two of them almost harmonizing like some sort of sick, newfangled version of 2 Tone.

It was that combination that got Layton to laughing, and soon everyone else in the house was wondering what all the noise was about up in that bedroom.

Six weeks later Jai was sliding his guitar out from under the hotel bed. He plugged in his digital tuner and made some quick adjustments. "The Scythe" was indeed the ugliest machine Layton had ever seen, and the first time Jai whipped it out Layton thought it was a joke.

Because Jai's family was extremely poor, he'd had to ask around until some retired metalhead was able to donate an old instrument. Jai stripped it down to nothing and spray-painted the body, but something was wrong with the paint and the results were frankly horrifying. Jai spent months learning some basic soldering and electronics and, along with Donovan's sound engineering expertise, was able to assemble a machine that sounded on par with the costly machines down at Axe World.

Layton gargled some warm water and started his vocal exercises and neck stretches (he'd pulled a muscle once during chorus rehearsal and couldn't turn his head for a week; he vowed never to suffer through another neck brace again).

"Alright," he said. "Let's fucking do this."

Jai bagged up his guitar and he and Layton stepped into the hall just in time to catch a scene they wished they'd hadn't: a girl half out of her mind with the grief of rejection was being compelled down the hallway by her parents, who were supporting nearly all of her weight. She seemed incapable of walking.

"Maybe the girls are going to be a little harder to woo than I expected," Jai said once she'd passed.

"Bit extreme, isn't it?"

Jai shrugged. "Maybe she pinned her hopes on success, just like every other sad, small-time, small-town loser that's here today."

"Aren't you originally from Framington, population 103?"

"Now you see why I'm going to play my guitar so hard my fingers bleed."

Layton glanced at him. "Maybe that's not such a good idea. It's a pop song, not Grindcore."

"I was being hyperbolic."

They kept walking. From behind various rooms they alternately heard screams of joy, wails of anguish, vocal exercises, televisions tuned in to various music channels, and instruments being tuned and practiced. Layton thought he might puke but he fought it back, knowing the stomach acid would make his throat burn.

"Breathe, Lay-Co," Jai said, slinging his arm around Layton's shoulder.

"I am breathing. I think I'm hyperventilating."

Jai laughed but it wasn't mocking laughter. He was enjoying this; at the moment he was preternaturally calm. But Layton also knew that at any moment, Jai might snap and threaten to kill himself, to quit music forever, or to smash his guitar to bits—all variations on the same outcome.

Layton wasn't sure he'd consider Jai his best friend, but of all the guys in the band Jai was the one Layton related to best. It felt like they'd known each other forever, but in truth they'd only met five years earlier, in the twilight of their junior high years, when Jai had moved to the city. Like Layton, Jai also spent much of his school hours desperately searching out new ways to survive or evade gym class. Each of them had separately tried various techniques, from faking illness to punching themselves in the face and blaming locker room bullying to playing plain ol' hooky. When all of those had run their course, Layton took to simply performing every sport, be it floorball or soccer or volleyball or any of the countless derivatives of ball sports, as poorly as humanly possible. He'd then spend most of the class sitting on the bleachers with the geeks, dorks, and queens, gossiping and playing with their phones. That's where he encountered Jai, and the two of them bonded immediately. They'd seen each other around and both assumed the other was gay, but their attraction wasn't sexual, only musical. "You're in chorus, right?"

"Yeah, and you're in orchestral, right?"

"For now. I'm going to drop out. I want to start a band."

Layton looked at him long and hard, then simply said, "I'm your singer."

"You are?"

He nodded. "Deal with it. I'm good. You're good. We'll figure out the rest."

"The rest is all figured out. I have three other guys who themselves are dreaming of being the lead singer, drummer included."

"Ugh. Drummers who sing. Is there anything more perverse?"

Jai had just started laughing when a basketball bounced off his face, giving him a bloody nose.

He flew off the bleachers and slammed into the floor—much to Layton's delight. "I'll take him to the nurse!" he said and carried off his new friend.

They'd been rehearsing ever since, all of it leading up to this day, it seemed, though it was a much stranger trajectory than they'd anticipated. As they descended the stairs to the lobby the noise swelled.

The room appeared to be an impenetrable wall of bodies. Everywhere you turned acts were singing, warming up, chatting, stroking their arms nervously, sipping from water bottles, crying, texting, napping on their feet.

"What a shit-show," Jai said.

"Good thing we've got Ted working his magic for us."

"You mean Thad."

"Yeah, whatever. Man, what will happen if there's another tremor? There'll be a genuine stampede. Kids will be trampled to death, along with the grandparents who came to watch."

"That's fine. It'll mean fewer contestants. Hey, there's Grannie and Donovan over there."

They made their way to the other band members.

"Britt's setting up the drum kit," Grannie said.

"He said it's crap but what can we do? They're making him use the house kit so that the sponsor's name is front and center when the show goes live tomorrow."

"Which stage are we on?" Jai asked.

"Number one. We need to queue up along the far wall. Then we'll have some time in a green room before we hit the stage. Come on."

The three of them punched their way into the crowd, but when Jai turned to check on Layton he wasn't there.

"Wait, guys," he said, and returned to find Layton standing in the same spot, his face paler than usual, his hands on his stomach and his eyes as wide as crash-hat cymbals.

Instead of trying to talk him out of whatever he was enduring, Jai simply placed his hand on Layton's shoulder and compelled him through the throng.

Then something truly weird happened on their way to the staging area.

The crowd seemed to pick up on some sort of vibe from #Five (or four-fifths of it) and parted to let them through, all the while studying the band members with guarded curiosity. They seemed to be scanning the band from top to bottom, assessing Layton's uncommonly lithe yet alluring looks and perfectly chosen clothing, the beat-up guitar bag on Jai's shoulder, the detached coolness of Donovan and his terrible-looking bassist's fingers, and the calculated determination of Grannie leading them forward.

To the other contestants and their supporters #Five looked like they belonged there, not necessarily like they'd won but like they didn't give a damn if they did, this was beneath them, they were real musicians, this was kid's play, etc.

"I need my squeaky mouse," Layton said. "Where's Clipper?"

"It's probably in your pocket, like usual," Jai said, then dug Clipper out of Layton's pocket and handed him the little rubber mouse than he rubbed and squeezed right before he went on stage or had to take a math test.

Grannie reached the sign-in table. "Granville Jordan for #Five, the hashtag not spelled out."

The security stooge checked the list. "You're on in four acts. Be ready to go up onto stage one as soon as it's clear. If any of the green rooms are free you can use one to rehearse, pray, gather your thoughts, whatever, but if you miss the call you're out. Once you're on stage you'll see the red light and you'll have between one and five minutes to prepare. When it's green you're playing."

"Between one and five minutes?"

"If the act ahead of you blows it'll be one minute until you take over. If they rock, you'll get a couple extra minutes so that they can play out their song. Any of you need barf bags?"

Grannie arched an eyebrow.

"Really?"

The guard jerked his pen toward a massive box of airline-style vomit receptacles, but Grannie knew that the crowd surrounding them was paying close attention and that such un-coolness did not align with their brand.

"We're good."

"Fine. Turn in your phones."

He handed them each a numbered baggie.

"Seriously?"

"No recording is allowed until tomorrow."

They sighed and did as told.

"I'm going to put you in green room number one. Good luck." The guard opened a door, the band passed through, and the noise and chaos faded away.

"Let me see the lyrics again," Layton said.

"I keep forgetting those stupid lines."

Grannie whipped out the lyrics sheet and he, Layton, and Jai looked it over.

"*Gawd,*" Layton said, pumping Clipper, his special mouse, in his fist, "why does she make us sing this crap?"

"Don't think about that now. Just focus on the music, the lights, the feeling you get being up there."

"Fine. Just give me a moment."

"Read them as you walk," Jai said, and led Layton by the elbow along the corridor.

Once the band had all but agreed to go along with Felicia's and Thaddeus' plan to take QuickFame by storm, she *then* presented her stipulation, which may or may not have been an ultimatum: that #Five only play songs she had written.

When QuickFame was over and the band had won or at least gone as far as they could and the band was courting recording contracts, then they were free to write and record their own material. But until then, the band would belt out her lyrics and strum her chords.

At some point the truth would be "leaked" as to the true authorship of the songs ("You will all claim to have been huge fans all along.") and Felicia would resume her reign as the queen of pop. Until then they had to keep their mouths shut about it—unless singing her words.

"'I didn't know I was cold until you gave me your shirt.' No, sweater. 'Until you gave me your sweater.' Well, shirt would be better. Hey that rhymes. Shit."

He stuffed the paper back in his pocket, closed his eyes, did a little dance, spun around, reached for the imaginary microphone.

When he opened his eyes again, they were in the audition hall.

"Christ," Britt said as he stormed toward the band, his little legs working a furious pace.

"Did you guys know they were going to let all these people watch? I thought it'd just be the judges."

"Are you sure?"

"I caught a glance when I was setting up the drums. I saw a massive dark hall filled wall-to- wall with the other acts, parents, supporters, and whoever. No media are allowed in though. Did they take your phone?" The others nodded.

"Security guards are prowling the aisles checking for rulebreakers who've snuck in other technology to film but so far no one has been caught."

A staffer with a headset appeared. "You can wait in the wings with me but no talking or you'll be expelled."

"Just like high school," Britt said, flashing metal horns.

They followed the staffer to the wings where she gave them the *shush* sign. As soon as she stepped away, Jai said, "Watch, watch, here comes the next act."

The spotlights lit up on stage 1, one of three compact stages mounted on a larger, rotating circular platform. It was cramped but not obscenely so—but the act onstage was only a three-piece, leaving them with plenty of elbow room. The band was made up of a dark-skinned female drummer, a male bassist of Asian heritage, and a white female singer-guitarist.

Their shtick was obvious: political fury. Their instruments bore anarchy symbols and their faces were canvases of youthful displeasure with the establishment.

"Name?" the judge asked from their darkened and walled-off special section, the judges' identities not yet revealed to the public.

"Rage Worship," the lead singer said. A beat passed and then she said, "Do you need me to spell it?"

The judge seemed to be talking to someone— Thaddeus perhaps—or biding their time. A hush settled over the audience.

"Is Plex McGuire here yet?" Layton asked.

"Nah," Britt said. "Not until tomorrow when they start filming."

At last, a signal was given—the light flashing yellow like a warning on a highway—and then green. Immediately the drummer counted off in double-time. The singer leaned in and bashed her mouth against the microphone, belting out the lyrics in rapid-fire while the guitarist laid down an undercurrent of sonic reverb. They were on point.

The lyrics were sharp, at least the ones that were intelligible, and when the vocals did come through clearly, the singer's throaty yet not un-girly voice rose above the chaos.

She had lungs and the anger to exploit their power.

The song didn't grow; it was galloping and raucous right from the get-go.

Then the singer ruined everything.

She decided to add some gusto to her dance steps, forgetting how confined the quarters were, and when she spun around, she bashed into the drum kit. The drums held up, but she'd lost her footing, and when she returned to her spot at the microphone she bashed her mouth into it a second time, sending it flying out of its stand. The bassist, distraught by this scene, lost the beat and missed a series of chords, leaving only the drummer's kinetic thumping and the amplified sound of the singer cursing as she tackled the microphone and scrambled on the floor.

A red light flashed. It was over. Immediately the stage pivoted from number 3 to number 2, leaving the singer isolated in that technical no-man's-land, not far from the judge's feet. The girl was probably studying those shoes, trying to figure out what monstrous corporate asshat was in there, judging her, ruining her life. Then the singer got up and ran off crying.

The audience offered some polite clapping. A man and woman stood up and rushed out of the room.

"Holy crap," Jai said, grabbing his guitar as the band made their way to stage number #1.

"That was awesome."

Layton had to kneel a moment, suddenly lightheaded. He wished he'd taken the vomit pouch.

"No talking on stage during the other bands' performance," a QuickFame staffer reminded them as she guided them to the back of the platform, "or you'll be disqualified immediately."

The band exchanged looks, then nodded at her and tried to stay calm.

Energy seemed to be surging through the audience like an ocean wave, the noise and chatter building toward a crescendo and then tapering to silence in a matter of seconds.

They also seemed to understand that the judge was dragging this out to increase the tension, perhaps to rattle the band on stage.

Finally, the lights came up on the stage 2, revealing the next act, another three-piece, this time all female.

Two of the musicians, however, had no microphones, each one of them holding either a tambourine or a triangle. The vocalist sat before a keyboard.

"Name?"

"The Adoptees."

"Are you all adopted?"

The singer looked confused "It's not a question I will answer."

"No worries. I was just wondering."

"Fine."

"But you do realize that we are judging you not only on your musical talent but also on your marketability and personality, right?"

"I don't care."

"Do you still want to perform?"

"Yes."

"Are you alive?"

The singer thought a moment, then said, "I feel my heart beating within the confines of my corporeal existence."

"Well then."

The light flashed yellow. Green.

The singer glanced to her left at the tambourinist, then to her right at the triangle player.

The triangle player nodded back and struck her instrument three times like a teacher trying to get the attention of roomful of five-year-olds.

The tambourine followed, then the piano: it was a ballad, and a somber one at that, a Tori Amos-style crooning full of self- pity and weird imagery.

The singer could sing. She could find her way through the overly complicated arrangement. But it was all so strange, off-kilter, and off-putting. Their presence did not match their talent. It would be difficult to market such an act, let alone to convince people to buy such an album. The song ran just under three minutes, ending with a mashing of the keys.

The audience clapped; it died quickly.

"Did you write that yourself?" the judge asked, clearly Felicia's voice. By now half the audience must have known it was her.

"I wrote it with my mother."

"It's very interesting. Thank you for performing."

The judge hit some unseen button and the light flashed red, ending the Adoptees' journey.

"You're on," the staffer said, giving #Five a salute.

"Britt!" Grannie called out, "hold onto the drums kit!"

"What?"

"Steady yourselves. This thing is going to lurch. And Layton, no dancing. Stay cool and focus on the music. Don't go down like Rage Against the Worship or whoever they were."

Layton nodded and remained kneeling. Britt spread his little feet wide and locked his drum kit in place while holding the crash hats to keep them quiet.

Grannie was still making adjustments to his keys and the sound system and Jai was fiddling with his tuning pegs. A motor kicked on beneath the floor and their feet started to vibrate.

"This is it!" Donovan said. "Stay fucking calm!"

The stage spun around slowly, then came to a halt with a heavy *clunk*, jostling the band and their gear. They recovered quickly though, and this time the lights came on immediately, blinding them a moment, but even when their vision settled, they saw nothing but the lights—no judge, no audience.

Layton knew this was just another test. *What is it like to play in a vacuum, when you can hear nothing but your own heart thudding in your eardrums and the music just waiting to be released from inside of you, like a curse or like diarrhea made of beautiful sounds?*

"Name?"

"Hashtag five," Layton said, his voice thin and trembling. "But not spelled out. Like, the actual hashtag."

"What's a hashtag?"

"You know, like on social media?" Layton said.

"The pound symbol from the phone," Grannie said, leaning into his microphone.

"Oh," the disembodied voice said. "Why didn't you just say, 'pound symbol'?"

Layton looked at his bandmates for help; they shrugged.

He turned back toward Felicia's voice to see if she was kidding.

"Never mind." The light flashed.

Layton nodded at Britt. Britt raised his sticks in the air, prepared to count off, then stopped.

He'd forgotten to disengage the lock on his high hat. "Sorry." He unscrewed the butterfly nut at the top, tested the length of the pedal's pull, then nodded and raised his sticks again. "One, two, three, four."

They introduced themselves to the world, along with Felicia's song.

The acoustics in the hall were better than they'd anticipated, much better than in Britt's garage, and for once Layton was able to hear the instruments clearly in the monitors.

It was nothing like his grandmother's birthday part.

It was a real show, albeit a three-minute one.

As for the song, it wasn't their style. It wasn't the blend of punk, pop, and post-rock that they'd used to establish their sound.

Felicia's music seemed written both for radio play and for the event itself, mere ear candy for people who don't know how to enjoy music, who need the sentiment spoon-fed into their ear. Layton had to shut off his brain when it came time to express those words.

Driving through the desert at night
racing the stars.
An old song on the radio calling our names
over the screaming of guitars.
I didn't realize I was cold
Until you gave me your sweater.
Oh just take me home and then go away
'Cause I can't stand feeling this way.

Standing at the edge of the universe watching
Tomorrow's yesterday explodes in the air
You release my heart
and the flashbacks start
And I realize that
I just don't care

He fought the urge to spin around. Even with the absurd music he needed to dance, to move, to express his love for what they were doing.

He caught Jai's eye as he set out for this miniature solo that they'd inserted into the song to show off his skills with The Scythe, which was followed up with another short run on the keys by Grannie.

Britt's job was to keep it on track, this hideous song, while Donovan laid down a dense foundation.

Can't I care deeply
And also be crazy?
So this is me screaming,
Standing in front of you saying, "I hope I die in your arms!"
If only I could go back to tomorrow.

As soon as Grannie was done with his brief but flawless solo, Layton cleared his throat and took hold of the microphone.

He inhaled, tensed up, and was just about to release it when the warning light flashed yellow.

None of them knew what that meant. Then the sound was cut. The band exchanged looks.

"What the eff, lady?!" Britt yelled.

Grannie threw a rag at him. "Shut it."

"Thank you," the voice said—Felicia. "Thank you. Frankly, I'm amazed. Pound-five, is it?"

"*Huh huh* hashtag five," Layton said, still breathless but no longer trembling.

He felt like he'd just taken cocaine—or so he imagined, having sworn to his grandmother that if he pursued a life in rock n' roll, he would avoid drugs and alcohol.

Still, he couldn't feel his hands and his mouth felt like something alien to his body.

"You're from Emmiline, right here in town?" He nodded.

"I'm curious about your song. Who wrote the lyrics?"

Layton blanched. *Is she fucking with us?* This time, however, he fought the instinct to turn and look at the others.

"I, uh—"

Britt dropped his drumstick and Layton nearly jumped out of his boots.

Felicia continued. "I mean, the words, they're all heartfelt and deep. You bring them to life with your instrumental skills and those vocals. I mean—wow. *Wow,* as Owen Wilson would say. *Wow. Wow.*"

"Um, thanks. Yeah, a uh, friend helped us with the lyrics. Ours are a bit darker and the music's usually a bit harder but we, um, wanted something that would speak to the hearts and minds of our fans. Our future fans. Make no mistake, our fans are out there. They're waiting for us. The question is, will you be the one to bring us there, QuickFame?"

Layton took a step back from the microphone. He felt like he'd could leap off the earth and catch a cloud in his hands. He'd drink that cloud and live forever.

"That's quite the ambition you've got. Well, no reason why you shouldn't put it out there in the universe. And yes, I hope to be the one to take you there. Yes, I 'discover' you."

She hit a buzzer of some sort and confetti rained down on the band.

No one said anything. The band waved the confetti away, still half-blinded by the lights—until the lights were shut off. A massive LCD TV was turned on along the far wall, the #Five appearing there as well.

#Five has been DISCOVERED!

The crowd rose to their feet. Layton could no longer hear his own hear pounding.

The noise was too loud. It devoured him like a beast.

He wondered if he would ever be able to escape.

***

Britt had smuggled in beer. No one knew how he managed to do such things, being a perfectly teenager-like 5' 4", a mere 120 pounds soaking wet (usually after riding his little motorcycle in the rain to go pick up some food or drinks). The things Britt accomplished were both disturbing and part of his legend. Slipping in through the sliding glass door with cases of warm yet perfectly drinkable Pabst, he was welcomed, kissed, hugged, and celebrated.

Layton shook his head and retreated back to his bed.

The others had opened the doors between the rooms to make a suite suitable in size for accommodating all the partiers. Among them were some of the other winners but mostly losers. In a matter of hours attendance at the hotel had been reduced by thousands—rooms paid for yet vacated out of shame—and somehow a number of those who remained managed to find their way to the #Five suite, insisting on reveling in the band's success.

That wasn't really the other guys' style, only Britt's, and he took it upon himself to turn a "sit in a circle and chat" moment into a full-on bash.

He'd made plans for the band for the evening, then disappeared; twenty minutes later he was flinging beers across the room.

Layton checked his weekender, hidden on the top shelf of the closet, making sure no one had touched the dress.

He wished he'd tossed the dress in the dumpster.

He didn't even want it.

It was ugly, just something to help him blur the sharp edges of his day-to-day persona, the one he wielded like a shield.

He didn't believe in violence, but he believed in protecting oneself at all costs. (In truth though, when he thought about it, he'd seen movies in which dudes used shields to behead their foes.)

"All good?" Jai asked, emerging from the bathroom.

A girl with mascara streaking sweatily down her cheeks slipped out with him and disappeared into the other room.

"Yup. What are you doing?"

"Just talking to my new friend. We're going to go hit the pool. You in?"

"I didn't bring a suit."

Jai laughed. "No one did. Don't worry about it."

"I'll just sit and watch, I guess."

"Don't be a party pooper."

Layton threw Jai a look. "If your party's success depends on my participation, that is one crappy-ass party."

Jai grabbed Layton by the collar of his jacket and dragged him into the party.

The pool area was well-lit and there was no lifeguard. Clothes came off. Bodies were revealed. Plastic recliners and pool floats filled the water.

Of #Five only Britt was really partying.

And he partied hard. If Donovan or Grannie didn't hide the beer, Britt would obliterate his teenage mind.

They had another performance the following day, this time with three judges.

"Screw this," Layton said, rising from a plastic chair to find that his butt was soaked. "What's on the other side of that wall?" He gestured toward a high concrete wall that'd been painted ocean-green.

"I don't know," Grannie said, "but we might as well find out."

Grannie and Layton circled the pool and scrambled over the wall, tumbling off the top and into tall, dry grass.

"Holy shit," Layton said. "Wow."

"*Wow*," Layton echoed. "Just like Felicia said. '*Wow*.'"

Overhead a massive electrical support tower hummed, red lights at their peaks warning off small planes. Just beyond it, in the valley below, lay Emmiline in all its filthy, twinkling, never- sleeping, nocturnal glory.

With the concrete wall at their backs the hotel's light was cut off, as was most of the sound.

They heard only the occasional squeal of a teenager girl and then water splashing.

They stepped off the path and hiked through the dry grasses.

In the distance, a wind turbine chopped up the dark night air, using the light of the stars to create a gentle strobe light effect.

It was as if they were still on stage, still performing.

And Layton thought to himself, *Are we ever not?*

Ever since he was a kid, he'd felt like he was always on stage, even if it nearly made him sick every time he stood up on his chair and banged a spoon on a pot.

Being gifted with a solo in the chorus' yearly concert was even more debilitating, but that feeling was as authentic as the act itself. His parents loved both the ad hoc and well-prepared presentations and they encouraged him, supported him, and paid for the lessons he needed to go from great to maestro.

The problem was his sister, Madeline.

On The Day in Question, Layton thought he was home alone.

Madeline was usually off practicing some sport or another or running for some meaningless "political" office in the student body or making out with her perfectly normal, perfectly plain boyfriend. Twelve years old, Layton still relied on the snacks his mother left in the refrigerator for him.

But of late he'd gotten into the habit of heading directly upstairs after school—to Madeline's room.

He went to her immaculately organized closet, memorized the order and positions of the clothes, then proceeded to try on his favorites.

He modeled them in front of her floor-length mirror. She had poor taste in shoes, and tiny feet, but crossdressers can't always be divas, so he crammed his digits inside.

He put on her makeup, though in truth he preferred the natural look. He had the face for it—his mother's face, luckily, and not his father's coarse, square-chinned macho jawline.

Then he donned the *coup de tat*: a crimson-red wig he'd purchased with his allowance after months of saving.

He wasn't sure if he was beautiful in that outfit, but he was at ease.

It wasn't like donning a new body exactly; it was more like moving to a country where the language was something he understood.

"Layton? What in the fucking fuck are you doing in my goddamn dress?"

Layton spun away from the mirror to find not just Madeline but also Naomi Weaver, one of the most popular girls in school. Naomi didn't typically spread rumors: she generated them through merely existing. She was a social media factory without even having a Facebook account.

"I'm just—I'm trying out for a play. It's *shh shh* Shakespeare."

Naomi was laughing; Madeline was crying. "Take it off!" She wailed. "Take off my goddamn clothes!"

While Naomi helped Layton peel off the dress—which was admittedly too small for him and neither his style nor his color (a puffy red thing with frills on the sleeves)—Madeline called her parents at work to tell them there was an emergency at home. Thirty minutes later they screeched to a halt and sprinted into the house with the car still running in the street. Madeline was sitting on the couch, sobbing. Naomi was standing in the corner of the room, unsure who to console. Layton was sitting in the armchair, his face covered with the makeup he'd yet to remove.

"Oh, Madeline."

She'd looked up at them. "*Me?*"

Layton's parents politely implored Naomi to keep this incident to herself. She said she would, and Layton believed her.

Naomi was ironically not one for spreading rumors herself, as other people's lives held little interest over hers.

Plus, she liked Layton. Or had. Now she seemed mostly confused.

Madeline could not be so easily consoled. She did not understand what she'd witnessed. *"I'm* the fucking girl in this family! Why can't he just be normal?"

She didn't attend school for two weeks. Rumors swirled that she'd had a nervous breakdown. Layton denied everything. He also promised his parents not to wear Madeline's clothes ever again; he would get his own. They did, however, implore him not to reveal this side of himself until he was in college. Or even after that. The world was cruel to people who knew themselves, especially when that identity was at odds with the world.

He'd kept the dresses in a sack ever since.

They were worthless dresses that he'd picked up from the thrift store or garage sales in neighboring towns, claiming they were for a drag show fundraiser. Most often he threw them out after a couple of fashion shows. They usually never fit, and his tastes were evolving, as was he.

"I can't believe we've never hiked up here," Grannie said as he and Layton stood beneath the electrical tower's concrete base.

Layton took hold of the tower, expecting it to be hot or to shock him.

Instead, it was just cold steel. But he also felt like there was something inside the structure and, like the music within him, it needed to be released.

Both the music and the electricity power life, he thought. *We're conduits. Felicia's songs are anti-electricity. They are rubber.*

The two of them sat awhile, enjoying the breeze and the quiet. Layton had never spent much time with Grannie.

He was sort of the odd duck in a band comprised of secretive suburban aspirants.

They called him "Grannie" because he was the mature one who kept the band's sound perfect, and the gear organized. He shepherded them in and out of rehearsal and kept them on a schedule. He seemed like an old soul for seventeen, and he even looked the part: his face already had some creases, no doubt the result of the stress of dealing with the rest of them. He was far and away the smartest kid in the school, acing every test and speaking fluently on a massive range of topics, from politics to art to romance to philosophy. It was a bit creepy.

"This wasn't how I thought we'd make it to the top," Layton said. "It feels so false."

"I know, but I agree with Felicia that we would be facing years of struggle. I mean, I like struggle as much as the next musician. That's part of our calling. But at some point, you just have to accept that there are other ways to win the game. There's nothing wrong with having a helping hand. If it wasn't this, it'd be some producer who's greasing the palms of some exec who can get our video on MTV or song onto Spotify or get our YouTube ranking jacked way up via some rigged algorithm. Who knows."

Layton shrugged. He supposed Grannie was right. The struggle was already boring.

He just wanted to make music and get a house where he could be himself.

And then transition. Then everything would be ok.

By and by they heard voices and then bodies thudding to the ground. Jai and Donovan strolled over with a few of the girls who'd been hanging around. They offered Layton and Grannie beers, but they declined.

The girls were not old enough to drink either and they suddenly became self-aware and took small, infrequent sips or set the beers aside.

One of them clung to the steel tower and started chatting with Grannie, and although he was clearly not interested in her in any way, the gentleman in him would not allow him to just give her the cold shoulder.

Another girl sat on the ground near Layton, tore out a stalk of grass, and stole a glance at him.

A pixie with short brown hair, she seemed as uncomfortable in her own skin as he was in his. "Did you perform?" he asked her.

"Yeah. I thought it went well but, you know, that fucking judge. What a bitch." Layton nodded.

"Too bad you weren't able to record it."

She knotted the grass into a noose that suitable in size for lynching a Barbie doll, then said, "There is a video of it online from another concert, in case you want to check it out."

He pivoted towards her. "Come on. Let's have a listen."

She got out her phone and brought up a grainy, shaky video of parental quality from a high school talent show.

"We won that show, by the way. Not that that matters for shit."

The girl was solo on the piano, singing a Rhianna cover with all her heart. Her voice was magnificent, her range as vast as the desert outside of Emmiline.

"You played solo in front of Fe—the judge today?" Layton asked.

"Yeah."

"Criminal. You've got chops. And you can play the keys."

He shook his head.

"Don't let the judge's opinion stop you. That's one person. She probably saw herself in you and felt threatened. You've gotten times the talent that any of the other fakers who showed up today."

The pixie laughed. "Thanks. That means a lot coming from you. I actually saw you perform, by the way. You guys were really good today, but I was bummed that we didn't get to hear the whole song."

"You should be thankful. Our original material is much better."

"You should play it then."

"We will at some point. When we're in control of our destiny."

The girl wrapped the grass noose around her fore and middle fingers and pulled until they turned white.

Layton thought that she was probably gay but didn't know it yet.

Or maybe she didn't know what she liked so she avoided all genders. This Layton understood, though he himself was still attracted to girls. Or, more aptly, women. He didn't like kids, not ones that looked like him: skinny, pale, still developing, insecure.

He wasn't in a rush to figure it out either, knowing that when he'd transitioned it'd probably be clearer.

If hormones were part of his regimen, he would be seeing changes he couldn't yet anticipate and emotions he'd yet to experience.

Another body thudded on the ground.

It took a minute for them to get up.

Then they strolled through the grass toward the tower.

"What's up, fuckers?" Britt said, teetering as he walked. "Man, killer view. Why didn't you tell us you were—oh, sorry, am I interrupting something?"

The girl rose. "No, not at all. It was nice talking to you. I'll be watching tomorrow too. I know you'll make it."

She walked off, leaving Layton alone with Britt.

Grannie had wandered off somewhere, perhaps with that girl but likely not.

"Woah, sorry dude. I didn't mean to block your cock."

"Shut up."

Britt snorted and plopped down on the base next to Layton. Layton leaned away.

Britt reeked of alcohol and someone else's perfume.

Layton didn't want the poison or his personality to rub off on him—but he suddenly didn't have a choice: Britt slung his arm around Layton. Then he laid his head on Layton's shoulder. He squeezed gently.

"I love you, man."

Layton looked at him out of the corner of his eyes. "You do?"

"Yeah. I wish I was you. So cool and sure of yourself."

Layton laughed, softly at first and then so hard his stomach hurt. His convulsions threw Britt's arm off and now it was Britt looking at him.

"What?"

"Nothing. You're drunk. I'm cutting you off. We have to perform tomorrow."

Britt thought about that, then sighed. Then he spat into the grass and made a face like he needed to find a toilet as soon as possible. But he didn't leave just yet. Again, he leaned over and slung his arm around Layton. He said nothing further. Layton didn't shrug him off and he'd stopped laughing. The two of them sat there a moment, watching the lights of the city pulse while the cables above them hissed with raw power.

3.
GET OUT OF MY AIRSPACE

Grannie was not surprised that the hotel's gym was empty of people at six in the morning. He ran his keycard and stepped into the laughably small room set up with a stairclimber, a beat-up treadmill, some dumbbells, and a padded bench, sat down to tie his shoelaces, yawned a few times, finished off the coffee he'd bought from the vending machine in the lobby, then got on the treadmill.

He walked a few minutes, then started jogging, all the while staring at a blank, bluish-gray wall evocative of a whale's hide.

The air vent in the ceiling provided only a gently cooling tickle and within ten minutes he was drenched with sweat. That was the goal. Grannie was determined to stay in shape, unlike when he was in high school—the first time. Back then he was nearly 200 pounds and went by the name Charles Tucker.

That was in a small town in Oregon named Pollis, and there had been forty kids in his graduating class. He doubted many of them had crossed the town line in the eight years since they'd thrown their caps in the air and collected their diplomas. The type of aspirations his classmates exhibited ranged from Head Feed Manager at the chicken farm to getting the Sunday shift at the dollar store.

And while he was sure that some of his former classmates were on Facebook, he doubted that any of them would recognize him should he appear on television.

Or so he hoped.

Grannie picked up the pace for another five minutes of running, thumping along at such a furious clip that people on the floor below the gym might think another tremor was hitting Emmiline. Grannie couldn't worry about that though and ran on, faster, arms swinging, sweat flying. Endorphins kicked in and he felt good, finally. It was nice to be alone. He savored his privacy, unlike Britt who seemed to gather as many people around him as some sort of attempt to hide among them, perhaps as a defense mechanism, hiding his height. (Or lack of it.) Britt had been sprawled out on the second cot when Grannie'd left the room, his head jammed against the wall. The kid was not only burning up his matches and burning the candle at both ends, he was pretty much melting: there was little holding him together. Worse, it rubbed off on the band, including Grannie. It made him feel like a kid again, watching Britt sneak in alcohol, chatting up girls who'd yet to take the SATs, ordering up porn on the TV on QuickFame's dime.

Grannie turned off the treadmill and pumped some weights. He didn't want to tire himself out too much, only to burn off the beer from last night's revelry. His family was genetically prone towards the endomorphic body type, and he knew that pounds could appear in mere days but take months if not years to shed.

He would rather cut off every other toe than get fat again. The four years of bullying back in Pollis had driven him near to suicide, and instead of coming to his aid, his parents told him to just eat less dessert, pray harder, and toughen up.

By the time he finished in the gym, members of the remaining 33 musical acts competing in QuickFame were starting to emerge from their rooms, yawning, singing softly, plucking guitars. Although the judges' tastes had clearly favored the 16-25 year-old demographic, they had given the green light to a number of acts from generations Y and X, the latter being old enough to have given birth to most of the members of #Five. Grannie, wiping his face with a coarse hotel towel, slowed his pace while passing through one of the lounge areas. There he saw a handsome, lean, ponytail-sporting guy fingerplucking an acoustic guitar with trained precision. While his skill was legitimate and his voice quite lovely, Grannie couldn't imagine this guy getting to the final round.

"S'up, brother," the guy said.

"Morning."

"You make it to today's auditions?"

"Yup. You?"

"Yeah." The guy adjusted the guitar's tuning pegs. "I've been plying this trade for a decade.

This isn't exactly how I thought I'd break out though."

"Probably not best to put all your eggs in this basket," Grannie said, waving as he walked off.

The guy's head jerked up. "Sorry?"

Grannie stopped. "I'm just saying—it's a contest. It's not really an evaluation of your skills. You're obviously very good, but they take into account things like looks, marketability, social media platform, all that junk."

"How do you know I don't have a platform? I'm marketable."

"You're, you know—never mind. I have to go get ready."

The guy stood up. "Say what you were going to say."

"Seriously, it's cool. Just, you know, look the judges in the eye."

"Screw you, man. Say it. Don't be a coward."

Grannie was starting to sweat again. He dabbed his forehead, then said, "Alright. You're old. For the market they're targeting, I mean. Teenage girls don't typically gravitate towards older guys who sing about world peace and sailing the open seas."

"How do you know what I sing about?"

Grannie shrugged. "Ok, so I'm wrong. What do you sing about?"

The guy put his guitar in his case. "You know, things that matter. So, what if I like the open sea? What's wrong with singing about the hell of war?"

"Nothing. Nothing at all." Grannie started to walk away again but the guy called out to him.

"Hey. You're not so young yourself. How old are you?"

Grannie hesitated. He hadn't put on any makeup yet and knew that the wear and tear of life was exhibiting in his face. "Seventeen."

The guy laughed. "My ass. Maybe in Benjamin Button's world but not in Emmiline."

"I turn eighteen next month. And I'm sensitive to the sun."

"Right. Well, fuck you, man. I'm not going to let your sour words neuter my dream."

The guy brushed past him and marched down the hall in the same direction Grannie was headed. Grannie gave him a moment, then slowly trailed in his wake.

Back in the room no one was up yet. Grannie kicked the cots until Britt and Donovan stirred, then banged on the door between the suites until someone finally stumbled over to unlock it. Layton.

"We need to rehearse Felicia's song," Grannie said. "It seemed like we were stumbling through the other one yesterday."

"It sounded pretty good to me."

"I love you, Layton, but you can't hear past your own voice. And 'Dangerous You' is hard rock or modern rock or whatever you want to call it. It's clunky and abrasive and oversaturated with fabricated angst, so we need to figure out how to get ourselves behind such spurious emotion."

"Spurious?"

"That's right."

"It's too early for such big words."

"There's espresso today." Grannie checked his watch. "Let's meet at breakfast in thirty."

As usual Britt was last to arrive.

The band had cordoned off a couple of tables and were going over "Dangerous You" when he arrived looking hungover, unshowered, petulant, and unprepared.

"S'up." The other four-fifths of the band could barely look at him. *"Good morning, Britt,"* he said to himself. *"Did you sleep ok?"*

Jai stood up and walked off.

"What's his problem?" Britt asked.

"You stink," Layton said.

"And you're irritating as hell," Donovan added.

A couple minutes later Jai was back with a paper cup full of steaming dark liquid in one hand and a tall glass of water in the other. "Two shots of espresso topped with regular coffee," he said as he set them down in front of Britt, "and water. Drink them both, get your shit together, limber up, and focus."

"I can handle my nutritional requirements myself, thanks."

Jai leaned in close, his face inches from Britt's.

"Drink the goddamn stuff or I will pour it in your eyes."

Britt looked up at him with his narrow, dark eyes reminiscent of a young Clint Eastwood, minus eight inches of height. "I don't think the body absorbs the caffeine that way."

"We'll just have to find out, won't we?"

"Dude, just relax."

"We are not here to relax, dickhead. We are here to kickstart our careers."

"I'm here, aren't I?"

"Your body is. Your spirit isn't."

"Aren't you an atheist? Anyways, go find another drummer if you want."

"Maybe after this we will."

"Be my guest. Just hope I don't spill the beans."

Britt sipped the coffee, made a face, took another sip.

"About what?" Grannie asked.

"Felicia's whole—" Britt waved his hands in the air "—orchestration."

"You mean that she spotted us playing 'Happy Birthday' for Layton's grandmother and told us we should compete?"

Britt snorted. "Like it was that simple. She's shuttling us through the entire thing, and we were playing some garbage by the Monkees, followed by a medley of hits from the 1930s. You know, the stuff of legends."

The table fell quiet, everyone scowling at their instruments, at Britt, or at the lyrics sheet.

After a while Layton leaned in and said, "Britt, are you really going to ruin this for all of us?"

Britt finished off the coffee and switched to the water. "No," he said sheepishly.

Grannie thought the kid might cry. "Maybe you could lay off the booze for the rest of the event," he said.

Britt nodded. "As long as you promise not to replace me."

"We wouldn—" Layton started to say.

"No promises," Jai said. "You stay dry, and we'll talk about that afterwards." His face was red, and he was squeezing a poppy seed bagel to death.

Britt slammed the glass down, water spilling onto the table. He looked at everyone's faces, then got up and left. The others watched him go, his little legs pumping away as he made his way through the crowd. The room was quickly filling up, a din of voices and half-tuned instruments ranging from tenor saxophones to harmonicas making it almost impossible to hear one another.

"Just let him go," Grannie said. "He'll feel better once the coffee—holy crap."

Their attention shifted toward the lobby.

"What's going on?"

"The media. Big time."

They watched as crews shuttled in carts full of cameras and gear while press reporters strolled about taking photos and interviewing people.

"This is getting too real," Layton said. "I didn't think it'd be like this until maybe the last day."

"The venue on the last day is also legit. It's going to be at the 13-666 Club."

"That's a real club!" Layton said, rising from his seat. "Real acoustics. A stage! Oh man. I need air. Some space. I'll be in the room. Jai, come with me. We need to go over this breakdown. I think the refrain needs fine tuning."

Donovan stood up. "I need to piss. All this free coffee."

Grannie was left alone. He sat there drinking the rest of Britt's water until a group of girls— women, close to his age—came over and stared at him. He sighed and offered them the table. They took it without a word of thanks. Their eyes were ringed with bright blue makeup, their cheekbones covered with stick-on sparkling sequins. Their hair was teased high and they were dressed in some sort of throwback aerobics get-ups. They looked like a pack of former sorority girls who'd been hired to prance around in the background of a *Flashdance* remake. Grannie, wondering how such an act could make it this far, was starting to suspect that the entire show was rigged.

In the hallway he kept close to the wall and slid past the media, raising a hand to block the harsh glare of their camera's lights, then headed for the lobby. He was mere feet from the front desk when a hand reached out and grabbed his shoulder. He turned to find a massive security goon with a shaved head looking down at him.

"Someone wants to see you. This way, please."

"Am I in trouble?"

The goon said nothing and cleared a path toward a door that said PERSONNEL ONLY. He ran his keycard and opened the door just enough for Grannie to slip through.

The goon gestured with the patience of a man who had many bodies to bounce, then slammed it behind him, shutting out the chaos.

A fabric-walled divider separated the room into two smaller rooms. Pinned to the wall was the run of the entire QuickFame schedule for the first two days, including all the acts' names and their audition times. Grannie leaned forward and was scanning the list out of curiosity when another door opened on the other side of the cubicles, and someone entered the room. Grannie knew who it was. After their first meeting at the birthday bash that redolence, almost something you could taste, had lingered in his mind, and occupied his dreams.

A small hand reached out from behind the divider, snapped, retreated. "Come." Grannie stepped into Felicia's compact, messy workspace.

"Just like home," she said, kicking aside a blanket and pillow. "Have a seat."

"You sleep here?"

"Believe it or not, QuickFame rented a room for me at a real hotel, but sometimes I get headaches and need to lie down. I get so damn overwhelmed by all the politics and idiocy that this industry inspires."

Grannie sat in one of the conference chairs. He wanted to pick up the pillow, sniff it, then clutch it against his lap like he were at home watching Netflix.

He could only imagine what it'd be like to do such a thing with Felicia.

He thought that she probably wore funny slippers.

"So," Felicia said, crossing her legs and leaning back as she finished typing something on her phone.

She was slow, using her forefinger to search for each letter. Done, she tossed it aside. "I just wanted to check in with you. You are clearly the de facto leader of the Hashbrown Fives."

"I don't know about that. I always thought of Jai and Layton as the leaders."

"They founded it, right? That doesn't make them leaders. They bought the car, but you drive it. You have a command over both the band and the music. You've earned their respect and you stay calm, and you influence the sound with your technical ability. Otherwise, the drums would be overbearing, the guitar tinny, the vocals whiny. You keep it all tied together."

"Thanks, I think."

"You've got a future beyond the band. You're an old soul."

"I get that a lot."

"Good. Exploit it. So, is everyone playing nicely at the moment, everyone on board with the program?"

Grannie rubbed his chin and studied Felicia's magnificent kneecaps.

He had never seen such an aesthetically pleasing and erotic knob of bone.

"Granson?"

"What? Oh, my name is Granville. Grannie."

"Fine. Granville. Give me an update."

"So, yeah, more or less. The doubters in the group have come around now that we're here and about to go on stage for the second time. But I have to ask: if we win, is it an authentic win, or are you and Thaddeus making that happen?"

Felicia uncrossed her legs and leaned with her elbows on her thighs, the tips of her toes dipping into the carpet. She was close enough that he could see the texture of her lips beneath her lipstick. "You can't win without the adoration and support of all three judges. That's indisputable. I'm just making sure you get the proper airtime. I can only say 'yay' or 'nay' and argue for you. And I'm willing to argue a lot. Andy and Heidi are morons. They don't know anything about hit music, at least not for teens and millennials."

Grannie nodded. As alluring as Felicia was, he felt the urge to get out of there. It felt exactly like an interrogation room in a security guard's office would.

His mind wandered back to the moment he first saw her, business card in hand, as she strolled toward the foot-high stage at Layton's grandmother's birthday part.

"My name is Felicia Scalding," she had said. "You may be aware of some of my work."

Grannie had bitten his tongue, knowing that moments like this were tests of his resolve and his ability to maintain the illusion of youth. He knew for a fact that he was the only member of the band who watched VH1, musical biopics, and so forth.

But no one said anything: they just stared at her *knowing* they should know her while not actually sure who she was exactly.

"I had a number-one hit in 1995, which I cowrote with Dexter Rhodes."

"Produced by Willis Pomeroy," Grannie had said, unable to help himself.

She'd smiled at that, then nodded, waiting for the others to come to a realization as to whom they were talking to; they didn't. Only Grannie knew that something momentous was taking place in that ridiculous venue filled with blue-haired women and mint cupcakes.

"You guys play a lot of shows?"

The other band members laughed. "Two. And a sixteenth birthday party. We're waiting for our manager to come back from Spain so that he can hook us up with some gigs."

"Don't."

"Don't?" Layton said. "Don't waste your time."

"Lady, isn't it past your bedtime?" Britt said.

Grannie shoved Britt back.

"Let her talk. Sorry. *Kids.*" He'd rolled his eyes for effect.

"What's your practice schedule like?" she asked them. But she was staring at Grannie.

"Four days a week, sometimes five. We'd do more but we have to wait until nighttime so that our rehearsal space is free from Leo."

"Leo?"

"Britt's dad. He's a dick."

"Maintain that schedule. Perfect your sound and your look, because I may have an opportunity for you."

The others were skeptical.

"A little thing called QuickFame," she said.

At that, Jai shoved the others aside and stood nose to nose with Felicia. "That asshat Andy Rainer is one of the judges. I hate that guy! Do you think he'd pick us?"

"So, you're all familiar with how the show works, right?"

Jai shrugged. "Like any other stupid show. Auditions, the judges argue, a few people go onto fame and fortune while the dreams of the rest are crushed like cockroaches."

"Exactly," Felicia said.

"Fame and fortune. A musical legacy. Concerts the size of small cities. Adoration and worship."

"We're in," Britt said.

"Call us," Jai said.

"Calm down, everyone," Grannie said.

"Please," Britt said, "*Please please please.*"

"It's not that simple," Felicia had said, fighting back her smile, and Grannie knew right then and there that she was not just a singer, songwriter, and producer. She was a puppet master, a maker of kings and killer of princesses.

"You still with me?" Felicia said to Grannie back in the cubicle. "Oh, yeah, sorry. I drift off sometimes."

"Fine. Enough chit chat. You need to get back to the band and get them warmed up and focused. Cheer them up, rile them up, slap them around, hold their hands, wipe their butts, do whatever it takes, got it?"

Grannie nodded.

"Before you go though, can I do something?" Before he could answer, Felicia spun around, grabbed a couple things from her workspace, then spun back. "I just want to fix up your makeup."

Grannie recoiled as if kicked in the balls. "I'm not—I mean— I'm only wearing a tiny bit. Just a little. So, I don't look too— young. On stage I mean. The lights are harsh, as you know."

The corners of her mouth curled upwards. She could have mocked him. She could have prodded for more and cracked open his secret with her manicured pink talons. "That's a good idea. Yes, I do know about the lights. I think they've added at least three years of degradation to my skin. Your makeup is just a little uneven and I want to balance it out, ok?"

Grannie muttered under his breath, then forced himself to relax while Felicia touched up his base.

He could feel pinpricks of sweat opening up along his hairline, the thought of which led him to once again thank his ancestors for maintaining the genetic disposition for healthy, long-lasting hair. No one in his family was bald and his father had barely started to gray.

Grannie once again felt himself slipping into his stream of consciousness obsession with age, leading him to question his motivation for reliving his youth a second time.

"You still with me, tiger?" Felicia said, her breath pushing out the last word a little too mellifluously. Grannie felt himself stirring to life and now really, truly wanted that pillow to clutch on his lap.

"Yup."

"You're more than just a keyboardist, aren't you? I can tell by the way you handle the sound mixes."

"I want to be a producer, mainly for the Quakes. I mean for #Five. I have a knack, the instinct for it, I guess. I can tell whether Layton's and Jai's vocal ranges are on point on a given day based on how hydrated and rested they are. I know their preferred genres and song styles, which rhythms they struggle with, what the no-go areas are for each member of the band, such as low or high or harmony." Grannie tapped his temple. "I've already got the perfect sound arc for our first album, almost like a prog-record with segues between each track. It'll be both edgy and commercial, the perfect mix for topping charts and for winning awards. Plus, I know the boys. I am careful to allow each band member time to shine, as inequality in the creative process has been a band killer throughout rock history. I've studied music, band history, the charts, production techniques, the styles of Spector, Jay Z, Dr. Luke, Max Martin, George Martin. I know them all. Walls of sound, backward masking, ProTools, the lot. God, I'm rambling, aren't I."

"No worries. It's what I wanted to hear. But how have you had time for all this? You're so young. You should be studying geography and English."

Grannie's chest rose and fell as his breathing accelerated. "There's time for everything if you don't party or play sports or waste hours on the Xbox."

"You have a girlfriend?"

"No time for that."

"Come on, everyone has time for a girlfriend at your age. You need the outlet. The *release.*"

Grannie was blushing.

"Perhaps when all this is over, you'll find love," Felicia said, then rose and led Grannie to the door. She was about to open it when he pressed his hand against it.

"One other thing," he said. "Why those songs? Aren't ours good?"

Her eyes danced around the cramped, dark room, then returned to his. "Of course, they're good. They're exactly what you should be playing. And what you *will* be playing. But Heidi and Andy would never approve of such songs. They're traditionalists when it comes to pop music. That's why I crafted those songs for you. What, you don't like them?"

"They're a little hokey, to be honest."

Felicia smiled.

It seemed coded but Grannie knew he neither knew her well enough and knew too little about women to decipher it. She was wearing less makeup than him, just enough to accentuate her dark eyes, her little ski-slope of a nose, her large, soft mouth that had climbed onto countless stages in hundreds of countries to sing ten thousand songs. He wondered how old he would be when he'd reached that milestone. What he would look like. Whom he'd be with. What it would feel like. And then Grannie, driven by something unspoken and perverse, pressed his mouth to hers.

Felicia leaned back. The smile was gone but there was something in her eyes.

"I'm sorry," he said, "that was weird."

"I'm a woman in the music industry. I'm used to it." Felicia headed back towards her cubicle.

"Oh, God. I'm not one of them, please. I'm sorry. That was a mistake."

She glanced back over her shoulder. "Was it?" She disappeared behind the barrier. "Now get on with it. Win this thing."

Contestants would all perform in the same audition hall in round two. The rotating circular stage remained, but each act would be allotted enough time to complete an entire song, as long as they didn't get ejected by an immediate triple-nay from the judges.

And they were assured that the stage would spin more slowly this time, leaving no singers behind.

Should two judges reject a band, however, and the third dissented, the judge could use one of their two wild cards to override the votes and automatically send the band to the next round. Otherwise, two or more rejections were enough to end a band's dream.

"It feels weird that we're slotted for the afternoon again," Layton said as the band gathered in his room to go over the song one last time. "I'm surprised no one has voiced a complaint."

"Everyone is too nervous to notice things like that," Grannie said. "They're too busy pacing and over-tuning their instruments and over-warming their vocal chords to the point of destruction."

"I just hope this doesn't come back on us," Jai said. "I mean, we're not guilty, are we?"

"Don't be a dumbass," Britt said.

He was lying beside Donovan on the bed with his little motorcycle boots perched up on the wall (their heels leaving a mosaic of streaks), slapping his chest with his rehearsal sticks. "Of course, we're complicit. You hire someone to kill your wife, you're just as guilty but of a different crime."

For once Britt was right, even though no one was killing their wife. Grannie got up off the floor and went to the bathroom. He shut the door softly and leaned over the sink to reapply some of the eyeliner that Felicia had wiped away. "Too death metal," she had said—as if she knew anything about such a genre.

"Your makeup looks beautiful, Grannie," Britt called out.

Grannie whipped the door open. Everyone was looking at him. "Shut the fuck up."

Britt shrugged. "Nothing wrong with makeup. If you're Donovan."

Donovan's head twisted toward Britt; his face aligned with Britt's knees. "Huh?"

"Just sayin'."

"Saying what?" Grannie said.

"It's a bit gay, isn't it?"

"What?" Donovan said. "What are you saying?"

"I'm saying that gay men are more likely to wear makeup, since they're basically trying to be girls anyways."

"What the fuck are you talking about?" Layton said, throwing a pillow at Britt.

"First of all," Donovan said, "you don't know anything about being gay. Second, men have worn makeup on stage for centuries. And many of the acts you worship wear makeup. Everyone from Hetfield to Snoop to Springsteen."

Britt shrugged. "I don't listen to Metallica anymore."

"You fricking dinosaur, Britt."

"Look, it's cool with me if Grannie wants to wear makeup. I just wish he'd come out of the closet."

"I'm not gay!"

Layton stood up. "This conversation is over. Britt, you're poisoning the band. Get the fuck out of here."

"No."

"Yes."

"For real?"

"It's that or shut up."

Britt sighed long and hard, then swung his legs down off the bed, tossed his practice sticks into his quiver, slung it over his shoulder, and yanked open the door. "I'm heading down there to see what the other acts are all about." The door slammed shut.

Jai sat up. His face was red, and his eyes were filled with tears. "You ok?"

Jai couldn't hold it anymore: his mouth made a sound like a wet tractor tire deflating and his shoulders rocked and heaved. Layton went to him and put a hand on his shoulder. Jai shook it off and looked up at him. He was laughing so hard he could barely breathe.

"What the hell is wrong with you?" Layton said.

He wiped his eyes and looked at the others. "Does Britt not know that he looks like an elf with that stupid-ass 'quiver' on his back?"

After a moment's pause, the others joined him with deep belly laughs.

"I noticed that but didn't want to put him down. Not that he can be put down much further."

"Unless he wants to live in the ground like a Hobbit."

"Stop!" Jai said. "Stop it!"

"What's the guy's name from Zelda? Link?"

"Britt is like what'd happen if Frodo and the elvin princess had a baby," Grannie said. "...And then he ran away and joined a motorcycle gang."

"More like a minibike gang."

"Stop! Just fucking stop!"

The band, minus Britt, made their way to the audition hall.

They descended the stairs and rounded the corner, Layton leading them, mouse in hand.

Then he stopped.

He immediately took a step backwards shoved the taller and larger Donovan and Grannie to the front.

"What's wrong?"

"They're doing it again. They're staring!"

As soon as #Five stepped into the lobby the gathered acts and supporters shifted their attention to the band.

It was as if they'd been expecting them. Some raised phones to take photos and photographers turned their cameras toward them.

One even approached with a microphone, his cameraman's light hovering over his shoulder and blinding the band.

"Are you Pound 5?" he asked.

"#Five,"

Grannie said as he continued walking, urging the band onwards.

"What's your strategy here today?"

"What?"

"No media were allowed in yesterday, as you know, but you managed to cause a stir, nonetheless. How do you plan to do the same with the panel of judges? They're all longtime insiders and stars. What would you like Plex McGuire to say about you?"

"There's no strategy, man, except to play our hearts out. That's all we've ever done and that's all we'll ever do because it's all we know how to do. There are no tricks. You rock or you walk."

The reporter stopped, flashed a leering smile at the camera, then turned back to Grannie.

"You're Granville Jordan, correct? How long have you been leading this band?"

"I'm not the leader. I'm just the keyboardist and sound engineer. But to answer your question, we've been plying our trade for two years."

"Cool, got it, but what I mean is, you're clearly industry-savvy. You're well-spoken and you're smart. Your band has a presence and talent that seems to rise above the others."

"I don't know about that."

"Well, I do. I've been reporting on music for a decade. Do you have any videos online that your fans can check out?"

Grannie turned to the band; they shrugged, then pushed past him to get to the green rooms. "Nothing public. Just some footage of us dicking around. We wanted to perfect our sound before we reached the stage. Now if you'll excuse me, we've got to get ready."

"Speaking of your sound—your songs. Reports are that your song yesterday seemed a bit, let's say, contrived? Was it written just for this event?"

"That's a strange question."

"Will you play original material today?"

Grannie's stomach went cold. A small crowd had gathered around the reporter. "The music is what it is."

"What does that mean?"

"Our sound will continue to evolve. We're young and we're just getting started."

"But you've been rehearsing for two years."

"Right, but, uh, we're still finding ourselves, our sound, how we gel. We were freshmen and sophomores in high school when we kicked off the band. Now we're on the verge of the killing age."

"Killing age?"

"Yeah, you know—can go to war and kill, can buy cigarettes, and kill yourself. Soon we'll be drinking ourselves to death and killing people in car crashes if we're not in the army killing people overseas."

The reporter blanched. "Interesting answer."

"I was just kidding." He added a small shrug.

"Right. Well, 'the killing age.' Perhaps the name of your debut album?"

Grannie shrugged. His knees felt like they might give out. He felt like he was going to get a scolding from Felicia.

"Yeah, maybe. That'd be cool. It'll be thematic, that's for sure. But I have to go. We're on soon."

"Thanks for your time, Granville."

"You can call me Grannie."

The reporter smiled. "That's what I call my grandmother. So, are you the maternal figure in the band?"

"Nah, nah, nothing like that. It's just a name."

Grannie gave the reporter a tepid smile and slipped out of the spotlight. They continued to film him as he shoved his way through the crowd.

A television in the green room was running a live feed of the QuickFame stage.

Host Plex McGuire was introducing the performers, bantering with the judges, and alternating between making somber but vapid generalizations and dropping lead-balloon jokes: when a bluegrass troupe had been ushered off the stage he said, "Folks, what's the difference between a banjo and an onion? No one cries when you chop up a banjo."

As much as Grannie tried to get the band to just focus on their own sad song, the others couldn't help but take in the horrifying spectacle that they themselves were now part of.

The band crowded around the TV and Britt tapped on the screen with his drumstick. "Look at them all! Gotta be seven, eight, nine—nine goddamn performers on stage."

Grannie turned up the volume.

The camera was feeding in angles that the live and future television audience wouldn't be privy to, such as a three-quarters shot from the edge of the stage that was able to catch the next act taking their places.

The group consisted of four men and five women dressed like they were setting out for a day of parkour or aerobic hip-hop class, replete with sweatbands and soft pants with sagging seats and crotches. All of them were wearing headsets.

"What is this crap? Some sort of NSYNCH-Brittany Spears mashup?"

The lights dimmed. The stage spun around. The lights came up. As soon as Plex McGuire introduced them—Harsh-Mellow— the band members waved to the crows while offering up smiles so inauthentic they might as well have been applied with glue.

"Hi everybody!"

"So glad to be here!"

"This is what it's all about!"

"What what's all about?" Britt said, then made a farting sound. "Quiet. It's about to start."

Andy Rainer gave the thumb's up to Plex. Plex gave the a-ok to the band. Harsh-Mellow's faces grew serious as they grabbed hold of their knees and cocked a shoulder out. Someone somewhere— not a musician—turned on a thudding beat, *thoom, thoom, thoom,* and the performers nodding their heads in synch, then hopped in the air.

As soon as all twenty of their sneakered feet hit the ground, they were off, spinning, dancing, and twisting, throwing, and catching one another, grinding, and heaving and gyrating erotically, all the while singing, each and every one of them never missing a word.

"My God," Jai said.

"The dancing is like something that crawled out of Satan's armpits, but the song is catchy," Layton said.

"If you listen to the words, it's actually quite sharp."

"Look though—" Grannie said.

"Something about lost love," Layton continued, "that reduced the subject to ashes. 'Ashes to car crashes,' I think he said."

"But—"

"They've got to be in good shape," Donovan said. "They're not even breathing hard."

"That's—it's—"

"Woah! Holy crap!"

The four men had thrown a woman in the air so high her head nearly smacked a spotlight; she landed in their arms, popped right back into place, and commenced laying down a hip-hoppy stream of confusingly upbeat sounds with morbid imagery.

"How'd they pull that off?"

"It's fake!" Grannie said. "They're lip synching."

The others looked at Grannie.

"One of their headsets nearly fell off and the sound kept going."

Jai took a deep breath, turned around, grabbed a chair, and threw it across the room.

It crashed into the buffet just as the door opened and the next act, a solo pianist-singer, came in. "Fucking pieces of lying shit!"

Layton eased Jai down onto the couch and told him to take it easy. "I'd get you a glass of water, but you just spilled it everywhere."

"I don't want any goddamn water!"

The others returned to the television.

They scrutinized every movement of the mouths on the screen, and half the time when the act was facing backwards, toward the camera feeding the green room, the performers' were too busy gasping for breath to be singing.

"That's why they spin around so much."

"Obviously we have to lodge a complaint as soon as we're on stage," Britt said.

"No way," Grannie said. "That would turn everyone against us. Our time in the spotlight has to be about *us*."

"He's right," Layton said.

"Then we have to corner Felicia first chance we get." The act wound down.

The applause was riotous. All the judges loved it.

Harsh-Mellow bounced and skipped their way off the stage. #Five passed them in the hallway, all of them holding back Jai as they headed toward the light.

"Plex McGuire is a fossil. Couldn't they have found a host with a little more vitality?" Jai was sneering at the autographed photo that'd come in their swag bags. "How many of these things has he hosted? A million? Not to mention World Model. I mean, that guy must have banged five girls for each nationality on this planet."

"I think you just answered your question," Britt said. "That's why he's here. Girls dig him."

"But a music competition? I'm not feeling it."

The band tuned their instruments and prepared while one more act performed—the solo pianist who went by the name Serenity.

She had a voice as shiny as a gold nugget that'd been birthed by a rainbow. It was sickeningly perfect and impossible to argue with, except that it was wholly inoffensive and guarded. There was no edge, no rage, no heartbreak.

Her song was a passionless love song composed in a vacuum, an exercise in schmaltz.

Felicia agreed and voted against Serenity. Heidi and Andy of course were in love with her.

She waved to the crowd and thanked the judges but her displeasure with Felicia was explicit. "Alright, bitches," Layton hissed. "This is it."

"Bring it together," Grannie said to Britt as the stage started to pivot.

Britt raised his sticks and whispered it: "One. Two. Three. Four o'clock. Rock!" He touched his sticks together as the stage delivered them to Plex McGuire.

The lights were less effulgent this time. Still the band was sweating but not because they were overheating like in round one: the pressure within them was pushing through their skin.

The audience before them, now visible, was placid and composed, half as many people in attendance today but the room still well beyond capacity, with rows of people standing three-deep along the walls.

The judges sat at a booth halfway between the audience and the stage, their hands folded before them, each of them armed with a notepad and pen, a glass of water beside them vibrating as the stage shifted into place.

Layton adjusted his microphone. Somewhere a girl called out to them, but it sounded more like a sexual sigh than actual words. Britt dropped his stick as usual just to get it out of the way, his little elvin ritual of old, and Layton took the opportunity to step back and drink some water. As he was stepping back to the microphone, however, someone emerged from the audience—a little girl. The others watched her but did nothing.

No one tried to stop her, not even Heidi Starr who saw the girl out of the corner of her eye and turned in her seat to watch her, a tiny, fair-skinned thing of maybe eight or nine years of age. She walked right up to the stage and offered Layton a rose.

Layton glanced at Grannie, who nodded back. Layton then climbed down from the stage and crouched to meet the girl. He had a brief conversation with her there and then, on live television.

Standing back up he said, "Our visitor's name is Wendy, and her sister Wanda is performing in a short while. Thank you, Wendy."

As Wendy made her way back to her seat, someone called out to Layton, saying they loved him.

"That's a bit nutty, isn't it?" Layton said into the microphone. "At least let us get famous before you distort your perception of us."

The crowd laughed politely.

"Alrighty then," Plex said. "Wasn't that just adorable. Since both Wendy and Wanda and #Five are from Emmiline, hopefully they'll cross paths again. Maybe there's a duet on the horizon for Layton and Wanda?"

Plex glanced at the judges. As soon as Andy Rainer gave him the go-ahead, he relayed the signal to Layton.

Layton gave the sign to Britt. Britt counted them off. They tore into Felicia's song.

While the lyrics were only marginally better, the cadence was a legitimate and poppy 180 beats per minute.

The song unfolded. The band restrained themselves, doing their best not to deconstruct it with their natural post-rock tendencies, remembering that it was a pop song.

It was cotton candy, not pasta, not a salad.

Layton, inspired by the sensation and the setting and unable to fight off the Footloose-like cardinal sin of dancing, executed his trademark little twist: he popped his right foot behind his left heel, immediately switched, then slid an inch or two to the side, all the while keeping his arms at his side with his fists turned upwards.

He did this over and over as if confined to yet another closet. Step, step, slide. Sing. Step, step, slide. Sing. Jai picked up on the vibe and started swaying a little.

Even Grannie was having fun at the keys. Britt was terrifyingly precise and focused, leading the others to wonder if he'd downed some Ritalin.

A she-wolf in a dress, Layton sang with as much conviction as he could muster. *When you find me there, you'll search no more. Never and then forever. And pleasin' together forever through rain or whatever.*

Jai and Donovan joined in: *The way you drag your nails down my face. Take me as I am— take my life. Drinking the ocean dry. Oh, you're the apple of my eye.*

Layton: *When we threw our coins into the river. At last, your unforgiving lies. I want to spend the whole night in your eyes.*

Jai tore through a brief guitar solo, which the band had again written in for him.

Britt remained surprisingly restrained in his drumming.

Layton, however, felt like he was holding back too much, coasting through the lyrics and not reaching for another octave on the refrains, even though he was quite sure he could. As long as he hadn't been smoking or stuck in some grimy bar with no ventilation—both of which he'd been doing prior to Felicia's arrival in their lives—his throat would perform when called upon. Jai delivered the song back to him and jumped back to the microphone to finish it off, bringing Felicia's song into its closing beats as they repeated the chorus.

The audience broke into applause. A small cluster of people even rose to their feet. A few cameras flashed while a cameraman swept past on a dolly and a cable-mounted unit bobbed overhead and a third one stage-right recorded their sweat and red faces, the band standing there looking shell-shocked and mostly terrified.

"Thank Christ that is over," Jai muttered, sticking his pick in his mouth.

"Thank you, gentleman," Plex McGuire said. "Wow. Just *wow*. What a performance by these five men from our very own city. I haven't heard something like that in quite a while. Let's hear what the judges have to say. Heidi?"

Heidi leaned forward. "Hello, Hashtag."

The band had a hard time believing they were being addressed by her. Though she'd had some work done on her face over the years, she retained a natural, effortless glamor that the weathered and jaded Felicia didn't.

"I will say right off the bat," she continued, "that that was not my cup of tea."

"Nor was it mine," Andy Rainer said, jumping in immediately. He seemed to have a hard time looking at the band.

Layton glanced back at Grannie. Grannie stood tall, smiling his slanty smile, and gave a little shrug. Layton turned back to the judges: "I'm sorry to hear that."

Andy glanced at him but only for a millisecond, then turned back to Heidi. "It just seemed to me that the song was difficult for them, like they were unsure of it. Are they ready to be pop stars?"

When Layton shrugged, Grannie nearly walked off. But Layton saved it, saying, "Pop—I don't know. Rock—yes. We didn't want to blast you all out of the room today, so we played something a little lighter. I assure you we have more up our sleeves."

"Such as?" Heidi said.

"Big riffs. Solos. Dancing. The room is small, the stage is smaller. We were honoring the limitations and the audience."

"Pandering, you mean," Andy said, now glaring at him.

Layton returned the glare. "Call it what you will. We're real musicians. We don't have a backing track and we're not faking anything."

"Meaning what?"

"Meaning," Grannie said, leaping in, "that's it's simply an honor to be here playing music for our future fans. The road ahead is going to be wild."

Andy Rainer leaned forward, his mouth almost touching his microphone. "Wild, perhaps. A sure thing? Well, not as I see it. Thank you for coming." Andy hit his button, turning on a flashing red siren overhead.

"Nor mine." Heidi slapped hers. Two red sirens turned the auditorium into the venue into a charcoal bloodbath.

"Woah!" Plex said, strolling back into the light. "We have a rejection. Two 'nays.' That means the band—wait, wait. Felicia?"

Without a word Felicia raised a large, placard depicting the QuickFame logo with a golden microphone in the air. In an instant the red lights flashed to green.

"No, Felicia saves #Five!"

The other judges turned in their chairs to look at her.

"This is your pick?" Andy said. She nodded.

"What about it appealed to you?"

"Where do I start? How about with the vocals? Dense but lively, a voice like, I don't know, steak covered with frosting, you know?"

"No," Heidi said, "I don't know. I don't eat steak covered with frosting."

"It's a metaphor. It's muscular underneath but it's also sweet and indulgent when it needs to be."

"That's a mashup of tastes," Andy said, "which I concur is the case. But it's not necessarily a good thing. They're unsure of their own style and of themselves."

"No," Layton said, fighting back tears, "we're not."

Felicia nodded vigorously. "They're the real deal. They love to do this. They have talent. I loved it and I love them. Now let's get on with it, shall we?"

Andy and Heidi sighed and leaned back in their chairs. Andy shook his head.

"There you have it folks. Different strokes make for real stakes on QuickFame. And when I say stakes, I guess I mean the kind that come covered in frosting. *Mmm*, yum!"

***

Britt and Jordan stripped down to their boxers and cranked the AC unit to its maximum while Grannie checked his makeup to make sure it hadn't smeared too badly.

A knock on the suite's dividing door summoned them to open it and Layton and Donovan appeared, both shirtless but still wearing their jeans and shoes.

"Grannie, come out here."

Grannie emerged from the bathroom, a ring of sweat around his shirt collar. He didn't like stripping down in front of the others—a vestige of his days being forced to play on the "skins" team in gym class.

"You need to talk to Felicia about what happened up there," Britt said.

Donovan tore his Plex McGuire photo into tiny squares. "And about the lip synching bullshit.

Obviously the QuickFame people are in on that. Someone had to be told to play the track."

"I want to play our songs," Layton said. "We can't keep faking it with this alt-pop crap or whatever it is."

"I'll change my shirt and head down there."

"And ask her how some of these other crap bands made it to the semi-finals. I mean, c'mon.

A gothy speed-metal strings quartet? Hasn't that entire genre been laughed out of existence?"

"I kind of liked it," Jai said, punching out Plex McGuire's eyes with a chopstick.

Grannie got a fresh t-shirt—black, identical to the one he had on—and returned to the bathroom. He sat on the toilet and took ten slow, deep breaths. He'd just finished exhaling the last one when his pocket buzzed.

"Yeah," he said.

"Great performance today," the caller said.

"Felicia?"

"You held your own and you stuck together as a group."

"We need to talk. Like, right now. Where are you?"

"I've got my feet in the air and a glass of champagne in my cute little fingers."

"I'll be there in two minutes."

"No, you won't. I'm not there. I'm here. And you'll be joining me in an hour. There will be a limo waiting outside the hotel. It'll take you to Plex's estate, along with the other surviving acts."

"What for?"

"What for? To celebrate, to get to know one another, to network and plant seeds should this all fall through."

"It almost fell through just an hour ago."

"All according to plan."

"It was?"

"Put on your best shirt. Preferably with buttons. I'll see you soon.

***

The band emerged out the front of the hotel to find a row of stretch limos waiting at the curb.

Fashionably late, #Five was relegated to the last one, a 1985 Cadillac Fleetwood with a sunroof that wouldn't close all the way and had no minibar.

Photographers lined the sidewalk, cordoned off by velvet ropes. They called out to the band, asking them to wave or smile or give their opinion on the other acts.

Grannie pulled Britt's arm out of the air. "Don't wave. Act like you don't care. We're above this. We've already won but we also don't care."

"You little rock star, you. You've got this whole fame thing all figured out already."

The limo carried them out of Emmiline and toward the foothills.

Soon they ascended the narrow and nauseatingly winding roads that separated the one-percenters from the rest of the world. Every now and then they would spot one of the other limos on a curve above them.

"This feels weird," Layton said. "Old-school, dirty weird, like we're going to be given Quaaludes, maybe raped, filmed, blackmailed, forced to sign a deal with the devil, et cetera. Some sort of Playboy mansion scenario."

"Don't touch anything you didn't pour yourself," Grannie said. "And don't touch alcohol. You will not know where to stop and if you want to win this thing, everything hinges upon the small decision you make. And you're too young to drink anyways. You never know who is watching. Could be a test."

Layton arched an eyebrow. "You're too young, too, big guy." Grannie turned to look out the window. "I know."

The limo struggled up the last climb, the steepest, but managed to get them there. The band waited for the driver to let them out; they waited some more.

Finally, Britt tapped on the divider with a practice drumstick he'd brought with him.

"Yeah," the driver said as he worked on the first three inches of a foot-long sub.

"Any chance we could get out?"

"Door's got handles. Pull them."

"Isn't that your job?"

"I'm hungry."

The guy showed them the sandwich he was eating. They filed out. They filed into Plex McGuire's mansion.

An hour later most of the other bands were staggering drunk. #Five isolated themselves, sipping from green beer bottles that they'd reclaimed, washed, and refilled with soda. All around them revelers hooted, slapped one another's backs, handed out business cards, shook hands, grabbed asses, pinched breasts to see if they were real, slapped in jest, slapped for real.

A fifty-something woman with a platinum blond coif and dressed in a creamy white pantsuit strolled up to the band while tugging on her gaudy gold necklace. "My, my, my, aren't we—"

"Fuck off!" Britt said, and the woman nearly tripped on the carpet as she skidded to a halt.

She *harumph*'ed and retreated the way she'd come. "What'd you do that for?" Grannie asked.

Britt shrugged. "Just playing the part."

"She could have been a music exec or married to one."

He shrugged again. "Then it just piqued her curiosity is all."

"You've got women all figured out, haven't you," Donovan said.

Britt gestured back at him obligingly. "I'm learning from the best, bitch."

"Screw you."

"Here? Let me get some real beer first."

"Go to hell."

"Hell would consist of twenty-four hours of dance performances by Harsh-Mellow. Oh shit!" Donovan snickered.

"I think I agree with you there, asshole."

Britt poked Grannie in the ribs with his stick. "There goes the queen! Sic' em, Grandma."

"I think I need a real drink for that."

Britt poked him harder. "Before she gets eaten up. Go!"

"Damn it."

One more shove and Grannie was thrown into the crowd. He weaved and bobbed, keeping his eye on Felicia, but stopped short whenever someone cornered her or summed her closer.

He'd stand and watch from afar but as soon as she'd extricated herself and made it another five feet further into the party someone else would throw themselves in front of her.

Felicia, I have someone you just have to meet.

Felicia, is that group with the Theremin player going to take the crown? Darling, give us a kiss.

Grannie proceeded and halted, proceeded, and halted, all the while studying Felicia's mastery of the crowd. Her facade never broke even when faced with the most inane drivel pouring out the side of some limp noodle's mouth.

Finally, she stepped out onto the side-yard veranda to catch some air and have a moment to herself. Grannie wouldn't let her though.

"You have to let us play our songs!" he yelled as he pulled open the huge glass door.

"Christ! You almost made me throw myself over the ledge."

"Sorry. I didn't think I would ever get a moment with you. I've been trailing you through the party for twenty minutes."

"I noticed."

"You did? Why didn't you do anything?"

"I assumed you're just infatuated with me."

Grannie's face grew hot.

They were mostly in the shadows but the climate in this part of the city was arid and unforgiving, and his sweat was surely catching the glint of the outside lights.

"We need to talk about what happened."

"Fine, but not here."

She took hold of his hand and led him back inside. Partygoers smiled and waved and beckoned her to come chat with them or introduce her to her little friend, but she ignored all of them.

She reached the foot of a dark hardwood staircase wide enough to accommodate a Hummer and pulled him upwards. Her hand was soft and strong, and she moved like Britt, with short quick steps but faster, more athletically and gracefully. He was overcome with arousal and wanted to let go of her hand but dared not. At the top she pulled him down the long carpeted hallway, bypassing a number of doors. The upper storey was almost empty save for a few voices laughing here and there.

She opened a door and led him into an office containing minimalist, gleaming white furniture. Along the south wall sat a glass case holding all of Plex McGuire's various awards, along with photos of him with famous people from genres and offshoots of the entertainment industry. The room's white couch was made from organic cotton, not leather, meaning Felicia's legs didn't make a farty sound as she plopped down onto it.

She slapped the cushion beside her. Grannie sat.

"Surprisingly tasteful for Plex."

"You can't assume you know someone just because you see them on TV. And you can't assume they're not garbage just because they hired a talented interior decorator."

Grannie nodded. "They hated our song. What the hell happened up there?"

"I didn't expect it but it's good. It makes you into the underdogs, moving forward despite the odds being against you."

"It makes us look like a joke. Look, Felicia, you are supremely talented at what you do but your songs are not for us. We need our music back. We feel like puppets up there. They saw our discomfort and how it was, like, just, you know—not good!"

"It wasn't good, I agree. But that's not a deal breaker for this type of thing. Look, did you see the performance by that guy Hals Angel?"

"The guy with the puffy lips? I saw maybe twenty seconds of it. It was awful."

"He's forty-three years old, has had multiple plastic surgery procedures, and has the voice that sounds like a rubber dog toy being crushed in a vise. How do you think he managed to get to round three?"

"Heidi overrode your and Andy's votes."

"Exactly. So, I looked into it. Well, more precisely I had someone who knows how to do such things look into it, a kid about your age." She paused a beat. "He's a hacker or investigator who wears a white hat, I guess. Anyways, he dug into Heidi's past and found that she and Hals have longstanding family ties. She's paying him some sort of favor. Maybe she was his babysitter and dropped him on his head or something. Who knows."

"So, it's rigged."

She sighed and waved her hand in the air. "It is and it isn't. Andy is going to pay back a favor or two, or maybe he already has his perfectly manicured claws dug into a group already.

"And the lip-synching morons?"

Her head jerked backwards as if poked in her little button nose.

"You know about that?"

"It was super obvious from our vantage."

She nodded, squinting. "I wasn't sure how to handle it but it's clear that something has to be done."

Grannie moved closer. "Like what?"

Felicia crossed her legs and leaned back. "I dunno. Maybe a video of their headset malfunction will be leaked."

"That reminds me. What about the hubbub with the fans and the media? It seems sort of, you know, contrived, us getting attention, the girl with the flower and so on. Are you instigating them and setting it all up?"

"Me? God no. I don't know anything about social media and making things go viral." Grannie exhaled.

"Good. That's a relief."

"But my social media team have a talent for it."

"Come on!"

"It's just part of the game. I want to create a story. That's what makes a band. That's what creates reality TV ratings. Are you interested in becoming stars? *Big* stars?"

"Of course."

"Also, it's good for me personally since it diverts attention away from all the arguing and sniping with Andy."

"It seems like Heidi is the one who's going to be our foe here."

"She'll come around. Tomorrow you're playing two songs. It's like an actual concert."

"And we'll play our own."

She looked at him.

"It'll be over tomorrow if we don't figure this out. There are some things that I have a knack for, an instinct, and this is it, music. I know what I'm doing with our sound. I help write the songs. This is what we need to win, to be ourselves. You can't snip our wings or lop off our balls with your very feminine, very mainstream songs. Please believe me when I say—"

Felicia pressed her mouth to his to shut up. She held it there until he ran out of breath. No tongue, no caressing, no eye contact. Just two sets of lips holding conference in the upper level of a mansion high up on the outskirts of Emmiline, city of dreams, city of murdered hopes.

She released.

"Wow," Grannie said. "Don't tell anyone."

"No one?"

"No one."

"I'll need another payment to seal the deal."

"Fine."

Felicia stuck her finger in her mouth then stuck it in his.

"We good?"

He nodded.

Then she pulled it out and left him sitting there on the couch.

***

It was even harder to make it to the gym at six a.m. the next morning. This time, however, he was able to snag a double espresso from a caterer preparing the continental breakfast. The bitter jolt of caffeine slowly started to take the edge off the few hours of sleep.

He sipped it as he shuffled along the mesmerizingly hideous carpet toward the gym, ran his keycard, tied his shoes, and climbed onto the treadmill.

He stared at the bluish-gray wall and thought of Felicia.

She was not his type. She was much older. She was still married, she said. The music industry had left her jaded, broke, and disillusioned. She had a short temper, was impatient, and didn't read books or follow the political revolutions occurring all over the world at any given moment, not to mention the impact of climate change on the industry—outdoor concerts soon too hot for most countries, surely to become some Scandinavian quirk, plus a curbing of unnecessary touring.

But there was virtually nothing about her he didn't like. Her breathe smelled like the syrup of a birch tree and her skin like the sand of a beach he'd only dreamt of. She was made of muscle and sinew and raw determination in the face of ridiculous odds.

She burned with a Latino fire that he found enthralling.

When life was pushing against her with gale force, she leaned forward and dug in her very tall, very sharp heels.

Just to be with her once...

Grannie increased the incline on the treadmill and picked up the pace.

He needed to keep the fat at bay. He wasn't a kid anymore.

4.
JUST ASK ME IF I FUCKING CARE

Anytime Britt wanted to know anything about the gay lifestyle, he simply asked Donovan. Donovan was out and proud and willing to discuss everything from sex (which he'd experienced more than all the other members of the band combined, including Grannie) to etiquette to politics to psychology.

Donovan's parents weren't too happy with his "choice," but that wasn't his problem. They'd have to come around, just like the band had. He had told the other guys about six months after they'd formed the band, hanging out one Friday night in Britt's two-car garage, a typical weekend event. They were taking a break at the time. Britt was perched on his father's Harley, even though his legs weren't long enough to ride it. Nor was he strong enough to handle it. Donovan wandered over and asked Britt to turn on the bike so he could honk the horn. He did; it was loud; the other guys were pissed.

"I wanted to get your attention," Donovan had said. "I have something to tell you. I am gay." They all laughed.

"I'm not kidding."

"We know you're not kidding."

Apparently, they'd been aware all along.

Or suspected strongly.

Donovan wasn't overt or flamboyant, but he did have some tells. Mainly he liked to flip his wrist, that highly typical if not stereotypical giveaway. (A punk band had even named themselves after such a gesture, and after Britt and Donovan had watched dozens of grainy videos on YouTube, they both half fell in love with that rollicking, screamy, old-school punk sound.)

Britt asked Donovan if he wanted to hop on the back seat of the Harley. "You need to get used to wrapping your arms around a man."

"Shut up, bitch."

Shortly after band practice ended, Britt's father Leo came home. The garage door rumbled upwards about fifteen seconds before Leo rounded the last bend of their winding suburban driveway.

Britt had been famished after working the sticks for three hours and needed his daily protein shake filled to the brim with creatine powder and Gainr 2000; thus, he hadn't yet put away his kit. His father put it away for him.

Britt sprinted into the garage and found the kit smashed the bumper of the truck and the wall of the garage.

"You'll fix the wall by the end of the week," Leo had said. "What about my drums?"

"Get a job, then you can buy another set."

The band had to pool their resources to buy Britt a new kit.

They kept it in Layton's basement and practiced there while talking about finding a new place to practice, but Britt's was the only place that gave them enough room to really cut loose. So, after an interval of peace between Leo and the Quakes, the band arrived there one Friday night to practice. They almost turned around and went home when they found out Leo was there. Leo didn't drink but he had the temper of a snapping turtle with rabies and somehow, he'd gotten word through one grapevine or the other that Donovan had come out as gay. He took that as a mark against his son and thus a mark against himself.

After interrupting the band five times to berate Britt for one minor domestic infraction or another, the Quakes simply turned off their instruments and decided to call it quits. They thought that's what Leo had wanted but in truth he just wanted to puff out his chest like a silverback and make sure that these queers in black jeans and tattered shirts knew that he was not into men. Leo, surprisingly, was not a small man. He'd built his wealth on granite countertops and tables and his trade revealed itself in his muscles, his forearms especially. Donovan once saw him crush a warm toaster with a single hand, which he then threw through a closet door.

Later that night, hours after the band had left, Britt showed up at Donovan's house. He had bruises on his shoulder from where the Claws of Leo had clamped down on him prior to hurling him across his bedroom.

Britt arrived at Donovan's with nothing except his favorite high hats (which had not been in use during the car-crash scenario), his quiver of sticks, and his backpack, which was filled with a change of clothes but not schoolbooks. Donovan's parents were members of a religious faith that peddled in pure, immutable guilt and even though they didn't like Britt much and were still coming to terms with their son's homosexuality (Donovan himself being someone they'd struggled to like prior to the revelation), they couldn't turn away the kid.

"He's just so small," Donovan's mother had said to her husband. "He must get chilly very easily."

Britt stayed there indefinitely, sleeping in the room Donovan's college-aged sister had vacated.

The bed was huge; each night he felt like he was swimming himself to sleep.

Felicia Scalding was more Britt's size. Her shoes typically elevated her an inch or two above him, but the day she came to visit Britt himself—*him*—at Donovan's house, she asked if it was ok to remove those shoes. Britt said yes. Then he asked if she wanted him to rub her feet, saying that he knew where Donovan's mother kept her creams and oils.

"That's sweet of you," Felicia had said.

"Nothing sweet about it. It'd be the best moment of my life."

Donovan wasn't home yet. He was in chorus practice or at a classical guitar lesson or something.

Nor were Donovan's parents, thank God. How to explain such a meeting taking place in their brown living room with its beige rug and frilly lampshades?

It wasn't hard for Felicia to sell Britt on her plan to shuttle the band to the top of the world in just weeks: first QuickFame USA and then the global competition. He didn't really believe they had a chance, and he wasn't sure Felicia believed it either, but he knew it would be a good ride.

"But you must do me a favor," Felicia said. "You have to be yourself. And by yourself, I mean you need to play up the worst qualities of your personality. From what I can tell you're the bad boy, the rebel, the wiseass. All bands need one of those, but you need to be smarter than the typical one who cites disreputable websites or spouts off fake news. I want you to be sardonic but educated. Read up. Stay in school. But be cool."

"That's easy. I read. Shit, I have a dictionary."

"Party hard but not too hard. Woo girls but don't knock them up. We don't need that at this stage. Love cleanly. Be honest with them but be firm with yourself. You don't have to hold back on your wants."

"Can I tell you what I want at this very moment?"

"No. Is Donovan home? I need to talk to him as well."

That night the bed in Donovan's sister's room felt larger than ever.

In some clubs it could serve as a riser.

Britt had always believed in Shakespeare's quip that the entire world is a stage, and that's why Britt was so inclined to snark and snipe and grind everyone down all the time: everyone was always watching and listening, so might as well play the part. Plus, it made him feel taller.

Britt had snuck back to his parents' house to get some things, including his motorcycle, a machine more suitable for a petite woman but fast enough to dodge the cops if he got a head start. After Felicia's visit, he went back a second time to get some clothes, parking down the street and walking up the driveway in the rain. He rang the doorbell and Leo answered it in his boxers and t-shirt, a bowl of ice cream in his Claws like Tony Soprano but slightly less tyrannical and far less charming.

"I just need some clothes."

"Your mother wants to talk to you."

"She can call me."

Britt skirted Leo and headed up the stairs. Leo followed him, slurping at his ice cream. "She asked for us to all sit down next week and have a chat. Friday."

"I can't. I'm going to be on a show called QuickFame. It starts soon and there's tons to do before then."

Britt opened the door to his room. It was a mess, the contents of all the drawers tipped onto the floor, papers and books strewn all over, the bed at an angle and the mattress devoid of sheets and pillows.

Leo had been looking for something. Drugs perhaps, or evidence of gayness.

"You can't do that. You have school."

"We got permission."

"You didn't get it from me."

"I forged your signature."

"You little punk. You can't do that!" Leo's face was bright red. Ice cream had dribbled down his chin and the front of his t-shirt, which depicted some cheesy Harley tribute band, *Hogg Wylde*.

"I can do whatever I want ever since you tried to snap my neck."

"I did no such thing."

"Donovan took pictures."

"I knew it. That queer. He got you to remove your clothes and then he photographed you."

Britt laughed as he went around the room stuffing clothes into his backpack. He didn't need much and when he went to leave, he found Leo blocking the door.

"QuickFame, huh? I seen that show. It's good stuff. Who's judging?"

Britt scoffed and brushed past his father. His father set down his bowl on a marble sideboard and followed him back down the stairs.

"Wait. Just wait."

"No."

"Please, son. Please. You want some ice cream?"

"Nope."

Britt wanted a photograph of his mother. He went to the living room and grabbed his favorite one off the fireplace mantel.

"Ok, you can take that. Sure, you don't want the one of the three of us at the beach last year?"

"No fucking way."

"Britt."

The Claws of Leo rose into the air. Britt expected them to inflict some last-minute damage on both Britt's psyche and his body. Instead, his father tried to hug him.

"I'm sorry."

Britt wrenched free. Leo, stunned, fell backwards into his recliner. His face sunk into his hands, and he started to weep.

"I always knew you'd be something. I know you've got talent. Even with all my meddling and trash talk you still became something."

He lifted his head. His eyes were red but not watery.

"You see, I was just trying to get you to experience a few hard knocks, which is what it's going to be like in the real world, not to mention the music world, which is filled with fairies and con artists and pedophiles. I was trying to get you to toughen up so you can fend them off."

"You humiliated me in front of my friends over and over. You called me Tiny Todd, Wee Man, and Supershrimp. Which is an oxymoron, you moron."

Leo stuffed his face into his hands again. "Just don't forget about me. And don't leave your mother behind."

"She knows I love her."

Leo rubbed his eyes and stood up. "If you had just done what I'd said we could have gotten along better. We could have been friends."

"I know I was a shit now and then, but you screwed it all up when you got violent. I see one bruise on Mom, and I'll come back here and kill you. I'll cut the brake lines on your motorcycle and your trucks. I'll poison your ice cream, Leo."

"Call me 'Dad.' I'm your father."

Britt looked at him, sneering. "'Dad'? Ha ha ha. Good one. *Dad*. Pops. Big Man."

"Watch it, Britt. I'm offering an olive branch here."

"Stick the branch up your ass."

Britt slung his bag over his shoulder and walked towards the front door. Then he stopped and went to the kitchen and started emptying the food from the fridge and cupboards into a grocery bag.

"Don't touch that food."

"You're required by law to provide nourishment for your offspring. Look it up."

"You said it yourself, I'm not your father."

"Mom does the shopping. We both know that, you idiot."

Leo's cheeks were as red as his eyes.

"You know what? You and your fag friends can go to hell. Snort cocaine, get groupies pregnant, get AIDS, I don't care."

Britt shrugged. "Alright."

"If you weren't so tiny, I'd pound you into the ground." Britt rolled his eyes and slammed the refrigerator door shut.

"Stop. Come back here."

"Goodbye, Leo."

"You know what? I hope they have a good stool for you, otherwise the TV camera won't be able to see you over your own drum kit."

"It's your shitty genetics that caused this, so you might as well stop riding me for it."

Britt left the front door open behind him as he headed out into the night. His father had left his truck in the driveway and as Britt strolled past, he whipped out his motorcycle key and dragged it along the side.

"Stop that, you little prick!"

He did it again on the other side, then took off running into the rain.

Now Britt missed the bed in Donovan's sister's room. The cot Locando Heights had provided had not one but two crossbars that made it impossible to get comfortable, forcing Britt to sleep on the edge and curl up against the wall. That's why Donovan was now in bed with Grannie—he couldn't stand the bars in his own cot.

Britt's dreams had been violent and repetitive. The alcohol didn't help, though in reality Britt was dumping out half of everything he acquired. He got drunk after two shots and one beer as it were. That is, if he could manage to get it all down. His stomach couldn't handle the alcohol, and if he was hung over, he couldn't keep the beat. But he had to maintain his image so he procured alcohol however he could, usually the old-fashioned way: by begging someone outside a liquor store. But sometimes he did it by wearing his motorcycle helmet inside the store and speaking in a low voice. For some reason clerks thought that if someone was tough enough to speed around on a cafe racer like that, he must be old enough to buy alcohol.

Grannie and Donovan were always awake before him, having slept better. Once they'd left for breakfast he'd crawl to the bed, try, and get another twenty minutes of sleep. The bed was closer to the AC unit and if he couldn't sleep, he'd lie there with the cold air blowing across his chest, visualizing himself tearing through a five-minute solo in a venerable club in the heart of the Old City. In this fantasy his shirt was off, and sweat was flying from his brow with each stomp on the bass drum pedal. He pictured the women that would be reaching out to catch said sweat like frankincense or some magical elixir. One of them would be his future wife. She would give birth to their child. That kid could pound on the kitchen pots and pans all he or she wanted and could become whatever he or she wanted to be, no matter how tall.

He'd never touch them in anger.

He sat up. First #Five had to win this contest. And to do that they had to do a lot more than play like champions.

Britt took a quick shower, dried his hair, and then messed it up, put on the same sweat-stinking clothes from yesterday, then rinsed his mouth with vodka and dabbed some on his neck. So far, the ruse had been working, though Britt rued the idea of another confrontation with Jai. That dude had serious issues and if he didn't deal with them or at least get a prescription, the kid was going to end up like Leo, only sooner—like before he was able to get that driver's license, he so coveted.

The hotel, surprisingly, was still booked to max capacity. Though only eleven musical acts were still battling in QuickFame, tons of people had remained to watch the final two rounds and the media and public were also crowding in. Britt put on his sunglasses, slung his quiver over his back—practice sticks in his hand—and stepped out into the hallway. He immediately locked in on three girls glancing over their shoulders at him. Whispering commenced. *Shh, shh. Hush. Stop.* Giggling. The coy game. Britt strolled past while drumming on his legs. *"Bah bah dum, bah bah dum,"* mouthing the words to his favorite Quakes tune.

People had amassed near the elevators, waiting their turn, but when they saw Britt, they stepped back.

"Please, go ahead."

"It's alright," Britt said. "No rush."

"Really, it's ok."

Britt moved to the front of the line. When the elevator arrived he hopped in and the others followed. They gave him some room to let him continue his thigh-drumming, his sticks going *whap whap whappity whap.*

A Leo-type guy leaned over and said, "That Heidi Starr is quite a—"

"Cunt?"

"Oh, um. I was going to say—"

"Bitch?"

"I—"

"Washed-up hag?"

"Something more like that. An angry has-been. But what I was going to say was—"

"She's got an edge to her, that's for sure. I'd like to soften her up." *Whappity whappity whappity.*

The guy laughed an awkward, uncomfortable laugh. "I think she had a point though. Our song was crap."

"No! It was right on. Reminded me of early Stones."

Britt stopped drumming and laid a tiny finger on his sunglasses and tilted them down so that the guy could see Britt's eyes. Everyone in the elevator had pivoted or was glancing over their shoulder. "It was grade-A garbage, man. Be honest. But it wasn't *our* song. Look for something more authentic this time around."

"I didn't like it," a teenager girl said. She wasn't a cheerleader-type or anything, but more of a choir-and-mathlete type, with glasses and straight brown hair. She had a certain style. She looked like she did yoga or maybe a martial art. "I thought it was derivative and trite."

Britt pushed his sunglasses back up. "She speaks the truth. What's your name?"

"Violet."

"Cool. Rad name. Maybe I'll be sure to dedicate a less-trite song to you tonight."

She laughed a dorky, snort-filled laugh. "Right."

"You don't believe me?"

The elevator's inhabitants were all holding their breath.

"I don't know," she said. "Whatever. It doesn't really matter since there's no way you're going to beat Scarlett Fever or the Whip Smarts. The other bands are terrible though."

Britt laughed. "Violet. *Violent* Violet. *Vicious* Violet. Violet is like purple, isn't it? The color of a bruise."

Violet seemed to be blushing, though Britt couldn't quite tell through the dark lenses of his mirrored aviator lenses.

"I appreciate your honesty. I haven't been involved with the music industry more than a couple of days and already I've seen that it's comprised mainly of liars and schemers."

The elevator dinged. Everyone stepped aside to let Britt through.

He delivered a miniature solo on the elevator wall, then stepped out, spun around, saluted them, and, finally, exhaled in relief. He wasn't sure if there was any seismic activity occurring today, but it certainly felt like the ground was unstable.

"You once again stink," Jai said, getting up to move to another couch in the ad hoc lounge that QuickFame had set up outside the green rooms.

Britt shrugged, set down his plateful of onion bagels topped with avocado, and took a long, hard pull on his coffee. "Glad I found you guys."

"Couldn't have been that hard."

"The caterers were already putting breakfast away. I had to beg them to get me something out of the kitchen."

"Maybe if you woke up on time for once you'd be able to stick to the band's schedule and not just your own."

"Take it easy, Jai," Donovan said, moving over to take Jai's spot beside Britt.

Britt started in on the bagel. It was good. He hadn't had an avocado like this in a long time. Since arriving at the hotel he hadn't been able to do his daily protein shakes. It didn't fit with his personal brand. He was supposed to be smoking cigarettes, but those things made it feel like someone was running a scraper down the inside of his lungs.

Afterwards his face felt like it was on fire. It messed up his drumming.

Jai waved off Britt and Donovan and turned his attention to the girl sitting next to him—Tona Kohl, the lead singer from Scarlett Fever. Her attention, however, was focused entirely on Layton.

"Check it out," Donovan said, jutting his chin toward Layton. He looked like he was trying to compress his body into the armrest of the couch to get further away from Tona.

"He likes girls, doesn't he?"

Donovan shrugged. "Far as I know. He dated Kim Prescott last year. She didn't kill herself or anything afterwards."

Britt finished his bagel and started in on the second while studying the other faces in the room. In addition to the entirely ravishing Tona Kohl, with her fiery orange hair, tattoos (full sleeves at age eighteen), perfectly distressed jeans, and loose top that showed off her pierced belly button (encircled with a tattoo of a Celtic sword).

The other members of Scarlett Fever were mingling or avoiding mingling: the muscular black drummer with dreadlocks that reached halfway down his spine, currently stirring something endlessly while staring off into space; the nerdy bassist with his polo shirt buttoned to the neck, which he was using to polish the lenses of his eyeglasses; and the ludicrously crusty, leather-jacket-wearing guitarist, who must have been pushing thirty.

His manbun was so tight it was pulling his eyes into an expression like that of someone racing a motorcycle down the highway without a helmet, while his tattoos were of the make-it-look-like-I- got-these-in-the-penitentiary sort and his starved, wiry frame was striving for the heroin-chic look. Britt saw him belch, then run the back of his hand across his nose just before digging into a bowl of red grapes.

Grannie was on the far side of the room chatting with alt-country solo act Cat Coggan. That was expected. The night before, rolling back to the hotel in the limo, they'd trash-talked that guy for nearly forty-five minutes straight. *Namby-pampby. Garfunkelesque. As sharp as a hammer. As wispy sounding as Bon Iver with strep throat.* Only Grannie had said he liked the guy's voice and style, that he was the real deal, that his lyrics were poignant and poetic, and his finger picking was not only magnificent, the sound he evoked from that battered Mexican guitar was unlike anything popular or alternative music had seen in years.

On another set of couches were members of Justice of Weather, an all-male, all-Asian nü-metal act, and Cherubicon, an all-female band whose math-rock-infused pop no one could quite put their finger on, only that they were good at what they did and their sound was inimitable and therefore precious, something to be fostered and commoditized before the conceit wore off and they were relegated to the category of "good but weird if you like that sort of thing."

Layton finally got up from the couch, making some half-baked excuse about needing to gargle some green tea. Tona watched him go, then pivoted around, coming face to face with Britt and Donovan. She rolled her eyes and flipped her hand in the air while offering a smile that followed a direct path through Britt's eyes, into his heart, where it boiled a moment, then shot down to his stomach, where it coagulated with the onion bagels and avocado, then spun wildly into his loins, where it wreaked havoc on his teenage hormones. To divert attention from his bulging pants, Britt offered her the last half of his second bagel. "Brekkie?"

"Thanks, I had a banana."

"Gonna be a long day."

"If I eat too much, I'll regurgitate it on stage."

"Eat too little and you'll pass out under those hot lights."

She looked at him with heightened curiosity. "Aren't you the little thinker. Shit, sorry, I didn't mean for it to come out like that."

"I may be short but I'm not little, if you know what I mean." The color drained from Tona's face.

"Christ, Britt," Donovan said, and vacated the couch—Jai leaping back in to fill the void.

But Tona only smiled and laughed. "Alright. I'll have that bagel."

As she reached for it, Britt noticed that the insides of each finger on her right hand was tattooed with a single letter, spelling out *b-l-a-z-e*, and on the other side of the finger *'n-b-u-r-n*.

"Let me get you some water," Britt said, rising.

"Coffee would be great, actually."

Britt shook his head. "That's too hard on your throat."

"Some milk then."

Britt scoffed. "You fricking serious? That pus and lactose will clog you up. Not to mention— it's milk. Nasty. You can have tea or water."

"Don't you want my throat to be compromised? Maybe I'll miss some notes and go down in a ball of flame, leaving an open path for #Five."

"We want to win on merit," Jai said.

"That's right," Britt said. "We want to win because we earned it, not because the other acts were less bad."

The smile toyed with her mouth again. "Fine. Water then."

Britt marched off and she turned to Jai. "Cute guy. He acts tough but he's a sweetie."

"He's already infatuated with you but don't let it fool you. He's the size of a gnat and has the impatience of one."

The smile vanished. "Well, I'm as messed up as they come. I eat men. I take years off their mother's lives."

"How so?"

"Something about me tends to evoke maternal issues in my lovers. Then end up calling their mommies in the middle of the night."

"Aren't you a bit young to be wreaking such havoc?"

She sneered. "Gotta have something to write about, you know? Live loud, sing louder."

"How about we write a love song together?"

Tona's face went blank a moment as she tried to figure out if this guy was for real or not. "I, uh, write songs with my band."

"A side project then."

"Depends on what happens here today."

Britt returned. With him was Grannie, who said, "Group meeting."

"Uh oh," Tona said. "Sounds serious. I should probably organize one of those too."

"You're welcome to attend ours," Britt said.

Tona accepted the glass of water and napkin. She finished the bagel, then emptied the glass. Britt stuck out his hand. "I'll take care of it."

Grannie poked him in the back, laughing.

Tona stood up. In her thick-heeled boots she was at least four inches taller than Britt. "I got it, doll. But thanks. I'm glad there are still good ones left in the world." She leaned in and gave him a kiss on his cheek.

"What the fuck was that?" Jai said as they all watched her walk off.

Two hours before showtime the band filed into the soundproof green room to prepare.

The couches were beat-up and reeked of smoke and urine. The carpet bore dozens of cigarette burns. The ceiling was stained yellow. They turned off the TV off and sipped water. They stretched. They took turns lying on the couches with their eyes closed and their feet in the air.

"This is depressing," Jai said. "It ends here, doesn't it."

Grannie grabbed a stool and sat in the middle of the two couches. "The Latina Queen is pissed, brothers. I begged and pleaded and reasoned with her about the songs. But listen up. I've come up with a solution.

The band listened closely, considering the idea Grannie presented. Then they got out their instruments.

After ninety minutes they agreed that it was good—good enough. They put away their instruments and tried to relax.

Jai kept his eye on Britt. "You sober?" he asked.

Britt, lying on the floor with his socked feet on Donovan's legs up on the couch, opened a single eye. "You talkin' to me?"

"No, the other goombah with a penchant for brushing his teeth with whiskey."

"Shut up, Jai," Donovan said.

"No, Jerry, I haven't been drinking today. I did shoot up in the bathroom though."

"Don't joke about that," Jai said.

"There's nothing to worry about. I'm not twenty-seven, so the curse hasn't struck yet."

With fifteen minutes to go a security goon rapped on the door. Everyone leapt up. They put on their shoes and took one last sip of water. They pissed. They cleared their throats. They fixed their hair (Layton) or made it worse (Britt). They fixed their makeup (Grannie) or dropped Visine in their eyes (Jai). They grabbed their instruments and stood by the door in silence. They could make out the vague thunder of applause as Scarlett Fever exited the stage, waiting until the four of them had made their way down the hall to a different green room.

"You ready?" Grannie whispered, then stuck out his hand. The others laid theirs atop it. "*One, two, three, four o'clock. Good. Let's rock.*" They threw their hands in the air.

The door opened again, and the guard led them to the stage where Plex McGuire was getting his makeup touched up by a tall blonde who was probably borrowed from a daytime game show. #Five was granted plenty of time to set up and to do a last-minute tuning and sound check. Meanwhile the audience murmured in the background. #Five had no idea how the previous performances had gone, with Cat Coggan set to perform last, after their two-song set. Then the judges would decide which three bands would head to the final round, a concert at the historically renowned and acoustically perfect 13-666 club down in the Chiroma Alley, the grittiest part of Emmiline, where the most venerated and culturally significant acts typically performed.

Grannie gave them a thumbs up; the stage manager signaled to the Plex.

Plex gave a thumb's up to the judges.

The lights came up and the camera blinked on. "Gentlemen! Welcome back. You must be thrilled to have made it this far. Quite a feat! Last night there was some disagreement as to whether you should continue, so, to be honest, you really have to wow us tonight."

Plex stared at Layton, fishing for some sort of response. "Uh, yeah," Layton said.

Plex smiled and laughed a wooden laugh. "#Five. Very cool. Tell us more about the name, especially for the folks at home who might not understand internet slang."

Layton frowned and fiddled with his microphone stand. "It's a stupid name. We just though it'd go viral."

He shrugged his skinny shoulders. "Just having a laugh."

"I see." Plex forced another smile. "Well, without further ado, let's hear some music, shall we?"

"That sounds like a great idea," Layton said. "This—"

"This one's for Violet!" Britt called out from the back.

Plex gave the little drummer boy a thumb's up and exited stage left where the same woman checked his makeup again.

Layton looked to Britt, Britt wiped his hands on his jeans and counted them off. Jai's pick awoke The Scythe.

They'd spent the afternoon tinkering with Felicia's song, another one of her ready-made radio ear-bombs.

It wasn't terrible but it had a leaden quality, with trite lyrics playing on the same dull themes and a messy harmony. #Five stripped it down and then built it back up, with Grannie serving as paramedic, layering in reverb, some voice modulation, and some grit while also lowering the bass and drums to let Layton's vocals mix more fluidly with Jai's strings.

We threw our coins into the river.
Then you dragged your nails down my face.
Take me as I am, oh, take my life.
At last, I'm home in your unforgiving eyes.
I want to spend the whole night drinking the ocean dry.

Jai went for a guitar solo while Britt went easy on the drums and Grannie laid down a steady layer of major chords. Donovan maintained the undercurrent, a steady *thrum thrum thrum,* his fingers—no pick—coercing the sound out of them.

You said you saw the other side of the moon.
And I said we'd never even left your room.
Oh, If I'm just bad news, then you're a liar.
Crush two stones with your fist, then set me on fire.

In a hole beneath the dead cemetery oak.
Let the night wear us down, overshadow us with its cloak.
Don't go you said, you wouldn't dare.
Oh, just ask me if I fucking care.

They rode out the song as Felicia had written it, which was just a repeat of the refrain and the same run of chords. They could have gone for something theatrical or masturbatory, exercising their vocal chops and instrumental skills, but this wasn't that. This was feeding sacred milk to the gods so that they'd stay happy and keep the storms at bay.

The song ended with a cheesy breakdown and some smashing of the high hats. Layton stepped away from the microphone and bowed.

The noise tapered off.

The audience applauded. A small cluster of people stood and cheered—Felicia's social media- tainted groupies.

Britt drank from a bottle of water and glanced stage left, towards the green rooms, and saw that both Violet from the elevator and Tona of Scarlett Fever were watching. Britt smiled at them both, then adjusted his drums. When he looked up Jai was watching him. Britt winked; Jai sneered and ran his sleeve across his sweaty forehead.

"Wonderful, gentlemen," Plex said, then gestured toward the judges. "Now over to our judging panel. Felicia Scalding, Heidi Starr, and Andy Rainer."

"Fantastic," Felicia said, breathing hard into her microphone. She looked to her left at Heidi and then to her right at Andy. Both of them were looking straight ahead. "So that song was called 'Wolf in a Cardigan.' Thoughts from the other judges?"

"I must admit that it's much improved over last night's performance," Heidi said. "For the moment I am glad and relieved that Felicia offered you a stay of execution. It was hard-rocking but not offensive, save for that dirty little bit that we'll have to bleep out."

"I'm really fucking sorry about that," Layton said.

The audience laughed; Andy grimaced, saying, "While it's an improvement, there's something missing. The song doesn't have a make-me-a-star quality."

Felicia's eyes bore down on him. "I disagree. Firmly. They have what it takes."

"I'm not convinced. I don't feel it in my gut."

"I do. And I have a firmer stomach. Heidi?"

Heidi raised her hands. "Don't get me involved. I'm on the fence right now. It's up to the band to show me whether the grass is green or not."

Layton made a farty sound into the microphone. "Something to say?" Heidi said.

"We don't believe in lawns," he said. "Just wild grasses. Unkempt fields. Towering elms."

Heidi looked as if someone had just written a poem for her. "That's lovely. Why don't you write songs like that?"

"Well, we—"

"I think their song was just right," Felicia said. "Touching and rich."

Andy scoffed.

"Alright, thank you, judges," Plex said. "I'm sure you'll have lots more to say later once all the performances are over. So, #Five, you'll be playing 'Money for Fear' now?"

"No. We changed our minds."

Felicia perked up. She glanced right, left, then back at Layton. "I think that's against the rules."

Heidi offered up a quizzical look. "How so? They can play anything they want. It's not like we know anything about the songs anyways. We just have the names."

"They can't—the names are important. I think—Plex, isn't that, like, you know, wrong?" Plex shrugged. "Makes no difference, I think."

Andy leaned toward his mic. "The band should play what they're most comfortable with. They should play what best demonstrates their musical abilities and star qualities."

Layton adjusted his mic stand. "Right then. This one is called 'Liquefied Pain.'"

The song started with little fanfare. Grannie and Donovan laid down a few introductory notes in unison, the drums built up to a rollicking beat, and Layton and Jai leaped in with harmonized vocals and guitar.

Take the devil by the horns, you said
and he'll serve you eternal
At least that's what I read
in your stupid little journal

Yeah, you never thought you'd leave
and lucky me I get to bring you home in a casket
But you were never really here so let's not pretend
at least we can never betray each other again.

This time Layton refused to stay put. While the stage's dimensions hadn't changed, his understanding of it had. His arms flailed about while his legs skidded sideways as if mimicking an ice skater. He pounded his chest and looked up at the ceiling as if able to see through to the sky.

Contact
Contact
Placing the yoke around my neck
like some sort of ceremony
Yeah, I'd rather marry you
than be subject to such sanctimony

When you were raging
You ran around in the dark screaming
Am I dreaming? Am I dreaming?

Sweat flew from his brow. He appeared to have been overtaken by zeitgeist, by an incubus who fed on the music within him. Behind him Britt reigned the song in by maintaining a steady, undeniable beat. The band became hyperfocused.

They forgot about the audience, the judges, the plastic host standing just feet away, the other band members hovering along the blurry periphery. They forgot about their ambitions and their regrets, their supporters and their naysayers, social media, and buzz and virality. There was nothing to do but play the music. Had one of the earthquakes started right then and there the band would have played on. It wouldn't have mattered to them, knowing they were all going to die, and as long as there was electricity in their instruments they might as well go out doing what they love, like the cliché said. No, the only thing that could stop the music now was for the earth to open up and swallow them—

Layton toppled off the stage. Felicia started to stand up, but Andy tossed a wicked look her way.

Layton still had the wireless microphone in his hand though and continued singing while lying on his back, writhing in a tangle of cords and wires. The camera zoomed in on him.

Contact
Dead zone
Reverb
Time to atone
Contact
Contact
End this
Transmission
Dead zone

Three times he and Jai repeated the refrain, with Grannie stopping the keys on the first, then Britt dropping the snares and using only the bass, Donovan, and Jai slamming home some chords in tight synchronicity. The last syllables were being spat out as if the words needed to be exorcised from their young bodies lest rock 'n roll take them forever.

The song crashed to its end. Their ears were ringing. Layton lay there a moment. Britt dropped his sticks, his hands cracked and bleeding. Jai felt panicked with the fear that they'd gone too far. They'd overdone it for such a conservative television program intended to placate the public, to fill the backgrounds of their daily lives with inconsequential noise. While not a novelty act like the lip-synching dance troupe, #Five wasn't supposed to be much different. Or so it seemed.

Then the hole in the earth opened up with a raucous echo. No—it was the audience erupting.

Applause. Cheering. Rising. Others stamping their feet to amplify their approval.

"Is this real?" Britt asked Grannie but he couldn't even hear the words coming out of his own mouth.

"Well, how about that?" Plex Goldar said as he strode back onto the stage. He picked up the microphone stand, then reached down and pulled Layton up. He put his arm around Layton's shoulders and gave him a squeeze, either to reassure him or to keep him upright.

Between them and the crowd the judges' faces hovered, inscrutable yet anxious. "What a performance. Did you enjoy it, folks?"

The crowd ramped up their applause. Plex and the band soaked it in a moment, and then he released Layton and batted the air, urging the audience to simmer down.

"We've heard from the people and now we need to hear from the judges. The road so far has been rocky for the band. Like our other nine semi-finalists, they emerged from a roster of 1,231 musical acts. Their second performance earned them severe criticism from two members of the judging panel, but Felicia Scalding saw something in them and used her wild card to offer them a reprieve. Now *this*. Judges, did you see and hear what I saw? Did you see and hear what the audience saw? Because I think most of us saw a performance by a troupe of legitimate stars. It was like these five young men were destined to come together and play that song. There was synergy"— Plex melded all ten fingers together "— and joy. There was harmony and there was glorious pain. Or so *I* thought." He smiled that manically bright smile of his. "Perhaps you disagree."

Felicia smiled, but it wasn't her trademark smile filled with mirth and deviousness.

It was tepid and restrained. "I loved it," she said. "What can I say? They're great."

Heidi said nothing, only gave two thumbs up.

Andy sighed and leaned in. "I think you summed it up well, but let's keep in mind that we have one more act to see before we make our decisions."

Then he gave the band an *a-ok* sign.

"There you have it, folks. Our judges are not only professionals, they are diplomats. As for you and me, we're just fans. And I think we're all now *big* fans of #Five."

The band bypassed the green room and fled to their suite. Within minutes there was knocking on the door and voices calling out to them.

"This is too much," Donovan said, grinning, his arm slung around Britt. "I love it. I think I might die. This is the greatest day of my life. I don't care if we win. We did the Lazarus, the Jesus— we came back from the death and performed music magic. That's more important than taking the whole prize. I would say our star was just made."

The banging on the door continued. Someone screamed Layton's name. *We love you!*

"Let's get out of here," Grannie said, pulling open the sliding door. They shut it behind themselves and jogged down the walkway to the pool area.

Jai kicked a plastic chair into oblivion. "Fucking shit, man!" he said, seemingly more furious than ecstatic. "We can never let someone try to contain us again. Not Felicia, not our parents, not ourselves. *Gaaaahh!*"

The others laughed and started to climb the concrete wall. They threw themselves over the top and flailed through the air before flopping to the ground.

"Just like Layton!" Grannie said. "*Ooohh, look at me, I'm having a seizure on stage! I'm the lead singer of Joy Division!*"

"Stop. Hear that?"

The voices and clamoring had spilled into the pool area. "Let's go."

They jogged through the grass toward the electrical tower and dropped down behind the concrete support, out of sight. They sat panting, Emmiline below them.

"Like kings in a castle," Britt said. "At least for one ni—wait a minute." He reached into his pocket for his phone, read a message, then shoved it back in. "We made it. In fact, we're supposed to be on stage right now for the announcement."

"Oops."

They smiled and shook one another's shoulders in silence. "Us, Scarlett Fever, and Cat Coggan."

"Hey," Jai said. "Who sent the message? Felicia?"

Britt snorted. "Tona Kohl."

Jai looked like he'd just been slapped. "How'd she get your number?"

"It was a Facebook message. She found me there, I guess. Pretty straight-forward, isn't it?"

"Why you though?"

Britt smiled and leaned back. "No, seriously, I—"

Layton pulled Jai back. "Easy, tiger. Britt's your buddy. We're a band. Don't let some girl get you riled up, especially when she's the opposit—woah. You feel that?" Layton pressed his hands to the ground.

For a moment no one spoke.

"Footsteps, I think. They're running around looking for us."

"No way. Wait—listen."

The ground started to shake. "Oh crap."

Then it rumbled. The cables overhead danced and the lights in the distance blinked. The turbine's blades slowly stopped spinning.

The tremor stopped. "Just a little one."

In the distance a bright flash filled the sky and a second later the echo of its explosion reached them.

"Damn! A transformer just blew."

The ground started to shake again, this time in earnest. The band leaned into one another, pushing their shoulders together and holding one another up, and let it ride.

5.
A LOVESICK NECROPHILIAC NESTLED SOMEWHERE IN TIME

Roman fished a nip of bourbon out of his pocket, drank it, then flung the bottle into the street where it bounced but didn't smash. As much as she wanted to, Tona didn't say anything. Seconds later a truck rounded the corner and crushed the nip with a loud pop.

"Idiot," she said.

Roman chuckled to himself and shoved his hands into his pockets, the thumbs on the outside. Tona always hated it when guys did that, but Roman's jeans were so tight it was probably impossible for him to get the last digits inside anyway. She couldn't believe the pants didn't make him sterile. Roman belched, then laughed again. When another car approached from the other direction at high speed, Tona briefly considered shoving him in front of it.

Their hotel was a mile from the Emmiline Heights but once the tremors started, cabs were nearly impossible to find. The members of Scarlett Fever wanted to walk anyways. Though some people recognized the band, at the moment everyone was too shook up to hound them or, God forbid, beg for an autograph.

At their hotel they skipped the elevator in favor of the stairs, and then the boys headed off to their room and Tona to hers, at the far end of the hall. Despite Roman's protestations she'd begged for this, saying that she needed her space lest she lose her mind out of anxiety and whatever else was born of such a contest. Didn't they want her to be calm and to preserve her lungs?

She shut the door behind her, leaned against it, and clenched her eyes. Then she went to the window, pulled back the curtain, and glanced out. There were no fires, no toppled buildings, no craters in the street.

She took off her boots and dug her toes into the rug. Then she went back to the window and glanced out.

She drank the orange juice out of the mini-fridge. She picked up her phone to call her mother but didn't dial. She went back to the window.

Over the next hour Tona did this so often she thought she was losing her mind, flipping back the curtains and peering out onto the streets of Emmiline over and over as if the correct combination of open-and-close would make time pass faster or perhaps summon the gods to bestow upon them the title of "Best Band of All Time As Determined By Three Washed-Up Pop Singers." But nothing happened, nothing changed. So, she pulled the curtains wide, perched on the sill, and sat there waiting some more.

She peered up the street toward the Emmiline Heights hotel complex where the other finalists were staying.

The sidewalks were busy with all sorts of activity that she'd never witnessed back on the coast of the Great Lakes: knife fights, men in fully chrome-plated cars wearing sunglasses when driving at night because of the glare of the street lights, prostitutes strutting around on shoes so tall they might as well have been circus acts, musicians busking in the subway so talented that she felt like a poseur and that she should just quit. But she needed to win. She needed the money. She needed an out—from all of it.

Her phone buzzed. She went to the bedside table to check it: Roman again, asking how she felt.

"Like shit, you idiot," she said to the air.

She lay down on the bed in the path of the humid breeze coming through the narrow slit of window that the hotel actually let you open. She tried to picture Roman down the hall with the others, his long hair pumped up with some sort of goop that kept it from going limp. She had always wondered what his secret was but had always been too afraid to ask. Spit? Pine sap? Soap? The thought of him sent another wave of nausea through her body. It wasn't that he was ugly—he was almost seductive, with his cocktail of grit and talent and intolerance for people who can't play guitar. It's just that he wasn't clear to her. He was contrary. He was like a snort of pollen mixed cocaine or a tractor with racing stripes.

If she kept his baby, he would be passing on genetics that were probably best left behind.

She wanted the thing inside her to kick as hard as it could, but she also knew that it was no bigger than a grain of salt or two. Maybe a seed, a nut.

She shifted her focus upwards, counting the separations in the ceiling tiles from right to left and left to right, getting two different calculations with each pass. She tried again but halfway across she thought that the designs resembled prison bars. That would be fitting. Trapped here, waiting for nothing.

She sat up, balled up her fists, cursed Roman, cursed herself, cursed ambition, cursed QuickFame. Just yesterday the band had debated dropping out, having decided that losing would kill their career, even if they made it to the finals. It would be embarrassing to lose a competition like this. Who wants to be marketed as "musical talent show non-winners"? Their fame would be built on dubious circumstances, not talent, not heart.

She tapped her fist lightly on her stomach. It didn't hurt. She tried to cry but couldn't remember how. She tapped her fists against her eyes, and though it hurt worse than she remembered, it didn't work.

Her eyes remained dry.

"Fuck this."

She sat up and went to the window again and looked down.

All these choices people were asking her to make. Touch. Love. Kill. Sing. Scream. Wail. Whisper. Caress. Convince. Seduce. Reduce. Commit. Betray.

She knew regret was as useful as non-alcoholic beer, but she couldn't help but feel suffocated by the accrued weight of thousands of these little choices suddenly settling on her like a mountain of old sympathy cards.

Her phone buzzed. A message from Aron. Beautiful married Aron who'd rejected her not once and not twice but thrice. *It's time to go.*

She got her coat and headed to the lobby.

Arriving back at the auditorium, Scarlett Fever found Thaddeus Goldar fielding calls with one cell phone and text messages with the other. The earthquake had thrown QuickFame's programming into disarray, the audience having been evacuated for awhile. Now they were being summoned back inside.

"Please remain calm," Plex McGuire was pleading into the microphone, "and take your seats. We have one more segment to film. We're offering tickets for tomorrow's finale at a fifty percent discount to anyone who can stay tonight."

Even after the seats were filled, #Five was nowhere to be seen. Scarlett Fever and Cat Coggan stood in the hallway adjacent to the stage area, which had quickly been cleared of instruments and gear, only a massive neon QuickFame sign now occupying the floorspace at the rear of the stage.

"What do you mean, 'No one can find them'?" Felicia screeched at Thaddeus, who was still on his phone. Felicia wasn't wearing her heels and compared to Tona she was downright child- sized.

Felicia got out her phone and stabbed at it wildly. "Little morons. What are they thinking?" She hung up, then raised her hand in the air as if she was going to smash the phone on the carpeted floor. Lucky for her Thaddeus caught her arm on the way down.

"Take it easy. They couldn't have gone far."

"What if they fell into a pit or something? Maybe a crack opened up in the earth and swallowed them."

He made a noncommittal expression. "That'd be good television, wouldn't it?"

"Not funny. But a good point."

"I'll find them," Tona said, separating herself from her band. "I've got Britt on Messenger."

Felicia went to her and wrapped her arms around her waist. "Thank you. Please save them."

When Tona found a quiet spot, she got out her phone and sent Britt a message. *They're lookin' for u. What's up?*

He wrote back: *Come outside. By tower on west side of hotel.*

It took her ten minutes to locate the spot. The band was sitting beneath the electrical tower, watching smoke billowing upwards in the distance. So, something had gone up in flames after all.

Upon seeing Tona, Jai leapt up and went to her. "Wow, congratulations."

"Everyone's looking for you."

"We're just letting them sweat a little."

Tona sat in the grass.

"Don't you, like, want to get this over with and find out if you've won?"

"Oh, we won," Layton said.

She twisted around so that he could see the incredulity on her face. "Even if we've lost," he added.

Tona *harumph*ed. "We have the totally opposite theory. Unless we win, we lose. Who wants yesterday's leftover meatloaf?"

"Meat Loaf," Britt said. "That was my first live concert. He's amazing on stage."

"You're kidding, right?"

Britt shook his head. "Leo took me. The guy who provided his sperm for my creation. He's a big fan."

"Why the hell does he go by that name anyways?" Tona asked.

"I mean, what kind of name is Meatloaf?"

Britt's eyes dropped. "His father was a dick, I guess. Called him 'meat' because he was big. Then his coach or teammates on the football team added the 'loaf.' As in 'turd.'"

Britt's face suddenly brightened. "Hey, Layton, did you know Meat Loaf once leapt off a stage and broke both legs?"

Layton gave Britt the same look Tona had given to him. "Nuh uh."

"Did so. Hardcore, eh? Good thing you're a vegetarian. You don't have all that flab for gravity to fuck with."

"You're making this up," Tona said.

"Am not. And he couldn't wear jeans as a kid since he couldn't find his size in his town. Isn't that the most fucked up shit you've ever heard? One of the future biggest-selling rock stars couldn't find jeans that fit him. Now he can have them custom made."

"Is that what you're going to do," Jai said to Britt, "or just continue to shop in the kids section?"

Tona cast a look at Jai, though he was at the far end of the circle and was hard to make out with the glare of the hotel lights in the distance.

"Don't be a dick," Grannie said.

"Instead of Meat Loaf you could be Chicken *Nugent*." No one laughed.

"Get it? Like chicken nugget plus Ted Nugent?"

Tona stood up. She offered her hand to Britt, then pulled him off the ground. "Come on. They're liable to give our spots to Kenny Juggler or Fountain of Eden if we don't get down there." They headed back to the wall. Britt made a platform with his hands and boosted Tona over.

The rest of them followed, Jai last. No one reached over the wall to offer him a hand.

"I hope you guys make it there," Tona said, hesitating in the doorway. For some reason she felt more comfortable with another band than her own. Maybe because no one here knew her. She could redefine herself, be anyone, say anything without repercussions or connotation.

"If we don't show up," Britt said, "grab the trophy on our behalf and rush back here so we can party."

"I would, but I don't think there's a trophy. All you get is another night in a hotel." She shut the door and pressed her ear to the door and listened.

They were buoyant. Boys celebrating. But they weren't tearing her down behind her back. Not like her own band.

Cat Coggan was crouching near some potted plants, smoking a cigarette, and playing with his phone, when Tona strolled up the stone steps to the Viper Room.

"Hey," she said.

He glanced up, then stubbed out the cigarette and went to her.

"Congratulations once again."

"Same to you."

He threw his arms around her.

Tona tensed up but Cat held firm. There was nothing lewd or coded in his affection. And despite the cigarette—which she suspected was one of those herbal hippie things—he didn't smell. He didn't even smell like he'd been playing music under hot lights in front of a ton of people and some judges. She realized it might have been an act, this Man of a Massive Soul, and Voice of the Angels, but there was something reassuring and almost shamanic about him.

Shamanic.

He released.

"The others are inside."

"Winners or losers?"

"A mix of both. Some seem not to have shown up."

"And #Five?"

"They're here. If they haven't gotten kicked out or arrested yet. I've gotta finish up some messages but I'll see you in there. Take care." He smiled; she fell in love a moment. Then he stepped away; the love faded.

Tona handed the girl at coat-check her jacket, then immediately veered toward the ladies' room and shut herself up inside a stall.

That fucking shaman. Was it his fault, all of this?

She got out her phone and brought up her mother's profile. Then she turned off the phone and put it away.

Her mother had made her go. What was it—a year and a half ago? She said the man could help Tona figure out her path, since she'd just gotten kicked out of yet another school (for never showing up, not for doing something stupid like the last time— breaking in on a Friday night to tip over teachers' desks).

Sitting in that Viper Room bathroom stall filled with wads of sopping wet toilet paper and cigarette butts and even a few cocaine vials, Tona could still smell the inside of the junky old RV in which the shaman had arrived, rolling into town like a tumbleweed but weirder.

Word had spread through town about him, as he had not been seen in those parts in ten years.

He'd saved lives, people said, through his insight into the Timeline of Human Existence—forwards, backwards, up, down, and all the nether-spaces that occupy it.

The shaman had worn a huge, maroon, woven shawl that hung past his bowing brown legs. His head was shaved and the lines around his eyes were more like crevasses than crow's feet. Tona had towered over him. She knew his seeing-power was bullshit, and half of her intention in being there was to point out how wrong he was, but before her ass had even warmed the crooked brown folding chair he threw her off by telling her she was a singer and if she didn't do it she might as well die. Then he said she had once shoved her mother across the room, and it wasn't dancing. By the time he told her she'd never have children, she thought this guy was a living god.

He told her to be careful, to make wise choices, to avoid men who wore their ghosts like a cloak. Men like Roman.

Time passed. She sang. She fought with her mother. Her first boyfriend didn't get her pregnant and neither did the second or third. So, two years later when Roman was ejaculating inside her for the fourth or fifth time, she wasn't really concerned.

In her defense, with all the orgasms and music, rain, and moaning going on, it was sort of unclear what exactly Roman was doing down there. But then she thought she saw a shadow in the room, which of course would be a crow—which of course would be the shaman.

Which of course was her omen, and she knew she was safe.

Her periods stopped just before someone from QuickFame saw their demo video online and encouraged them to try out.

She bought a home pregnancy test, and it showed a big pink plus. As if this were a positive thing.

The shaman accepted credit cards, but she had paid in cash. She realized later that the lapels of her jacket were covered with pins of her favorite bands, tipping off the shaman to her love of music.

And her mother had already visited, spilling her guts about their violent throw-downs in their suburban enclave.

She wanted to tell her mother about the pregnancy.

She wanted to tell Roman.

She didn't want the baby, but she didn't want to be that bitch who didn't want a baby because she had songs inside her, songs she didn't even get to sing because the boys didn't think they were good enough. (Now and then they threw her a bone and let her keep or rewrite a line or two or a chord sequence, but that was about it.)

One of the vials popped underfoot as she stood up and blew her nose with the last few squares of toilet paper.

She wasn't crying but something in the bathroom was getting to her sinuses.

That was not good. She had to perform her heart out the following night, singing so mightily that Cat Coggan and #Five would soon just be a fond memory, just like all-white rap act Brutal Voodoo, metal band X-Ray Salad, pop singer Lizeth Breedlove, and the other four non-winners.

By the time she found her band and the others, a melee was brewing. Britt Elwyn had gotten his little hands on some alcohol, which wasn't exactly on lockdown at the Viper Room. He was dancing atop one of the tables while a bunch of tarts in tight dresses threw poker chips at him.

It was '90's night, the club was at capacity thanks to the QuickFame crowd, and the judges were the guests of honor. They'd been wisely sequestered in their own section, which was blocked off by security guards. Those who wanted to talk to the judges had to state their business, at which point Thaddeus Goldar would either approve or reject them.

"Just a cranberry juice and seltzer," Tona told their server. Only Roman was old enough to drink, Aron being a mere twenty and Gavin nineteen. Still, they had beers in their hands.

On stage a DJ was slamming together '90's hits with house beats. It was danceable but borderline nauseating. He was just killing time, apparently, because #Five had been summoned to the stage for an encore of sorts: they were going to perform an acoustic version of Andy Rainer's old hit "A New Twist On Love."

Donovan, the sweet, out-of-the closet bassist, managed to coerce Britt off the table. The rest of the band helped him up onto the stage.

Someone scrounged up some guitars and a set of bongos, which set Britt off on a laughing jag, so instead of banging on the goat skins the DJ laid down a drum track.

Strangely enough, only Grannie knew the lyrics to Andy Rainer's song, so he took over on vocals. When the song kicked off, Layton jumped in with some *Wooo oo ooo*s and *ah ahh ahhh*s. Then he picked up on the chorus. The song started to come together in a messy but refreshingly unforced and unproduced way. Tona forgot about everything for a moment.

Then Britt, who'd been dancing around the stage like the half-drunk goofball he was, banged into Jai, knocking the guitar out of his hands. Jai picked it back up and swung it at Britt; Britt ducked out of the way, but Donovan was standing behind him and the guitar whacked his right hand.

The song quickly fell apart and Grannie gave a knife-across-the-throat signal to call it quits.

The audience ate it up.

Britt was first off the stage. While getting a drink from an unsuspecting or simply indifferent waitress, he spotted Tona sitting alone at a tiny round table. He needed a chair. Unable to find one, he simply approached a large table occupied by a group of losing QuickFame contestants, leaned with his little hands on the surface, then said point-blank to one of the girls that he needed her chair. She and her punky friends (all of them taller than Britt), looked at him a moment, then she stood up. He took the chair and dragged it across the club, set it in front of Tona's table, and plopped down with a decidedly Tigger-esque manner.

"Buy you a drink?" he said, setting down a highball glass of bourbon on ice.

"Please tell me they're not selling alcohol to minors tonight."

"They don't dare ask me if I'm of age."

"Britt!"

"Is that a yes? What are you drinking then?"

"No fucking way. I plan on winning tomorrow or at least trying my absolute best."

"Cool. Makes sense." Britt jutted his chin towards Roman and the rest of Scarlett Fever, hovering nearby like a crew of bouncers. "These guys need new batteries or what?"

Tona twisted around in her chair and glanced at her band. "It's cool, gentlemen. This guy's ok."

"Maybe physically," Roman said, "but don't drink nothin' that he gives you." Her crew stepped back, fading into the crowd.

"Jesus fuck. What's up their asses? Each other?"

Tona didn't want to laugh but did. "They're nervous and they don't trust anyone."

Britt leaned in, sliding his glass with him. "You trust me though, right?"

She leaned in too. "No. Way."

She leaned back. "Not tonight anyways. Maybe we can talk about your trustworthiness once the winner has been declared."

"Sure, sure. We'll have lots of time to talk then. We'll be crossing paths all the time."

"Oh?"

"Yeah. If you win, you'll be in Emmiline all the time for recording, performing, meetings, and all that shit. If I win, I'll be flying you out here from Michigan every week."

She laughed. "Somewhat presumptuous, don't you think?"

"Not at all. We're destined to be together, you and I. Don't you think?" She crossed her arms.

"What?" Britt said. "You don't think so? Is it because of my, you know, differentness?"

"Differentness?"

Britt nodded. "You didn't notice?"

Tona feigned ignorance. "Notice what? And is that even a word."

"It sounds like a word." Britt sat up straight, then repositioned his chair. "Look at me."

"I am looking."

"I mean straight on."

She moved her chair. "Now I am facing you straight on."

"Notice?"

"Notice what? That you're—no, that your—oh my fuck. Your ear! The left one is slightly lower than the other."

Britt's repositioned his chair at a slight angle. "Now you know about my differentness."

Tona bent forward with laughter.

The sight and sound evoked in Britt a warmth that spread through his arms and into his stomach, almost like a cancer you wanted. A cancer called love. *Fuck, I need to write that down.* Someone bumped his chair though, and he snapped out of his reverie.

"Hey, what's going on here?"

Britt looked up at Jai. "Oh, hey Jai alai."

"Don't call me that. You know I hate that name."

"Sorry, Jai alai."

Jai thrust his hips into Britt's chair. "Stop."

"*Stop*," Britt said, mocking him with a nasally voice and ugly face.

"Simmer down, boys," Tona said, composing herself.

"I'm simmered." Jai saw someone vacating a chair nearby and grabbed it. He sat. "I feel great. What a day!"

"That was indeed a wonderful performance."

"Up there?" he said, jerking his thumb toward the stage. "No, that was awful."

Britt moved his chair closer to Tona. "Kinda crowded, Jai alai." Jai glared at Britt.

"We were having an A-B conversation. Maybe you could C yourself to another table?" Jai snorted.

"Relax, hamster. We're *all* celebrating. No need to isolate yourself."

"This here is a private party." Tona stood up.

"Where are you going?" Britt said.

"Someplace that doesn't reek of testosterone."

They watched as she walked off.

"See what you did?" Jai said.

"I was doing fine until you showed up."

"She's way above your league. Key word being 'above.'"

"Oh *har har*." Britt shoved his chair back and chased after her. Jai pursued him.

Grannie, Donovan, and Layton pursued both of them.

The rest of Scarlett Fever pursued #Five.

They congregated in the lobby where Britt was attempting to apologize to Tona.

She didn't seem angry, just bored, flipping through the records in an antique jukebox.

"I wrote you a poem," he was saying. He reached into his jacket and pulled out a folded piece of paper.

"Oh yeah?" Jai said as he snuck up on them. "Let's hear it."

"Let it go, Jai," the others said.

"Let's go find a table."

Jai snatched the paper from Britt and held it in the air.

Britt leapt up and down, bouncing like Tigger again, trying to snatch it back but to no avail.

Jai held the paper overhead and unfolded it with a single hand and started reading.

Dead Love

Sweet Tona
The most stunning shark queen
To ever swim through Emmiline
Eyes dark as coal
How could I ever
look at another
knowing you're alive

"Aww, isn't that cute. What'd you think, Tona?"

"I think you're an idiot."

"Me?" Jai pounded himself in the chest.

"What about Drummer Smurf here?"

"Going after his height is the cheapest, easiest insult you could offer. Is that supposed to impress me?"

"You're choosing him over me?"

Tona crossed her arms and guffawed. "I'm not choosing anyone. I'm here to perform, not to be wooed."

Roman inserted himself into the fray, taking Tona by the arm. "Let's get out of here."

She wrenched free. Jai in turn grabbed Roman by the arm. "Hey, old timer, leave the girl alone."

"Who you calling old, you nerdy little Pakistani fuck?"

"Nerd? I'll take that. Nerds are cool. And anyways, I'm as American as you, white bread."

Other partygoers were stopping to check out the scene.

"You are most certainly not cool," Roman said. "You're like a—a—a flea. You're making everyone itchy."

Jai scratched his head. "Hmm. I did notice something."

Grannie stepped forward. "Alright, let's cool down. We're all friends here and we all have a big show—"

Roman gave Grannie a shove in the chest. "We're not your friends, bro." Jai shoved Roman.

"Don't touch him."

"I'm about to touch you with my fist."

"Shut up!" Tona yelled.

"Would all of you idiotic sperm factories just shut the fuck up! I'm not interested in any of you. I think you're all pieces of shit and I don't want you near me."

Jai stood there stunned. Britt put his hand on his shoulder. "Come on, dude. Let's get some rest."

"Don't touch me."

"Whatever, Jai alai."

Britt turned to leave.

Jai lunged for him, but Layton and Grannie were already there, pushing him back.

"I'm calm, I'm calm," he said, but he was nearly hyperventilating. They stood there waiting for his neck to return to normal, from blazing red to white. His eyes too.

"You need to focus on what's important, Jai. Right now, romance is not at the top of that list, is it?"

"Fuck you!" Jai stormed off, shoving bodies aside. But when Jai passed Scarlett Fever, Roman couldn't resist the opportunity.

"Idiot."

Jai stopped. Beside him was the old jukebox. Without hesitating, without envisioning the consequences, he grabbed hold of it, planted his foot on the wall, and threw the machine to the floor.

And onto Roman's foot.

Felicia rushed into the lobby to find two security guards lifting the jukebox off Roman. "Jesus Christ! Was there another earthquake?"

"No, just a hurricane named Jai," Layton said. "What happened?"

"He and Britt got worked up over Tona Kohl." He gestured toward her, crying in the arms of Aron, the drummer.

Felicia's eyes widened. She seemed to be fighting back a smile.

"He might be arrested. Roman's foot is good and smashed. Ambulance is on its way."

"Let me handle it. Please go find Thaddeus."

Felicia went to Jai, sitting on the floor while a bouncer stood nearby. She crouched and put her hand on Jai's tear-stained cheek. "I thought Britt was the bad boy, but it's clearly you."

"Fuck him. He's a stain."

"Britt is just putting on an act. He isn't bad."

"I'm not bad, am I?" He shook his head. "I'm just so—fucked up inside. Sometimes all I want to do is smash skulls together and then set the world on fire." Jai's shoulders heaved in concert with his sobbing. Felicia put her arms around him. She held him. This angry little kid trying to stuff himself into men's clothing. She pulled him tight and rocked him back and forth while softly singing a lullaby that her mother had sung her.

> *You like playing hop and running the top*
> *You like to contemplate the bigness of the sky*
> *But when you start to daydream,*
> *Your mind goes blank*
> *And you start to cry*

> *Tralala la, tralala la*

The paramedics arrived and carried Roman away on a stretcher. As Tona passed by, Felicia reached out and squeezed her hand.

"Rock 'n roll, eh?"

Tona's mouth smiled but the rest of her face didn't. "Why do women put up with this shit?"

She pulled her hand back and followed Roman out to the ambulance.

6.
THE KILLING AGE

At first jail wasn't as bad as Jai expected it to be. Being a juvenile, he had a cell to himself. The bunk had a mattress on it, which seemed not to be the case in the holding cells occupied by the legitimate career crooks, which contained only steel planks for sleeping. The toilet flushed. Water emerged from the pipes. A guard came around every four hours with a snack. It was quiet. Jai had time to think.

Then it got even better.

The evening rush started and criminals of all walks of life were shepherded into various cells, sometimes six each. Jai watched from the corner as they filed past in handcuffs (he'd been brought in without incident, unshackled). Some were bruisers, thugs who'd fought, stolen, and looted as a vocation, out of boredom, or out of necessity. Others looked like career criminals, scum who'd been born onto the splintered floor of some Old City efficiency apartment. Others looked domestic, plain: husbands, fathers, uncles, neighbors who'd finally been exposed as the abusers, pedophiles, perverts, and all-around creeps they were. There were homeless men. Geezers with oxygen tanks. Guys with one eye. One hand. One lung. Guys so strung out they should be in rehab. Some of them caught Jai's eye and whistled at him or winked or smiled. Others stared through him as if he were already dead.

Just when he thought that all of them had been brought in for the night, a guard stopped in front of his cell.

"Open twelve!"

The door opened with a heavy clunk. Beside the guard stood a tall and lanky black kid wearing shorts so long they were nearly pants and a white tank top. The kid's upper arm bore a horrifically rendered tattoo depicting the Nike swoosh and a basketball net that looked more like barbed wire than sporting equipment. Though the kid didn't look older than sixteen, he was nearly a foot taller than Jai and the tattoo looked like it'd been sitting there for years.

The door slammed shut. The guard leaned in and said, "No fighting. You fight, I come back with my friends. We haven't cracked any skulls all week and we're getting antsy. You understand?"

"Definitely, sir. No fighting."

The kid sneered at Jai, then at the guard. "Whatever."

"Unless your lawyer gets here before midnight, you won't be arraigned until ten o'clock tomorrow morning. So, get comfortable. Blankets and last meal will be distributed at eleven. And no fucking or sucking. That's as bad as fighting. Unless you're secretly a girl. In which case." The guard smiled, revealed a missing incisor, hooked his thumbs in his belt, then turned and left.

Jai's chest was tight. He suddenly realized he needed to take a dump but there was nothing between his cellmate and the steel toilet with no lid. He decided to hold it until his lawyer arrived.

"S'up," Jai said, jutting his chin at the kid.

The kid sneered at him, then sat on the lower bunk. "Oh, I was—no, it's cool. I'll take the top."

"Good."

"Hey, do you have a phone? I can pay you to use it. Eventually." The kid looked at him. "In my ass, you mean?"

"Yeah, like one of those tiny things you can tuck up there."

"First of all, I don't. And second, they checked my hole when I was brought in."

"Oh. Right."

He stared at Jai. "Wait, you're saying they didn't make you spread and bend?"

"I know. Isn't that whack? Assholes. I mean—assholes, obviously, that's the topic, but dickheads—no, I mean, that's not the topic. Cops, man. Cops are such a drag. Fucking jerks!"

The kid shook his head and lay back with his hands behind his head. Jai stood there a minute, wondering if he should pace, take his bunk, or cry himself to death. Instead, he said, "So, uh, what's your name?"

"Bro, I don't need to tell you my name. We're not friends. Just leave me be, ok?"

"Alright."

Jai climbed up onto his bunk and lay like the other kid, with his hands behind his head.

It was just like in the movies.

The ceiling above him was covered with gum, boogers, other smears he didn't want to think about, and all sorts of tags and graffiti scratched into the concrete. It was depressing. He really needed to take that dump now. Instead, he tried to just release some of the gas that'd accrued behind the fecal blockage.

"I can hear that" the kid said from below. "Sorry. I need to go."

"Then go."

"I can't. Not with an audience."

"You think I'm going to watch?"

"Not with someone in the same room."

"You probably grew up with your own bathroom, didn't you."

Jai didn't answer. His house had had three, though none of the doors had locks. He usually went at school. Jai rolled over. Then he rolled toward the wall, which was as nasty as the ceiling. He rolled onto his back again.

"You're keeping me awake."

"Sorry."

Jail tried to keep still. The anger had largely passed, though it still surged through him whenever he thought about Tona, Britt, the decision to tip over the jukebox, and pretty much anything else from the last twenty-four hours—except their performance. That mitigated the rage for a moment. When the reminiscences of QuickFame passed though, he was left stewing in the wake of the anger, wondering what gave rise to such emotion. No one else in his family was like that.

No one was insane or did drugs or was abused or in jail. It was a very staid, safe, plain American life—

And perhaps therein lay the problem. It was too easy. His parents had come over from India in the seventies, set down roots, established their computer business, and built up a small local empire. Jai hadn't had to struggle, so, he thought, maybe that's why he was inventing one.

"Why you dressed like that anyways?"

"Sorry, what?"

"I asked why you're dressed like a goofball."

"Oh, this? I was actually wearing a tie too. A narrow black tie. It really tied the outfit together, so to speak."

"You didn't answer the question."

"I'm in a band."

"Oh. Whatever." The kid fell quiet for a couple of minutes, then said, "You play the trumpet or something?"

"I'm an incredible guitarist, believe it or not."

"I don't. What's the band?"

"#Five. As in the symbol, not spelled out. It's also the symbol for 'number.'"

"Thanks for the rundown on the hashtag. I was not aware as to its cultural significance."

"Sorry. You never know who knows this stuff."

Somewhere in the cell block someone screamed, "Hymie, you fuck!"

It sounded like they were threatening to kill the referenced individual. The main door at the end of the block opened and three guards strolled past. They said something, rapped their clubs on the bars, then retreated the way they'd come.

"So, what'd you do?" the kid asked once the melee had settled. "I tipped over a jukebox onto a rival band member's foot."

"Ha ha. That's legit. Were you the opening act or something?"

"No. We're all contestants on QuickFame. Have you seen it?"

"What is it? A show?"

"Yeah. It's a super-high-paced music contest that turns nobodies into stars in less than a week. We're finalists. Or were. Now I'm here, so who knows what's going to happen. We're set to perform tomorrow night in the last round, and they can't replace me."

"What about the other band? Is the guy going to be able to play?"

"I don't know. That's why I need a phone. I need to find out if I'm even still in the band."

"You just said they can't replace you."

"Maybe that's just my wishful thinking."

"That's hardcore. I bet it went viral and shit. What's your name?"

"Bro, I don't know you," Jai said.

The kid laughed. "Fuck that. I know you now. You're in #Five. I'm Eddie."

"Jai Garnett."

"Jai Garnett. I gotta remember that name. You're gonna be some big-time star one day and I'll be able to tell my homies that I shared a jail cell with you. They'll ask what you did, and I'll tell them how you tipped over a soda machine on a guy because he was in another band."

"No, wait. First of all, it was an antique jukebox. And you can tell them that it was all because of a girl. Tona. Tona Kohl. The most gorgeous thing I've ever seen. I fell in love the moment I first saw her. And then, when she sang, it was like she was singing just for me."

"She wasn't though," Eddie said after an interval of silence. "That's why you tipped over the antique jukebox on her dude's foot."

"I didn't—he wasn't—I—that's weird. I wonder if you're right."

"She's in one of the other bands, this Ton of Coal?"

"Tona Kohl, yeah. She fronts a metal band. She doesn't sing so much as growl like a panther in heat during a full moon. You're fucking doomed if you get near her when she's like that. But the truth is, she's soft inside. I can tell. But I'm not. I'm made of fire, and I tend to ignite everything I touch. Like King Midas but an asshole."

The lower bunk creaked as Eddie got up and leaned with his arms crossed on Jai's bunk.

"So, what's the deal? Are you going to get out of here in time for the show?"

"I dunno. Depends on whether they come to get me or not. It's not like I have a lawyer."

"You gotta, bro. You have to get shit squared away, make amends, and get back on the show. Do it for me, man. Get up on stage and say, 'This one's for Eddie,' then give me your live television imitation of Hendrix."

Jai tried to smile but couldn't fake it.

"We'll see. I'm not sure I even want to be in the band anymore."

"What? You crazy. Fuck that shit. Don't be a dummy."

He shrugged.

"It brings out the worst in me, especially the competition, but also the noise, the chaos, the competition, the egos, the smarmy music biz execs. I don't know if I can take it."

"What have you got to be so full of angst about? You just some goofy middle-class boy with nothing to worry about."

Jai sighed.

"Screw you, Eddie. You don't know me."

Eddie slunk back to his own bunk.

"Whatever."

They were silent a long while.

Then Jai said, "I have mood swings that just overtake me. I'm probably bipolar. Perhaps borderline schizophrenic."

"Where's that come from?"

"I don't know. You're right, I've got a good life. No problems, good grades, good friends. I even get along with my brother and sister. It's, like, Brady Bunch shit. But something trips in my brain and I just go berserk."

"What's it like?"

"First, I'm overcome by periods of calm that can last for a day, sometimes two, then this feeling settles in my skin like all my blood has just turned to oil or like a ghost-blanket has grabbed hold of me. It strangles me and I can't breathe. I can't think straight. Even though I know there are two choices, right and wrong, the creature of darkness won't let me make the right choice. The only way to fight it off and not kill myself is to act out in rage. It releases it."

"Sounds like you need medication for starters, bro."

"I have it, but it won't let me play the guitar the way I want to."

"There are people here you can talk to."

"I do that. I go to groups, I see a therapist, I see a medical doctor, I meditate and do breathing exercise. It works for 95% of the time and then there's that moment where, like, I can see the anger coming down the tracks like a train, but I just can't get out of its path. So, I jump on, ride it for a sec, let it destroy whatever's in my path, then jump off and assess the damage."

"Woah."

They didn't talk for awhile. Men yelled; someone sobbed; another prisoner was escorted down the hall and tossed into an already crowded cell.

Eddie popped up again. "The guitar is your outlet. You have to keep playing. You quit doing that, the creature will consume you."

"You might be right, but I might have burned that bridge tonight."

"Start your own band. Do you sing?"

"I do backup but I'm only able to match harmonies. I can't hit the highs and lows. I have a very average voice."

"Then stick with the band, bro. You can't give up on it now."

Jai shrugged. "I don't even know if I'm getting out of here in time."

"Let me handle that."

Eddie disappeared from view. Jai heard grunting, clothes swishing, some cursing. Eddie reappeared. In his hand was a phone not much bigger than Eddie's thumb.

"What in the fu—did that come from your butt?" Eddie's face was blank.

"I'm not touching that."

"It don't stink or nothing."

"Just on principle."

Eddie laughed long and hard, then tossed his sneaker onto the bed. "It's got a secret compartment in the heel."

Jai sat up, bashing his head on the ceiling. "Who do I call?"

"Who do you trust?"

"Grannie."

"Your grandmother?"

"Nah. Our keyboard and tech guy. He's like our brood mother though. He watches out for us. When I'm around him I feel calm. I just can't remember his number."

"Give it back. I'll take care of it. What's his full name?"

***

Grannie, Thaddeus, and a heavily disguised Felicia climbed out of the Sööper car—a matte black Audi with tinted windows—and climbed the stairs to the police station.

"Shouldn't be long," Thaddeus said. Despite the chill in the air, he was sweating. And despite the time of night the police station was bustling with activity. Thaddeus spotted Sid Conner, a lawyer who'd handled his divorce and some litigation involving some artifacts that Thaddeus had imported from Afghanistan during the war.

The two men shook their chubby hands. "If we move quickly, we can probably have him out of here tonight," Sid said.

Felicia tried to hide behind Grannie and the lawyers. She had on sunglasses, a large-brimmed hat, a jacket with a high collar, and a baggy sweatshirt and sweatpants—with her stiletto heels.

"Sounds good. Do we have a meeting room?"

"Yes, but there's a hitch."

"Hitch?" Felicia said.

The lawyer glanced at her. "Yes, Ms. S—"

She raised a hand to stop him from saying her name aloud in this godforsaken place.

"There's a contingency. Jai is requesting that I also represent his cellmate, a juvenile named Eddie Jefferson. Well, he'll be eighteen in two weeks."

"What's he in for?"

"Attempted kidnapping, extortion, grievous bodily harm—"

"Jesus H. Christ."

"Jai said that Eddie claims it was self-defense. Supposedly someone was trying to break into his parents' home, and he held the would-be burglar hostage until his accomplices came up with ten thousand dollars. Unable to do so, the accomplices attempted to free their friend and received the blunt end of a baseball bat, which either Eddie or Jefferson Senior was wielding. I don't have all the facts yet, but I think we can also get him out on bail."

"How much?"

"One hundred thousand. That'd require ten thousand up front."

"Forget it," Thaddeus said.

Sid fixed his tie.

"Ok. Then I guess we can leave."

"What do you mean?" Grannie said.

"Jai refuses to leave until we agree to post bond for Eddie."

"Do it," Felicia said.

"I don't have that kind of money."

"QuickFame does. There must be some sort of emergency fund or something."

"I don't—there might—it's not—I'm not important enough to have access to it, nor would anyone there help me. They'd ask who and what this is for and that would expose this entire scheme, Felicia."

"Shh. And don't call it a scheme."

The lawyer glanced at his watch.

"I just don't think this is right," Thaddeus said. "It seems like extortion. Are we sure Jai isn't making this request under some sort of duress?"

Thaddeus removed his handkerchief and dabbed his neck and upper lip.

"You'll find a way, Thaddeus. You always do."

She adjusted the lapels of his jacket and brushed off some lint.

"No."

"Yes."

Felicia spun back to the lawyer. "Do it," she said, shoving him toward the front desk.

"We'll need wire transfer details."

Felicia gestured at Thaddeus. "Go, Ted."

Thaddeus ran his sleeve across his forehead. "No."

"Stop using that word. It's offensive."

"I'll be in the car," Thaddeus said with as much dignity as he could muster, leaving the others standing there.

The lawyer glanced at the clock on the wall, then compared it to his watch.

"Well, um."

Grannie pulled Felicia aside.

"You can take it out of our prize money should we win."

"And if you don't win?"

"Then you can insert a clause into our signing bonus when we get a record contract."

"And if you don't?"

"We will, damn it! Believe in us."

"I do, sweetie. It's just that I'm only now starting to crawl out of debilitating debt. This would be a major financial blow for me. Have I told you that I have a team of investigators following my every move? They dress like G-men, with dark sunglasses and suits and pantsuits for the women. They crawl behind me like slugs with cameras. Only QuickFame can get me out of this hole and— and everything else we're going to do."

"Then wouldn't it also be a major blow if we lose after making it this far?"

She touched his face.

"I'm a gambling addict, Granville."

"This isn't gambling."

"It's very similar. I'm gambling with success, with lives. You know, people call me all the time, but I don't recognize their numbers so I can't answer, and it's a crapshoot just answering my phone. What if it's Streemy telling me they want to pay me shitloads? What if it's a legbreaker with a Jersey accent as thick as his forearms? I can't breathe. I can't move without fear. I'm suffocating in my own skin."

"Look, I'll help you get through this. I'll stay with you and make sure you don't get back into the habit."

"Excuse me," the lawyer said. "We've got three minutes to sign the paper and to supply wire transfer details."

"What do you mean, 'stay with me'?" Felicia said to Grannie.

"I'd been labeled a pedophile. I mean, I know the whole 'sexy teacher' thing doesn't come with the strings that pervy old men have, but it's still weird, you know? That'd expose me to ridicule."

"I'm not talking about a carnal relationship. I'll just be watching over you."

Felicia lowered her sunglasses and looked him in the eye. "You really are a pure soul, aren't you? I don't think you've got one dark cell in your body."

Grannie put his hands on her shoulders and pivoted her toward the front desk. "You have no idea."

An hour later the two inmates were stepping out into the cold night. Jai tilted his head back and looked up at the stars, which were actually the lights of airplanes cutting through the haze. "Free at last!"

Grannie kicked a rock off the sidewalk.

"You were in jail for six hours, moron."

"You don't know what it's like in there."

Sid the lawyer stepped closer to Eddie.

"We'll need your contact details so that we remain in touch regarding this matter."

Jai stepped between them.

"He's coming with us."

"What?" Felicia said.

"What?" Thaddeus echoed.

"Huh?" Grannie interjected.

"I'm hiring him as a security guard. That's how he'll earn the bail money."

"In one night of work?"

"He'll be coming to Australia for the finals."

Grannie laughed up at the night sky.

"You've got it all figured out, huh? You freak out, smash the foot of a guy in a rival band, get arrested, then claim that we're going all the way to the finals?"

"We're already breaking the key elements of rock n' roll, dude: hearts, bones, and laws. We're on our way to rock stardom. Even if we don't win, Eddie's services will be vital in keeping us safe while we're on tour and doing our thing. He'll be a roadie, security, a music tech, a—"

"Fine! Whatever! Get in the car."

"I'm hungry," Eddie said.

"We get some food?"

"Good idea," Jai said, sliding into the back seat with Thaddeus and Eddie.

"Grannie, you're gonna have to take Felicia on your lap."

Grannie looked at her. She looked at him, the corner of her mouth being tugged upwards by a mysterious notion.

"I'm winking at you," she said from behind her sunglasses.

7.

THANKS FOR RUINING MY LIFE
BEFORE I WAS BORN

Andy Rainer found Jesus. He thought. Or Jesus had found him.

Andy wasn't quite sure. He thought at the time that it had been a genuine vision, but it could just have been some sort of blinding light. In his business there were many such lights—light that over the years had started to destroy his eyesight. Regardless of the vision's legitimacy he found himself praying a few times a day, though not to anyone in particular: he simply clasped his hands together, bowed his head, and pleaded for good things to come— or to at least to be spared from nefarious elements like temptation, lust, greed, pride, etc.

Christ, there is nothing but temptation in this industry. It's the entire driving force for music.

"Fuck it. Amen." He touched himself on the forehead, right where his third eye should be, but also where a priest had touched him once during communion and finished getting dressed. He had planned on wearing his darkest suit for the last night of QuickFame, but when he put it on it seemed to bulge in the middle. It looked unseemly.

He looked fat, old.

He had a good long crying jag, ate a low-carb protein bar, got on the exercise bike for an hour, then sat praying for a few minutes before making another attempt at his closet.

This time he went for blue jeans and a black V-neck sweater.

Dressed, Andy peeled back the curtain and peered out the window of his tour bus, which he'd asked the driver to park out back. At the time had thought that some peace and quiet would be best, and there was absolutely neither of those things in the halls and wings of the 13-666 club, located in Emmiline's hallowed Chiroma Alley.

He'd never set foot in such a seedy venue and didn't plan on staying for longer than it'd take to seal the deal and get the winner chosen.

He'd hop back in the bus and speed out of here, hopefully never to return to one of these awful shows.

Like the other judges, he was using it to boost his music industry credentials so that he could elevate his star again.

He would soon need to move on from singing, which was exhausting, to focus solely on writing, producing, dieting, and searching for true love.

The whole contest seemed pointless anyways.

Cat Coggan was going to win.

Andy had one wild card left, Felicia had none.

With Heidi on board with Andy's plan it was all but a sure thing: Cat would win, he'd hire Andy to serve as a producer on the record—as Cat had assured at their meeting in a dark alley before the second round of QuickFame—and Andy would earn residual incomes and get his foot in the door for bigger projects yet to come, such as managing Cat's musical output and helping to shape his sound and career. #Five was good, yes, but they weren't his flavor, and they didn't want Andy's help with their careers. He liked solo singers like Cat—like himself—who'd forged their own paths without being propped up by superior musicians.

As for Scarlett Fever, they seemed cooked and fried and tossed in the bin: one of the little shits from #Five had thrown an entire juke box across the room at the Scarlett Fever guitarist in a dustup over the female lead singer, or so it was being rumored on social media. Felicia herself had said it was true, she was there, it was amazing, the juke box was heavy, and the singer was so full of Hulkian rage the machine all but threw itself *blah blah blah*. It all seemed unlikely, but Andy didn't care. He liked a little bit of drama, and the incident hadn't affected his singer and the inevitable winner, Cat. But with a broken foot, how could that guitarist work his pedals and keep the beat, let alone stand?

#Five. *Pound Five? No, Hashtag.* He snorted. *I'd like to pound the fuck out of them.*

There was no doubt #Five was the real deal, but their songs stunk.

They had what it took to be stars of their own making and they didn't need this contest, but their music—what was wrong with these kids?

The lyrics were absurd, more like something from a 2Tone B-side track circa 1995. He wouldn't put it past Felicia to be feeding them songs that she thought would be a hit with both the judges and with the voting public, who would be chiming in from all over the world in the finals.

Because of such meddling nothing was yet assured. The winner would be ultimately selected by judges, but it would be done electoral college style: viewers would be watching the performances live as each of the bands alternated one song after the other for three songs, until 9 p.m. Emmiline time.

Cheating wasn't likely, as voters had to register with a real email address and their corresponding IP addresses would be logged. Sure, there were ways around such things, but QuickFame had a tech crew working for such contingencies and at best such meddling could only skew the voting system by two or three percent.

Once the votes were tallied the judges would have the final say. But if, like, a billion people voted for #Five and 100,000 voted for Cat, he couldn't simply declare him the winner.

That'd be too obvious. That'd be typically American, and Andy's proudly Canadian heritage would not allow for such fascism.

Andy wanted to throw up. He opened another curtain. *Why did I ask to be parked where no one could see me?* He got himself a diet soda from the minifridge and sat on one of his couches sipping it and doing his best to stave off the Black Cloud of Existential Dread. He quickly realized that he looked pathetically forlorn, like that awful Keanu Reeves meme that would never be scrubbed from the internet and leapt back up to shut the curtain. He turned off a couple of the lights as well, then put on some music. Tom Jones. Nice.

He thought about setting up the mood lighting for when the writer arrived for the interview, but he wasn't sure whether the publication was sending over a man or a woman. Andy hadn't really been paying attention when his agent had called to discuss it.

A few minutes later someone knocked on the door. Andy's hard-heeled loafers tapped their way across the bus's hardwood floors. When the door hissed open, he found one of the security staff standing there with another guy wearing a slouch beanie and sporting an impressive red beard, trimmed in the latest style.

"Good evening, Mr. Rainer. I'm here to discuss your book."

Upon realizing that the reporter was a man, a wave of ennui washed through Andy.

"Alright. Come on in."

He stepped inside; the door hissed shut. The man offered his hand. "Carl Rian."

"Pleasure to meet you."

"Ok to keep my shoes on?"

"As long as you didn't step in blood, shit, or a pile of hypodermic needles on your way here, it's ok with me. And you never know in Chiroma Alley. Get you a drink?"

"Water would be fine."

Andy got a glass from one of the cabinets, then handed it and a bottle of ice-cold water to the writer.

"So, you're here to interview me?"

The writer sat down on one of the narrow but reasonably comfortable couches and got out a pad and paper from his shoulder bag. "Oh—no. I think some wires got crossed. That's not what this is about. I've been hired by Chafin-Fraley to help you with your book."

Andy sat on the opposite couch. "My book? Are you an editor?"

"Editor, coach, author, ghostwriter."

"Ghostwriter? My publisher hired you to write *my* memoir?"

"Not exactly write it, no. I'm here to help you find the core of your life's narrative arc, to suss out the moments where you made key decisions that lead you to your achievements, ending with now or with what's next. It seems like your story is unfinished, but the path that has led you here has surely been full and vivid. I just want to help you frame that in a literary and compelling way."

"And I've failed in that regard? I know I'm not a writer but—"

The writer hesitated but didn't equivocate.

"The editors at Chafin-Fraley feel that the structure is linear and overly focused on the sequence of events, which is one of its two main weaknesses.

"What's the second?"

"Perhaps that should wait."

"Come on, man. Just have it out."

"Ok. You're playing it close to your chest. You're holding back."

"In what way?"

"You're not exposing yourself. I've found that the majority of performers and artistic types I've worked with have dark secrets that have compelled them to pursue their art to the point where it nearly kills them. I assume that that's the same with you. Am I wrong?"

Andy sipped his soda, now mostly flat. Maybe the writer wasn't such a dick after all. A bit pompous and direct, but that was a nice change in an industry where people could say one thing to your face while texting otherwise under the table. "Well, I only have an hour or so until the show."

The writer started to stand up. "If this is a bad time, I can arrange something else with your agent and pub—"

Andy waved him off. "No, no. This is perfect. It helps me keep my mind off the live television production." Andy's gaze settled on a point in the distance, almost as if he were staring out the window, except that the curtains remained closed.

The writer sat again. "Do you get nervous being on stage and TV?"

Andy laughed. "Au contraire! It's the one place I feel at ease. I feel alive up there. I feel like my true self." Andy kept laughing as if enjoying a private joke whose punch line the writer was too obtuse to grasp, then sighed, set down his diet soda, and turned to lie back on the couch. "No, it's when I'm alone that things start to come apart. Then it's nothing but me and my thoughts."

The writer contemplated this a moment, scratching his notepad but not writing anything. "What's it like being up on stage in front of thousands of people?"

Andy smiled to himself, his soda resting on his chest. "Up there I'm anonymous."

"Hm. You mean because you can be anyone or anything they want you to be?"

Andy nodded. "It's not really me, you know? I've got fury inside, and hope, and love, but on stage it's all about good feelings. I carry on the tradition of the troubadour, of romantic bold men who express their love of life to thousands of people at a time. James Taylor, Jimmy Buffet, Neil Diamond, the Rat Pack. No one really knows those people off the stage, nor do they want to. They don't want to see my dirty underwear or the dust on my books that are never read because most nights I feel nailed to the couch. One day we'll have holographic concerts by the great singers long since expired, but it's pointless. You're already looking at a facsimile on stage. It's just a carbon copy of me, the version that puts out joyful music that doesn't offend or alienate or cast political aspersions."

The writer was taking notes like mad. Andy gave him a moment, then continued. "It's a form of altruism, really."

"How so?"

"On stage I am focused solely on the people. Sure, I write music for myself but mainly for the people. Once it's out there, it's for them to do with as they please. Art is for others."

"So, what happens when you're not on stage?"

"That's a different story."

Andy twisted around to sit up and leaned with his elbows on his knees.

"When I'm alone with my thoughts, Carl, I am overwhelmed with fear, doubt, and low self- esteem."

"Where does that come from? What happened to you to bring that on?"

Andy's shoulders rose and fell.

"Where to start?"

"Maybe with your strongest memory. I didn't see anything in the book on that topic. You start the book with college, when you joined the drama troupe and earned leading roles in the campus musicals."

"That's true. I did not include my mother. On purpose."

"To anger her?"

"Exactly."

"I don't mean to pry but—well, how to put this delicately? Was she—?"

"Responsible for making me who I am today? Yes. And a righteous cunt? Indeed. She ruined my life and drove me to stardom."

"It sounds like this is a crucial component of the book. Can we include it, all the pain and rawness and honesty?"

"I have to think about that."

"Could you at least tell me her story?"

Andy sighed and told himself that he was under no circumstances to shed a single tear. He leaned back, crossed an ankle over his knee, and commenced bobbing that foot up and down. "She was a real queen of the arts, or so she fancied herself. She became an alcoholic at an early age and never quite recovered, so I became her proxy in the arts. My father split early on. He'd had enough of her antics and addiction, despite numerous attempts to make things better. He left me a letter apologizing for not taking me with him, that he'd come back for me once he'd gotten settled and had hired a solid lawyer, but he never did."

"I'm sorry to hear that."

"I saw him again though. When I'd reached the big circus, Madison Square Garden, he emerged from the crowd. I gave him a bop in the nose and told him to fuck off and die. Anyways, back when he had left us, Marcella, my mother, lost it for a couple years. We were evicted and it was up to me to take care of her, go to school, pay the bills. It was hell on earth, and I strongly considered suicide, or even murder-suicide, first her and then me. But it was also heaven on earth because my mother loved me and when she was sober or only half-drunk, we made amazing art together, with her on the piano and me on this little plywood stage that we carried around from apartment to apartment. As you can imagine I picked up some of her habits and psychoses. Her behavior vacillated given the day, the tide, the season, her moods, and of course whether she was able to procure alcohol."

"This sounds like something you've never told anyone."

"Correct."

"Your struggle was almost Dickensian. I can't imagine leaving it out of the book. It adds a lot of texture to your story, Mr. Rainer."

"Andy."

"Andy. Not to be too blunt or bold, but my perception of you is that of a somewhat shallow and bland person."

Andy flashed a look of pure indignation at the writer.

"I'm sorry. It's just the image you convey on television, through your music, and in print."

"You're probably right. I don't exactly seem full of profound wisdom when I'm singing things like 'Hot thoughts and lovely balloons at our summer vacay. No more tired days for me or you, at least not for a week or two.'" He laughed. "Idiotic, I know. And then there's my mother's paranoia about me getting fat, which led to my nightmarish relationship with food. While I'm sure there exist other men who can bring on the gag reflex simply by imagining their mother's cooking, I've yet to meet one."

"Are you saying you're bulimic?"

"Not at the moment, but that's because I've got a nutritionist keeping me alive on a starvation diet, at my request."

"I'm sorry to hear that. I think your experience could help a lot of people though, and it would earn sympathy from fans old and new."

"I don't know. Maybe. Do I want to expose myself like that? I'll look like a crybaby. Everyone already thinks I'm gay, which I'm not. I love the ladies."

"So was music an outlet for you during your youth, dealing with your mother's addiction and heavy hand?"

"Music was really the only thing I was capable of doing. I was shit at sports, not great with drama if it wasn't a musical, a lackadaisical student."

"How did you discover your voice?"

"Oh, that's easy." Andy closed his eyes. "Marcella dragged me to church whenever she was alive on Sunday mornings, but rather than sit there sweltering with the fogies and babies, I joined the choir."

Andy perked up; he was beaming, his fingers dancing in the air like a maestro's.

"The choir director stopped rehearsal one day to ask who in tarnation was singing *like that*. No one dared answered, so he said, 'Whose voice is that challenging the angels for supremacy, the one who's upper end just scraped the edge of heaven itself?' The people around me nudged me forward. I got my first solo that week. The rest is written in stone, like the commandments themselves."

"We just need to get it down on paper," the writer said with a smirk, but Andy was too lost in his own history to pick up the humor.

"So, uh, would you consider yourself religious?"

"Me? God no. I'll do what it takes though."

"To do what?"

"To stay relevant."

"What does relevancy mean to you?"

"Are you a shrink or a writer?" Andy said, his face darkening. He spun around, lay down again, and propped up his feet on the counter.

"I'm just trying to get to the bottom of your beliefs. I want to know what drives you and what paralyzes you."

"Felicia Scalding," he said after an interval of silence.

"Ah. You've had quite a combative relationship over the years."

"Yes. I feel the need to crush her. To obliterate her from the public eye."

"Because of her success? I mean, it seems to me like you've achieved much greater things over the years, especially of late. Your star continues to shine."

"No. Because of some things she said once. She didn't know it, but they were recorded. It was never made public but an anonymous friend in common relayed it to me."

"That's too bad."

Andy raised an eyebrow. "Don't you want to know what she said?"

"Only if you want to tell me."

"Isn't it important for the book?"

"If you think it has value in telling the story of your life, it could be."

"She said that my songs are as wooden as a nutcracker but with less personality and as authentic as a three-dollar bill printed on toilet paper."

The writer worked hard to keep his expression neutral. "That's harsh."

"The fucking cunt."

"Sort of clever though."

"I know! That's what's even worse! She really got my goat."

"I can see why that would offend you, Mr. Rainer."

"Please, call me Andy." He sat up. "I've got to get to the performance. So, did we get to the core of my life?"

"I'd say we're closer. I'm seeing some trends."

"Good. I want to pick this up again. What's the next step?"

"I'll call your agent on Monday to arrange another meeting."

"You can come to my place. I live up in Emmiline Heights."

"Oh, well, um, sure."

"Is that weird?"

"I guess it'd be ok."

"I don't throw orgies or anything." He winked. "Not anymore."

***

Andy ran a lint roller over his outfit, grabbed his phone, exited the bus, and headed into the 13- 666 club. For some reason as he walked, he could hear one of #Five's songs running through his head—the incredible song they'd performed the previous night. He hadn't liked #Five as a band, nor the members individually, until they'd performed that last piece, which was probably their own material. At that moment he started to see them in a new light, as his new pastor (who was also his AA sponsor) encouraged him to do—to look for the positive in something, even when you step in dog crap.

The more he thought about it, the more obvious it was becoming that Felicia was steering #Five toward the win the same way he was working with Cat Coggan, but Andy wondered what had happened now that they'd switched to their own material. When he thought about it, it was entirely unclear who the winner would be. He liked that.

And he felt deathly ill.

He needed other opportunities. The book was likely going to be a flop, despite the writer's hard-hitting dissection of his past, and Andy couldn't imagine churning out any more holiday singles.

The most recent one just barely squeaked past the Streemy execs, who claimed that Andy's style of nasally crooning was dead. All money lay with millennials now: if the kids don't approve of a track, it doesn't matter whether your grandmother can find it on the radio or not.

"Welcome, Mr. Rainer," a security guard said as he held the door open.

"Hey there, thanks a lot. Have a great night." He shook the guy's hand and tipped him ten bucks.

Then, stepping into the bowels of the club, he stopped short. "Fuck me."

The walls of the 13-666 were painted black. The ceiling was black. The chandelier was probably black but when lit up its prisms took on a purple hue. The columns were black. The staff wore black.

"It's like some sort of arson crime scene."

The club's lone green room was reserved for the bands, forcing the judges onto the floor early. Luckily, their area was completed segregated. Andy liked that. He was first to arrive, apparently, and it seemed uncool to do so, so he hung out on the wings and watched as the audience was conveyed onto the club's main floor. VIPs were being escorted down a chute to the second-level balcony, while those without tickets were being relegated to the cramped and distant third-level balcony. DJ Collide-o-scope had been brought in from Alaska to do whatever it was he did with records and a laptop.

At the moment it sounded like a Marvin Gaye record was being violated by a robotic vacuum cleaner.

The stage, also painted black and framed by largely decorative black curtains, contained three drum kits: one for Scarlett Fever, one for #Five, and even one for Cat Coggan, who'd brought in a full backing band for the night. Everything was tuned and ready. As soon as one band had finished their song, the next band would have the length of a commercial break to prepare for their song— about three minutes. It was slightly mad, pushing the limits of nonprofessional acts like this, but it made for good drama. Andy enjoyed seeing bands humiliated on stage, just like how Felicia had been humiliated by Michaela George when she walked off stage mere minutes before their massive performance at Wembley Stadium all those years ago. Millions of dollars were lost on that show. Thousands of disappointed fans would never recover, nor would Felicia, neither financially or emotionally. Her career had largely spluttered out since then.

"Ahh, shit." Andy pressed his hands to his side where he felt stabbing pain. It'd started a couple years ago but struck at mysterious times. He was convinced it was schadenfreude embodied, physical pain registered in the body when reveling in the suffering of another person. It was also where his mother used to jab him with a knitting needle whenever he wasn't singing on key or was asking for another snack.

"You ok, Andy?"

Speak of the she-devil: Felicia Scalding.

"Never better," Andy said, forcing himself to stand upright. "I was doing some sit-ups in my bus and probably overworked a muscle."

"Exercise will do that to you when you pass fifty."

"I'm not fifty!"

Felicia laughed. "I know you're not, you dweeb. You don't look a day over forty-nine."

"Hardy har har. Where have you been storing that comedic nugget?"

Felicia's phone buzzed. She got it out and read a message. "Twelve million viewers have already registered to vote and thousands more join every minute."

"Better hope the system doesn't crash like on Song of Life. What a shit-show that was."

"If that happens it'll come down to the three of us. No band can win without two-thirds majority."

"I know how it works, Felicia. And yes, that'll be a disaster. Heidi is championing her favorite, you have your pet project, and I am supporting the one band of actual musical merit because they deserve to win and *only* because they deserve to win."

Felicia scoffed. "You're so innocent, aren't you? Like a virgin. Maybe you should get laid, Andy."

Andy waved her off.

"You don't like me, do you?" she said.

"Ha! You know, I was just talking to my—my friend—on the bus and we were discussing the horrible things you have said about me all those years ago, Felicia. I don't know why but I suddenly feel liberated enough to tell you that I know. You tried to tear me down behind my back. So here is what I have to say to you."

"Oh, Andy—"

"Thank you."

"What?"

"Thank you, Felicia. You made me realize that although my songs are not profound, that although I downplay my true emotions in order to make music that people will enjoy and maybe dance to at a bar mitzvah reception, I don't play the Emmiline hate game. I never stooped to your level. I am what I am, and I'm proud of it."

Felicia clenched her eyes shut. "Andy, you're right. I'm sorry for those things I said. I was insecure but also full of myself. I felt the need to tear people down left and right."

"No wonder Michaela George walked off in that auspicious moment."

"Hey! I thought you just said you weren't going to stoop to my level."

Andy looked at his feet.

He really needed another low-carb protein bar in his stomach before showtime.

"You're right. That was a low blow."

"That was the worst moment of my life. Well, until recently. This past year has been hell. I don't even deserve to be here, to be honest."

The two judges stood staring at the black stage.

"I hate this place," Felicia said.

"Me too. It's downright funereal. Where pop music goes to die."

Felicia laughed. "You're funny, Andy. We should get drinks sometime. I can get blitzed and apologize again for the transgressions of my youths."

"What if we fall in love?"

"Then we'll just have to make beautiful music together."

Andy smiled, staring off into the space. Next thing he knew, Felicia was standing on the tips of her toes and kissing him on the cheek.

"But you're not my type," she said. "Sorry."

She walked away as the doors to the hot and humid club were opened and the audience flowed in like lava.

Heidi took her seat just before the live show commenced. Andy was seated in the middle with the women on either side of him, even though he'd requested he not be front and center, i.e., in a position that could be deemed patriarchal. But it was too late. Plex was warming up in the wings, saying, "Red leather, yellow leather" over and over, followed by "the sixth sheik's sixth sheep is sick," and "when one black bug bled black blood, the other black bug bled blue."

The makeup artist came around one last time to check the judges' makeup. "Good as it's going to get in this coal mine," she said, then marched off to paste another layer onto Plex's shiny brow.

The audience was surprisingly restrained, perhaps exhausted from leaning against one another for over an hour. The bands were nowhere to be seen. Andy checked his list again: Scarlett Fever would kick it off, followed by #Five, with Cat Coggan third. If they did go over their allotted five minutes, the warning light would give them ten seconds to wrap it up or risk humiliation on live television when their song was cut off. Then the cycle would be repeated, each band taking turns, playing a total of three songs each right up to the end. Online and telephone voting would start only after the second round, close to the one-hour mark. Then the madness would begin as the twenty million or so registered users chimed in with their very valuable, very informed opinions as to who the winner should be.

Soon enough Thaddeus Goldar was on the floor, giving the audience a run-down on what was happening and what kind of behavior was expected of them. Should they try to jump onto the stage or assault one of the musicians in the wings or shout profanities, they would not only be ejected, they'd be arrested. They'd also be humiliated on social media and in the news, their face likely plastered on the front pages of newspapers.

"And have a great time, everyone!"

The lights came down, offering a moment's reprieve from their intense heat.

Although Heidi and Felicia were paragons of poise and equanimity, Andy could feel sweat trickling down his spine and pooling around his balls. He needed to adjust but it wouldn't be decent, not with the women surrounding him and thousands of people standing mere feet away. With few options he waited until the women were distracted with their phones or conversations, then jammed his water bottle into his crotch and created some air flow. Then he waved over a low-level staffer and requested another bottle.

Showtime.

"Wow, what a night!" Plex said as he strolled onto the stage. The moron. Vapid. A Ken Doll of a human. "You're part of the second-ever QuickFame contest, the world's most rapid ascent from nobody to star!"

The applause sign flashed on, and the crowd put their hands together.

"We started with 1,231 acts on Monday and Tuesday. By Wednesday night it was down to just 33."

He lowered his voice and the crowd hushed itself and leaned in as if being told a secret. "Then eleven. Now three. And in two hours: just one." He held up a finger. Andy found himself imagining how many anuses it had wormed its way into. "Who will that one band be? The four thrashers from Michigan with the orange-haired nightingale-slash-metal-head for a singer? The five clean- cut boys from our very own Emmiline, each of whom brings a valuable skill to the stage?"

Andy snorted to himself. More like "#Four." There was no way that kid got out of jail in time.

How did QuickFame even let him continue to compete?

"Or the golden-throated troubadour with the soul of Neil Young and the grit of a young Springsteen, who tonight has not just his well-traveled acoustic guitar but a full band to bring his songs to life? Who will it be, folks? Will your votes swing the judges, or will they throw a wrench in the works and award the prize to someone else? It all depends on what these musicians give us tonight. So, clear your ears, open your hearts, breathe deeply, and put your hands together for the QuickFame U.S.A. Finale!"

8.

THE STARS IN THE SKY
ARE ALREADY LONG DEAD

Layton's research indicated that Oxford Street was the prime location for clothes shopping, dresses in particular. Designers here were doing things that had never been done before, mainly experimental designs that played with geometric forms, materials, colorways, and old ideas combined with the new. They often sold out in hours and were never made again. Even a photograph of a person trying them on could net tens of thousands of likes on social media.

Layton didn't plan on recording anything for austerity or to be shared.

He just wanted to see what he looked like in something other than a frilly denim toss-off that not even an impoverished Iowan farmer's wife would consider using to wipe up spilled milk, let alone wear.

He got dressed, pulled on a baseball cap and sunglasses, and snuck out of his hotel room shortly after Grannie had gone to get some exercise. It was barely seven in the morning. He knew the shops didn't open until close to noon, but he couldn't risk running into anyone he knew.

Everything changes once your face has been plastered all over live television and even more so when you hook up with the lead singer of one of the other bands after knowing her for a mere forty-eight hours.

Exiting the lobby into the half-dark, half-golden morning, Layton suddenly realized how half- baked his idea was. What was he going to say to the clerk? "Can I try on this dress? It's for my sister, and we're about the same size." If he were anonymous like a few weeks ago it would have been different. Now he couldn't count on anything. The world was now one giant proctologist, shoving its fingers into your most private parts and examining the findings under a microscope.

He could always window shop. He could take pictures, then make plans for designing his own once he was back home. And he heard that the second hand stores—"op shops," they were called here—down on George Street had last year's fashions at manageable prices. No one would notice if you'd throw a dress into the pile with jeans and tops.

Layton shook his head and kicked the curb. He wasn't sure how much longer he could hide like this.

Like the emperor who wore no clothes, except that I wear clothes to hide the queen inside.

Or is it even hiding? he further wondered.

You can't hide what's plain to see. You can only lie about its nature.

Coffee shops were just starting to open. Layton knew that the country had invented the flat white and wanted to try an authentic one, not that watery American version that flat-brimmed-cap-wearing baristas were slinging in Emmiline. He walked, then walked some more until he found a flat-brimmed-cap-wearing guy with long blond locks emerging from beneath it in the process of raising an awning. He was wearing board shorts, a tank top, and flip-flops, and he had the physique of someone who paddled a longboard through the surf for half the day.

"Hey, mate. Just opening up."

"Cool. You make a flat white?"

"Aw yeah. No problem."

A few minutes later the barista whipped up a perfect flat white with almond milk. Layton carried it to the corner of the cafe and sat with his back against the wall, sipping and receiving his first hit of caffeine for the day.

The barista, wiping down tables, waved at him. "Aw no, mate. You can't sit there."

"Why not?"

"The sun's shining and the air's fresh. You gotta some sun, eh?"

"I don't know."

"I highly recommend it, mate. This is the quietest it's gonna be all day. So pissful."

Peaceful.

He said peaceful.

So, Layton found himself on the terrace, watching the city come to life. He expected wild animals to hop down the street. Instead, he saw only buses. The birds looked normal. The sky was tinged with haze, but the sun wasn't blazing hot. He felt at peace a moment, happy, dreaming of the fashion boutiques he'd discover in this strange new city. Then he looked up at the eaves overhead, saw a creature that'd obviously just emerged from the bowels of hell, and sprang to his feet, sending his table and the coffee flying to the ground.

"It's just a spider," the barista said as he made another drink for Layton. "Scary, yeah, I know. I seen the bastards climb twelve floors to my apartment. I got screens though. You get used to them after a while, but I guess a foreigner would be spooked. Here. On the house."

"No, no. I have to pay. It was my fault."

"Naw you don't."

Layton stuffed five dollars in the tip jar, thanked the guy, and took his drink with him, intending to find a place devoid of spiders the size of a child's hand.

He took out his phone to check the time. Eight o'clock. He wondered what time it was back home. What his parents were doing. What his human shit stain of a sister was doing. What Tona Kohl and the rest of Scarlett Fever were doing.

Even Cat Coggan.

"How did I get here?"

Layton walked and sipped his second flat white. He'd never tasted anything like it; he briefly considered moving here forever. Then he thought about the spiders climbing the sides of buildings, not like superheroes but their enemies, and quickly ruled that out. Then he remembered the snake he'd seen once in Emmiline, a giant beige thing with a triangular head slipping into a hole the size of a quarter in a friend's house. They never found the snake and Layton had to give up that friendship. Spiders weren't so bad, maybe.

He checked his phone, then slowed his pace as he turned onto Oxford Street. Most of the boutiques were closed. He toured the street, peering into windows but seeing little of interest. The hipster-surfer-chic look wasn't his thing.

After walking four or five blocks he crossed the street and started back towards the hotel, but further along he spotted someone setting up a sandwich board on the sidewalk advertising a post- New Year's sale.

Layton pulled his cap so low that it was crushing his sunglasses against his face and raised his coffee to his mouth as he approached the store.

"Oh shit. That is divine."

He needed the vest on display in the window. It's design was nothing special: a simple gray tweed with subtle white striping with ample spacing between the rows.

No, it was the cut of it that he liked, with the neck high and sharp and a small V-shaped notch at the hem.

Vests are stupid. Who wears them? The serve no purpose unless you're, like, lost in the wilderness and the thing is stuffed with bark or dead birds or something. And I hate camping.

He took a heavy pull on his coffee.

But rock 'n roll is stupid too. It's ALL one big fashion show. Even the anti-fashion bands are hypocritically fashionistas of another sort.

He laughed out loud. "Anti-fash."

"Is there something you like?" someone asked, startling Layton, and causing him to throw his flat white onto the sidewalk.

"Fuck, not again!"

"I'm sorry. I didn't mean to scare you."

"It's my fault."

"I've got a pot brewing in the back if you'd like a cup."

Layton shrugged. "Nah, it's ok. I was just looking at—my sister—maybe I—"

"The vest?" He nodded.

"The owner made that herself. It's surprisingly soft, unlike most suit vests, which are stiff and meant to sit flat beneath a jacket."

"Isn't it made for, you know, girls?"

The clerk looked at the vest, then at Layton. He felt inclined to cover himself. Or run. The clerk couldn't have been more than a few years older than him. Her hair was straight and blond, her skin dark with sun but not obscenely so. Even her teeth were perfect, so straight, and white that she could have modeled for a toothpaste ad.

He imagined that she spent most of her afternoon at the beach with the guy from the coffee shop, polishing their standup paddle boards and sharpening their oars, or whatever it was you did with an oar (he imagined they needed to be sharp enough to fight off all the great white sharks that prowled the waters around Sydney). "I believe it's cut for women, yeah, but you might be able to squeeze into it. You want to try it?"

"No, I—It's not my—I don't know."

The clerk went inside, then reappeared in the window, bearhugging the mannequin torso as she lifted it off its stand.

A minutes later the clerk was setting up Layton in the tiny dressing booth in the back corner of the shop. "All set?" she said, then slid the curtain shut.

Layton collapsed onto the minuscule stool and sunk his face into his hands.

If I'm so sure of myself, why am I so goddamned confused?

He found the girl attractive. The problem was that ever since discovering that he was a woman inside, he had expected to be interested in men—but he wasn't. When he truly thought about it, the male body held little sway over him. Even his own body repulsed him, with all that muscle and hair and sharp edges. He'd been hoping that as he came to terms with transition his sexuality would transition as well; it hadn't. It wouldn't. He realized that now. He was not only going to become a woman in the future, but he would also become a lesbian.

He could already hear his sister's laughter, his parents' confusion. Only the band would understand and support his decision, though their main concern would primarily be whether his voice would change drastically enough that they'd have to reinvent their sound.

And Layton realized that #Five was not his band. #Five implied five bodies that comprised one entity, five personalities compressed into one vision, one musical identity. They had always been Shivvr and the Quakes. Their mission in life was to release tectonic energy in the form of music.

If only Felicia Scalding would let them.

When Layton had returned home the morning after the QuickFame finals, even Layton's parents had sensed something was going on. His sister, too, with her meddling and suspicious ways, kept spying on him and was texting constantly as soon as he'd appeared in the kitchen in his Happy Clothes (sweatpants and a cardigan).

She gave him his space, vacating a room as soon as he entered it, afraid he might develop other, weirder "psychoses."

"It was quite a show," his mother had said as she embraced her son, "but what was going on up there on that stage?"

"It's hard to explain."

"Do you want to talk about it?" his father asked.

"Definitely not. I need some rest and some time to myself, ok?"

"Of course. I'll bring you some dinner in a while. Alright dear?"

He shrugged and carried his weekender up to his room, then punted it into the corner. He tore off a couple of posters featuring rock stars he no longer idolized, from a young Mercury to an aging Morrissey. He tugged off his boots and flung them out the window, then slammed it shut lest they find their way back up the wall and through the window.

You big baby.

For the next two days he cycled through the events in his mind, over and over, like a sickness, like a mental patient. He wondered if he was going to snap and perhaps throw a juke box across the room like Jai.

It was an antique jukebox and he just barely managed to tip it over, you ass. You were there.

As his days at home stretched out, he relaxed somewhat, but the details started to blur. It wasn't something he wanted to forget; there were so many lessons to be gleaned from the experience, both about life, music, himself, and the base, corruptible natural of the human soul.

So Saturday morning he woke up early, ate breakfast alone before his family raided the kitchen—where he might encounter Madeline in that awful bathrobe she claimed was the same style as the one Princess Kate wore—then locked himself in his room and removed his journal from the cheap little safe he kept in his closet. He cleared off his desk, locked the door, then started writing.

***

Despite how badly the machine had crushed the foot of Roman, Scarlett Fever's guitarist, it'd only broken two bones. In order to stay precise, he'd kept his pain medication at half the recommended dosage. He was in constant pain and took every opportunity to voice loud complaints or simply bitch out anyone remotely associated with #Five. As for Jai, he slunk around like an unwanted puppy because Tona was now doting on Roman like a mother hen, even shedding a few tears (and Roman shared a few; there seemed to be something between them that no one was privy to, something deviant).

Weirdest of all was the new guy, Eddie, who was following Jai around. Jai claimed that he was his own personal security staff, but when Layton cornered the kid, he said that Thaddeus and Felicia were paying him to keep Jai calm and out of trouble, along with the rest of the band.

One would think that having a jukebox crush your guitarist's foot would have turned the tables for #Five, shifting the underdog status to Scarlett Fever.

Instead, the strangest thing happened: when the lights came up and Plex McGuire kicked things off by introducing Scarlett Fever, the audience booed.

It started with a small cluster of people in the upper levels, and though others standing nearby tried to shut it down, another cluster on the main floor not only picked up the booing, but they also amplified it.

It somehow surged through the club, unstoppable, infectious, and misunderstood, like an internet meme gone bad, but it inexplicably continued. Soon the booing filled the black walls of the 13-666, which was fitting in a sense: these people were doing the devil's work, and in that moment, Layton considered Felicia evil incarnate. She surely had orchestrated this—she was the only judge not to react to the haranguing, whereas Heidi and Andy rose from their seats and surveyed the audience with horror.

It took two or three minutes for Plex McGuire to reign in the audience. Then he scolded them. "Shame on you. Shame. These musicians have put their hearts and souls on the line, performing their material for you with heart and soul and—and—*blah blah blah.*" He actually said that. *Blah blah blah.* "Words. Just words. I shouldn't even have to use them. I've never seen anything like this and only action suffices in a moment like this. If it were up to me, we'd empty the club and usher in a much more deserving audience. But since time is of the essence and we're live on television, you own this. Shame on you. You don't deserve the music this band is going to offer you."

Plex gave the clearly distraught Tona Kohl a moment to collect herself, and then Scarlett Fever held a powwow right there on stage, on live television—great drama, a viral moment.

A hush settled over the audience. Tona composed herself and took the mic. Aron brought in the beat. Gavin answered with the bass.

Roman added a layer of sonic reverb with his guitars, the sound so dense it rivaled that of Jai's (as it should have, him having fourteen years more experience than the teenager). Roman's foot was bound up in a cast he'd spray-painted black, which should have added an element of pure rock 'n roll but somehow looked slightly pathetic and grotesque, like a blackened chicken wing. The song was probably Scarlett Fever's crown jewel, and one that they'd been saving just for a moment like this. It was a mix of the best '90s alternative, akin to Nirvana and Mud Honey, and newer sounds like Silversun Pickups mated with the heaviness of Queens of the Stone Age and of course Tona's ridiculously guttural growl. It hit hard but it was tied together with a deep hook, a chorus marked by a rich melody, and a heavy breakdown that verged on disintegration just before Tona pulled it all back together with a riot-grrrl-esque scream.

"Wow!" Plex had said following Scarlett Fever's performance. Those word still echoes in Layton's mind, because he thought it too. "Wow, folks. What did you think of that?"

Then the crowd flipped again: the applause for Scarlett Fever nearly blew the roof off. The floor shook from the stomping the purplish chandeliers shivering with the noise. Tona was in tears again but for different reasons.

"What in the fuck is going on out there?" The members of #Five kept asking themselves. "Bipolar to say the least."

"Fuckin' Felicia," Britt said.

Grannie corralled the band together while Eddie stood guard a short ways away. "Focus, guys. It's good that they started off so strongly. Now we have to do them one better."

"We can't do that with Felicia's shitty song!"

"We don't have a choice."

"Sure, we do. We can do 'Hot Crazy Lover' or 'Up To My Neck In Your Blood.'"

"We haven't practiced those."

"I don't even remember the lyrics," Layton said. "Fuck!"

"Just focus on 'Peace and Wisdom.' Play it as if it's our own, with feeling."

"That's like trying to read a greeting card at a poetry slam."

Layton looked to Grannie; Grannie gave him a noncommittal look of sympathy, then led the band onto the stage. They took their spots. At the last second, just before the production manager threw the camera to Plex McGuire, Britt *pssst*'ed at the others.

"Four o'clock?"

"Rock!" they whispered back.

The audience welcomed them with genuine yet restrained applause. #Five played the song as best they could, but it was yet another watered-down light-radio-rock tune. It had no station in their hearts. They were playing a song, not performing music. When the song petered to its end, Plex didn't offer them any wows.

"Great stuff," he'd said to the band, then turned to the audience. "More great stuff from the five Emmiline boys."

The commercial break and dimming lights shielded their shame as they rushed off the stage to the green room while Cat Coggan and his backing band made their way to their instruments, but when #Five stepped inside the cramped room they found a grimacing Roman in the arms of Tona and two more angry musicians raiding the catering.

The room reeked of sweat and deli meat and leather.

"Follow me," Grannie said.

He led them down the hall and they crammed themselves into the bathroom.

Again, Eddie stood watch outside while inside Jai leaned against the door and slumped to the floor.

Layton peeled off his shirt and splashed water all over his face and chest. "I can't breathe."

"You can," Grannie said. "Take it easy."

"We failed."

"We didn't fail," Donovan said. "We made asses of ourselves. We look idiotic. We normally play songs that speak to the gods but here we play turds that a plumber wouldn't dare touch."

"Do plumbers actually handle turds?"

"You know what I mean."

They sat in silence, their chests heaving. "It's over," Britt said.

Grannie threw a wadded-up paper towel at him. "It's not."

"Your makeup is smeared."

"Shut up."

"The voting starts after the next song," Layton said.

"We need more than boos against the competition to win," Britt said. "I bet right now we're in last place."

"Coming in second would be ok. Third, no. We're underdogs, not homeless cats."

"What?"

"I don't know! Leave me alone."

They sat there another minute or two.

Then Grannie stood up. "Time to go. Scarlett Fever will be clearing out soon, and we can prepare in the green room."

Jai stood up. "Prepare what? Oh, you mean that we have to polish that musical turd before shitting it into the ears of all our new fans."

"No," Grannie said. "Britt was right. We play 'Hot Psycho.'"

It was as if all of their faces were punched upwards at once.

"Stop smirking. Do you even remember the lyrics?"

"Of course, I do."

"Britt needs a microphone too. We all do for the '*psycho psycho psycho bitch*' refrain. I'll have to rig it up as fast as I can."

"Can we say that on TV?"

Grannie led them back to the green room. "I guess we'll find out."

Cat Coggan did his Cat Coggan thing but with more acoustic guitars, a bass, and an academically trained drummer culled from a jazz band.

It was precise, well-written, erudite stuff, and utterly soulless once you probed beneath its bearded, poorly tattooed surface. The band garnered ample applause, as they should have. He would surely go on to have a brief but successful career before being relegated to a lifetime of performing on the summertime festival circuit.

Scarlett Fever all but danced onto the stage for their second song. #Five abandoned the green room to watch from the wings. Tona was on form now, gleeful with their newfound support. Even Roman was jamming, keeping the beat with his chicken wing foot. The audience was bouncing, clapping to the beat, headbanging along with her. Tona played off it and played off the judge's increasing bias. The song was slower placed than their other material, but it featured a new variation on Tona's wailing: all-out screaming. It sounded painful. It *looked* painful. It sucked the audience in and sent the band coasting into the voting phase.

Plex escorted them off the stage with his hollow witticisms, alerted the viewers to the impending commencement of voting, then made a farty sound with his mouth right after cutting to a commercial break. "I need some fucking water, people!"

We took the stage in silence; Layton wrote in his journal.

#Five was sure not to glance at Felicia—as if they'd be able to read her face. Though she'd only had bit parts in two low-budget cinematic bombs, she was a good actor in real life. A few minutes later Plex welcomed everyone back, *blah blah blah.*

He wasn't hiding his disappointment with #Five. Everyone surely thought them not idiosyncratic but unsure of themselves. They knew they'd lost the audience. All that was left was to play their music.

"Pull out all the stops!" Britt had yelled at the top of his lungs from the back of the stage while Plex blathered at the live and studio audiences.

Plex turned and looked at him. "What?"

"Let us play, damn it."

The host smiled into the camera. "You heard it folks. They're ready to rock. Are you ready?

Next up #Five will be playing—" "'Hot Psycho'!"

He turned around again. "Change of plans."

They could practically hear the blood sliding down the back of Felicia's neck.

"Change of plan, dear viewers. They're switching things up, no doubt because the other bands are really bringing their A-game tonight. Let's hear it for—"

"One! Two! Three! Four o'clock, rock!" Britt hammered his sticks so hard he dented one of them and immediately had to fling it aside and grab another, all without missing a beat. Layton latched onto the rhythm; one he hadn't heard in a long time. He grabbed the microphone and pulled it close to his heart, his chin against his chest as he intoned the lyrics in his lowest, most insidious tone of voice.

Hot psycho bitch
You're standing so close but still a world away
Hot psycho bitch
Touch me once and you'll know it's true
Hell would be
Spending eternity in a motel room with you

The others joined in.

Hot psycho bitch
Hot psycho bitch
We're standing still in time
Because as much as I fucking hate you
I don't want you to die

They'd spent nearly three months writing the song, but the lyrics were almost filler. The subject could have been anything: dick, dude, prick, ass, killer, whatever. The point of it was to showcase each member, giving them a chance to shine.

It was similar to what they'd done in round two but with a long run on the drums for Britt, giving him a chance to show off his high-hat skills.

A chance for Jai to not just speed through some intricate pick-work but to express his and The Scythe's capabilities with the pedals, layering his own guitar with multiple reverberating assaults.

A moment for Grannie to meld the synth with Layton's robotic vocals, layer them, return them, layer them again.

Meanwhile Layton was at his most macabre: his soul had been possessed by the music and only a nightmare could stop it. It was the band's song. It represented them as humans. It was written by Shivvr and the Quakes, not some dumb band on television. Layton danced. He flailed about and windmilled his arms with abandon, not caring how it looked but how it felt—going where the music took him. He leapt off the stage and continued his song a short distance from the judge's area, the three of them in their comfy seats with a nook for storing a bottle of water with the sponsor's name facing the camera.

The band saw the song out as wildly as they'd brought it in, restraining themselves from smashing their instruments only because they had one more song to play. It sped to a halt, like a commuter train that'd jumped its tracks and slammed into a building, all with a smile on its face, finally free from the constraints of the rails.

"Wow!" Plex said, his face as bright as the lights above him. "Where did that come from? Who is this band?" He turned to gesture at them, but they were already gone.

"My—my Emmiline boys!"

They brushed aside Cat Coggan and his rustic friends and made their way towards the bathroom to catch their breath and figure out.

We had no idea what we were going to do next.

Britt was sitting on the sink with his feet soaking in cold water.

"Felicia is going to kill us." The others nodded in agreement.

"We'd better throw her a bone now that the votes have started," Jai said. "Which song are we going to play?"

They turned to Grannie. He said, "We've only got two choices."

"We have an extended break, thanks to the intermission and recap. That's like five extra minutes."

"We can't risk it."

They nodded. Grannie was right. It was hard enough summoning up their own material that they had barely rehearsed.

"Let's just rest here awhile and—"

Shouting could be heard outside. It sounded like Eddie was fending off someone from intruding. The second voice was strident and piercing, worse than feedback from amplifiers turned up to eleven. The bathroom door bowed as someone threw themselves against it; luckily, it was still locked.

"Open up, you punks."

"Oh shit."

Grannie pulled Jai off the floor and opened the door. "Hello Felicia."

Felicia glared at Eddie, who was staring at his sneakers, then stepped inside and kicked the door shut. "So, this is where the magic happens."

"Depends on what you mean by 'magic.'"

"My 'magic' I mean idiocy and assholery."

"No magic here then."

She crossed her arms. "What song are you going to play next?"

"Yours. 'Modern Chaos.'"

"And then?"

"One of ours. We need to go out strong."

"Wrong."

Grannie and Jai sat down on the floor.

"Come on, Felicia," Layton said. "Your songs su—your songs aren't for us. They're not our style. We can't win on them."

"Bullshit. It got you this far!"

Britt climbed down from the sink "*We* got us this far. Our songs."

"We had a deal," she said.

"Nothing on paper," Layton said, "and nothing with merit or integrity. The point is to win, isn't it? Right now, that's not looking good."

Felicia stood pouting while staring at the tiled floor of the men's room. "Was that song about me?"

They laughed quietly.

"If we make it to QuickFame OneWorld, you have to use only my material," Felicia said.

"No," Britt said.

The others shook their heads.

"Then I expose all of you. All of this."

"You expose yourself then, like a flasher showing off his wrinkly old balls in a high school parking lot on a Friday night."

Her face twisted up; she seemed to be thinking about that. Layton assumed she was doing her best to shake off the image of the wrinkly old balls. "Fine. We write the songs together, but I get full credit for them."

Britt: "No."

Jai: "No."

Donovan: "Not going to happen."

"Fine. You play all of your material except for my song goes last. We develop it together, cowrite it, go public with it, then take it all. It works for all of us. We keep our secrets to ourselves."

Britt shrugged. The others stared off into space. "We'll consider it," Layton said.

"You'd better get back there," Grannie said to Felicia. "You have, like, one minute."

She glared at each of them in turn. "After everything I did! The whole shadow social media campaign, the audience support—"

"None of it matters if the music isn't good," Layton said. "Who gives a fuck what some idiotic teenager girls are screaming in the hallways or online? Tomorrow they'll be Instagramming their cleavage and we'll be forgotten."

"I won't forget," Felicia said through the side of her sneering mouth. "I'll never forget any of this, and I hope you don't either. Now clear out. I need to take a girl piss."

Felicia arrived back at her booth just in time for Cat Coggan's second song.

It was a faster- pace piece with a galloping rhythm that got the audience stomping. It was played to perfection, with not a beat missed or a note off-key. It sounded like something a band might release on their third or fourth album, and even though the band's stage presence was staid if not outright dull, the music overcame such a lack of showmanship. The audience expressed their satisfaction, and the judges discussed the song at length, largely praising the band.

All the while, behind the judges' head a clock had been counting down, and now it showed just seconds until voting was open.

Plex McGuire strolled up to the barrier holding back the sweaty, packed audience and said, "Last time we saw twenty-five million votes. Will it be fifty this time? Who are you voting for?"

He offered a microphone to a chubby woman wearing a "Born in the USA" Springsteen tour shirt. "Cat Coggan. He's classic rock but with a country heart. He makes me proud to feel like an American."

He asked her neighbor, a much younger girl with braces and glasses. "#Five. For so many reasons. First of all, they're gorgeous. They make me wet."

The crowd, and the judges, gasped. "Honey, did you really say that?"

She stared at Plex. "My sister Maggie told me it means you love someone."

Plex gave her a sympathetic look. "Oh, honey." Then he reached over the barrier and gave her a hug. "Your sister needs a good spanking."

Within minutes Scarlett Fever had a lead of one thousand votes. #Five was slotted in second and Cat Coggan was just behind. As the minutes ticked past, the numbers swelled. At one point #Five surged to the forefront but it was short-lived. Cat Coggan was stepping on their heels. Then Scarlett Fever pulled away again, surging. It was like watching a numerical horse race.

Then Tona's voice cracked. Or she cracked. Something seemed to break inside her.

Their third song had opened strongly with a heavy techno-inspired dance tune peppered with metallic guitar riffs. It was odd but it worked. Tona carried it through to the final verse, her voice soaring but showing signs of distress. It was the lyrics that seemed to trip her up. *Baby, baby, cry for me a little longer.* She choked on those words. It was visible in her face. And on the refrain, just before closing, her voice wobbled and then broke altogether, leaving the line unfinished. The band, comprised mainly of a bunch of poorly traveled hacks with little stage time, stumbled along with her. The song limped to its conclusion, then petered out.

As a result, #Five surged to the lead just before their third performance.

Thirty million people had voted. Cat Coggan was slotted into last.

But Felicia's song, "Modern Chaos," was #Five's weakest yet, a truly bouncy boy-band tune with lots of *Woah oh ohs* and *Yeah yeah yeahs*, probably something she'd lifted from the Monkees catalog. #Five played it to its limits, taking the sound was far as it could go without bastardizing it and turning it into a different genre.

The other two judges were perplexed, as was Plex. The bantered, debated: Was this band the real deal or was it searching for its soul? What kept pulling—or kicking—the band in different directions? Perhaps even Felicia was at a loss. Layton found her inscrutable. In that moment he despised her with every fiber of his body. He wanted to take Jai's Scythe and lop the head off the snake.

#Five sloughed off the charts to third place. Cat Coggan did his thing a third time.

The votes rolled in.

Plex bantered with the judges; a few audience members were interviewed, none of whom thought #Five was it, none of whom were wet for the band.

Layton and the band, however, couldn't stop smiling and slapping themselves on the back.

They took the green room hostage, forcing Cat Coggan and his minions into the men's room. "We fucked the song in the ear, didn't we?" Jai said.

"Best we could," Grannie said.

"At least no one can come back at us later and say that we didn't give it all we've got."

Layton found beers in a cooler and offered them to everyone. Only Jai and Britt accepted, though Britt took only a sip before setting it aside, saying, "I'm sure some goons will make it into a chart-topper some day, but it's not our music. So, are we ready for 'I've Only Got One Shivvr For You'?"

Jai hurled a beer at the wall, spraying the room—and Grannie and Donovan—with glass and beer. "I fucking hate her!"

"Calm the fuck down!" Grannie said, picking glass off his clothes.

Eddie leapt into the room expecting to find someone bleeding from the jugular. "Sorry, man. Just letting loose. It's cool."

"Asshole," Donovan said as soon as Eddie had shut the door and taken up sentry again.

"I fucking hate her too," Layton said.

Jai turned to him. "You do?"

"Yeah. She's a manipulative—" his voice dropped "—cunt."

"No, she isn't."

"She is too. She's got us wrapped around her little Latino finger, trying to figure out how to bring life to these musical corpses."

Jai recoiled slightly. "*Ohhh*. You mean Felicia."

"Who the fuck are you going on about?"

"Tona!"

"Tona? I thought we were talking about Felicia!"

"Yeah, well, fuck her too. She is a cunt. And so is Tona! I can't believe she doesn't like me the way I like her."

"She's a lot older."

"A lot? Two years?"

"You're a sophomore in high school, dude. Tona hangs out with bikers and drug kingpins." Jai sat down. "I could be a kingpin. Of something."

"Bowling perhaps?"

"Alright," Grannie said, clapping his beery hands together. "Let's go over the lyrics one more time."

As he handed out lyrics sheets the room fell quiet, with only the distant thudding of Scarlett Fever's last song audible, the others couldn't take their eyes off Grannie's hand: it was shaking. Layton realized that he too was shaking. He looked around the room and saw that Britt was hugging himself as if chilled. Jai's fists were clenched at his side as he attempted to calm himself down, breathing slowly in and out. Donovan was pale, on the edge of puking.

"Let's count it off now, ok?" Layton said. "When we're on stage, we'll be 100% focus and determination. We have to play like we've never played before, even if Jai breaks all of his strings and Britt drops both of his sticks and my voice gives out and Grannie accidentally unplugs his cords or the earth opens up and swallows us whole— don't stop playing until you hit the bottom. Crash and burn. Go out with a bang, literally, showing the world your innards."

The others nodded. Layton put his hand out. The others layered theirs on it. Grannie. Jai.

Donovan. Britt.

"What time is it, my totally fucked up brothers?" Someone banged on the door.

"Time!" Eddie called out.

"You heard the man. Time to rock."

They made it to the stage halfway through the commercial break, giving them just enough time to check their tuning and make sure everything was still plugged in. The audience was chattering; they seemed resigned, ready to vote in Scarlett Fever. Tona's voice had held throughout their final performance. It was a strong song, perhaps not their best and in no way groundbreaking or audacious but good enough to continue their run of consistent, gutsy female-led post-metal.

Voting continued, the number continuing to accelerate towards fifty million, maybe even sixty registered users. It'd be open for another thirty minutes after the last song, at which point Plex and the production crew would host a recap of the entire week.

"Good luck, assholes," Roman said as he hobbled off the stage with his hand on Tona's shoulder. She smiled tepidly and said nothing.

"Twerps," Aron the drummer said. "Dickfarts," Gavin the bassist said.

Eddie stepped forward with his chest puffed out, but Britt nudged him back and made a mousy farting sound with his mouth, garnering a laugh from even Gavin himself. The bands parted ways without resorting to fireworks.

#Five got ready.

Felicia looked on from her special chair, her legs dangling above the floor, her face a mosaic of fear, disgust, hope, and wonder. Layton could tell that she had no idea what would happen next.

Plex's face was serious. "Red leather yellow leather. Red letter yellow tether. Shit! Someone get me a gin and tonic, for fuck's sake."

Britt counted them off. Jai, Donovan, and Grannie brought in the long instrumental intro. Layton swayed to the beat, presenting to the audience his trademark silly yet alluring dance moves. Then the music stopped. Britt counted them off again, starting the song anew—the same exact beat but twice as fast—and the instruments followed. Layton spun around and dipped the microphone to the floor as if it were an eighteenth-century aristocrat who refused to give in to his love no matter how hard he wooed it. And a third time Britt ended the song, leaving the 13-666 suspended in complete and utter silence, every soul in the room holding their breath, unsure what they were experiencing. And a third time he brought in the beat, this time even faster.

The instruments answered, Grannie's, Donovan's, and Jai's fingers sprinting across their respective instruments.

It was as much a feat of musical athletics as it was a magical aural achievement.

This was the rhythm they had been building towards, using those gaps as stepping stones across a chasm of mediocrity that so many other bands had fallen into.

Layton leapt into the air like the singer he would forever idolize—Dennis Lyxzén of Swedish band Refused, that lithe, stylistically irreproachable screamer—his feet seeming to nearly touch his ears. When he returned to Earth, he tore into the song, his tongue and throat pumping out the lyrics so furiously it seemed impossible for him to breathe.

Like ghosts killing the living out of fear of being alone
Madness breeds in your eyes
Killing dreams before they've even hatched

Fluttering sycophantic crybaby me me me
What will it take to get you to stop talking?
Why won't you go away? Start walking.
Running. And running. Burning away.
Please not one more day –
With you.

He did breathe though. Layton had spent months practicing inhaling through his nose while chuffing out the lower notes with pure force. The unrelenting cadence of the song demanded a physicality that only someone like him could manage, despite never in his life having run more than a mile in a single go.

He could only execute this performance once, for it ruined his throat and exhausted him entirely. Tonight, he summoned up a vigor that he wasn't even aware lurked within him.

Three minutes of this and the band never missed a note. Beethoven, sure. Michael Jackson, whatever. These kids were doing things with music that hadn't yet been explored, especially not on live television.

Britt carried them into the last minute and a half of the song, and that's when the purple-black lights above started to shake. The audience grabbed hold of one another. The judges clutched the armrests of their chairs. The other bands' musical equipment fell over on stage. The ground trembled as yet another tremor concussed Emmiline from beneath, almost as if Earth itself were being summoned to life by this song, which was being played not by #Five but by Shivvr and the Quakes.

They played on heedless, ignoring the screams of the audience, which might have been from joyful fans but could also have been terrified grandparents.

The last time I saw you
you were climbing the tower
with a rifle on your back
I said—that girl's never coming back

Didn't we already talk about this?
You can't be both the judge and the executioner
There's gotta be space between your lies
and the memories

Hang on, little girl, hang on
And wait for the dust to settle
so we can see which road to take
By the time we're rollin
  the devil won't even know our names

Sweat poured off Jai's forehead. Britt's palms were bleeding, as were Grannie's knuckles. Donovan couldn't feel his fingertips. Layton sprang into the air one last time. When his feet returned to the still-shaking earth, the band was ready, driving the coda home with a scream and another tear through the refrain.

Suddenly it was over. The song, the tremor. A quake had indeed hit, and the audience stood shaken to the core. The building would never be the same. The air was vibrating. Somewhere a wire sparked, and smoke filled the air.

Layton's hand had been cramping when he wrote all of this down, the recount spanning two dozen pages. Nighttime had fallen. His phone had rung, and hundreds of messages and alerts had flashed on the screen until he simply turned it off.

It was hard to figure out what, at that point, had happened among the judges. Collusion perhaps—some sort of agreement, both unspoken and predetermined.

But the messiness of it left a taste in his mouth like that of a dirty old guitar string.

The audience had applauded for so long that it was unclear if the tremor had stopped or not.

The band, unsure whether to leave or stay, simply took as much time as possible disconnecting their instruments. They waved to the crowd. Someone shouted that she loved Layton and this time, rather than telling them to fuck off, he raised his hands to his chest and made a heart symbol. He could practically hear the votes clicking past.

"Well, judges. That's some food for thought, isn't it?" Plex said, clearing addled by the earthquake and the Quakes alike. "I think that song came from the devil himself, but it was delivered by angels. Who's to say which force will win tonight? Are our souls at risk?"

Finally, the production team ushered the band from the stage, but even they seemed reluctant to do so. When a techie touched Donovan on the shoulder to make sure he didn't fall off the stage, his hand came away glistening with moisture and almost hot to the touch.

"Never seen anything like that," the techie said. "If you weren't put on Earth to play music then I'm the King of Persia."

"You'd be the emperor," Donovan said.

Cat Coggan stepped aside to let the band through, his eyes fixated on the ground.

Plex welcomed Cat and the audience back after the commercial break. Cat nodded and waved, and he and his temporary band played their song. Towards the end Cat broke a string on his beat-up hipster-hippie guitar but played on, nonetheless.

While such grit and pluck would have earned major accolades on another day, tonight was hardly enough to garner a few extra cheers.

Still, it was a good song, a lovely country power ballad belted out in his smoky, inimitable Cat Coggan voice.

When the song ended, he remained seated a moment, a look of resignation washing over his face.

"Fifty-seven million votes," Plex said after the recap of all that'd been said and done over the course of the week, from the very first audition to the most recent performance.

"Unbelievable."

The stage had been cleared and all the bands had been assembled, a comfortable distance between them all.

Plex continued. "So, Heidi, Felicia, Andy—will you side with the will of the people or will you hold a coup?"

"There has never been a band like #Five," Felicia said. "I am proud to support them. They have my vote."

The audience gasped.

Plex was taken aback.

"But Felicia, they remain in second place."

Felicia hadn't even looked at the numbers; she did so now, scrolling through the stats on her tablet.

"That doesn't matter. No one has ever seen a performance like that."

Heidi smiled and brought her beautiful lips to her microphone.

"Their performance was wildly inconsistent. As much as I love Scarlett Fever, they don't yet have the chops to deliver the goods. When the poo-poo hits the fan, they fall apart. The pressure of being a star is enormous. You can't implode like a red giant." She sat back. Then she leaned in again. "A red giant is a star, by the way. I think they're big and they explode. Very gassy and bright. Don't be gassy!"

"A split decision, folks. Andy?"

Andy didn't move.

"Andy Rainer, singer, and songwriter of yet another smash holiday hit. What do you have to say for yourself?"

"I, uh…"

Plex managed to maintain his smile but the longer it went on the more it resembled the grimace of a man who'd drunk the water in a country that didn't use toilet paper. "My friend Andy. What say you?"

"It's very complicated."

Heidi and Felicia looked at him.

"I am very confused. I feel torn. You know how in old movies the cowboys tied a bad guy or even good guy to a couple horses and then sent them running in different directions until his limbs were ripped off? That's how I feel. Not like a big gassy star. I feel torn. I'm a good guy, I think. I think that Scarlett Fever has a wonderful future ahead of themselves, but Heidi is right, they aren't ready and don't deserve the crown. Cat Coggan, however, is the real deal.

That voice makes me consider retirement. It makes me want to buy a pickup truck and drive to a cabin in the woods and smoke a doobie while watching a glorious mountain sunset."

"That's quite an endorsement."

"But I can't vote for them."

"What?" Heidi said.

Plex gestured at the huge screen behind the bands. "What is your instinct telling you, Andy? The votes are clearly steering towards Scarlett Fever."

"There are more factors to consider than just numbers."

"Who bought you off?" Heidi said.

Plex stepped forward. "Now Heidi."

Felicia laughed. A buzz cascaded through the audience.

Andy stood up. He appeared to be ranting. No one could hear him; Plex told him to calm down and use his mic. To this Andy all but collapsed into his chair.

"#Five gave me the chills. No band has done that in a long time. Maybe the Four Tops when I heard them on their revival tour. No, #Five's weak songs are not good. The band is at war with itself, like it's trying to release its inner demon. Right? Am I right? Don't we all have demons we need to release?"

Felicia climbed out of her chair and hugged Andy. Then she leaned into his microphone. "Andy is a wise man. His words show us why he is such a mainstay of the music and entertainment industry. He and I vote for #Five."

Plex looked for Thaddeus Goldar, standing in the wings with the production manager. For once calm and collected, Thaddeus gave Plex two thumbs up.

"Two votes out of three?" Plex said. "Is this final?" He turned to the judges.

Heidi was weeping.

"This is how you want to go? You want to contradict the will of the voting public?"

Felicia nodded vigorously. Andy nodded his head less vigorously but nodded it, nonetheless.

Confetti rained down. The QuickFame trophy—a golden microphone—emerged from a door in the stage floor. Moments after Plex handed it over to #Five, Heidi stormed the stage and grabbed the microphone from Plex's hand. When he reached to get it back, she placed a hand on his arm and squeezed gently and softened him with her superpower: the eyes of a former model. He looked down at it, then stepped back.

"I'll let you finish, Plex." Heidi looked out across the audience, then turned to the bands. "Hey #Five, I'm really happy for you, but Scarlett Fever played one of the best songs of all time. One of the best songs of all time!"

The audience applauded, but it wasn't exactly thunderous.

Layton thought the ground might be shaking; he couldn't tell. His legs seemed like they were about to give out, either from tension or from the performances he'd given.

He set the trophy on the ground.

He wasn't sure they'd won. He wasn't sure he wanted it. He walked off the stage.

He ascended to his room, gathered up his things, and exited the hotel through a side exit and summoned a cab. He didn't head home though. He asked the cabbie to take him to the edge of Emmiline, to the last train station. There he sat on a bench until morning.

***

Layton slid open the changing room curtain. "I'll take the vest."

"Lovely. Anything else?"

He took stock of the store's wares. "What have you got in my size?"

The girl followed his gaze, bouncing from rack to rack and display to display. "What exactly are you looking for?"

"That's a great question."

9.
PEACE AND WISDOM

Grannie slept through his phone's alarm. Then he slept through the phone calls. The adrenaline highs and subsequent lows of the past week had carved a void from his soul, leaving him feeling lethargic and borderline depressed. Plus, he'd barely slept after sharing a room with Britt and Donovan for nearly a week.

The night of the QuickFame finals he'd gone straight home like most of the other members in the band. It felt strange not to celebrate, but it also felt somewhat wrong to revel in their success. They weren't sure they'd won. Or, rather, they were sure they'd won but not sure they'd deserved it. Grannie had slipped out the back door of their room, circled the pool, leapt the concrete wall, then descended toward the highway. There he ordered a Sööper car to get him home. He took a bath, scrubbed his face clean of all the makeup, applied a healthy layer of moisturizer, and went to bed.

He didn't eat. He didn't get up to exercise. For three days he'd just laid there with the blankets pulled over his head, getting out of bed only to use the bathroom or fills his arms with food that he then carried back to his room.

Monday morning, he slept through the first round of banging on his door but not the second. "Grannie! Wake up!"

"No."

"Someone's here to see you."

"Fuck off."

"She's hot."

Grannie pulled the blanket off his face.

"You might recognize her from that show you were on."

"Damn it."

"She's coming up."

"No. I mean, let me get dressed at least." *And piss.* "Entertain her for a couple minutes."

"Not a problem. I'll make her one of my classic Cheeze Whiz and bologna sandwiches."

"Please don't. I don't want an ambulance parked in front of the house right now."

Grannie pulled on the same jeans he'd worn to the finals three days ago, then a Doctor Doomsday t-shirt that he probably hadn't washed in a few months. He wasn't even into the band anymore but couldn't bring himself to toss the shirt, since his last girlfriend had given it to him. He unlocked the door, stood there a moment listening to the faint voices coming from the kitchen downstairs, then padded to the bathroom. He relieved himself, slapped on some deodorant, then brushed his teeth. But his makeup—it was downstairs in his duffle bag, beside the door where he'd left it when he'd come home.

"Oh well." At the top of the stairs, he called down, "I'm good," then returned to his room and shut the door.

He plopped down onto the mattress on the floor—no bed frame, no box spring—and climbed back under the blankets.

Felicia let herself in. For the first time since he'd met her, she was wearing a casual outfit: jeans, sneakers, a tight sweater that hugged her incredibly fit body. She too wasn't wearing makeup, or at least not much of it, and with the sunlight coming through the tall windows of the house that Grannie rented with three college kids, her natural beauty rose to the forefront. She almost looked like a totally different person, the veneer of the music industry scraped away from her typical stern look of apprehension and mistrust.

"Shouldn't you be in school?" she asked.

"I'm not going back there."

"You're banking on your new fame to get you through life?"

He laughed.

Felicia looked around the room, which was markedly different than those of the younger boys in the band. Namely it was a mess. There was no pretense of trying to impress. As for a place to sit, the desk and chair were covered with music gear and clothes. "Do you mind?" she asked, indicating the mattress. Grannie pulled his feet in and propped himself up against the wall. Felicia plopped down, sat there a moment, then flung her arms over her head while exhaling a massive sigh. "Think I'll sleep for three days too." She shut her eyes.

"My roomm—friends told you?"

"Yup. Post-partum depression?"

"Not exactly."

"Misgivings about what went down?"

He nodded and shrugged at the same time. Though her eyes were still shut, he knew she could sense it.

"You're not seventeen, are you, Grannie?"

Grannie looked out the window. Though the sun was shining it was set to be a cold day. He wondered if it was time to go running again. To get some color back into his skin. To eat some healthy food. "Haven't been for eight years."

Felicia laughed. "Wow. I was off by a few. I thought you were maybe twenty-one" She opened her eyes and studied his face. "No makeup today."

"You either."

She closed them again. "I guess we both look our age then."

"Sorry I disappointed you. And deceived you."

"Do the others know?"

"In the band? No. I mean, I don't think so."

"So, you're one of those imposters who returns to high school and tries to do it all over again but with the wisdom of a person who has suffered through it all before."

"Sick, isn't it?"

She shrugged. "The music industry is full of imposters and this city is populated with them. To me it isn't the worst crime in the world. Lots of people lie about their age. Usually, they don't do it when they're so young."

"Not exactly a boy band then, are we?"

She didn't answer that. Instead, she said, "No, it doesn't disappoint me. Actually, it makes me feel better, since our incidental little smooches were not quite so—lascivious."

"Dirty."

"Risqué."

"Illegal."

She propped herself up on an elbow. "The age of consent is seventeen. It wasn't illegal."

Grannie thought about that. "Huh. I shouldn't have been so afraid then."

She stared at him.

He tried to decode that look of hers but still wasn't able to dissect it properly.

"You want to know something funny?" she asked.

"Do I?"

"Someone has been emailing me and sending text messages. I mean, they've been sending me messages for years but of late their frequency has increased. I think I got the first message shortly after I got my first email address, actually. They never sign their name, and the address is generic. I have no idea who they are, but they frequently send me strange messages full of strange wisdom, aphorisms, quotes, and poetry. Or maybe they're song lyrics. I'm not quite sure."

"A stalker?"

"Could be, but I doubt it. I don't seem to matter enough to earn stalkers these days. My goal was to change that with QuickFame. Anyways, one of the things the person in the cloud said—"

"What cloud?"

"The person in the cloud. Isn't that what the internet is?"

"Not exactly."

"Oh."

"We'll deal with that later."

"Ok. Anyway, the man or woman from the internet's cloud or tubes or whatever said to me that regret is simply hope in disguise, meaning the hope that we will do things differently next time— or else we will find that we are locked into a certain lie about ourselves, leaving us incapable of change. I have so many regrets, Granville, because I also have so much hope. I regret the choices I've made for myself, for others, for music, all the choices that have impacted the people I care about. I hope I can do better."

"Do you regret forcing us to play your songs?"

"Actually, I hoped you'd all start to like them."

"We don't. I'm sorry, but it has to be different in QuickFame OneWorld. The stakes are even higher."

"If you indeed want to go to OneWorld, you'll have to play my songs. Otherwise, Thaddeus and I will pull the plug."

Grannie scowled. "How will you do that?"

"It can be done any number of ways."

"Goddamnit, Felicia. Why do you have to be like this?"

"You guys are my pet project. If it weren't for me, you'd be playing birthday parties and taking math tests."

"And we'd be happy."

"And you'd be living a lie."

"Just like now."

"Except that this lie will get you rich and famous and turn you into idols. The lies are in the past anyways. All I did was make sure you got the proper airtime so that the judges and the public could witness your talent."

"They only witnessed it because we defied you and played our own stuff. Your songs don't evoke the music in our hearts. I know that sounds ultra-cheesy, but we can't take it seriously, and if we can't perform it with integrity, people will see right through us.

"You just have to—"

"Listen, that little aphorism of yours about regret? It must have a flip side to it. If you have the foresight to grasp that something is happening right now that you regret and yet you go through with it anyways, what does that say about you? Why pin your life on botched hope when you can choose the right path at the right moment?"

"You're young, so it's not always easy for you to recognize what exactly is the right moment and the right choice."

"I'm not as young as you thought. And the other guys? They're not so young either. I don't mean their age."

"Don't fool yourself. They haven't been kicked around by life enough yet. You, on the other hand." Felicia poked his leg.

Grannie slid it away. "Don't try to soften me. I'm not that easily manipulated."

"Fine. I'll shut up. Or should I leave?"

"I don't care."

Felicia slid toward the edge of the mattress and rolled onto her hands and knees, but when she pushed off the old, rough floor, she yelped.

Grannie flung the covers aside and leapt up. "What's wrong?"

"Splinter."

"Shit. Fuck. I hate this place. I need to move out and get my own apartment, don't I? It's time. I need space and peace. These guys don't know anything about anything, and they just sit around all day drinking beer and eating Captain Crunch and—"

"Granville!" Felicia had tears in her eyes. "Do you have tweezers?"

Grannie told her to wait there and ran downstairs. He found his roommate Charles parked in front of the TV, playing Aqua Wars.

"Where are my tweezers that you stole to use as a roach clip?"

"Dude, why is Felicia Scalding in your bedroom?"

"It's—private."

"Aren't you supposed to be in school?"

"I'm twenty-five."

Charles' jaw dropped. Then the controller dropped from his hand. "I always thought there was something strange about you."

"You mean other than pretending to be a high school kid? I mean, why would a teenager be renting a room anyways?"

"Yeah, I mean, I don't know. No. Yeah. You're weird." His hands made a circle in the air. "Like all-around weird."

"I need my tweezers."

Charles got him the tweezers, as well as Grannie's first aid kit, which Grannie hadn't known he'd stolen. "I got a boo-boo awhile back," Charles said.

Grannie disinfected the tweezers, then returned to his room where Felicia was trying to bite the wood out of her hand. "Stop that." He kneeled beside her on the mattress and turned her hand towards the light. "Don't move. It's deep." The splinter evaded him, and he started to dig deep into her flesh.

"Ow!"

"Sorry. Should I stop? Do you want to go to the emergency room or something?"

"For a splinter? No, you do it. I'm tough."

Grannie held her hand in his and got back to work. He was concentrating so hard he forgot who the hand belonged to, where he was, what he'd just done, and what he was facing.

"Move in with me," Felicia said.

"What?"

She gave a little shrug.

"Stop wiggling around," he said. "And no. I'm not doing that."

"Good. I regretted it as soon as I said it. Ow! Damn it, Granville."

"Your hand is tough and tiny. It's like extracting a briar from a coyote's paw."

"Hmph."

He got back to work but she continued to wiggle.

"Is there Mrs. Grannie in your life?"

Grannie held her hand tighter. "Not anymore."

"What happened, if I may ask?"

"She went away to college."

"What was her name?"

"Misty."

She laughed. "Misty Mountains?"

He looked at her. "She wasn't a porn star. She's studying biochemistry and wants to help develop better vaccines. Misty Sullivan."

"Why didn't you chase after her?"

"I had the band. Our paths did not align."

"You could have found another band. Maybe with kids—people—your own age."

"I relate to the younger crowd."

"Because you can be their mentor. Ow!"

"Got it."

Felicia fell backwards onto the mattress.

"Whew! I feel like I just had an orgasm."

Grannie blushed so hard he thought he might pass out. He shifted toward the edge of the mattress and cleaned off the tweezers. Felicia's eyes were closed, her face in the sunlight. Despite the sun a few flakes of sun drifted past the window. She whimpered slightly. Grannie felt the need to touch her, so he got a cotton ball and some hydrogen peroxide and cleaned the gouge in her hand left behind by the splinter. He suddenly loved this crappy apartment and more specifically the floor. She didn't say anything as the peroxide sizzled but when he wiped her hand clean, she grabbed hold of him. Her eyes were still closed. Her chest was rising and falling. His heart was thundering against his sternum.

"Come here."

"I am here."

"Closer."

"That would be a bad idea."

"Why?"

"I fall in love easily."

"What's wrong with falling in love?"

"It's what happened afterwards that sucks."

"You're thinking too much. Just go with your impulses."

"Felicia..."

She opened one eye. "Fine. Just let me sleep here a bit then. Your sheets smell nice." She rolled over and curled up. Then she whimpered again.

Grannie sat there a moment, trying to assess whether it would be inaction that would cause regret or giving in to the part of him that wanted to curl up with her—that part being every single cell in his body.

He got her a pillow and one for himself, then pressed his body against hers and closed his eyes. When Grannie's roommates slammed the door mid-morning and stumbled off to class, Grannie disentangled himself from Felicia and got out his laptop. On a whim he dug deep into a corner of the dark web, searching for stolen unreleased tracks by major artists, checking to see if there were by chance any of Felicia's. He found three, though all were from her post-top-100 gray era. The tracks were heavily electronic, with only a guitar providing an authentic vibe. The rest was drum machines and synthesizers and some fairly thin vocals.

Fortunately, the track was raw, with all the instrumentals, beats, and vocal layers separated. Grannie brought the vocals into ProTools, then added two fresher and more modern layers of beats, both heavy and snares. Then he added a track of Jai's guitar playing, slowed it down somewhat, brought it down a key, and stretched out the low tones. He added some glitches and pops and another layer of Felicia's vocals, along with some reverb and some masking.

Felicia's hand reached from beneath the covers and pulled his headphones off. "What's that sound?"

"Nothing."

"It sounds familiar."

"Does it? That's weird."

"Hey, dickhead. No more lies between us."

Grannie removed the headphones. "It's your track called 'You Can't Stop The Girl.' Remember it?"

"How did you find that?"

"I have my ways."

"You're listening to that shit?"

"It's not shit. You just had a crappy producer and cowriter. I've cut out the chorus and kept the refrains. It's a bit too house-style for my taste, but it works better for this song."

Felicia's hand groped around until she found the headphones. She dragged them under the covers and put them on, then gave Grannie the signal to play the song.

When it was over, she sat up, her face still creased from Grannie's stiff old pillow. "You made that just now?"

"Took me about an hour. I thought I'd let you sleep." Grannie shut his laptop. He felt stupid.

"It almost doesn't sound like my song."

"I'm sorry. I didn't mean to—"

"It's far better."

"Cool! With the right production it could have been a hit, especially if I had access to a studio. See, I could take out the guitar and put in a piano loop, and then if you wanted to rerecord the chorus with more poignant lyrics it would really pop."

"Can you email that to me?"

"For what?"

"To send to Streemy."

Grannie thought about that. "I don't think that's a good idea."

"Why not?"

"First of all, because I didn't have permission to use it. It's stolen. Second, Streemy will just fuck it up again. They'll water it down, autotune it, make your voice sound as glossy as a magazine cover model looks. They'll trim the fat and soften the edges so that it doesn't sound like music at all, as is their usual style, the stupid assholes."

"So, it's just going to live on your computer?"

Grannie drummed his fingers on his laptop, thinking. "How about this? I do another couple version of it with my own keyboard work and maybe even get Jai to record a guitar riff or two and then I release it onto a couple of online platforms. I'll also supply a white-label remix of the best version of the track for DJs working the club circuit. Let it go viral on its own merit, at its own pace, and see what happens. Then, once it's out there, we tell people who did the song. You."

"You."

"Us. Together. A team. Me as producer and keyboardist."

Felicia smiled a sleepy, content smile. "Alright."

"I'll get to work."

"But not right now."

Grannie stood up. "There's tons to do."

"No." Felicia swept the blankets away. She'd yet to put on a lick of clothing.

"Oh God."

"Did you just come? You big baby."

After another round of sex, they fell asleep again. Another hour passed. When a car horn blared nearby Felicia woke with a start. She fixated on the ceiling for what felt like eternity but what in reality was less than a minute. Then she checked her phone.

Grannie woke up soon after. Though Felicia had been entangled in his arms just moments ago, she was now hopping up and down as she wormed her legs into her jeans.

"What's the rush?"

"I need to do something, and I need you to come with me."

"Can we at least get breakfast first?"

"We'll stop at Starbucks for lattes."

"Gross! No thanks. How about we hit Grindcore instead? It's a doom metal-themed coffee shop down in the—"

"Fine, whatever. Can I use your toothbrush?"

"Oh. Um, I guess so."

Felicia opened the door and strolled to the bathroom. Grannie lay there a couple minutes. Then he heard a strange sound and sat bolt upright. "Are you peeing with the door open?"

"Yup!"

"We're already at that stage?"

"Don't worry. I draw the line at pooping."

A Sööper car pulled up ten minutes later. The driver recognized both Felicia and Grannie as they slid into the back seat. "You guys know each other personally?" he asked.

Felicia squeezed Grannie's arm as a sign to let her handle it. "I was so impressed with the band that I decided to help #Five prepare for QuickFame OneWorld."

The driver hit the gas hard.

"That's gonna be something, having the finale on the steps of the Sydney Opera House. Better hope there aren't any more earthquakes."

"I'm sure there won't be. But there could be sandstorms."

"Now *that* would make for great TV. Can I take a picture?"

"Please don't. And please don't tell anyone you saw us together. Not on social media. Not to your friends. Ok, maybe a few months down the road you can tell your friends at a dinner party. If you can do that for us, we'll do something special for you, ok?"

His face implied that was somewhat on board.

"What kind of 'something special'?"

"Autographed album? Personal appearance at your next birthday?"

"Hmm. Ok. Oh, and how about Michaela George? Could she come along?"

Felicia turned her attention to the window.

"No? Not an option?"

They traveled in silence the rest of the way to the coffee shop.

Felicia waited in the car, scrolling through the list of messages, texts, alerts, calls, and news items that she'd missed while screwing a musician twenty years younger than herself.

"I'll take you up on that offer," the Sööper driver said. "My wife's turning forty-two in August."

"Sounds lovely. Here's my card."

Grannie returned with their drinks; two charcoal-black coffee cups filled to the brim with the darkest coffee available on the West Coast.

The driver pulled into traffic. "Heading to 54 Welch Street now, ma'am."

Grannie spit some of his coffee back into the cup. "Welch? What the eff? That's Layton's house."

Felicia blew on her coffee and took little sips. "He needs you."

"For what?"

"He's in crisis."

"What kind of crisis?"

"Existential, I think. I have a feeling he's going to back out of this. Or the band."

"How do you know this?"

"He called Thaddeus since I wasn't answering my phone."

Grannie rubbed his face up and down as if trying to work the caffeine into his bloodstream. "He would never do that. He founded the band, or at least Shiv—"

Felicia glared at him, shutting him up. "Not here."

They traveled the rest of the way in silence, save for the music on the radio—Foo Fighters, which the driver sang along with—until the car rolled to a stop outside of Layton's house.

Felicia dealt with the Sööper app. "Can you wait for us? It'll be an hour."

"I can, but it'd require Layton Coy joining you for a duet at the birthday party." Grannie paused, halfway out of the car. "What are you guys talking about?"

"It's cool," Felicia said. "I can order another car."

"No, no. I was just kidding. Just playin'. I'll wait here. It'd take me thirty minutes just to get back to the city anyways."

Felicia and Grannie headed up the walkway. "What the hell was all that?"

"I'll explain later."

Madeline opened the front door before the visitors had even reached it. "What now?"

"It doesn't concern you, sweetie."

"He's my brother. Of course, it concerns me."

"From what I've heard and witnessed, you don't give a shit about that massively talented individual."

Madeline's face pinched together with fury. "He's a pervert. He's weird and he—he—he 's a faggot and he wears dresses."

Grannie blanched but Felicia didn't flinch. "I'm sure he looks better in a dress than you do, Madeline."

"He's a boy!"

"Only by design."

"Exactly! I mean—no. He's—God made him that way."

"And God made you a raging bitch. Which one is worse?"

"Shut up, you shriveled old cunt!"

Felicia nudged the door open. "Old, yes. Cunt, maybe. Shriveled, not entirely. Is he here?"

Felicia looked around, then called out for him. "Layton?"

Madeline stormed off, leaving the two of them stranded in the brown-and-corduroy-dominated living room. "That was fun. Shall we?"

They climbed the stairs. Grannie knocked lightly. "Dude. You in there?" When no answer came, he knocked harder. A minute later the knob twisted, and the door creaked open. They stepped inside just as Layton, wearing his pajamas, climbed back into bed.

"Are you depressed too?" Felicia said, sitting at the desk. Grannie took the bean bag.

He noticed that nearby sat the remnants of Clipper, his rubber mouse, now chopped up into tiny bits, the complicit scissors lying nearby.

"I don't know. What's it feel like?"

Grannie said, "Something halfway between being crushed to death by a boulder and drowning in a darkness so thick you can't breathe. A weight so crushing you can't move."

"I think I'm halfway there."

"Why?"

"You know why, Felicia. Felicia *Scalding*. What a name. When you get your finger on something it tends to burn, doesn't it?"

"That's not very nice," Grannie said.

Layton sat up. "It's not very nice to force us to play those songs. Worse, Granville, it's worse for you to do Felicia's bidding like some sort of toady. You ply us and talk at us and make us give in."

"You wanted fame and eventually fortune. This is the shortcut. Attention spans are weaker than ever, you know?"

"That means selling out?"

"How can we have sold out when we haven't yet sold anything?"

"Actually," Felicia said.

They looked at her.

"We have an offer. From Streemy."

"We?" Layton said.

"I'll be serving as producer."

"How did you set that up so quickly?"

"That's what QuickFame does. People come to you."

"What about the songs though?" Layton said. "Are we going to use our material or are you going to make us sing that crap?"

"We'll cross that bridge when we get there. First, I need to make sure you are still a band. We need to deal with this—" She gestured at the lanky boy bundled up in quilts and blankets. "Will you continue, Layton? Or is this your way of telling us that you're not interested in pursuing your hopes and dreams?"

Layton sat up slightly. "That's not really the problem. I mean, it is and it isn't."

"Well, which is it and how can we help?"

His chest rose and fell. A tear rolled out his left eye slid down his face.

Grannie climbed off the beanbag and sat on the bed beside Layton. "Dude. Look at me." Layton shook his head.

"I mean really look at me. Please." His eyes opened.

"What?"

Grannie held his gaze and said nothing. Layton seemed to think it was some sort of staring contest.

Then, slowly, his eyes widened, and he took Granville Jordan's face.

"Grannie," Layton said, smiling. "Our matriarch."

Grannie took his hand. "I'm twenty-five."

What followed was one of the world's ten longest laughing sessions in recorded history.

It concluded only because Layton could no longer breathe, and his throat was burning—and then someone knocked on the door.

"Everything ok in there?" Madeline said from the other side.

"Fuck off!" the three of them yelled in unison.

When she was gone Layton said, "I guess I have to tell you my secret now."

"That you like to wear women's clothing?" Felicia said.

"Who told you?"

"Madeline. Just now. Not that I couldn't tell that you have crossgender inclinations my first visit." She nodded towards his posters.

"It isn't that though. I'm not a dude."

Felicia nodded. "I see. What are you going to do about it?"

"There's nothing I can do until I turn eighteen and until I save enough money to start my transition."

Felicia joined them on the bed. "First of all, you need to talk to a psychologist." The boys looked at her.

"Just to confirm your suspicions and feelings. If all is good, the psychologist will then document his or her findings. You can show that to your parent and doctor. I can give you the number. I'll pay for the appointment myself."

"You'd do that? Is this one of your ploys?"

"No ploy. But the procedure is not cheap. Hormones, surgery, cosmetic surgery if you chose to do that, new wardrobe, beauty treatments—it's all going to cost you. That I can't pay for. You're not going to pay for it pumping gas three nights a week. Does that not give you more motivation to crawl out of this dungeon and get singing again?"

He nodded.

Felicia patted his knee.

Or what she thought was his knee.

"Good. Answer your phone when I or Granville call. And I mean every time we call."

On their way out they found Madeline sitting in an armchair in the living room, dressed in the blue piece she'd worn to prom.

"Well, aren't you pretty. Putting on a show for us?"

Madeline crossed her legs coyly.

"Cat Coggan should have won. He's ten times better than Pound-Five."

"Since you don't know that our name is 'Hashtag-Five,' I'll assume you've never seen us perform and are just trying to stir up more shit."

"I watched. All my friends think it's shit too. You'll never get a record deal."

Felicia fished her phone out of her purse, fiddled with it, then held the screen in front of Madeline's face. "See the words under that executive's name?"

Her eyes slitted. "As if I care. As if *anyone* cares. Once you get crushed in Sydney, you'll be laughed back to Emmiline and forgotten. No one at Streemy will want to touch you and that boy-thing upstairs with a hundred-foot pole."

Felicia took hold of Madeline's dress and rubbed the material between her fingers. "Your sister will need a nice dress when she makes her debut on stage."

Madeline's face darkened. Then the tears came. "What?"

She stood up. "Shut your evil face.

That's a crime against God."

"No, sweetie. This dress is a crime against God."

Madeline swatted the air between her and Felicia, then ran up the stairs.

They stepped outside. The sun was on the horizon.

"I can't remember," Grannie said as he waved to the Sööper driver.

"Is it morning or night?"

"Granville, this is the dawn of a new day."

10.
YOU CAN'T STOP THE GIRL

"Mushi," the petite South Korean girl said from her table at the press conference in the Sydney Opera House.

"Not 'mushy' like rice but 'mushi' as in 'hello,' because I am introducing myself to the world. I had never played before an audience until QuickFame Asia."

"What kind of upbringing did you have?"

The girl's eyes fell.

"I was born in North Korea. My father serve in People's Army. He was able to get my mother and me out of country only because he have some power and influence. We never see him again. He was caught and sentenced to life in a prison camp. He tried to escape and get us freed but he was captured just beyond the Chinese border and killed on the spot. As a result, Mushi-Mushi only makes happy music. I do not want to bring people down. As for your question, I had never left South Korea until now. I mean, except for my escape through China, but I was so small you could have hidden me among the potatoes, and no one would have noticed that one was wiggling and making baby sounds."

The reporters and gathered crowd chuckled.

"Have you ever been to America?" someone asked.

"I have never, but it is my dream to play there and make many good friends with Americans. There is such dreaming in that country. You see it in their faces and in their large automobiles. They think they can carry the world on their backs. I would like to give them songs to play in their trucks."

"Would you bring your entire band?"

Mushi hesitated, her eyes wide and unblinking. She then leaned in and said, "I do not understand your question."

"Would you bring your band along?"

"They do not speak English."

"So, you'd become a solo act?"

Mushi's mother—and manager—seated to the right of Mushi leaned over and whispered something to Mushi.

Mushi nodded and said, "My band is my friends. My friends have many talents, and I would like to make them happy."

Mushi looked over at her other four bandmates, all of whom sat to her left, smiling, their legs crossed and their hands in their laps.

The reporters talked in low murmurs amongst themselves. Mushi saw them stifling their laughter, casting furtive, condescending glances her way.

"What do you think of the other bands?" another reporter asked.

At this Mushi's face brightened.

"It is an honor to play with such wonderful acts. They are all deserving winners."

"Even #Five?"

She nodded.

"Of course. I hope to go on tour with them. We are already discussing future plans."

"Really?"

"You do not agree? Do you not have ears? Layton Coy's voice is unlike anything on the radio. If he goes solo, he will be immortalized in the pantheon of the greats. If he remains in his band, he will lead them to rock 'n roll glory. But they must not play their weak songs. They must be themselves. They are rock n' roll through and through. Mushi-Mushi is pop. We know this. As for the other bands, Blazing Camel is very talented, though alt-country is not my favorite type of music. Herd of Rockets is all spectacle and do not deserve to be here. Glycerin Satellite is quirky and jarring, and though I like it, I need to see what they are capable of."

"Are you and Layton Coy romantically involved?"

"Next question."

"What of the rumors of Layton Coy's secret life?"

Mushi's cheeks turned red.

"That is none of my business. It is none of yours either. Your concern is the music."

"Ok, fine. What about the rumor that the band was given special treatment throughout QuickFame USA and that their music is not entirely theirs?"

"Please. I am here to talk about Mushi-Mushi's music, not about #Five."

"What do you think about the fact that Jai Garnett said Mushi-Mushi is little more that corn syrup filtered through drum machines and synthesizers and poured into your ear?"

Mushi laughed. "He is pain in ass. I will pinch him hard next time I see him."

The assemblage of reporters again murmured among themselves. They seemed baffled not by the camaraderie but by the lack of contention among the performers. There was no animosity like in the continental competitions.

"Did you watch the other competitions from around the world?"

"Yes, all. Even the preliminaries."

"And what did you think of the winning bands?"

"Such good. Very talented."

"Were you surprised that Scarlett Fever did not win?"

Mushi hesitated. She looked at her mother, who leaned in and whispered something to her.

Then Mushi said, "It was confusing. I thought Cat Coggan would win, even though his music sounds old. Scarlett Fever sings good songs, but Tona Kohl does not have strength of spirit on stage."

Mushi's mother whispered something again and Mushi said. "No more talk about other bands."

"Alright. Which songs will you be playing?"

"We have new material."

"Will you be playing it live?"

Mushi, taken aback, looked at her mother. Her mother said something; Mushi shook her head and scowled. "I do not understand the question," she said into the microphone.

"There are rumors that your music is all prerecorded."

"That is unkind! You must never say such a thing. We sing with our hearts."

"Right, but do you sing with your voices?"

"I—of course we do. Mushi-Mushi sings. I sing. We all sing together. No, we do not play instruments on stage, but we are smart girls—women—who bring life to music. You—unkind!"

"Thank you much," Mushi's mother said, standing up and removing the earpiece connecting her with the translator. "We is stop."

The other members of the band, none of whom spoke English beyond the few phrases they had to learn for the lyrics, stood up as well.

Mushi collected herself. "Thank you for your questions, everyone. I look forward to seeing you tomorrow at the competition. *Annyeonghi kyeseyo!*" She flashed two fingers, then stuck a wad of gum in her mouth and shuffled off the stage in her trademark stunted, pigeon-toed style of walking.

The band hurried along behind her, Mushi's mother chasing after them.

They circled the throng of reporters and headed for the exit. Stepping out into the lobby, Mushi spotted a few members of #Five ordering up free smoothies and coffees at the pop-up cafe. Mushi raised a hand to her entourage—*stay*—and approached the band.

"Hello hello," she said with a smile.

"Oh, hey," Grannie said. "How did your conference go?"

"Very nicely. But I do not understand why your band was very unkind to me in your own press conference."

Layton sipped from his blueberry-avocado smoothie.

"That was Britt and Jai being edgy and controversial. They don't mean it. It's an act."

"Why must you act? Why not be yourself?"

Layton exchanged looks with Grannie and Donovan.

"It's just the scene, Mushi. People like a show. They like attitude. They like controversy."

Mushi's mother scampered forward, leaned in, and said something into her ear. Mushi raised a hand to shush her.

"This I do not understand," Mushi said. "Why cannot you just say positive things? Why is it so hard to be happy?"

Layton snorted into his smoothie, spurting out pureed blueberries and almond milk. "Not everyone is happy. And if we're being honest, what's so goddamned honest about your music? It seems pointless to deny the pain and agony of life and love, making it all seem like glitter and sunsets. Not to mention that your vocals are all watered down with filters."

Mushi's huge dark eyes narrowed.

"You are much crueler and straighter-forward speaking when you have friends to back you up."

"Hey, keep us out of it," Donovan said, a smoothie in one hand and a flat white in the other. "I like your music."

Grannie nodded and shrugged diplomatically.

"Layton, I talk to you alone?"

Mushi stepped aside, crossed her arms, and waited. Layton glanced at his friends who averted their gazes and sipped from their own coffee and smoothies. Layton sighed and joined Mushi.

"I think maybe you are not liking me so much as when we met a few days ago. I know American romances have short lifetimes, but this seems like world record."

"I like you. You're pretty."

"Layton!"

"What!"

Mushi glanced over her shoulder at her mother who was looking on with a look of mild terror. Some passersby and a couple of straggling reporters slowed down to watch.

Mushi crossed her arms and switched to a whisper. "You do not want to be with me anymore?"

Layton took a long pull on his smoothie, leaving behind a blue stripe on his upper lip.

Right when Mushi reached up to wipe it away with her tiny pale finger, a couple of camera flashes went off.

Her hand snapped back.

"We can hang out," Layton said. "Hang out? Like buddy and buddy?"

"I need to focus on the competition. It's kind of hard when you're hounding me all the time, asking for smooches and stuff. And it's like you're going to—you know— not go further."

Mushi released a subtle but audible squeal. "I just meet you. I not do sex so soon."

Layton drank more, leaving another stripe. Mushi didn't help him with this one. Mushi's mother scampered over again and spoke in a hushed voice, eyes low. Mushi nodded. "I must return to my hotel."

"Ok, cool," Layton said, visibly relieved. "See you later? I mean, see you around? Or maybe at the competition tomorrow. I'm anxious to see what kind of music your computer comes up with."

"Aiii! You jerk!" Mushi's hand shot out as fast as a dragonfly at the height of the summer and smacked the smoothie cup at the perfect angle, sending it pouring down Layton's new vest but nary a drop on herself.

"Shit! Fuck! Psycho bitch!"

Cameras flashed.

Voices murmured.

Mushi was gone in an instant. Her entourage followed.

"Where the hell is Eddie when we need him? Isn't this why he's here—to keep away deranged fans?"

Grannie handed Layton a wad of napkins. "Nicely done."

"She's sweet but clueless and her music is an affront to the human ear. If you can even call it music."

"I heard you singing to Emo tunes on the plane."

"Shut up."

"And that Best of Grindcore playlist."

"Shut up!"

Layton spun on his heels and marched off.

Donovan watched him go. "I'm not chasing after him. I'm no one's bitch."

Grannie couldn't help himself from telling Britt what'd just happened.

"Seriously?" Britt said, stretched out on his queen-sized bed. Grannie was stretched out on his own. The balcony door was open, and the sun was in full force, though the heavy breeze kept the room cool. Being on the twentieth floor, the room afforded views of both the city and the Opera House steps where they'd be performing on day three, the finals, if all went according to plan.

"Yeah, Layton pretty much tossed aside the leader singer of a band that is surely going to explode. They have a video on YouTube. Did you know that? After their QuickFame Asia win, the video jumped from five thousand views to hundreds of thousands, now on the verge of a million. Maybe our ounce of fame is going to Layton's head or something, and he feels like he can just toss people aside at will. What do you think?"

No answer came. "Britt?"

Britt stepped out of the bathroom, pointing toward his mouth full of foam. "*Mphh flllph rrph.*"

"Why are you brushing your teeth? Where are you going?"

He spat and rinsed. "To find Mushi."

"Why?"

Britt slapped on some deodorant. "You're moving in on her now?"

Britt put on his jacket and sunglasses, unhooked his phone from the charger, and slid a pair of practice sticks out of his quiver.

"You do realize that you trashed her band at the conference, right?"

"That gives an in-road, doesn't it? 'Hey, Mushi, I'm really sorry that I—'"

"*Moo-shee*, Britt, not 'mushy.'"

"Right. Thanks. Wish me luck."

"You're crazy."

"That's my persona, right?" He stopped in the doorway. "By the way, where were you last night? I woke up to piss and your bed was empty."

"Oh—yeah. I went for a walk."

"Where?"

"To some park."

"That's weird. Your shoes were still here."

Grannie looked around the room.

"I have my running and workout gear with me."

"Which was in the bathroom. Hey man, it's cool. Secrets fuel this band."

Britt opened the door, then glanced back again.

"By the way, you look good without makeup."

Grannie's mouth opened but he wasn't sure what to say.

"See ya, Granville."

Britt sprinted to the elevator. When it arrived, the car was nearly full. Britt didn't require much room, however, and elbowed his way in.

From behind his mirrored aviator glasses, he stole furtive glances at the other occupants, trying to figure out if any of them were contestants from other bands. A pair of guys in bowties was probably Devine Bliss, the British duo that resembled twins but in truth shared no blood. Along the lines of Daft Punk, their sound was tonally groundbreaking, with loops and beats that were on the edge of freeform.

As for showmanship, their shtick was indifference, nonchalance, and all-out digital assault.

Britt liked it; he also detested their inability to play actual instruments.

To illustrate his displeasure, he rapped out a complicated marching band beat on the elevator doors, along with some just-for-shits-and-giggles stick spins and flips, all of which helped to keep his mind off Mushi.

Out of the corner of his eye he saw the not-twins exchange a look.

The doors slid open at the lobby and Britt's little legs took off. A couple of reporters called out to him, and while he loved the attention and normally would have stopped to chat and play up his public persona, he didn't even bother to give them the middle finger. He hoped to catch up to Mushi before she got to the apartment that her band, Mushi-Mushi, was renting, which Layton had said was an upscale unit that she'd rented through AirBnB.

Britt was thankful for his sunglasses: though the day was not particularly hot, the sun was glaring. He had a bit of a headache, having drunk pretty hard the night before. If he wasn't being particularly mindful, he'd inadvertently slide from fake binge drinker to full-on dipsomaniac. Mushi wouldn't like that. She didn't touch alcohol. Cigarettes. Meat. Gluten. Oil. Watermelon. *WTF?* He stopped on the sidewalk, the sticks nearly tumbling from his hands, people elbowing him as they rushed past. He wondered why Mushi held sway over him. He'd only talked to her once or twice when she'd visited Layton's suite, and even then, she had been clinging to Layton like a life ring in a Caucasian sea of musicians. What was it—her looks? She was certainly cute and, to Britt, exotic. Her sweet voice? Though she spoke excellent English, it was tinged with a distinct elitist air, the influence of her tutor obvious in her rigid syntax and lack of contractions. Her eyes— Britt got lost in them. And that dark hair.

Her narrow hips and skinny legs and arms almost entirely devoid of muscle tone. Luckily, she wasn't much taller than him, whereas Layton had towered over her.

Does he even like girls?

As he walked Britt fired off a text to Layton, asking how to get to Mushi's apartment building.

Why?

Just because.

You've got a crush on my sloppy seconds?

Did you—no, don't tell me.

No idea what the address is. Here's a screenshot.

The map was unintelligible to Britt. He turned his phone sideways, zoomed in, twisted it, but couldn't figure out what street he was on in relation to the apartment building.

"Fuck a duck!"

He kept walking. He was starting to sweat. He shed his black coat and fanned his shirt in an attempt to dry off his armpits. Eventually he stopped in a convenience store to show the clerk, a mustached guy with a strong Indian accent. "I have no idea where that is man, except for that park. It is about two kilometers that way."

He pointed the direction from which Britt had just come.

"Seriously?"

"Yes, very serious."

"I just walked those two kilometers."

"For this I am sorry, but it was not me who gave you the directions."

"Shit. Crap. Dang it. How do I get a Sööper?"

"A what?"

"Like, you know, a cab."

"I can call one for you."

While the clerk made the call, Britt got some sort of Australian sports drink called Maximus, drank half of it, then brought it to the counter.

He then reached for his wallet.

Which wasn't there.

"Shit. I don't have money."

The clerk slid the Maximus across the counter, away from Britt.

"I already drank half. You're just going to throw it out?"

"You are American? Here we pay for things, mate."

"Hey, what the fu—of course I pay for things. I need to pay for the Sööper—the cab. Obviously. So, it's not like I'm trying to pull a fast one."

"A fast one?"

Britt waved him off.

"Forget it. The point is that I forgot my wallet. I was rushing."

"You are Russian? I am sorry. I thought you were American."

"No, rushing! In a rush. I still am. Can you help me out? What's your name?"

"Ardit."

"Ardit. Listen, my band won a competition called QuickFame USA. Now we're here to win QuickFame OneWorld. Have you heard of it?"

"It sounds vaguely familiar."

"If you can let this slide, I'll give you and your shop a shout-out on live television and thank you for your altruism."

Ardit crossed his arms.

A moment later the cab pulled up outside. Britt stepped out and flashed the guy his index finger. *One minute.*

"How's that sound?"

"This is not my store. I would never advertise this place for the cocksucker who owns it."

Britt's shoulders slumped forward. "Ok."

"But I do have a website you can speak of. It is called www.arditexpeditions.au. It is my dream business. Private tours of the desert."

"Great! That's even better. Write it down for me."

While Ardit did so, Britt snatched back the Maximus, finished it, then grabbed another. Ardit scowled as he handed over the paper. "You had better win. I need many viewers to see my URL."

"Definitely. Also, can I have twenty bucks? Otherwise, I can't pay for the cab. It's a prime-time show, man."

Ardit's scowl tightened. "You are cunning individual. I am not sure which is worse—American or Russian."

"Americans are the worst but I'm legit, Ardit. No fraud here."

He lifted his sunglasses.

"This is a matter of the heart."

Another customer came in, the door jangling.

"Fine, fine." Ardit handed over the cash, which Britt was pretty sure had come out of the till. "Please do as agreed or I will contact the Russian embassy and make a complaint. Now go. Your cab is leaving."

Britt was about to offer his hand for a shake but at the last second handed over his drumsticks instead. "Let me sign these. They'll be worth a lot some day."

Ardit took the sticks, examined them, offered an expression of satisfaction, then tried a little *tappity tap* on the counter. "I always wanted to play drums."

"I appreciate you helping me find this place," Britt said as he paid the driver. "Keep the change."

"Oh, thanks mate. That ninety cents will really feed my family."

"Shit, man, it's all I've got. What about *my* family?"

"Get out."

"You get out."

"It's my cab, guy."

"Be nice or I'll contact the embassy."

"That sounds promising."

Britt slid out of the cab and forced himself not to slam the door. He put his jacket back on, cleaned the sweat off his sunglasses, and sized up the building. It was large.

He had no idea where Mushi was staying.

As soon as he stepped inside the cool building, a security guard roughly five times the size of Britt stepped forward with a hand as large as a stop sign extended before him. "You're not a resident of this building."

"I'm here to see someone."

"Are you on the list?"

"I'm not sure which list you're talking about but probably not."

The guard stepped past Britt and held the door open for him. Britt didn't move. "I'm here to see Mushi. Of the band Mushi-Mushi."

"Give her a call and ask her to come down and put you on the list. She'll need to provide a photo as well."

"I don't have her number."

"You two sound like close friends."

"Come on, man. It's a surprise visit."

The guard gestured outwards, back into the relentless sunlight. Britt wished he'd brought more drumsticks. He sighed, shoved his hands in his pockets, and was starting to exit the building when someone called out to him.

"Britt?" *Breet.*

Another member of Mushi-Mushi was walking past with a towel on her shoulder. Britt couldn't remember her name for the life of him. *Noon? Star?*

"What? Britt? You?"

Britt nodded vigorously. *Sue? Yung?*

"He's not on the list," the guard said, crossing to his little desk to retrieve a file containing names and photos. "No little boys named Britt."

"Britt!" *Breet.* She hooked her arm in his.

"Mushi?" he said.

She nodded. "Mushi-Mushi!"

Shit. She dragged him to the elevator. She pressed the button and stood here smiling as it returned to their floor. She was nearly as short as him but thicker than Mushi. Still cute. But not Mushi. Britt couldn't recall what her role was in the band, then remembered that none of them did anything except sing and make some vaguely dancing gestures. As they stepped into the elevator, Britt realized that in the video of their competition finals that he'd watched, there seemed to be more dancing and bouncing around than singing. He had no idea what they were singing about, though the song was peppered with some English, namely, "Really love you," and "Such a cute time with you." Britt started to wonder about the performance itself, and whether maybe they were lip-synching as well. A cold sense of doom settled into his stomach as the doors shuddered open.

They'd traveled upwards one floor.

The girl knocked on an apartment door; it opened to reveal Mushi's mother. Her face was the paragon of matriarchal discontent.

Whatever came out of her mouth sounded like chastising, a true verbal assault, for the girl's eyes lowered to the floor and she looked like she might cry. Then the mother turned to Britt. "Bad band boy. Go. You go."

Someone called out from the apartment. Mushi's mother started to close the door, but a little hand caught it and pulled it back open.

"Britt!"

Britt slouched, his sunglasses still on. "What's up."

She threw her arms around him. "Britt! Sun brought you here?"

Sun. Her name is Sun—as in soon. "She got me past security."

"Oh, that big dumb man. He is like elephant with Australian accent. How does he fit through door? Come in, come in."

She shut the door in Sun's face.

"You want drink?" Mushi nudged her mother back and headed to the kitchen.

"Got beer?"

Mushi laughed. "Please have sit!" She was barefoot, the mother in socks and sandals.

Britt slid his boots off and realized that his feet were on fire, sweating and rank. The motorcycle boots were a women's model, since it was hard to find men's shoes in his size, but they were taller than men's and didn't look as strange with the risers he used. His foot, however, was decidedly masculine in shape and the boots pinched his feet in all the wrong places.

He slid the boots close to the door, then went inside, holding himself back from nudging the mother farther away.

The apartment was sunny but cool, the furniture minimalist and gleaming, perhaps arranged according to the principles of feng shui. Britt shed his jacket and sunglasses and sat on a couch so white and shiny he was afraid his dirty old jeans would leave behind some sort of embarrassing stain that the guests might mistake for a worse, more embarrassing stain.

Mushi emerged from the kitchen with a tray bearing glasses and a pitcher of some sort of thick orange drink. "You like mango?"

"Um, sure. I think."

She laughed. Always smiling and laughing. Like this was a K-pop video. Which, Britt hoped, it was: the videos he'd watched (usually with the sound turned off) all seemed about girls wooing or being wooed.

Britt drank the icy mango juice while the mother perched on a stool on the other side of the room where she occasionally glanced at her phone but primarily stared at the back of Mushi's head or Britt's uncouth American face.

"Do now worry about my mother. She is a creature of old and does not speak English. We can talk about how she cannot please Father in the bedroom, and she will only sit there and smile."

"Please, let's not talk about her and Father in the bedroom."

Mushi tittered and covered her face.

"Ok. What should we talk about?"

"Us."

"Us?"

"Should we go to the bedroom to talk about it?"

Mushi's face turned white.

"I'm kidding."

"Ah. Ha ha ha! I see."

"Are we going to stay friends even after the competition?"

"Of course, Britt. We will be friends forever."

She reached across to squeeze his hand. "So why you come today?"

"I wanted to apologize for what I said during the press conference. It's all theatrics. Just for show, I mean."

"I know that."

"I heard you were mad though. Very angry."

"Not about that. I am angry because of Layton. I do not understand why he treats me so poorly. We had a rapid romance and then it was like a fire explosion in the sky." Her hands rose up and burst above the mango juice.

"He's like that. To be honest, I think he's, you know, still figuring things out."

"What do you mean?"

Britt made a dismissive face. "I don't want to talk about him." He glanced past her at the mother. Seeing that she wasn't going to be cut into this dialogue, she got up and stormed off to another part of the apartment.

"Thank God," Mushi said. "She is like moth, always flapping at me, her moon." She made a moth with her hands and fluttered it in Britt's face. He pretended to bite it.

"That must be hard having your mother as your manager."

"Yes, but since I am only seventeen, I cannot do it any other way or I would not get permission to travel, miss school, rent apartment, hire cab, go to concerts. She is also my tutor."

"But not in English."

She laughed yet again. It was infectious. She was also wearing very little makeup, revealing her true face, softer and kinder than when it was dolled up, sexifying her to an extreme that made Britt feel as if he were violating some sort of covenant had he not been a year younger than her.

"Oh, Britt, I want to show you our video we made. It is just a test video for when we make an album, but we have big hopes. You must tell me your honest opinion. Should we go with this style or not?"

Mushi sprang from her chair and walked across the room. Britt liked the backs of her legs. Her firm little buttocks. Her hair reached nearly to her waist when not pulled together in corn rows or some other silly style. She pressed a button on the wall and a panel slid open to reveal a television.

She pointed her phone at it, swiped; a video popped up on the TV.

She returned to the couch and sat beside him.

She looked tense, exhibiting the body language of someone who was flying for the first time. "Watch."

Mushi was front and center in the video. The video featured a retro-chic set-piece full of bright pastels, old Chevys, Coke bottles, and boys with greasy black hair and white T-shirts.

There were, inexplicably, some rap breakdowns featuring Britt's new friend Sun before mercifully switching back to the typical K-pop style of mesmerizingly flat vocals spouting off the blandest of lyrics.

The video seemed to largely be a showcase for the fashion designer's skills and the dance choreographer's chops rather than for singing and music. Maybe that was the point—to fully distract everyone from the cringe-inducing, off-key vocals by slathering the girls with enough makeup to make them seem of consenting age. There wasn't a single musical instrument to be seen in the video and probably hadn't been one involved in its production. Grannie could have assembled a better mix in his bedroom.

She finally shut it off after three interminable minutes. "Wow. So, you play chess?"

She was puzzled. "What?"

"In the video you're playing chess. You know, the game?"

"Oh, no. I do not understand that game. I like Angry Birds. You know this game?" The cold settled in his stomach again. *But she's so sweet. And cute. And kind.*

"Please tell what think about the video."

Britt's eyes were trained on the TV where Mushi and her band, Mushi-Mushi, remained frozen in one of their dance poses, which could have been a pose struck by any one of ten thousand pop acts around the world, their shoulders going on direction, elbows another, hips backwards, knees forward, eyes up—those huge dark eyes that sucked him in, tickled his soul, chewed it up, spat it out. He wondered what kind of video #Five would produce, especially if forced to perform one of Felicia's songs. Felicia herself would no doubt be on set, barking commands and telling the boys how to pose, how to pout, how to look moody and aloof.

Some Streemy exec would probably be there too, whispering into her ear.

The music would be autotuned, filtered, softened, the vocals sped up and heightened and the drums tamped down to just a hiss in the background.

"It's not good."

Mushi's body instantly jerked an inch to the right. "No?"

"It's derivative."

"Deriv...?"

"It means it's not original. It just plays on everything that everyone has done before you. I can't think of an original thing about it. Even the retro thing has been done by Gaga, Cyrus, Bieber, some Japanese pop-metal bands, et cetera. And the music—well, that's not my thing. You probably have a nice voice, but the sound engineer will not let it speak for itself, so to speak. I can't hear its flaws, highs, or lows. It's flat. And you guys dance so fucking much! What's the point? Why not just sing and play music? Or do any of you even know how to play an instrument?"

"I am classically trained in piano. I also play flute and oboe."

"Then put that in the video. That will earn you some integrity."

"My fans do not want oboe music."

"Make music because it's bursting out of you, not because some faceless, nameless statistic wants to see your boobs bouncing around on their laptop. In other words, don't pander to your fans."

"Panda...?"

"Pander. Sorry. Never mind. I probably just came across as a total snob and asshole. I'll see myself out."

Britt stood up. As he made his way to the door he thought he could smell his boots. He was starting to slide his feet into them while putting on his jacket and sunglasses when someone grabbed him by the neck and twisted his face around. He was expecting to find the mother armed with a kitchen knife or pepper spray; it wasn't. It was Mushi. She pressed her mouth against his. He tasted mango and caught the scent of cherry lip balm.

"*Okaaay*," he said once she'd pulled away.

"No one speaks the truth to me."

"That's sad. Rock 'n roll is all about truth. That's why we play it. Pop music doesn't have to be about hiding your intelligence behind feelings. Sing what you want. Flute, oboe, screaming— just make it count."

Her eyes were glistening. "Stay a little longer. I want to show you my favorite pillows."

"Pillows?"

She nodded. His hand was in hers. "And your mother?"

"I will tell her to leave."

"Oh. Wow. I love pillows, by the way." She laughed, then kissed him again.

Two hours later his phone was buzzing like mad. Late for his band meeting, he borrowed twenty Australian dollars from Mushi to get back to the hotel.

He flew on invisible wings down to the cab, coasted along the hot dry roads, and tipped the driver generously.

His feet floated him through the revolving doors and into the lobby where a reporter immediately strolled towards him, saying, "She's here. What do you think of that?"

"Who? Felicia?"

"No. *Her.*"

The reporter jerked his thumb towards the lobby lounge where a figure in black and sporting huge dark sunglasses sat as still as a Grammy Award.

Britt's mouth opened and he was about to ask who it was when he noticed the hair.

The color of fire but angrier. "Tona?"

She turned and looked at Britt; he waved.

In a split second she was on her feet and jogging over to him.

She wasn't wearing her thick-heeled boots and with the risers in Britt's they stood nearly eye-to-eye. She threw her arms around him and kissed his cheek. Their sunglasses banged together. Cameras flashed all around them.

"What's wrong?"

"You were the only one who spoke the truth to me. You're the only who actually cares about me."

Shit. Not again.

"What happened to Roman?"

"He's a moronic piece of STD-filled shit who had another girl on the side. Who was also pregnant."

"And you—the—your belly?"

She shook her head. "I didn't want his DNA in my body another second."

"Wow."

"I've got a room upstairs. Come with me."

An iceberg slid down Britt's throat and settled in his stomach.

"Um, ok."

She grabbed his hand and led him to the elevator. Once it'd arrived and emptied out, she turned around and said to the group of travelers waiting to ascend with them.

"Fuck off."

The doors shut. Tona pressed Britt to the wall.

He could still taste mango. Cherry.

Should I tell her I just lost my virginity?

11.

UP TO MY NECK IN YOUR BLOOD

Donovan locked the hotel room door and set the safety latch, then collapsed on the bed. If the world of rock 'n roll offered such few moments of privacy, he knew he was going to struggle. He needed his time and space to think, to jerk off, to deal with the constant influx of messages and alerts on his phone. He couldn't think or be himself when suffocated by hordes of clingers-on and teenage groupies and strange middle-aged men in sweatpants toting backpacks full of stuffed animals.

Who the fuck let that perv into our room anyways?

He laughed to himself. He needed to tell his older brother Casey and dialed him up through Whatsapp.

"I think Britt let the guy into the suite," he told Casey. "He's always doing shit like that."

"You mean shit that will rile you guys up and get people like the perv into situations that just might get them arrested?"

"Pretty much, yeah."

"So, what'd the creepy guy do?"

"He just sat in the corner of the room staring at us with his backpack of stuffed animals on his lap. He was probably stroking himself beneath it."

"How do you know it had stuffed animals in it?"

"Britt asked him! He said, 'Man, what you got in that backpack?' and the guy smiled this nasty mouthful of gnarly teeth, all brown and twisted like a British person's, then unzipped the backpack and poured them out onto the floor. The backpack was just some average-sized Eastpak, but the guy'd really crammed the animals in there. Dolphins, bears, mice, parrots, you name it. Some were quality animals, and some were those foam-stuffed things from carnivals and such."

"What'd you guys do?"

"Man, I just watched, but Britt and a couple others dove right into that fucking pile. They started flinging the animals around the room like they were Santa and his elves, Britt being the chief elf of course. Some people fought over the animals and tore a bunch of limbs off. The guy totally freaked out, just bawling, and clawing at people, trying to get his animals back, going, 'No, no, no.' Then he flipped over a table and tackled Britt. Eddie, our new security guy, or security kid, jumped on the guy. He flipped onto his shoulder and carried him to the elevator, then tossed him inside."

"How did the guy get in your room in the first place?"

"No one knows. He had a ticket to QuickFame OneWorld though, and a couple pictures of #Five from a website. He'd printed it out and written our names underneath each person."

"Holy shit."

"Yeah. Total creepville."

Casey sighed into the phone. "You're really living the life."

"Yup. So, how's accounting school?"

"Shut up, man. It's not accounting school, it's finance. I'm planning on doing accounting for hedge funds. I'll be able to launder all your illicit earnings and funnel it to tropical islands around the world. So don't snark on it."

"Sounds positively thrilling. And how are Brenda and Nick?"

"Mom and Dad are fine. They invited me and Anna to some church event this weekend, but I lied and said that I had to practice my calculator techniques."

"Right. Cool."

Donovan strode to the tiny kitchen and got himself some pineapple juice, then carried it to the balcony and sat looking out across Sydney.

"How's the rest of the band dealing with the sudden trajectory into fame and fortune?"

"They're a mess. What a fucking nightmare. As for fortune, there's none of that, but when it comes to fame and all the trappings of romance and industry schmoozing, they all get an F-. Jai and Britt are fighting over the same girl—the singer from Scarlett Fever—while Layton positively recoils from girls' touch unless they're willing to jump his bones. He's romantophobic."

"Gross. He must get a lot of offers though. How about you? Getting any?"

"I'm working on it. Dudes are so hot here, but I don't know how to approach them. It's a cultural thing. I just can't read the signals. Oh, listen to this. Grannie and Felicia have gotten eerily close. We suspect that she's robbing his cradle. Maybe they can do that down here on the opposite side of the earth and get away with it."

"What the fuck!"

"I know."

"Why is she even there?"

Donovan paused. He chewed on his lower lip. "She's our, uh, mentor. After the USA show she thought she could offer us some advice for the global competition. I wish she hadn't. Man, I just wish she'd disappear. I wish they all would, actually. I'm practically tearing my eyeballs out with what I'm seeing. Tantrums, bickering, backstabbing. We're fucking teenagers, for Christ's sake."

"Don't bring Him into this."

"Who?"

"Christ."

"Yeah, Brenda and Nick wouldn't like that."

"You joke about it, but maybe it would help you to put your hands together once in awhile and talk to the man in the sky. It'd help you get some things off your chest. He's like a therapist but for everyone. And He doesn't charge anything."

"And He doesn't talk. Or answer. Or do anything. Give me a break. And I don't have anything I need to get off my chest."

"Nothing?"

Donovan stood up.

"I'm not getting into trouble."

He walked to the kitchen and got more pineapple juice.

"Donovan."

"What?"

"Something happened to that Korean girl and your band had something to do with it. I was watching too, you know."

"Maybe they did. And?"

"Maybe you could have stopped it."

Donovan drank the pineapple juice, then filled the glass with water and drank that.

He returned to the balcony and leaned on the railing. The ground was so far away. If he had to jump and take one person with him, who would it be? At the moment it was a toss-up. But it'd probably have to be Britt, who until just recently Donovan would have considered his closest friend.

The previous night, on the QuickFame showcase at the Ko-Walla Club, which collectively introduced the bands to the world, Britt had done something really bizarre.

Just before Layton was about to kick off the song, he jogged over to the microphone and grabbed hold of it, saying, "I'd like to dedicate this song to my friend Ardit, a local bloke who helped me out in a fit of desperate romance. Please visit arditexpeditions.au. And tell him Britt Elwyn sent you."

Layton had laughed and shrugged it off, and the band recovered quickly enough.

#Five had then performed their song to near perfection, or as near to perfection was possible for a full reconfiguration of one of Felicia's songs, which after much work in the days leading up to their arrival was finally rewritten to the band's liking, with Felicia's approval.

Following #Five was the Brazilian winner of QuickFame SouAm, London Mountains, whose music bridged the gaps between reggae, nü-metal, and post-punk. It was mesmerizing. And hard to follow up. But that was Mushi-Mushi's burden.

Once the stage was set for the Korean would-be stars, all of the dancer-singers that comprised the band took their places except for Mushi. The music was turned on and the other four Mushis stood there waiting, one fist on their hips and their heads nodding along with the beat. This went on for whole minutes. The audience clapped along with them, thinking this was a build-up of some sort. Then it breached five minutes. Six. Seven. A few of the Mushis stopped nodding their heads. They stood there looking around. When it seemed like there was nothing left to do but pull the plug, Mushi at last shuffled on the stage with her head hanging low, staring at her feet.

She had been wearing sweatpants, a t-shirt, and a single white clog. The other Mushis looked at one another as the real Mushi walked up to the microphone.

She bonked her head against it a couple of times, causing feedback to barrage the audience.

Then she removed the microphone and nudged the stand to the edge of the stage one centimeter at a time until it finally toppled off into the pit between the stage and the audience. As soon as a technician had reset it, she did it again.

"It is dead," she said while staring down into the tech pit.

"The music is dead. I am dead."

She was crying. "Our music is fake."

She turned and gestured at her dancers and singers.

"All this is fake. These are not my friends. You are not my friends. Friends tell each other the truth. Only Britt Elwyn from stupid boyband #Five tell me the truth. He was my friend for a day. We made beautiful music together but not the kind with instruments. Not that my band uses any instruments, as he was kind enough to tell me. Now I find out from television that he is making music with another woman. A real musician. One who writes own songs and plays own instruments. So here I am telling you that Mushi is dead. Britt Elwyn did not kill it. He just showed me where my body will be buried. So, I sing one last song to you."

Mushi had then raised a middle finger to the crowd and sung "Happy Birthday." Done, she dropped the microphone on the ground and walked off.

She hadn't been seen since.

One fewer contestant would be in their way now, but it wasn't how it was supposed to go.

"You might be right, Casey," Donovan said into the phone.

"I regret not doing something about it, but to be honest, it wasn't just that. Something else happened."

"What?"

"I dunno. Maybe it's no big deal."

"Tell me."

"Grannie took one of Felicia's unreleased songs—God knows how he got hold of it— remastered the vocals, laid down new beats, integrated some of Jai's guitar from one of our own songs, then leaked it to the major forums for use in clubs."

"Sounds like he's thinking about his solo career."

"That's what I was thinking! He's using our music for Felicia's benefit and for his own. It's become a major hit in clubs, which is really nothing, since it can't be monetized, but for him and his career it's a major thing."

"Isn't that good?"

"Is it?"

"You sound jealous, Don."

"I guess am jealous."

"What are you going to do about it?"

Donovan bounced up and down on the bed, thinking. "What should I do?"

"You could, you know, talk to Grannie and the others about solo projects. The band has barely formed, hasn't put out any material, and has two days remaining in QuickFame OneWorld. I think that sends mixed messages, don't you?"

Donovan was nodding, his eyes shut and the sun warming his face.

"You still there?"

"Yeah, thanks. Gotta go. Love ya, bro."

Donovan put on his mod-style boots, his jacket, and sunglasses, then crossed the hall and banged on the door. Eddie opened it. Jai was sitting in the lotus position on the floor, doing breathing exercises.

"Hey. Where's Grannie and Layton?"

"Jai's calming himself down."

"I can see that."

"It's cool, Ed," Jai said, stretching out his legs with a groan and some wincing. "They're out, I guess, and where the hell is Britt?"

"He's probably with Tona Kohl."

Jai stood up. "You're joking, right?"

"It's all over the news now. I tried calling him, but he's not answering. But I'm sure he's in the hotel. I asked the front desk where Tona's room is but he said to fuck off. In his kind Australian way, I mean."

Jai started pacing. "Britt and Tona. Britt and Tona. I saw her first! I'll kill him."

"She's just not into you, man. Why can't you see that?"

"But Britt? The elvin drummer boy?"

"He's got a big heart."

"Shut up, Donnie."

"Don't call me that."

Jai crossed the room again and stood before the largest wall.

He raised his fist, cocked it back, and launched—but Eddie was there to catch his arm. "You want to end your career before it gets started?"

Jai stared at his hand a moment, then collapsed on the floor and returned to his breathing exercises, though it mostly looked like he was just panting in and out.

"You ok?" Donovan asked Jai.

"I just don't get what's going on."

"Me either. It seems like everyone is doing their "something else" besides the band."

Jai studied Donovan's face, waiting for the punch line; there was none. "What's wrong with that?"

"We need to stick together!"

"You can see now that this isn't kindergarten. This is rock 'n roll, dude. We do what we want when we want and how we want. That's why Britt's running off with all our women."

Donovan scoffed. "You sound pretentious and idiotic. Go back to watching cartoons."

"Actually, I've been sitting here meditating for over an hour, but fuck you very much."

"Is that what you call it? It looks more like Lamaze class."

Donovan flung the door open before Jai could fire off another zinger.

Halfway down the hallway Eddie caught up with him.

"That dude has serious anger management issues. How do I keep him, you know, down to earth? Hordes of fans and random stalkers I can handle, but his mood swings are unpredictable and dangerous."

"He needs another infatuation. Can you find him some other lead singer to fixate on?"

"Well, he did mention the backup singer from Blazing Camel. I don't think he has a chance though."

"Me either, but it might be good to let him think he does. You're doing a good job though. Just sticking by his side and making him feel like someone's there for him is good."

"Cool."

Donovan kicked the elevator door while waiting for it to arrive. He'd never been a wrathful person. Not like this, like Jai at his worst. He wasn't sure where such rage was coming from. He'd fought hard to quash the schizoid notions that religion had birthed in his brain, the constant tug of war between moral and societal, inner and outer, hot and cold, sky and earth, light and dark. He embraced the spectrum, believing all humans capable of all deeds depending on the context. He supposed that this was his dark moment, one he'd come to regret, but in that moment, he couldn't see another way out.

The fury wasn't a mask he was wearing—fury was wearing him like a suit.

The elevator ejected him into the lobby where a half-dozen reporters were lingering.

Upon seeing him they beelined for the elevator, ready to vomit out the same old questions for the tenth time. Except that they didn't.

"Is it true that Britt has already been arrested for a DUI?" He stopped.

"No. Where'd you hear such a thing?"

"Just a rumor. Is it true that Layton Coy wears dresses?"

"No fucking way."

"Oh?" A reporter showed him a grainy photo taken from a drone or a helicopter that'd been hovering outside Layton's hotel room.

"That was—it looks like he was—we were fooling around."

"Fooling around? Like, you know, sexually?"

The rage flowed back into Donovan's face. "Fuck you, man."

"Is he gay?"

"Because he put on a dress? Don't be an ass. *I'm* the gay one."

"What do you think about Grannie releasing a remix of Felicia's song? Is he leaving the band?"

Donovan could hardly breathe.

His ears were ringing.

"I—I don't know."

"What would you say to him if he were standing here right now?"

"I'd say he needs to focus on our band. I mean, what the hell, bro?"

"So will you say that to him?"

He nodded. "Totally. Duh. I'm on my way to talk to him right now."

"Oh, so you're headed to the Milo's, where he has been spotted dining with Felicia Scalding.

Our photographer is there." The reporter showed Donovan a cell phone picture.

"Right. It's, uh, just around the corner, right?"

"Three blocks north, one block west. On York Street. You are staying in the band, right?"

Donovan heard the words, translated them in his brain, flipped them upside down, chewed on them, then ingested them. In his stomach they fed the rage and the feeling of being on the outside looking in. "I guess. I mean, the boy band shtick isn't really my thing, with the goofy songs and all that, but it's fun. It's cool for the time being."

"You mean you might leave the band if better options present themselves?"

"I didn't say that." Donovan was sweating heavily. He needed to clear his eyes, but he didn't want to remove his sunglasses and let the reporters see the fear registering in his irises; he thought he'd probably look like a victim of shock.

"But, you know, whatever. Who knows?"

"You do realize you're just the bassist, right?"

"What?" Donovan turned to the reporter but couldn't figure out which one had asked the question.

They were smiling inanely while trying to goad him into saying something typical of a teenager. He then realized that he was indeed a teenager, and he should say something stupid. "Have you ever been on stage, asshole? Do you know what it's like up there, trying to keep the beat and enjoy the show and not shit your pants or miss a note? Go suck a fat one. Preferably mine."

Donovan exited the hotel through the revolving doors. He looked left, right, and forward, but had no idea which way was north or west or any of the other directions. It didn't help that the sun was so bright it filled the sky. Because they'd seen him hesitating on the sidewalk like a moron, the reporters followed in his wake, prompting Donovan to pick a direction at random and set out at a good clip. What he didn't know was that one of them was following him.

At the end of the block, he turned left only because there was shade there.

He kept walking until he reached a convenience store. He stepped inside, opened a refrigerator door, and let the cold air wash over him.

"That costs me a lot of electricity," the man behind the counter said. In front him, on the counter, was a handmade sign that read, *Ask Me About Ardit Expeditions Today!*

"You're Ardit?"

"The one and only."

"Go fuck yourself!"

He slammed the refrigerator door so hard it bounced back open, then left the store. He then turned around and went back inside.

"How do I get to Milo's?"

"Six blocks north, two blocks west."

Donovan gently shut the refrigerator door. "I'm in the band with Britt."

"Ahh. I thought I recognized you. Would you like a Maximus? On the house." He gestured toward the drinks in the refrigerator Donovan had assaulted.

"Sure, thanks. Now, when you say north, do you mean that way?"

Donovan opened his Maximus on the sidewalk. He felt like all he'd done since arriving in this civilized desert was ingest liquids, few of them containing alcohol. As he wiped his mouth clear of the purple liquid, he spotted someone slinking down the sidewalk on the opposite side of the street, his shoulders hunched, wearing a hat and sunglasses as a disguise. Donovan raised his hand to call out to him—then stopped. He capped the drink and started following the lead singer of his band.

The man with the press badge followed Donovan.

Layton was shopping. Gleefully, it seemed.

When he went into a store, Donovan sat on a bench across from it. He sipped his Maximus while his friend was in there trying on high-end fashion.

He must have been successful, for he emerged ten minutes later with a shopping bag in his hand and a grin on his strange, angular face. Donovan pocketed the drink and followed him again. A couple of times he removed his phone to take some pictures. The figure following him did the same, only he photographed both Donovan and his target.

Donovan grew bored with all of Layton's shopping and was about to head out in search of Grannie and Felicia when the game changed. Donovan went into another store. A lingerie store.

He has a girlfriend?

Donovan knew Layton liked women, but he was rarely sentimental enough to buy them gifts. Of all the members of #Five, Layton was the most unconcerned lover, practically a Lothario, never hooking up with the same person twice. He was in the store a long time. An oddly long time. Usually one just asks the clerk to find something in the right size, box it, bag it, flee. Layton was in there forty-five minutes.

Finally, he emerged, and the chain formed again, with Donovan following at a good distance but never losing sight of Layton. He never once turned to look behind him. Nor did Donovan.

Layton stopped and checked his watch; he then pivoted and headed right towards Donovan.

Donovan stopped in his tracks, then backed up, colliding with a cafe table where sat a picture- perfect Australian couple enjoying lunch. "Watch it, mate!"

"Sorry, sorry. It's the—heat. I'm not used to it."

"Better get some liquids in you then."

"All I've done since I've arrive in your country is piss on it!"

By the time Donovan had gathered himself, Layton was gone. He looked up and down the street, finally spotting him on the opposite side, heading back the way they'd come. Donovan followed from the far side, where it was fortunately cooler. He watched in amazement as two girls stopped Layton on the sidewalk, recognizing him despite the disguise, and asked him for his autograph. Layton set the bag on the ground behind him, signed a magazine, gave the girls hugs, then waited until they were gone before snatching up the bag and all but running back to the hotel.

They were nearing the entrance at the same time as Grannie. Layton waved to him; Grannie stopped. The two of them hugged.

What in the actual fuck?

Donovan stood there a moment, watching, but couldn't help himself.

"What up, bitches?" he said and raised his arms as he approached.

"Are you ok?" Layton asked. "Your face is really red."

"What, I don't merit a hug? Only you two are on such happy terms?"

"What? No. Of course not." Layton hugged him.

Grannie hugged them both.

The figure photographed it from the corner of the hotel.

"Let's head inside," Layton said.

Donovan jutted his chin at the bag behind Layton's back.

"What have you got there?"

"Nothing."

"Just some girly undies?"

He tugged down his sunglasses and winked at Layton.

"You got something on the side?"

"Uh huh. Someone I met."

"Met where?"

"At a, uh, another clothing store."

Donovan put his hands on his hips.

"Cool, cool."

He turned to Grannie. "And you? Lunch with Felicia? You guys are getting pretty buddy-buddy too, eh? It's just like high school, cliques, and all."

"It wasn't that—it's work."

"You mean a meeting to discuss the song you released?"

Grannie looked at Layton; Layton shifted the back further behind his back, giving the lurker a better angle.

"It was just for fun," Grannie said.

"Or the start of a new career? Tell me something, bros, does this band actually have a future?"

"What're you talking about? Of course, it does?"

"It's starting to feel like a bunch of solo acts working together until greener pastures come into view."

Layton pressed forward.

"Maybe it's you who's hoping to go solo. Like Krist Novoselic. He's had a *huge* career since Nirvana folded."

His eyes rolled in his skull.

"It didn't fold, you asshat. The lead singer killed himself. Perhaps because he had too many demons."

Donovan lunged for Layton's bag, but Layton twisted away.

Grannie stepped between them.

"Chill, Donovan. Layton, take a step back."

"Don't tell me to chill."

"Then calm the fuck down."

"I am calm!"

"Your face is about to burst open."

"I got sun is all. They have lots of it here, in case you didn't notice."

"Let's go inside and cool off then."

"Fuck you! You're not our papa."

"Do you even want to be in this band?"

"Yeah, duh. I mean, I think so. Why wouldn't I?"

"You belittle everyone, and you feel threatened by everyone's side projects. I mean, what the fuck, man. It's ok to do something with your energy, which is all we're doing. We're young and there are so many possibilities. We have confidence now that we've been on stage and succeeded. Roll with it, ok?"

"It was rigged! The whole fucking thing!"

"Shh, dickhead," Layton said.

"Yeah, keep your voice down, Donovan. Come on, let's go upstairs."

Grannie led Layton through the lobby. They raced for the elevator before the reporters spotted them, but as soon as the elevator doors were shut Layton swung the bag of lingerie at Donovan, hitting him in the head. A few pairs of underwear and a silky top flew out.

"What the fuck, man!"

"You're such a punk-ass little bitch, Donovan. Why can't you just enjoy this?"

"I love playing music and I love this fucking band. It's my number one priority and I just wish it was yours. Instead, you're off buying lingerie for some random bitch."

Grannie and Layton stared at the clothes lying on the ground. When the elevator slowed to a halt to let on a passenger, Layton grabbed them and stuffed them back in the bag. The three of them separated, waited for the passenger to get off two floors higher, then turned to face one another again.

"It's my priority too. I'm not going anywhere. No one else is either. You're just being insecure."

"I'm sixteen. Of course, I'm insecure."

Layton shrugged and turned to face the doors. "I'm not. Not anymore. I know who I am. I thought you did too."

The doors opened. Layton stepped out first, then pushed Donovan against the wall. "Are you in or out?"

"Get your ugly little vampire hands off of me."

Donovan twisted free and stormed off.

"Let him go, Layton. He'll come around. Or he won't."

"Bassists are a dime a dozen."

"It's his band too. He's important."

"Self-important is more like it," Layton said, giving the back of Donovan's head the middle finger.

Grannie took Layton by the arm and led him back toward his room. He was shivering, cold.

No—crying. Then sobbing.

12.

A CANCER CALLED LOVE

Details returned to Felicia.

She opened her eyes, then immediately shut them again when the bright Sydney light drilled its talons into her brain.

She recalled having had lunch with Grannie at a lovely sidewalk cafe in the Rocks area. Grannie was sweet and had insisted on paying. After that they'd walked around, and Felicia felt so in love— with the preserved architecture and the sophisticated air of the place. She even pocketed a real estate guide she'd come across. She remembered strolling past the Opera House to get a look at it.

"Tomorrow," Grannie had said.

Then he'd wanted to get back to the hotel to reconvene with the band and go over "Unstoppable," which the band had reworked heavily, so they parted there.

"I'll do some shopping and touristy stuff," Felicia said. They'd kissed long and hard. They batted their eyes and stretched out their arms, their fingers holding onto one another until finally, at last, slipping from each other's grasp. They walked backwards and waved until Grannie turned the corner and was gone.

"Christ on a crutch," Felicia said once she was finally free. "I feel like a babysitter."

Her feet had picked up the pace. Then she'd stopped.

She shook her head and muttered to herself, then picked up the pace again. She'd taken out her phone to call Cheree—she remembered that—except that Cheree was more of a luddite than herself and was still using a Nokia designed for grandmothers, huge buttons, and all, so getting her on Skype wasn't an option.

"Stupid bitch."

She'd considered calling Thaddeus. *No. I'm done with him.* She wished Chad was available.

He was only one ocean away now, somewhere in Asia.

Be strong, Felicia, you dumbass.

She had kept walking after that. She remembered entering a pub to get an adult beverage, which for some reason she still felt foolish drinking in front of Grannie. "Something sweet and not too strong," she'd said, but she hadn't been imbibing much of late and her tolerance was lower than when she'd stolen that wine at her first communion and spent two days clutching her bed in a stupor of dizziness and nausea.

This drink in Sydney, however, was a local version of an appletini or something. It was delicious; a second followed. While waiting for it she noticed an electric slot machine in the corner. A "pokie," they called it here. A guy dressed in fishing gear was leaning against it, his forehead against the glass. Felicia laughed. She remembered laughing long and hard at that—how stupid the guy looked. How stupid she'd been to waste all that money on gambling. Hundreds of thousands of dollars.

A couple million frittered away on frivolities like the boat, a condo in Hawaii, a recording studio that she never used and whose address she couldn't even recall. She could have invested and retired. She went on laughing and ordered another drink.

She woke up hours later in the Star City Casino, her forehead against a pokie. Her skull was pounding, and she had a bit of vomit on the front of her shirt. More of it sat in the bucket of coins in her lap. She didn't remember anything between the pub and the casino, such as how she'd gotten there, where she'd gotten the money, and what day it was. She couldn't find a clock on the wall and her eyes wouldn't settle.

"*Shlur*," she said to the lanky, Stetson-topped man working the machine beside her still upright, his head not pressed against the glass. "*Shlur*. What time *ish* it?"

"I don't wear a watch when I'm here," the man said.

"Bad luck."

"Fuck."

"You ok?"

"No. I have an *addickshun*. You shouldn't enable me!"

"Mm. Sorry about that."

The man carried his bucket to another pokie.

Felicia fished her phone out of her purse, but the battery was dead. She took that as a sign.

She stuck her hands into the bucket of vomit-spackled coins and started feeding them into the machine.

The machine sucked the bucket dry one dollar at a time and by and by the bucket contained only vomit. Felicia tossed it aside and stumbled toward the bathrooms, or where she hoped the bathrooms would be. Other gamblers stepped out of her way to let her pass, some of them whispering and pointing. On her way towards wherever she was heading she passed a lounge with a bank of TVs. A crowd was gathered, shouting at the television, but it wasn't showing a horse or dog race or a sporting event. On the screen was her very own Grannie.

"Oh dear."

The people in the lounge were placing stages on who was going to win the first of two rounds of QuickFame OneWorld.

The performance was live.

Felicia took a seat in a massive pleather lounger, squirted some drops into her eyes, then leaned forward and watched her creation do its best without her.

The first thing she noticed was that Donovan was standing at the edge of the stage with his back to the band. He was staring out at nothing—not at the crowd, the judges, or anything. The rest of the band seemed equally disconnected. Felicia cupped her ear and listened to see if they were popping out her lyrics as she'd instructed them, with spunk and energy and a bit of spittle.

"*Shurn* that up!" she said.

No one looked at her.

"*Pleesh! Shurn* it up."

A woman in a cocktail waitress outfit glanced at Felicia, then produced a remote and increased the volume.

"You little donkey farts."

Felicia ignored the other gamblers casting glances her way. Felicia saw nothing but those sweet faces and heard nothing but the wailing of a song that wasn't hers.

It's their thirst for blood and fame
Their shiny watches and wretched faces

Please forgive us, we don't know what was done in our name
Our lives were ruined even before we were born

Despite the disconnected vibe, the judges were making notes. Their eyes were wide, their faces expectant. Of the judging panel Felicia knew only Heather Sullivan, who had fronted a 1990s one-hit-wonder band that went on tour with 2Tone. As for Domingo Tucker and the singularly named Remi, she didn't know them from a glory hole on the interstate.

Felicia wondered if this was a new ploy by #Five: a fuzzed-out shoegazer sound, like something you'd hear on college radio at ten o'clock on a Friday night, something arty and off the wall. The band was precise and sonic though. Grannie created a wall of sound from the instrumentals. The vocals were too washed out for Felicia's taste, but it worked in the context.

The song was dark and political and would never top a chart. This wasn't the heyday of grunge. This was now. People wanted mind-candy, something to rinse their brains of the day's horrors.

A couple of times the judges nodded to the beat. They almost seemed deferential to the band. And the audience liked it. Maybe they didn't love it but when the noise faded out, the applause was heavy though not thunderous. Somehow it was enough for the judges, who appreciated the diverse output of the band. They discussed the song at length. They argued in the vein of Felicia and Andy, though with more eloquence and less emotion. They were, if very drunk Felicia thought about it, much better at their jobs than she and her cohorts had been. These Aussies were probably not being bribed and didn't have ulterior motives.

"*Blarrgh*," she said, shoving herself off from the chair.

She spent the next thirty minutes getting herself through the casino to the sidewalk. Someone ordered her a cab, but whom she wasn't sure. It whisked her to the hotel, the windows lowered to combat the smell of her vomit. With the sun down, the breeze was tinged with a seaside coolness that brought some life back to her body and some sense to her mind.

She paid the driver what she hoped was an appropriate amount, then used her refreshed brain cells to figure out which floor she and the band were staying on. She stopped frequently to lean against the wall and catch her breath. Despite everything she found herself craving an appletini.

Members of other bands gave her a wide berth as they marched off to celebrate or mourn.

Felicia knocked on a door that might have belonged to someone from #Five but no one answered. She tried the one next door and came eye to eye with a muscular, dark-skinned boy in a suit and tie.

"At *lasht*."

"Are you drunk, ma'am?"

"Eduardo, get of my way."

"I think maybe you had better come back later. The band is trying to focus."

"Move, Edmundo!"

Felicia shoved Eddie aside and entered the room.

"Quite a show, gentlemen. Or should I say 'gentleboys'?" She cackled. "Maybe we should change your name to that? Obviously, you don't want to be Hashpound Five. Nope. *Nuh-uh*. You're all too limp-dicked to get the job done without Mommy here to make sure you sing the right notes."

Eddie shut the door and resuming his duties as security officer.

"I think Felicia is a tad tipsy," Britt said.

"Quiet, tiny man."

Britt laughed; the others looked on in horror. Felicia grabbed a pile of clothes and gear off a chair, looked for a place to set it, then simply flung it in the air.

She sat and held her head a good long while.

Grannie brought her a glass of water.

"I suppose you haven't seen the news."

"I saw that you made it to the finals along with Lunar Pulse, London Mountains, and—who was it?"

"Muscle Memory."

Felicia's face twisted up.

Only the left side of her mouth had any lipstick. "Dumb name."

"They're a good band," Jai said. "That's not what Grannie was referring to though."

Felicia sat up.

She drank half the water, paused, tried not to regurgitate it into the glass it'd just emerged from, then set the glass on the floor.

"Someone was following us around, sniffing out stories. Apparently, we're full of them. He caught a little bit of everything."

"Like wh—?" Felicia raised her hand to her mouth to stifle the gag reflex.

"Britt and Mushi. Britt and Tona Kohl."

They all looked at Britt who shrugged and made a *what can ya' do?* face.

"You and Grannie," Layton said.

"Obviously you're screwing," Britt said.

"Are not."

"There are pictures, Scalding. Which raises the question of age."

"Oh."

"Grannie cleared it up for us. Consider us shocked. But the media will have some questions. They think he's in high school. It sounds like we perpetrated a fraud in QuickFame USA."

"Perpetrated? You don't talk like a kid."

"You're more of a kid than we are."

Felicia's eyes bounced from face to face. "You all are babies! Infants. You're all in my womb at this very moment."

She patted her belly, which only put her closer to vomiting. Her eyes then settled on Layton. "You tell them?"

All eyes shifted to him. "Tell us what?" Britt said.

"Does this have something to do with the lingerie?" Donovan asked, then shrugged. "I haven't read the news myself."

"There is a picture of Layton trying on some women's clothing," Grannie said. "A girl working at a clothing shop snapped it."

Jai laughed. "And Donovan is talking about how the band is falling apart."

"Is it?" Felicia asked, suddenly very present.

No one answered.

She focused on Donovan, squinting to make sure she was looking at the right face. "Are you in or out?"

He stood up and paced. "This band is my life. I have nothing else. *Nothing.* I'll tell you this though—I'm not playing those shitty ass songs anymore. It's Shivvr and the Quakes or nothing. We can't pretend to be some boy band just to get a record contract."

"I need you to play my songs or I won't get paid! I'm in debt, you dicks. I have an *addickshun*."

"That's what all this is about?"

"No. Yes. And no. I want my name back. And I want to be a star-maker."

Her little fingers made magician gestures in the air above her head. "Poof. Hello there, #Five, biggest band on the planet."

"We won't be recording your songs either."

"Then you won't be recording anything."

Felicia clenched her eyes shut. She was crying. "No no no."

Grannie went to her and rubbed her shoulder. She shrugged him off. "This means I cannot license the songs and earn royalties."

Layton made a *thhhpptt* sound with his mouth. "That's not our goddamn problem. We're not your conduit to fame."

"Stop using fancy words. It's making my head hurt. You of all people. I supported you. I helped you come to terms with your—" She didn't finish.

"I know. That's why we won't tell anyone about what you've done. You've helped us all in some way. Now we're helping you by no longer enabling you to meddle and manipulate."

"Stop rhyming. You're not a rapper."

"It's not a rhyme. It's alliteration. You'd know that if you had a lick of poetry in you."

"Fuck you!"

Donovan went to the door and opened it.

"Time to leave, Felicia. We need to get some rest. The finale of the world's biggest music concert takes place tomorrow night."

"No."

"Please."

"I hate you all. I *made* you."

"No you didn't. We were already thriving when you stumbled into our graces. Now stumble out."

Grannie took her elbow and helped her from the chair. "I'll take you to your room."

Britt and Jai shook their heads and went to the kitchen.

"This is my band," Felicia said.

Grannie compelled her toward the door. "It's not, Felicia. Just stop."

"You stop, you gigolo. Boytoy."

"Uh huh."

Grannie shut the door behind them and led her to her room. He fished her key out of her purse, then helped her onto the bed, took off her shoes, and threw the blankets over her.

"Stay with me."

"Not when you're like this. You're disgusting. You're not even you. I'll get you some water and then I'm leaving."

She grabbed his hand. "Please don't. I don't want to be alone. The balcony door—" she pointed at it "—it's a long drop."

"That's manipulative. I have to perform tomorrow."

She closed her eyes.

Grannie set a pitcher of water on the bedside table. His hand was on the doorknob when he turned to look at her once more. Tears were soaking her pillows.

The balcony door was just a few short steps from the bed. The city was thriving below them.

Felicia woke to an empty room. She rolled over and touched the other pillow, which still held the imprint of Grannie's head. The pitcher of water was empty, but she didn't recall drinking it.

She packed her bags while her phone charged. She put on some dirty clothes and didn't shower. When her phone had enough juice to power up, she saw a slew of messages, texts, and alerts. One in particular stood out. The anonymous.

What's going on with your band? Have you lost control of your pets? Maybe you need to tighten their collars. I hear that your little boy toy likes to wear one.

It was eleven in the morning. The finalists had press conferences starting at three in the afternoon. The bands also had meetings scheduled with a couple of talent agencies and some music executives. Felicia had told them not to attend any of the meeting without her present as some sort of counsel. But with her there they'd probably pull a Mushi (who Felicia thought she had spotted wandering through the casino wearing a single shoe).

She shut off her phone again, checked under the bed for stray sex toys, clothing, money, and other things she'd left behind in the past.

She then opened the door and looked left, right, up at the ceiling, and back into the room before stepping out. She shut the door behind her as quietly as her stiff, dehydrated body would allow.

She took the stairs, all twelve floors' of them, her suitcase going *thump thump thump* behind her. When she reached the ground floor she could barely stand. She was sweating pure alcohol. It smelled like apples, which brought her near to puking.

A door opened and closed somewhere above her in the stairwell. Felicia took a deep breath and kept descending. She could hear her phone continuing to chime at her. Near the bottom floor, slightly dizzy and her head pounding, Felicia sat on the stairs and finally took a look at her phone. She scrolled as quickly as possible as her eyes tried to settle on the words, at last coming into focus as the most alarming alert appeared.

You gotta read this, Fel! Cheree had written. *Bad bad shit! Fight the power, grrrl!*

Felicia breathed a sigh of relief when she saw that the link led to some obscure blog called *Music Bitch*, then sucked it right back in when she saw that the post included wide-ranging revelations about #Five and Felicia, all of it accompanied by photos. The images alone were incriminating.

```
Layton Coy: ladies man, singer extraordinaire,
lyricist, teen prodigy, and… wearer of lady's
clothes? That's right, bitches, Layton Coy wears
dresses, if this image is to be believed. And
```

according to our sources, this is legitimate. It's not some slapdash Photoshop job. Layton was seen shopping in multiple women's stores. There he tried on various items of clothing. A receipt below shows what he bought. Then a drone caught him trying on said undies!

What exactly is all this about? Is he playing for the other side? Is this a career-killing move?

He's not the only one with demons in the closet however. Britt Elwyn apparently is a raging alcoholic at the tender age of 16. Rumors are that he's already driven his motorcycle into his drum kit, had a DUI, passed out during shows a couple of times, and nearly punched his father unconscious. He's like that dwarf from the Hobbit only, you know, sexy and talented. Not only that, he's also a ladies man. Or boy. They're all boys, aren't they? (Or are they…? More on that down below.) Yes, Britt Elwyn not only cast aside Mushi of QuickFame Asia-winning band Mushi-Mushi, he then sent her into a downward spiral by immediately picking up with none other than TONA KOHL.

That's right. He walked out of one Sydney hotel room and right into the other. S-C-A-N-D-A-L. (Rumors that Tona aborted a fetus sired by Layton Coy are unsubstantiated, but you can run with that image if you'd like.)

Then there was a photo of Felicia. And Grannie. They both looked old and awful.

Felicia Scalding. Where to start? Well, this isn't a forum for investigative journalism, which is what it would take to delve into the ins and outs of Felicia's disastrous human existence. Nay, this is a mere music blog written by a literary mortal.

All we can do is analyze the evidence laid out before us.

The pictorial evidence indicates that pedophilia isn't below Felicia Scalding. In addition to her massive debt, gambling problems, disastrous love life, and perverted friendships with industry insiders, she has stooped to a new low: fornicating (allegedly, dear readers, allegedly!) with Granville "Grannie" Jordan, keyboardist extraordinaire for #Five. I have no idea when this started, but it looks pretty sincere, so it must have been building for awhile. And by "awhile" I mean a couple weeks not days. They only met following QuickFame USA, so… or did they? (More on that below.) Weirdest of all is the fact that Granville recently produced a club version of Felicia's hit You Can't Stop The Girl, which he then released raw for further experimentation and is now being played in all the hip joints in all the right places. Worst of all, there's no monetization involved, so it must be some sort of collaborative rebranding of Scalding and her goofy 2Tone songs.

The other band members have their issues as well. Jai Garnett, I've been told, is heavily medicated: he's schizophrenic. It runs in his family. Apparently he needs to stay on an even keel or he'll start breaking things. Things like ROMAN SMITH'S FOOT. That's right, bitches. Apparently the rumor that Roman dropped an amp on his foot was pure fiction. Instead it was Jai who threw a juke box (what??) across the room at Roman. Where it landed on his foot.

Okaaaay. Right. That's up for debate, but what's not being debated is that Jai is the maniac responsible for his injury and perhaps thus responsible for the band's loss at QuickFame USA. Lawsuit, anyone?

Of course not. Tona Kohl, now with Britt Elwyn (is she his babysitter?), would surely never allow that to happen.

Last in the lineup is the bassist (aren't they always last?) Donovan Paris, the gay Frenchman (I just made that up. Get it? Paris?). The very out and proud musician is also outwardly expressing his increasing distaste with the behavior of the band. He's threatening to leave. Where he'll go no one knows. It's not like the band can't find another bassist. I mean, he's a bassist. I could probably step in to help.

My source, however, reveals that #Five itself isn't what it's cracked up to be. It's not the discovery that Felicia Scalding is claiming ownership to. The band was a legitimate musical powerhouse long before Felicia Scalding came a long and forced herself upon the band in the same way she forced herself upon the unsuspecting high schooler who plays the keys. Multiple sources

```
claim to have seen the band playing in basement
shows around town before QuickFame. They didn't
have a real presence back then, and they weren't
popular, but they were certainly talented and
poised to "pop." Most curious is the tidbit that
their songs were hard and thoughtful, not the
"woah-oh-oh" confection being foisted upon us.
So who's pulling the strings? And why?

The puppet was not even a puppet. It was a full-
on human being long before Felicia Scalding
claimed to bring it to life.

The truth is out there, folks. Keep feeding me
the tips and I'll sort through them. (Anyone have
any intel on the rumor that their security
staffer is a convicted felon with a rap sheet as
long as those handsome legs?)
```

Felicia turned off her phone and shut her eyes. A minute later she opened them and turned on her phone.

She logged into www.one-eyed-cardsharp.com and dived into the first game of poker she could find. It lasted all of one minute before her phone's battery ran out of power again.

The band was the one thing that hadn't seemed like a gamble. The boys all seemed so sure of themselves and yet pliable.

She'd thought she could hammer them into shape.

The shape of a Grammy or a gold record.

"I've got work to do," Felicia told the empty stairwell.

She then pitched forward and vomited her guts out.

Felicia watched from the shadows as the bands took turns performing their sound checks. The members of #Five seemed surprisingly cordial with the other acts and with one another, almost like they'd forgiven each other for all the lying and scheming—the secrets they'd kept from one another.

Her secrets! She owned the rights to each and every one of them.

If only I could patent such things. If only I were smart enough!

She muttered to herself and checked her phone to see if she'd received any more bizarre messages from her cyberstalker—she hadn't—then watched as #Five tested their instruments and gauged the echo that the outdoor venue caused. It was bad. They would be confused by the reverberation. But so was Felicia: she had no idea what they planned on performing.

#Five needed to pull out a performance in the vein of Queen or The Beatles or even Fleetwood Mac to claim the crown of Biggest Band Ever of All Time and Forever. Such a show was unlikely. Felicia was quite sure #Five didn't have it in them, the pure spectacle.

Sometimes the performance needed to overpower the music itself. Only her own song could do such a thing, and she had gifted them her biggest, best, most danceable song to perform. They in turn, despite everything she'd done to get them here, had turned their backs on her and, even worse, on her music.

She was pretty sure the band didn't have another song of their own to unleash, certainly nothing epic or genre-defying.

If they were not going to perform her song, there was no music left for them. They'd burned all their matches. Unless by some unfathomable act of artistic glory they'd stayed up all night penning a new work. Then again, she knew they were too young to do such a thing, too immature and impatient. The band was about to fizzle out before her and millions of other eyes. The veneer had been scraped away and what was left was lackluster. Literally. The band lacked their virginal shine. So, what could they do?

Play a cover song? Steal something from another band? Play something by Scarlett Fever? An old blues ditty with tinkly piano? A song they'd already performed, which would surely be awarded no points by the judges? Or what, all of the above?

Ha ha. Fuck them.

Felicia was pretty sure they wouldn't even make it onto the stage. They'd humiliate themselves. She pulled her hat low, went in search of a cab, and returned to her tiny boutique hotel. There she set up her laptop and phone and ran multiple gambling sites and apps.

She still had plenty of money left over from her appearance as a judge on QuickFame, but there was something about seeing the numbers in her account dwindle as her losses mounted. It was almost as if she were buying back her integrity.

As she waited for the other players to place bets she scrolled through messages on her phone. The boat had sold at a loss. Now she wanted it back.

She decided to fire her lawyer and sent him a terse email, then immediately regretted it, and sent a follow-up. *Just kidding, laughing out loud, as all the kids say. What else can I sell? Is there a corner of my soul left to put up for auction?*

She then returned to her favorite blog, Music Bitch. Whoever was feeding the author inside tidbits had continued to do so with increase accuracy, detailing the up-to-the-minute developments with #Five, including their outfits. This person was on-site. She or he was among the bands, mingling, schmoozing, spying, perhaps snuggling. Maybe it was one of the band members themselves.

Felicia's laptop chimed. She flipped through the browser tabs until she found the offending site. Except that this time it wasn't offending: she'd won at last. Twelve thousand dollars. Digital confetti rained down. Other players congratulated her. She felt hollow inside, all but dead.

It was a sign.

Felicia did a web search for local investigative agencies.

An hour later she was sitting in a minivan with Flip, a chubby guy sporting a mustache but armed with all kinds of technology. He was giving her tips on how to blend in, starting with a wig: blond. Like Cheree but purer. It was hideous and it itched but she had to admit that it gave her a totally fresh look.

"I'll be in the crowd, as will Willy, Bobbo, Conrad, and Little John himself. It's a big team, but I guess this is a big job, finding your stalker." He added a whistle for effect.

"What?"

"Nothing. I mean, we just don't usually work with big spenders like this. It's nice though.

Usually, it's some penniless wife looking to catch her man in the act of, you know, coitus."

"How do I look?"

Flip fixed her bangs.

"Add your large-brimmed hat and the big sunglasses. Yeah. You look like a rock star in mourning."

Felicia exited the minivan and headed for the venue.

She flashed her credentials—her leftover badge from QuickFame USA, with her finger hiding the "USA"—and swept past the security guard before he could do a double-take. The crowd was already thick as a hive in spring, surprisingly diverse in both color and age for this side of the planet. Perhaps they didn't get many concerts like this one and crawled out the cool shadows of their burrows and whatever they lived in. The sun had been oppressive at its height in the early afternoon but as it started its descent the main floor became less crematorium-like. Misting machines consistently sent out clouds of moist air and pretty blond women walked around with tanks on their backs reminiscent of insect repellant devices but in truth distributing a sweet electrolyte drink in the compostable cups being provided by one of the sponsors. Everyone was so goddamn happy, Felicia felt compelled to sneak some ecstasy or even LSD into their tanks.

Every now and then Felicia spotted one of her detectives snooping around. They seemed awkward but competent and determined to find her stalker-blogger-nightmare. Soon she received a chirp on her phone from Flip, the goofiest of the bunch. He was adjacent to the stage, waving her closer.

He was busy bribing a security guard, who let Felicia into the backstage area for a mere two hundred Australian dollars. Felicia told Flip she was fine on her own now and sent him back into the crowd to continue the search. Backstage no one paid much attention to her.

She blended in, just another industry lackey or washed-up pop singer—one among dozens who'd glommed onto the spectacle.

She spotted Grannie setting up Jai's pedals and cables. First, she had to get through Eddie though.

"Hi doll."

"Ma'am. I can't let you through here."

"Listen, I got you out of prison, Edwin. I allowed you to join the band. You're an important part of this entourage now."

"I appreciate all that you've done for me. I hope to repay it with my service and fortitude."

"Lovely. Now get the fuck out of the way, Eddo."

Eddie remained firm. "Can't do that."

"Can."

Felicia sighed, then swung her purse around. "Fine. Can I at least give you a hug?" Felicia lunged forward.

In an instant Eddie was writhing in her arms. Felicia waited until it looked like his eyes were going to burst out his skull, then switched her Taser off and let him fall to the ground.

"Help! Help! I think this man is having a seizure!"

Once he'd gasped back to life Felicia stepped over him and let the real security and paramedics take over.

She found Grannie going through his gear in the wings. "Sweetie."

Grannie glanced up and over his shoulder, then returned to his work. "Oh God." He shook his head and returned to his work.

"You come already?"

"Very funny. Seriously, I'm really busy at the moment." "Granville."

He looked up again. Then he stood and faced her.

"What in the fucking fuck are you doing here? And why the stupid disguise?"

He shook his head. "Forget it. I don't want to know."

"I miss you." She reached for his arm; he wrenched it free.

"You need to go."

"Alright. I'll let you focus. I know you must be stressed out." She turned to leave. She was near the edge of the stage when he looked then called out to her. "Wait."

She stopped.

"Why are you here? I thought you went back to Emmiline."

She turned and removed her sunglasses.

"I just had to see you guys go all the way. It's like seeing your baby born and go off to college in a matter of months. Can't miss the graduation, you know?"

Grannie looked like he might cry. Instead, he laughed. "Child prodigies. That's us."

Felicia cut the gap between them by half. "I'm really proud of you guys."

He nodded, said nothing.

"Just wondering—what are you playing?"

"It's a secret."

"Come on, Granville. It's me, your sweet Felicia."

"Not so sweet after all, are you? Pretty malicious stuff that's been leaking to the press."

"That's not me, you asshole!"

Grannie snorted and went back to work. Felicia stood there watching him a minute before her shadow fell over him again. "Did you guys decide to play 'Destiny With The Night'?"

He said nothing.

"Grannie? Hon'?"

"I'm busy."

"If you could just tell me I'll know whether to stick around or not. It'd kill me if you decided not to play it, so I'd leave. I'd understand, after all I've said and done, but I can't pretend it won't hurt."

"You'll live."

She scowled but Grannie wasn't looking. "That's not nice."

"Neither are you."

"Don't be snarky."

"I can be. I'm a rock star now, didn't you know? I'm sure you've been reading all the blogs and such. Even the mainstream media is picking it up. It's ok though, I gave a statement revealing my true age. It'll be running tomorrow. You'll be exonerated in the area of child rape at least."

Felicia's face turned white. "So, it's not my song then."

Grannie stood, uncoiling a cable for his keyboard. "Fuck you, Felicia. Fuck your stupid song."

"So, what is it then? What will you play?"

Grannie plugged in his keyboard, powered it up, ran through a few runs of the keys. The keyboard stand was off-kilter and the instrument rocked back and forth. "Go away or I'll call security. I need to concentrate on this."

Grannie knelt down to adjust the stand's feet. Felicia didn't move.

"Go back home, Felicia, and write some more silly pop songs. Find another boy to twist around your finger. Go ruin some other guy's life. Drive someone else to their early death."

"That's just—you—shut your ugly old man face!"

Grannie shook his head, laughing. It was his body language more than anything that enraged her.

"But I love you."

"You love nothing except the sound of your own voice."

In one swift move Felicia grabbed a microphone stand and drove it into the back of Grannie's skull. He keeled over like a sack of sugar that'd split in the middle, his face smashing into the keyboard stand and bringing the entire thing down with him.

Felicia stood over him, panting, sweat streaking out from beneath her wig. "Grannie? Honey?"

"Holy shit," a voice said behind her.

Felicia jettisoned the microphone stand and turned to find Flip the chubby detective standing there with a digital camera in his squishy paws.

"This isn't what it looks like," she said.

"What do you think it looks like?"

"Ignore this! This is nothing. A lover's spat. Clear it from your memory."

"I'm not a computer, Ms. Scalding."

"That thing in your hands."

Flip moved the camera to behind his back. "He was attacking me."

"Come on, Ms. Scalding, I saw. And now he's injured. I need to inform the police."

"It's just a gash."

"He's unconscious!"

Felicia stood up and offered him her sweetest eyes. "There's a bonus in it. A nice one, ok? Quick, before the others show up."

She shepherded him off the stage just as some technicians carried in an amp.

Flip considered this. "How much?"

"You tell me." She rubbed his arm.

"Why are you touching me like that?"

"I feel dizzy. You see, he hit me before you walked in."

"No, he didn't. I was standing there longer than you think."

"Shut your mouth."

Flip reached for his phone.

"I'm sorry! Look, money. I have Australian dollars. How much to keep your pie-hole shut?"

Flip smiled; a tooth was missing. "A lot."

Felicia dragged him away. "Let's negotiate elsewhere."

Flip screeched to a halt at the international terminal and hopped out to get Felicia's bag out of the trunk. She gave him a kiss on the cheek while trying not to picture his disfigured teeth, then sprinted inside. The terminal was cool; she was not. She kept her sunglasses on all the way through the ticketing process, right up until the security check. While in line she clamped her hands over her ears to keep the awful noise of humanity out of her head, the crying and talking, laughing, and singing along to songs that deserved to be lost in the annals of pop culture history.

She still had her Streemy VIP pass, granting her a reprieve in an exclusive lounge. She flung her carry-on onto one lounger and plopped down on another.

"Get you anything?" a stout server with massive breasts asked her.

"Got those appletini things?"

"Sure do. On ice?"

"As cold as my heart, darling."

"Aw, don't say that. You seem sweet." Felicia sighed.

"I can fake anything."

The server returned to the bar where she turned on the television so that Felicia would have something to watch.

And what it revealed was Grannie.

Felicia sat up.

"What in the actually fucking fuck?"

"Drink will be right up, ma'am."

"Can you increase the volume?"

"DRINK WILL BE RIGHT UP, MA'AM!"

"I mean on the television."

"Oh. Right."

A reporter was standing outside the Sydney Opera house, reporting on the developments.

Grannie had been attacked.

He claimed that he wasn't sure who had done this to him. Perhaps someone from a rival band—someone retaliating for crushing Roman's foot prior to the finals.

"Was it someone from London Mountains?" the reporter posited.

"No," Grannie was saying "No way. Those guys are legit, and they don't need to resort to such things. Are you fishing? Is this a racist angle you're taking?"

"No, no. I mean. *Ahem.* As I was saying. What was I saying?" The reporter touched her earpiece. "Apparently the crowd remains excited to see #Five tonight."

The report cut to the main stage. The crowd was chanting and clapping impatiently. *Hash-tag.*

Hash-tag. Hash-tag.

Felicia downed her drink and checked her ticket to find out when her gate closed. Mere minutes.

"Can you ask them to hold my plane?" she asked the server.

The server laughed. "That was a strong drink, eh?"

Felicia drilled the bar top with her fingernails. "Come on, come on."

"Granville," the reporter said, "You will be playing tonight with the band, correct?"

"The rock never stops."

"Is that a yes?"

"As long as I can remember the notes, I'll play. How much time do I have? What time is it? One-two-three-four-o'clock-rock. Right?"

The reporter glanced at the camera, then back at her subject. "Are you feeling ok?"

"Never better. Just wish we could find our lead singer. *Ha ha* "

"What do you mean?"

Eddie appeared at the edge of the screen, his eyes bloodshot and his tie askew. "Interview is over."

"Where are we going?" Grannie asked.

"Small problem." He whispered into Grannie's ear. "Layton's missing?"

"What?" the reporter said.

Eddie raised his hand to block the camera.

"Is the band imploding again?" the reporter asked.

"Everything's fine. We just don't—he's—Lay—it's all under control."

"Is it?"

"We've got to do our sound check."

"That's right," Grannie said, then played air guitar. "Sound check. Hat check. Hip check!"

He drove his hips into Eddie, nearly flooring the poor, unstable, recently shocked kid, then blew a kiss to the world and bounced off.

"Back to you in the studio," the reporter said, and the camera cut to the main stage. On the television screen the band was filing out. Britt. Donovan. And then a minute later Jai and Grannie, the latter of which garnered massive applause. He was wearing a beanie over his blood-soaked bandages. He flipped a shy wave to the crowd, making Felicia die a little inside.

Felicia was almost proud—of him, of herself. She'd done it, whether she'd meant to or not.

She'd made a mortal into a star with one tiny act.

"Another, please," Felicia said, sliding her glass across the bar. Lastly their lead singer appeared.

The applause stopped.

He emerged in a skirt. A beautiful, slim affair that fell to his knees. Up top he wore a long T- shirt, tastefully loose, with just the neck hole.

He had on some chunky heels that he must have searched all over to find in his size.

He didn't have on a wig, which was probably best.

It would have looked like a costume.

Only she and the band knew that it wasn't.

"This is not our song," Layton said into the mic. "It's a little of everything. And yes, I am the lead singer of #Five. Thank you for having us."

Then, much to Felicia's relief, the applause returned. Once they'd realize it was legitimately him, they just wanted the music. They were ready to accept him as he was. At least down here. In Emmiline—that was another question.

Lay-ton. Lay-ton. Lay-ton.

The song kicked in—"Billie Jean" by Michael Jackson.

"Are you fucking serious?" Felicia asked. She sipped her refreshed drink and checked the time again. One minute. By the time she'd set the drink down, the song had switched again. Now it was Queen. "Under Pressure."

No.

They wouldn't dare. A medley?

There was no way they'd had time to put together such a thing. Only one person could do that, and he'd have to lead them through the entire—Grannie! That's duplicitous little shit. He was going to pull out all his magic tricks for this one. Indeed, Grannie was steering them through the musical seas, not Britt. Instead, Britt was forced to pick up the beat each time a new song kicked in. He managed it deftly, waiting a second or two to figure out the rhythm, the volume, the ferocity with which to strike.

Felicia's hip buzzed. She removed her phone from her pocket and set it on the bar. It chirped again. She glanced at it, looked away. Then she glanced back. Another message from her anonymous cyberstalker had come through.

On the television the band had leapt into another song— Nirvana's "Smell's Like Teen Spirit," the breakdown no less. The band was flailing about on the stage. It was wild. Just when the crowd was really getting into it, the Quakes shifted again, seismically: they slowed it all the way down to Eric Clapton's "Layla." Layton's voice was sonic, mesmerizing. The camera honed in on a girl with tears in her eyes.

Felicia scoffed and glanced at the message on her phone.

How's it feel? Full circle? Do you now recognize the evil of your ways, Fello?

Only one person in the world called her Fello. "Michaela?"

Cheree snapped her gum as she drove. She had her headphones in so that Felicia could try and sleep, but Felicia could hear it—the soundtracks to Pitch Perfect and Pitch Perfect 2. Cheree's face was done up with a sheen of glittery moisturizer and lip gloss, which she was inadvertently ingesting each time she blew a bubble. The woman never seemed to age. Or evolve.

"Thanks again for driving."

"What?" Cheree yelled.

"THANKS FOR DRIVING."

Cheree pulled out her headphones. "No biggie. I always wanted to go to Taos. *Tay-ohs.*"

"Taos. Like in 'towel.'"

"What towels?"

"Taos."

"I got some napkins around here somewhere." Cheree reached into the back seat, the car swerving.

"No—stop! Just drive."

"What is it? Stop or drive or look for towels?"

Felicia pressed her fingers to her temples, her teeth clenched, her head filled with such rage that she thought she might bash her face through the windshield, like a deer trying to escape the car, not leap over it.

"Just drive, Cheree. Please. The town's name is pronounced Taos."

"Oh. *Towel-ohs.*"

Felicia put on her sunglasses. "Something like that."

Cheree's Prius started to strain as the hills turned to mountains. The peaks were capped with snow while all around them the land was arid and exotic. Felicia imagined filming a video out there. She had a song with a distinctly Native American beat; she could don a headdress, an authentic skirt, have a set full of teepees and—*Shit, Felicia. You really are stupid. Cultural appropriation went out of style at the same time as fringed leather jackets.*

Taos appeared in the distance. The GPS system started chiming in with instructions.

Still Cheree missed half of them, adding miles and time to the trip.

"Can you stop at a gas station or something? I don't want to show up there and first thing I say is, 'Fuck you, I hate you, you suck, can I use your bathroom?'"

"Sure thing, doll. I need some more Trident anyways."

A few minutes later Cheree steered them into a truck stop. Before the car had rolled to a stop Felicia kicked the door open and took off running.

"Are you ok?"

Felicia waved over her shoulder and sprinted around the building.

Ten minutes later Cheree found Felicia sitting on a curb, slumped over, her feet splayed out.

Cheree sat with her.

There wasn't much to look at except the departing traffic and a vista across the high-mountain deserts.

"You ok, hon'?"

"Maybe I shouldn't do this. It could be a trap."

"Um, yeah. We did just drive across three states to get here. That wasn't for nothing, I hope. Obviously, you had a lot of time to think about things. I know you. Once you get it in your head to do something, you do it. Remember when you were playing that huge show in Schenectady, and you wanted to ride a bicycle across a high wire and then drop down into a net? You did it. And the bicycle was on fire."

"It was *me* that was on fire, but that part was an accident. Luckily, the fall into the net dampened the flames."

Cheree opened her gum and shoved a stick in her mouth. "By the way, I have some news. I've been debating whether to tell you or not. It's about Chad."

Felicia looked at her. "He's dead to me. I don't care."

"Yeah, exactly. He's dead to all of us."

"What?"

Cheree took her time, working the gum into a nice shape. "That trip to Nepal didn't go so well for him. I mean, it did go well for awhile. He got really good at climbing mountains and raising money for the orphans of the natives or whatever it was he was doing there, but then he decided that since he was acclim—acclimitated—climated changed—whatever it's called, you know, when you can breathe on mountains? Anyways, he decided he wanted to go to the top of the world. Mount Never Rest."

"Everest."

"Right. Whatever. He made it to the top though and touched the sky. For a moment he was higher than any human on Earth, the closest person to the sun. Isn't that something?"

"But then—"

"He didn't make it down. I guess that happens a lot. You use all your energy to get up there but don't save it for getting back down. He's actually still up there, frozen in place. He might be there forever."

Felicia stared off into the desert. "I know you loved him."

"I don't know that I did."

"You said you did."

"I said a lot of things. What I felt was different. He just filled a hole in me."

Cheree laughed.

"Stop it! You know what I mean."

"At least he died doing something he loved."

"Oh please. As if that matters. He was—I want to—there are better ways to, you know—to live—to go—" Felicia's face sank into her hands. Her shoulders rocked. Soon she was sobbing.

"What's wrong, hon'?"

Felicia shrugged.

"Let's get out of here. After I pee again."

An hour of driving and the Prius was silently coasting to a stop on a quiet street on the outskirts of the city. The houses, spaced well apart, were all adobe and Pueblo in style or some variation of such, but this one in particular looked like it had been built by hand from a pile of mud and river debris. Cacti and wildflowers served as a lawn, with a stone path winding through it. Pine trees shadowed the property.

"Quite nice," Cheree said. "This can't be it."

"The computer says so."

While staring at the house they saw the curtains slide open a few inches, then fly back into place.

"Someone's home."

"Damn it." Felicia sighed. "Alright. You can wait here, Cheree." Cheree undid her seatbelt and got fresh gum. "As if."

The two women strolled up to the front door. They stood there a minute, and then Felicia used the fox-face brass knocker to announce their arrival. They heard the latch being undone. The door opened.

"Hi Felicia."

"What in the fuck? Teddy?"

"Thaddeus, actually. Maybe you could try and get my name right."

"I almost didn't recognize you. You look like you've lost fifty pounds. And your face isn't all swollen and blotchy."

He smiled. "Thanks. I've cleaned up my diet and lifestyle."

"Great. Now what the fuck are you doing here?"

Thaddeus stepped back.

"You'd better come in. It's hot."

"Not until you explain."

"Please. The cool air will slip out. Michaela doesn't use air conditioning."

The women exchanged looks, then stepped inside.

They removed their sunglasses and looked around. The inside of the house was indeed much cooler than outside.

Cheree snapped her gum. "Nice place. Feels real homey."

"And you are?"

"Cheree Parker."

She offered a dead-fish handshake.

"Oh! I remember you. You were quite a dancer." Thaddeus took hold of the fish and shook it. Then he wrung his hands together.

"Yes, so, well, the short version of the story is that after you mentioned that someone was following you around at QuickFame USA, I had security look into it. One of my guys pinned down the perpetrator, and after some intense grilling—I mean, like, literally, we went to my place and had some steaks on the grill, this being before my dietary transformation—he revealed that he was working for Michaela George. I found that really upsetting and I threatened to make it public and to tell you. Instead of doing that, he told me why Michaela was having you followed."

Felicia felt the familiar constricting of her chest, her heart threatening to burst through her sternum, just like when she was being hounded by debt collectors. *Did the person following me see me attack Granville? And Eduardo?* Felicia took out a handkerchief and pretended to blow her nose while sopping up her cold sweat.

Cheree crossed her arms over her chest and snapped her gum. "Which is why?"

Felicia broke out of her anxiety paralysis and raised her hand to shush Cheree.

"That still doesn't answer how *you* got here."

"You have a real knack for using people and fucking them over, Felicia. We agreed that you would give me credit for #Five's rise through QuickFame. Instead, you took all the credit for discovering them. You said we'd go to Streemy together and I'd get a co-producer credit. My first ever! But instead, you pursued it entirely on your own. You cut me out. Sound familiar?"

Felicia's eyes narrowed to boomerang-slits as she cast a cutting glare at him. "No."

Then her face relaxed. She looked down. Her shoulders slumped and she let go of her purse. "Yes." The purse slid from her shoulder.

Thaddeus continued. "Through the spy I met, I got in touch with Michaela and explained to her what had happened. She said that the only way you were ever going to change was by getting you to see the wickedness of your ways. So, we joined forces."

Thaddeus smiled like a country bumpkin, blushing. "Then we joined hearts. *And bodies.*"

Cheree raised a hand. "Eww. TMI."

"We're in love. Or at least I am."

"So where is she?" Felicia said, her voice hushed with resignation. "In the garden or on the veranda."

"Is she expecting me?"

"I suspect so. Head on out there. I'll bring out some iced tea in few. Maybe Cheree can help me in the kitchen."

Cheree sat in a stiff recliner topped with a coarse Hopi-style rug and examined her fingernails.

"As if."

Felicia exited through the sliding doors and marched out onto the veranda, clutching her purse like a shield.

She spotted someone sitting in a lounge chair.

As she got closer, she saw Michaela's unmistakable copper-red hair glimmering in the sunlight.

Butterflies and birds flittered about the immaculately tended back yard filled with small cacti, a few tall trees and a dozen smaller ones, stone paths, a fountain, and a small garden.

"So, this is where you've been hiding all these years."

The head turned slightly.

"Hello Felicia."

"You ruined my life, you stupid bitch."

"Because I walked out of Wembley?"

Felicia laughed. "Yeah! Duh! For starters."

"Do you know *why* I walked out just before we were to go on stage?"

"Because you're a foolish, idiotic, unfathomably selfish, cowardly... jerk!"

Michaela crossed one leg over the other, then tucked a lock of her wavy hair behind her ear. Though her hair had faded, Michaela could tell that she didn't dye it and it hadn't yet started to gray. Felicia spent thousands of dollars keeping her own hair chestnut-brown.

"Is that what I am?"

Felicia nodded so hard she almost gave herself whiplash. Michaela slid out a chair and gestured for her to sit.

"I don't want to sit."

"I want you to sit."

"I want you to tell me why you've been following me and leaking things to the press and— and—and being a mean person! You cunt!"

Michaela gestured at the chair. Felicia kicked it. She could hardly breathe.

The sliding door opened, and Thaddeus emerged with a tray of iced tea. Without a word he set it down on a small glass-topped table and went back inside.

Just before the door shut, Felicia thought she heard Cheree laughing.

Michaela poured iced tea and handed a glass to Felicia. Felicia finally sat on a chair that looked like it'd been built out of local logs, then dumped the iced tea on the veranda.

Michaela sighed.

"Perhaps I was indeed trying to ruin your life. To be honest, at times I wasn't quite sure."

"What did I ever do to offend you so much?"

"You turned into ruthless businesswoman Felicia. You know, 'girl power' doesn't mean acting like you have a dick. You became a total dickhead too."

"I didn't." Felicia squinted in the sun and put on her sunglasses. "Did I?"

Felicia shook her head, then reached for the iced tea and poured herself a glass.

"I probably did some things that weren't very kind."

"You and I wrote a lot of songs together. Some of them were almost entirely my words and beats. Then you joined forces with Dexter Rhodes and together arranged something with Streemy so that only your songs would be used. I lost all my chances to earn royalties for those songs. You are indeed a conniving, scheming bitch."

"I don't even remember doing that. It was all kind of a blur. I have a problem. Michaela. I gamble. I have an addiction."

"Thaddeus's man discovered that. That's just a symptom though, and not your problem."

"What's my problem then? What the hell is wrong with me?"

"I don't know. And I therefore don't have a solution for you. I just thought that if someone did to you what you did to others, you might come to see the evil of your ways. All I knew was that you needed to be touched somehow."

"Touched? Like by a stalker or a creep?"

"As in affected. You were always so damn stubborn, Felicia. You still are. Your face is the paragon of rigidity at the moment. Breathe! Don't you see that you are free?"

"Free of what? Money? Security? Success? A career"

"Were you ever free from those things or were they holding you hostage? Look at your debt, your gambling addiction, your insidious interference with the QuickFame process."

"Thaddeus told you all this? It was his idea!"

"Is that important now? Or is the important thing that while trying to build your career you destroyed others'?"

"I don't know!"

"Of course, you do. You have nothing left. You're broke and all but homeless. Your boy band refuses to work with you. Your husband has left you—"

"He died."

"Oh. I'm sorry."

"It's ok. He left me for another woman and a pack of orphans. And just so you know, I took #Five to the top. They may not have won QuickFame OneWorld, but they succeeded and are on their way."

"They always were, Felicia. You just demanded to be part of it, to capitalize on others' success. Why don't you just do your own thing and focus on one song at a time, rather than ten thousand? Better yet, why don't you just sit here awhile and enjoy the sunshine?"

"We have sun in Emmiline too, just so you know."

"The air there is tainted. It's toxic. That's why I came out here."

"That begs the question: how do you make a living if I fucked you out of almost all of the royalties? Your advances must have long since dried up."

Michaela set down her glass and leaned towards Felicia. "I write songs. I've put out a couple CDs and digital albums under my pseudonym, Jolie Desantis. I play locally. No one seems to recognize me, which is both disturbing and refreshing."

"Oh. That's... interesting."

Michaela lay back in the lounger and let the sun wash over her face. A breeze played with her hair and helped Felicia cool off for a moment. Some copper wind chimes provided occasional texture to the otherwise still afternoon, but when the air settled the place was all but silent.

No traffic, no airplanes, no trains, or toothless men screaming at pigeons or humping a parking meter. Every now and then they could hear laughter coming from inside, usually Cheree.

"Do you want to try it?" Michaela asked out of the blue.

"Try what?"

She stood up and went inside, then returned a couple minutes later with an acoustic guitar.

"You play that?" Felicia asked.

Michaela nodded and tuned it. "Why don't we write a song together?"

Felicia laughed. "I don't write hippie stuff."

"What's 'hippie stuff'?"

"You know, howling at the moon and banging on that thing."

"Like Joni Mitchell? Carly Simon? Joan Jett? Sarah McLachlan?"

"Ok, ok. Whatever. But no thanks."

"Why not?"

Felicia shrugged. "I don't really know how. I need someone to produce beat, some paper, an idea."

Michaela sat on the edge of the lounger, facing Felicia. "You've got all you need inside of you. Just listen to it, then play a chord. Listen to it, play another chord. Tie them together. It's that easy." Michaela strummed the guitar, letting the notes hum in the air a moment, then strummed it again. "Hear it? What is your heart telling you at the moment?"

Felicia closed her eyes a moment. She heard Cheree laugh again. She heard the wind chimes chiming. She heard Michaela's fingers pressing against the guitar keys. "I've got it."

"Good. Let's hear it."

Felicia stood up.

She grabbed the guitar from Michaela's hands and lifted it Joe Strummer-style, high enough that it was scraping the boughs of the pine tree above her, needles raining down on them. She paused there a moment, looking down at her reflection in the glass table, her eyes peering back at her—crazy, manic eyes that told the tale of a life lived in the fast lane but with someone else behind the wheel. *I lost everything, got it all back, lost it again, and all for what?* As she stared down at that face, her old face, her arms started to shake, her fingers inadvertently strumming the strings and releasing a playful *twang*.

She brought the guitar down, smashing the glass table. "Fuck you!"

Cheree and Thaddeus hurried out the sliding door. "They're wrestling on the ground!" Cheree said, her gum flying out of her mouth. Thaddeus grabbed Cheree and pulled her back.

"No. They're not."

"She's got Felicia in a headlock!"

"That's a hug, Cheree."

Michaela was sitting with Felicia on the rocky veranda, safely away from the broken glass, Felicia's head against her shoulder, Michaela rocking her back and forth in concert with the trees swaying around them.

13.
AN OLD SONG ON THE RADIO CALLING OUR NAMES

Britt's new motorcycle was faster than his old one, with a bigger and throatier engine, but it was easier to control and did what he asked of it. Best of all, he'd gotten the guy to craft a custom holder for his drumsticks, which sat behind the passenger seat. The latter was occupied at the moment.

"Not so fast this time!" Tona said into her helmet's headset as they rolled to a stop at a red light.

"I don't like the way it feels in the corners."

"No problem, baby."

"I mean it."

"Well, define 'fast.'"

"Just stick to the speed limit."

"I don't have limits."

"I do, you prick!" She wrapped her arms around him and squeezed. The light changed; Britt opened up the throttle, leaving behind some rubber on the pavement, screaming past the line of oncoming cars. Then he slowed down, and as he got closer to the house he slowed down further. The familiar landmarks appeared, none of them different than when he lived here.

He knew every dip and twist in the road, its texture imprinted on his memory and compressed into his bones. Then appeared the long, winding driveway, the house looming at its end like the castle hosting a king of nothing, a man in exile, a mere merchant of marble.

"Nice place."

"It looks ok on the outside but inside it's pure shit. Just like Leo."

Britt brought the motorcycle up to the garage and killed the engine. He and Tona climbed off.

"You ok?"

"It's nothing," he said, setting his helmet on the handlebars.

"Is anyone here? It looks like—"

As if on cue the front door opened and Leo appeared. He'd grown a beard and put on some weight. His face, however, was different. It looked—relaxed.

"I'll get E-Man to open the garage for you," he said, then went back inside.

Tona and Britt exchanged looks. "E-Man?"

Britt shook his head. "No idea."

The garage doors rattled and shuddered, revealing snappy black running shoes, suit pants, a suit coat, shirt, and tie—and Eddie.

"E-Man?"

"Your pops has been slinging that at me."

He shrugged. "It's cool."

Britt and Eddie embraced bro-style, with their clasped hands between them. Then Eddie and Tona hugged like adults.

"How long have you been here?"

"Just a few minutes."

"You didn't drive? Where's your car?"

"No car. Just that." He gestured towards a Harley in the driveway, which Britt had assumed was his father's.

"Oh shit. We are so racing back to downtown."

"No way!" Tona said, shoving him into the garage.

Sitting in their usual spot was Britt's practice kit, untouched after all these months left dormant, not even dusty. Beneath the kit though sat fresh black flooring.

"I installed the rubber awhile back," Leo said as he turned on the lights.

"The old stuff seemed ratty. The mini-fridge is stocked up with waters and such. You're still not old enough to drink beer. Are you, Tona?"

"Me? Oh, ha ha. No, but thanks."

"Cool. I'm sure the others will be here soon, so I'll let you get to it." Leo went back inside.

"He seems nice."

"'Seems' being the key word. It's an act."

"He's trying," Eddie said.

"I know. I can see that. But it's gonna take a lot more than some discount rubber flooring before I forgive that son of a bitch."

Britt took off his jacket and sat at his drum kit. In the months of being away he'd completely changed his set up and needed to reconfigure everything. Nearby he found a package of new sticks, Zildjians, his favorite. Leo must have gone and bought them as soon as Britt had sent him a message asking if it was ok for the band to come practice one last time in the garage.

By and by the sound of an engine echoed up the driveway. A beat-up Honda Accord with a baby spare up front and two different-colored doors clanked its way toward the garage before sputtering to a stop. Jai climbed out, kicked the car's rear door, then went to the trunk and removed The Scythe II—the original having been smashed at the end of their Sydney performance—and a new amp. When he looked up, he saw Tona and Britt watching him; he waved. "S'up, brother. Sister." He slammed the trunk as hard as he could, then pressed his face to the rear passenger window. "Wake up!"

Someone sat up in the back seat. He rubbed his face, then with great effort reached up to pull the door handle and kicked the door open. Donovan slid out, then went to the front and got his bass and amp out of the passenger seat.

"We thought maybe you were having another fit," Britt said to Jai.

He grimaced. "I'm on medication. It evens things out a bit. I'm still getting the dosage right though, since it makes my hands feel weird."

"Nice car, by the way."

Jai set down his case and kneeled before it as if honoring the gods. "Isn't it though?"

"Don't you think you could have afforded something new with the advance from the record deal?"

"What's the point? I won't be able to drive it when we're on tour. And anyways, you're getting ahead of yourself. We haven't even written the album yet."

Britt slung The Scythe II over his head and plugged in his amp. "The songs we've got so far are enough to get us a following in Japan. Or at least South Korea." He winked, then plugged in his guitar and started tuning it.

Tona checked her watch.

"They'll be there," Eddie said as he helped Britt make some more adjustments to his drum kit. "Now that they're on the edge of being rock stars they're allowed to be assholishly late."

The door opened and Leo appeared with a tray of drinks. "Lemonade. I squeezed the living shit out of the lemons myself. And Cokes."

"Maybe Grannie would like a beer. When he shows up."

"Very funny."

"He's twenty-five."

"Very funny."

"I'm serious."

Leo set the tray down.

When he saw that Britt wasn't kidding his started to scowl.

"How is that possible?"

"Sometimes people just pretend, you know? Kind of like what you're doing now." Leo's face darkened.

"I'm trying, Britt."

Britt dropped a stick, then bent down to fetch it. "I know, Dad."

He sat upright, his cheeks red. His eyes darted to Tona, who was playing with her phone, then to Donovan, who was fighting back a smirk, then to Jai, who was focused on his guitar, to E-Man, who seemed poised to interfere should things go south, then back to Leo, who was either on the verge of tears or an eruption.

"Thanks for the drinks," Britt said.

"No problem. I'll let you guys do your—what in the holy hell?"

"Hi there, Mr. Elwyn."

Nobody had heard Grannie's electric car pulling up. He'd slid in behind Jai's shitmobile, and then he and the lead singer of Shivvr and the Quakes had approached the garage with trepidation, waiting for the scene between Britt and his father to play out. But Leo had spotted them first. His jaw dropped, and then the jaws of Donovan, Britt, Tona, Eddie, and Jai dropped in unison. Once the shock had passed, they stood up and started whistling and clapping.

Leo rubbed his eyes. "Layton?"

"Actually, now it's 'Layla.'"

"You're a woman now?"

"I always was, Mr. Elwyn. My body just didn't know it."

"How did you—you're allowed to do that to your body?"

"Dad—Leo. Chill."

Layla stepped into the garage. Her hair had grown five or six inches since the others had seen her and, with Grannie's help, she'd learned some advanced makeup techniques. Her breasts weren't much to speak of, but the look suited the changes her body was undergoing, with slightly wider hips, long model-like legs, and a smoother, less intimidating jawline. "Since I'm eighteen I was able to start hormone treatment."

"Wow. Just—wow."

"Am I hot?"

"Yeah!"

"*Leo.*"

"Ok, ok. I'll, uh, go inside and wrap my head around this. And around the fact that Granville is also not quite who he said—who he thought—his age, I mean—fuck. Killing me." Leo shut the door behind him.

While the others admired Layla up close, Grannie set up his keyboard. He'd grown a beard and had put on five pounds, none of which was muscle and none of which he was pleased with. "Alright gents and ladies. Are we going to do this shit or what?"

Layla set up the microphones. Tona got up to adjust the stand to her height. "Thanks for letting me do vocals on this track."

"Just don't outshine me."

"Like that's possible."

Grannie waved his arms in the air. "Bring it in, bitches." Everyone gathered around him. He put out his hand. Layla placed hers on top. Then Jai. Donovan. Britt. "You too, Ed. Don't be that weird lurker."

Eddie's massive hand covered the pile. But there was one more yet. "Come on, lady."

Tona joined in. "Ready? One."

"Two."

"Three."

"Four."

"Five."

"Six o'clock."

They all paused a moment, staring at that array of limbs. The things those limbs were capable of. The places those limbs had traveled. The punches they'd thrown and the instruments they'd destroyed.

The music they'd created.

They were so focused on those limbs and the faces behind them that they didn't notice another car had pulled into the driveway. Its windows were tinted. The rear passenger-side window lowered halfway and a tanned face sporting huge sunglasses appeared.

Smiled.

Nodded.

Whispered.

"Rock."